DATE DUE		
MR 15 '01		
JAN 1 7 2006		
JUL 2 1 2010		
JAN 2 1 2016		

The
Peshawar
Lancers

The
Peshawar
Lancers

S. M. STIRLING

A ROC BOOK

ROC
Published by New American Library, a division of
Penguin Putnam Inc., 375 Hudson Street,
New York, New York 10014, U.S.A.
Penguin Books Ltd, 80 Strand,
London WC2R 0RL, England
Penguin Books Australia Ltd, Ringwood,
Victoria, Australia
Penguin Books Canada Ltd, 10 Alcorn Avenue,
Toronto, Ontario, Canada M4V 3B2
Penguin Books (N.Z.) Ltd, 182–190 Wairau Road,
Auckland 10, New Zealand

Penguin Books Ltd, Registered Offices:
Harmondsworth, Middlesex, England

First published by Roc, an imprint of New American Library,
a division of Penguin Putnam Inc.

First Printing, January 2002
10 9 8 7 6 5 4 3 2 1

 REGISTERED TRADEMARK—MARCA REGISTRADA

Library of Congress Cataloging-in-Publication Data

Stirling, S. M.
    The Peshawar lancers / S.M. Stirling.
    p. cm.
    ISBN 0-451-45848-6 (alk. paper)
    1. Comets—Collisions with Earth—Fiction. 2. International relations—Fiction. 3. Great
Britain—Fiction. 4. Russia—Fiction. I. Title.

PS3569.T543 P47 2002
813'.54—dc21   2001048515

Printed in the United States of America

PUBLISHER'S NOTE
This is a work of fiction. Names, characters, places, and incidents either are the product of the author's
imagination or are used fictitiously, and any resemblance to actual persons, living or dead, business establishments, events, or locales is entirely coincidental.

In Memoriam:
To Poul Anderson
1926–2001

Acknowledgments

To Melinda, Yvonne, Walter, George, Daniel, the two Terrys, Sandra and Trent, of Critical Mass.

To Harry Turtledove, for the gift of *Hobson-Jobson*, which was an immense help; and to Eric Flint, for recommending the *Cultural Atlas of India*.

To Mark Anthony, best chiropractor in the West.

For inspiration, I'd also like to thank Kipling, Mundy, Lamb, Merritt, Howard, Sabatini, Masters, Fraser, Burroughs, Wren, Kline, and all the others, the grand storytellers of adventure and romance.

Quotations from *The Golden Road* and *Hassan*, by James Elroy Flecker.

"What shall we tell you?
Tales, marvelous tales
Of ships and stars and isles where good men rest
Where nevermore the rose of sunset pales
And winds and shadows fall towards the West . . ."

Chapter One

Captain Athelstane King rinsed out his mouth with a swig from the goatskin water bag slung at his saddlebow. Even in October this shadeless, low-lying part of the Northwest Frontier Province was hot; and the dust was everywhere, enough to grit audibly between his back teeth. When he spat, the saliva was as khaki-colored as his uniform or the cloth of his turban. It made a brief dark mark on the white crushed stone of the military highway that snaked down from the Khyber Pass to Peshawar.

Looks the way I feel, he thought. *Dirty, tired, pounded flat. Necessary work*—nobody who'd seen a village overrun by hill-tribe raiders could doubt that—*but not much glory in it.*

Right now the Grand Trunk Road was thronged with the returning men and beasts of the Charasia Field Force, following the path trodden by generations of fighting men—for most of them, by their own fathers and grandfathers and great-grandfathers. Feet and hooves and steel-shod wheels made a grumbling thunder under the pillar of dust that marked their passage; camels gave their burbling cries; occasionally an elephant pulling a heavy artillery piece squealed as it scented water ahead with its trunk lifted out of the murk.

Horse-drawn cannon went past with a dull gunmetal gleam, rocket launchers like bundles of iron tubes on wheels, and machine guns on the backs of pack mules. There were even a few self-propelled armored cars. Two of them were *not* self-propelled any longer, and were being pulled back to the workshops by elephants. King's smile held a trace of malice. The newfangled Stirling-cycle gas engines were marvelous for airships, or the motorcars that were rich men's toys on good roads. In the field, the day of the horse-soldiers wasn't over *quite* yet.

Staff officers with red collar tabs galloped about, keeping order in the endless steel-tipped snake that wound down from the bitter sun-baked ridges of the Border. The right margin of the road was reserved for mounted troops, and there the Peshawar Lancers moved up in a jingle of harness and flutter of pennants and rumbling, crunching clatter of iron-shod hooves on gravel. They trotted past the endless columns of marching infantry and the wheatfield ripple of the Metford rifles sloped over their shoulders.

King ran a critical eye over them as they passed; the *jawans* had shaped up well in the hills . . . for infantry, of course. There were Sikhs with steel chakrams slung on their turbans, Baluchis with long, oiled black hair spilling from under theirs, and Gurkhas in forest green with their *kukris* bouncing at their rumps and little pillbox hats at a jaunty angle above their flat, brown Mongol faces. There was a regiment of the Darjeeling Rifles—young men of the *sahib-log* doing the compulsory service required of all the martial castes—and even a slouch-hatted battalion of Australians.

King frowned slightly at the sight. They were devils in action, but an even worse headache to the high command back in camp. And their ideas of discipline were as eccentric as their dialect of English, which they had the damned cheek to claim was the pure tongue of the Old Empire.

One of their officers answered Colonel Claiborne by saying he didn't understand Hindi! Damned cheek indeed.

His own men were in good spirits as they rode homeward; they were a mixed lot—half Sikhs and Punjabi Hindus of the Jat-cultivator caste, the rest Marathas and Rajputs for the most part. Swarthy, bearded faces grinned beneath the dust and sweat, swapping blood-thirsty boasts and foul jokes, or just glad to be alive and whole. Each carried a ten-foot lance with the butt socketed in the ring on his right stirrup iron; their cotton drill *kurta*-tunics and loose pjamy-trousers were stained with hard service, but the carbine before each man's right knee was clean and the curved *tulwars* at their belts oiled and sharp. Pennants snapped jauntily beneath the steel points that rose and fell in bristling waves above.

They'd had a few sharp skirmishes, and the usual *jezailachi-*sniper-behind-every-rock harassment you could expect on the frontier, but the plunder had been good, and they were returning victorious.

"Quite a sight," King murmured to the soldier riding at his side. "Fifteen thousand, horse and foot and guns—enough to give even the Masuds and Afridis a taste for peace, not to mention the Emir in Kabul. Or so they all assured us, at least, when they signed the treaty."

With a bayonet at their backs and a boot up the bum, he added to himself.

The man beside him spat into the roadside dust in turn; he was a little younger than his officer's twenty-five years, broad-shouldered, with a full black beard and sweeping buffalo-horn mustachios, and snapping dark eyes above a curved beak of nose. King had spoken in English, and Narayan Singh understood it perfectly—had he not followed the young *sahib* from infancy as playmate, sparring partner, soldier-servant, shield-on-shoulder, and right-hand man? Had not his father been the like to the *sahib*'s father before him? But when he replied, it was in Army Hindi, as was fitting.

"The cobra spits, *huzoor*, and the Pathan speaks—who will grow rich on the difference?" he grunted. "The tribes will stay quiet until they forget men dead and captives led away and villages burning. Then some *fakir* of their faith will send them mad with lies about their stupid Allah, and they will remember the fat cattle and silver and women of the lowlands. On that day we shall see the hillman *lashkars* come yelling down the Khyber once more."

King grinned and slung the water bottle back; Narayan Singh was undoubtedly right. The *lashkars*—tribal war bands—would come again; raid, banditry and blood feud were the Afghan idea of being sociable, having fun with your neighbors and kin, like a polo match or tea party among the *sahib-log*. A *razziah* into the Imperial territories was more dangerous than stealing from each other, but also much more profitable.

"It could be worse; we could be in the Khyber Rifles. Comfort yourself with that, *bhai*," he said. "*We* won't be stationed in some Border fort, sleeping with our rifles chained to our wrists."

Which was the only way you could be sure, when a hillman came ghosting over the wall looking for a weapon better than the flintlock *jezails* their own craftsmen could make. A Pathan of the free high-lander tribes could steal a man's shadow, or rustle a horse from a locked room.

Another rider came trotting down the line toward him, also in the uniform of an officer in the Lancers, but with gray streaks in his brown beard and the jeweled clasp of a colonel at the front of his turban. The regimental *rissaldar*-major followed him, with a file of troopers behind.

King saluted, trying not to wince at the pull of the healing wound in his right arm. "Sir!" he said crisply.

Colonel Claiborne returned the gesture and frowned, an expression that made the old dusty white *tulwar* scar on his cheek draw up one corner of his mouth. "Dammit, you insolent young pup, I said you weren't fit for duty yet!"

"Sir, the doctor said—"

"Dammit, I'll have you know that I know a damned sight more about wounds than some *yoni*-doctor from the Territorial Reserve, and *I* say you're unfit for duty."

King forced himself not to smile; the regiment's current medico *was* from the reserve and *was* a gynecologist in civilian life. "I just wanted to see my squadron settled in before I took leave, sir."

Claiborne let approval show through his official anger. That was the answer that a good officer would give. "I assure you," he said dryly, "that the Peshawar Lancers—yea, verily even the second squadron of the Peshawar Lancers—will survive without your services until you return from convalescent leave. Dammit, you are *dismissed*, Captain."

Then the colonel smiled. "I'd hate to have to explain to your lady mother why you'd lost your sword arm, lad. Go on, and go soak away some of the frontier at the Club. You'll be spending the *Diwali* festival at home, or I'll know the reason why, dammit if I don't."

King saluted again. "Since you put it as a direct order, sir."

Then he touched the rein to the neck of his charger and fell out of the column. The *rissaldar*—senior native officer—of the second squadron barked an order; the unit reined in, wheeled right, and rode three paces onto the verge before drawing to a halt like a single great multiheaded beast. Only the tips of the lances moved, quivering and swaying slightly, catching the sun in a glittering ripple as a horse shifted its weight or tossed its head.

The maneuver went with a precision that was smooth rather than stiff, the subtle trademark of men whose trade was war. King rose in the stirrups to address his command:

"*Shabash, sowar! Sat-sree akal!*" he said, dropping effortlessly into Army Hindi, one of his birth-tongues, Imperial English being another, of course. *Honor to you, riders! Well struck!* "Go to your homes and women, and we shall meet again when the swords are unsheathed; the colonel-*sahib* has ordered me on leave."

The *rissaldar* raised his sword hand: "A cheer for Captain King *bahadur*! A cheer for the *Afghan kush*!"

King grinned as he waved his hand and cantered off. It was capital, to be called *champion* and *killer-of-Afghans*. A hand smoothed dust-stained mustachios. Even if it was deserved . . .

The cave where Yasmini slept was cold; she was curled into a ball under the piled sheepskins, but it was not the damp chill of this crevice in the Hindu Kush that made her shiver. It was the words and sights that ran through her sleeping brain. She knew them all too well, these visions; they were nothing like true dreams.

Instead, they were simply *true*, though they might be of places and deeds far away, of things that might have been, of things that might yet come to be.

This time it was of the past—some sense she could not have named told her it was the single past that could lead to this cave in this night. . . .

A cold wind from the west flogged snow through the streets of London, piling it in man-high drifts against the sooty brick at street corners and filling the cuts made by a thousand shovels near as fast as they could be cleared. Great kettles of soup steamed over coal fires in sheltered spots, and children too young to do other work shuttled back and forth with pannikins of the hot broth. Under the wailing of the fanged wind they could hear the dull *crump . . . crump* where parties from the Royal Engineers tried desperately to blast a way for supply ships through the thickening ice on the Thames. The men and women who toiled to keep the streets cleared were bundled in multiple sets of clothes, greatcoats, mufflers, and improvised garments made from blankets, curtains, and any other cloth that came to hand. More pulled beside skeletal horses to drag sleds of fuel and food, or boxed cargo down to the docks.

When the horses died, they went butchered into the stewpots; hideous rumors spread about human bodies disappearing from the piles where they were stacked. . . .

The immaterial viewpoint that was her suspended consciousness swooped like a bird through the wall of a building guarded by soldiers in fur caps and greatcoats, a building where messengers came and went incessantly. In a chamber within she saw a man with long dark curls and a tuft of chin-beard dyed to a black the deep lines of age on his face belied, dressed in a sober elegance of velvet and broadcloth cut in an antique style. He turned from the window, shivering despite his thick overcoat and the blazing fire in the grate.

The face was one Yasmini recognized, long and full-lipped, with a beak of a nose and great dark eyes; a Jewish face, clever and quick and intensely human. And she could feel the *being* of him, not just the appearance . . .

Benjamin Disraeli rubbed his hands together, putting on an appearance of briskness. Even Number 10 Downing Street was cold this October of 1878; sometimes the prime minister wondered if warmth was anything more than a fading dream, if blue sky and green leaves would ever come again.

"I fear must beg your pardon, gentlemen," he said to the half dozen men who awaited him around the table of the White Room.

She understood the speech somehow, even though it was the pure English of six generations past, not the hybrid tongue of the second century after the Fall. It was as if her mind rode with his, a deep well full of memory and thought, where concepts and ideas rose with a darting quickness, like trout in a mountain stream.

A wave of his hand indicated the meager tray of tea and scones. "You will appreciate, however . . ."

He had never taken more than a dilettante's interest in the sciences, but it was clear that an awesome amount of talent was involved in this delegation. Stokes, the secretary of the Royal Society; Sir William Thomson down from Glasgow, despite the state the railways were in; Tait likewise from Edinburgh; Maxwell from Cambridge—

It was the Glaswegian who spoke: "We would no ha' troubled ye, my lord, but for the implications of our calculations concerning the impacts the globe has suffered. Even now, we're no sure if 'twere a single body that broke up as it struck the atmosphere or a spray, perhaps of comets . . . consultations took so long because travel is so slow, and telegraphs no better."

In his youth, Disraeli had been something of a dandy. There was a hint of that in the way he smoothed his lapels now. "I am sure your speculations are very interesting, gentlemen—"

Inwardly, he fumed. *The world has suffered the greatest disaster since Noah's Flood; God alone knows how we will survive until the spring; and yet every Tom and Dick and Harry sees fit to demand some of my time—when that commodity is as scarce as coal.*

Perhaps those who crowded into every church and chapel and synagogue in London—probably in the whole world, with mosques and temples thrown in—were wiser. They were helping keep each other warm, and at least weren't *distracting* him.

The annoyance was a welcome relief from the images that kept creeping back into the corners of his mind, images born of the papers that crossed his desk. Fire rising in pillars from where the hammer of the skies had fallen all across Europe, so high that the tops flattened against the upper edge of the atmosphere itself. Walls of water striking the Atlantic coast of Ireland and scouring far inland, wreckage all along the western shores of England, where the other island didn't shelter it; far worse in most of maritime Europe. Reports of unbelievably worse damage on the American side of the Atlantic. Chaos and panic spreading like a malignant tide from the Channel deep into Russia as the governments shattered under the strain.

Only the supernal cold had kept plague at bay, when the corpses of the unburied dead lay by the millions across the ruined lands.

"Perhaps we could discuss the scientific implications of the Fall at some time when events are less pressing—when the weather has improved, for example."

The professor exchanged a glance with his colleagues, then cleared his throat and spoke with desperate earnestness: "But my lord, that is precisely what we must tell you. The water vapor and dust in the upper atmosphere—there will *be* no improvement in the weather. Not for at least one year. Possibly . . ." Thomson's face sagged. "Possibly as many as three or four. Snow and cold will continue all through what should be the summer."

Disraeli stared at the scientist for a long moment. Then he slumped forward, and the world turned gray at the edges. Vaguely he could feel hands helping him into his seat, and the sharp peat-flavored taste of whiskey from the scientist's silver flask.

Moments ago he had been consumed with worry about the hundreds of thousands of refugees pouring in from the flooded, ruined coasts of Wales, Devon, and Cornwall. With finding ships to bring in Australian corn. Now . . .

He came back to himself—somewhat. A man did not rise from humble beginnings to steer the British Empire without learning self-mastery. Doubly so, if he were a Jew. He hadn't asked for this burden. *All that I desired was to dish that psalm-singing hypocrite Gladstone*, he thought wryly. Now Gladstone was dead in the sodden, frozen ruins of Liverpool, *and the burden is mine, nonetheless.*

"Correct me if I'm wrong, gentlemen, but as far as I can see you have just passed sentence of death on ninety-nine in every hundred of the human race. If any survive, it will be as starving cannibals."

One of the scientists dropped his gray-bearded face into his hands. "It is not we who have passed judgment. God has condemned the human race. My God, my God, why have you forsaken us?"

"Nay, it's no quite so bad as that, sir," Thomson said quickly. His voice was steady, although the burr of his native dialect had grown stronger. "Forebye the weather will turn strange over all the world; yet still the effects will be strongest in the northern latitudes, and even there worst around the North Atlantic Basin—the Gulf Stream may be gone the while, d'ye ken . . . In Australia they might hardly notice it, save that the next few years will be a trifle more cool and damp."

"But what of England, Sir William? What of her millions?"

The scientists looked at him. With a chill twist deep in his stomach, he realized that they were waiting for *him* to speak. . . .

Yasmini screamed and thrashed against the blankets. A hard hand cuffed her across the ear, and she shuddered awake. A flickering torch cast shadows across the rough stone of the cavern wall above her, and glittered in the eyes of the man who held it. Count Ignatieff was dressed in the rough sheepskin jacket, baggy pants, and high boots of an ordinary Cossack; but nobody who saw those eyes could ever mistake him for an ordinary man. It was more than the cold *boyar* arrogance, or even the fact that one eye was blue and the other brown. She suspected that he thought of himself as a tiger, but it was a cobra's gaze that looked down at her.

"*Veno vat*, Excellency," she said. "It was a dream—"

"A true dream, bitch?"

"Yes, Excellency. But not a vision of any use; *pajalsta*, Excellency. One from the past. It is the vision of Disraeli, once again. Only Disraeli, Excellency."

He struck her again, but for all the stinging pain in her cheek it was merely perfunctory, if you knew the huge strength that lurked behind the nobleman's sword-callused palm as she did.

"For that you should not disturb my sleep," Ignatieff said.

His left hand toyed with an earring in the shape of a peacock's tail; it was the sigil of initiation in the cult of Malik Nous—or Tchernobog as some called Him, the demiurge worshiped throughout the dominions of the Czar in Samarkand as the true Lord of This World.

"We must be in Kashmir within two weeks. Dream us a way past the Imperial patrols." Ignatieff kicked her in the stomach. "Why do you keep seeing that damned old Jew, anyway?" he demanded.

"I do not know, Excellency—it is my very great fault, Excellency," she gasped, trying to draw the thin cold air of the heights back into her lungs. "I most humbly apologize."

But Yasmini did know, although there was nothing of conscious control in her dreams. It was the eyes that drew her—those great brown eyes, eyes that held all the pain of a broken world.

Peaceful, Athelstane King thought, as he and his orderly rode eastward at a steady mile-eating canter-and-walk pace; Narayan Singh had two spare horses behind him on a leading rein. With those, and swinging northeast around the military convoys that filled the Grand Trunk Road just now, they made good speed.

Peaceful compared to the tribal country, at least, if not by the standards of home.

Near Peshawar, the dry rocky hills of the Khyber gave way to an alluvial plain, intensely green and laced with irrigation canals full of olive-colored, silt-heavy water from the Kabul River. Plane trees lined the road, arching over the murmuring channels on either side to give a grateful shade; the lowlands were still warm as October faded. This close to a major city and frontier base the roads were excellent, even on the country lanes away from the main highway, and it was a pleas-ant enough ride on a warm fall afternoon.

Tile-roofed, fortified manor houses of plastered stone stood white amid the blossoms and lawns of their gardens, each with a watchtower at a corner and a hamlet of earth-colored, flat-roofed cottager-tenant houses not too far distant; this area had been gazetted for settlement more than a century ago, right after the Second Mutiny. An occasional substantial yeoman-tenant farm or small factory with its brick chim-ney kept the scene from monotony. Around the habitations lay the fields that fed them and the city beyond; poplin green of sugarcane, grass green of maize, jade-hued pasture, the yellow of reaped wheat stubble, late-season orchards of apricot and pomegranate, shaggy and tattered at the same time. Cut alfalfa hay scented the air with an over-whelming sweetness, and the neat brown furrows of plowed fields promised new growth next year.

People were about; mostly *ryots*, peasant cottagers, the men in dirty white cotton pants and tunics, women in much the same but with longer tunic-skirts and head scarves instead of turbans, both with spades and hoes, bills and pitchforks over their shoulders. There were also oxcarts heaped with melons or fruit or baled fodder, moving slowly to a dying-pig squeal of axles; a shepherd with his crook and dogs and road-obstructing smelly flock making the horses toss their heads and shy; a brace of horse-copers from the Black Mountain with a string of remounts for sale.

King took a close look at faces and gear as they went by, giving him the salaam and smiling, looking rather like hairy vultures with teeth. *Hassanazais or Akazais*, he decided.

Those were Pathan-Afghan frontier tribes in the debatable lands; beyond the settled, administered zone, but not beyond the Imperial frontier . . . not quite. In theory both were at peace, autonomous but tributary to the Sirkar, the government of the Raj. No doubt the horse-copers had *kitubs*—official papers—with the appropriate stamps, seals, good-conduct badges, and letters of recommendation from the Political Officers attached to their clans, all as right and tight as be-damned.

King and Narayan Singh both kept wary eyes moving until the pair jogged out of sight and for a half hour afterward, lest the officially approved traders unofficially decide on impulse to shoot the Sirkar's men in the back and lift their horses and weapons. To enliven the tedium of spying for the Emir, or half the bandit chiefs on the Border, or both and several others besides; and a modern magazine rifle was worth more than any dozen horses, to the wild tribes.

A few minutes later, a stout gray-bearded *zamindar* trotted by on a dappled hunter. A pair of sandy-haired Kalasha mercenaries from up in the hills above Chitral were riding at the landowner's tail with carbines in the crook of their arms, which was wise; he wore pistol and saber himself, which was also prudent. You didn't go unguarded or unarmed this close to the Border, with loose-wallahs and cattle-lifters and *jangli-admis* about. Nor were the local Pathans much tamer than their wild kin, even if they'd learned better than to show it over the last century.

"Good evening, Captain!" the squire called in a cheery voice, lifting his riding crop to his turban in salute. "Capital work you lads have been doing, eh, what?"

Athelstane answered in kind; in fact the Army slang for punitive expeditions of the type he'd just finished was *butcher and bolt*, and depressingly accurate.

Not quite what the newspaper correspondents dwell on, though, he thought.

His smile was broader for the next passerby, a woman in a ponytrap with a tasseled sunshade. She was likely a wealthy man's wife, from the opulence of rings on fingers and toes and the emerald stud through one nostril, and the jeweled collar and leash on the pet monkey that climbed and chattered beside her. Her sari was of black silk shot through with silver, a fold of it over her yellow hair and the other folds showing full curves.

"Ma'rm," he said as they passed, bowing his neck and touching one finger to his brow in polite salute.

Sighing, he ignored the pouting invitation of a full lower lip and the flirting blue-eyed glance sent the tall Lancer officer's way from behind her ostrich-feather fan.

Last thing you need now is a bloody duel with a husband, he told himself sternly. And nothing could be private; there was a maid in the cart with her, and half a dozen armed retainers following behind. *Dogras*, he thought, looking at their blue turbans and green-dyed beards. They bristled with spears and matchlocks and knives, one resplendent in back-and-breast armor and lobster-tail helmet.

Think about the first whiskey-peg at the club instead. Think about Hasamurti's delectable rump.

"Now I know thou'rt wounded in truth, *huzoor*," Narayan Singh said dryly from his side, as they trotted on toward the outskirts of Peshawar town.

King cocked an eye at his companion: *Huzoor* meant *sir*, but there were ways and ways of saying it.

"What precisely did that mean, *Daffadar* Singh?" he asked.

Narayan Singh snorted. A *daffadar* was a noncommissioned man, but there was no excess of deference in his voice.

"When a pretty woman passes by smiling and making eyes, *sahib*, and we ride on, I know you are wounded indeed. Wounded and near death!"

Countryside gave way to villa-fringed outskirts and the broad straight streets of the Civil Lines—the military cantonment was on the south side of town. The streets were filled with wagons and light horse carts, pedicabs, cyclists—Peshawar had almost as many bicycle manufactories as Ludhiana—and an occasional silent motorcar. The country scents of growth and manure and water gave way to a smell of humanity and coal smoke from the factories spreading south and east. Their horses breasted through the crowds of Peshawar Old Town itself, the narrow twisted streets near the Kissa Khwani Bazaar, the Street of the Storytellers, with the old Sikh-built fort of Bala Hissar frowning down from its hill.

The lanes were overhung by balconies shielded with carved wooden *purdah* screens, and below, the buildings were full of little *chaikanas* where patrons sat on cushions drinking tea laced with cardamom and lemon and smoking their hookahs. The streets were loud with banyan merchants selling dried fruit, rugs, carpets, hairy *potsheen* coats made from whole sheepskins, karakul lambskin caps, and Chitrali cloaks from little open-front shops; full of the smell of packed humanity, sharp pungent spices, sweat-soaked wool, horses. And of veiled women, an icily superior ICS bureaucrat waving a fly-whisk in a rickshaw drawn by a near-naked coolie, a midshipman in a blue jacket visiting his family on leave, bicyclists frantically ringing their handlebar bells, sellers of iced sherbets crying their wares . . .

"Good to be back to civilization," King said with a sigh.

"Han, sahib," Narayan Singh said, as they drew rein before the wrought-iron gate of the Peshawar Club. "Good to sleep where we need not keep one eye open for knives in the dark!"

King laughed and nodded, as grooms ran to take their horses.

Chapter Two

Miss Cassandra Mary Effingham King—Ph.D., F.R.S.—tilted her glasses down her long straight nose and looked over them. That gave her a view out the slanting windows that ran along the airship's side galleries, and at the ground a thousand feet below, distracting her from the knot of anxiety in her stomach.

It isn't the height that's bothersome. She had been born in Kashmir and had been an alpinist from her early teens, yet another of her eccentricities. Clinging to a cliff with a sheer drop beneath didn't worry her.

What disturbed her about flying was the knowledge that she was hanging under millions of cubic feet of hydrogen gas.

Illogical, she scolded herself, mentally reciting statistics. *Air travel is safe. Safer than a railroad journey. Safer than a steamship.* Considerably *safer than a motorcar.* Much *safer than rock-climbing, for Durga's sake!*

Logic seemed to have little to do with it. It never did, which was why she always took trains when she could. No matter how much she lectured herself, her stomach muscles still seemed to feel that they must strain to hold the airship up. The more so, given her responsibility for the precious cargo resting under guard in the baggage hold. Not just the cost of it—a *lakh* of rupees, on top of the *crore* for the project as a whole—but the endless niggling effort to make something on the very edge of her people's abilities.

She leaned closer to the railing and looked up at the solid-seeming bulk above her, thrown in shadow with the westering sun on the other side of the craft. The *Diana* was the newly launched pride of British Imperial Airways, an orca shape eight hundred fifty feet long sheathed in silver-gray doped cotton, more than two hundred feet around at the broadest point, a third of the way between blunt nose and cruciform tailfins.

Cassandra had always been given to analysis under stress; to a scientist, the firmness of numbers was soothing. Her trained memory reeled off details automatically; truss rings, laminated bamboo geodesic skin framework, radial steel wire bracing, gasbags like giant cylinders with a central hollow to pass the triangular keel; strengths, stresses, densities, useful lift.

One of the eight Stirling-cycle engines that drove the *Diana* was in a pod not far above the level of the gallery, humming away—more data, gas burners, heat exchanger and regenerator, triaxially opposed pistons and enclosed crankshaft in an oil bath, gases as working fluids, power-to-weight ratios. An elegant, quiet machine, with only the whirring of the four-bladed teak-laminate propellers to break the rushing wind, and beneath it a faint mechanical hum.

She took a long breath, remembered what she'd learned from *yogis* she'd met, made herself *see*. Control the breath. Slow and steady, steadying the heartbeat. Let perception flow through the senses without interruption.

They had left the rich bottomlands of the Ganges plain behind by noon. Below lay the dry sandstone ridges of the Shiwalak range, the southernmost ripple of the Himalayas, occupied by the client kingdoms of Basholi and Kangra. The *Diana*'s shadow moved over them, across rolling cactus-speckled hills interrupted here and there by abrupt escarpments where the folded bones of the earth reared suddenly. Human habitations were the dried-blood color of the stone, huddled hamlets and tiny fields scratched from a bitter earth, with here and there the crude belligerence of a chieftain's fortlet.

Dogras dwelt here, Sikh and Hindu, men poor and proud and fierce—though their aristocrats sat in the House of Lords in Delhi, coequal with nobles whose lineage ran back through the centuries of lost Britain. The land's other export was fighting men, whose wages bought what their meager farms could not grow.

Feudal relics, she thought with a mental sniff; she was firmly on the Liberal wing of the Whig party. *Backward.*

The yogic technique worked, bringing her out of her funk. She became aware of the slight, pleasant chill of the air, so welcome after Delhi's heat and dust and endless crowds—four million people in one city! Nearly as many as dead London, at the height of the Old Empire. None of the other great cities of the Raj—Bombay, Calcutta, Cape Town, Singapore, Melbourne—was even half that size. No city whatsoever outside the Empire was a third as large, save perhaps Peking. It was a wonder anyone could draw breath in the capital, or think two coherent thoughts without interruption.

The *Diana* was working its way north into a head wind, rising gradually toward the high passes, and a slight subliminal quiver ran through its fabric. The air held a scent of glue and fresh wood from the laminations of the structure, the doping compound on the fabric, the smell of hot metal from the engines.

She sighed and pushed the glasses back up to reading position. Papers lay scattered across the rosewood-topped wicker table before her. She picked one up:

> . . . impact of a small comet—600 yd. diameter icy body striking the Earth's surface at the velocity . . . mass $M = 4\text{x}10$ to the ninth pounds . . . kinetic energy $E = 1.2$ GT . . .

No, I'm too distracted to do two plus two, much less equations. The drawings of the Observatory project were as familiar as her own face in the mirror, even though construction wasn't her specialty. It would be more efficient to have specialists to handle each aspect of it, but even the Empire's scientific establishment wasn't quite that large yet. Everyone had to turn a hand to the needful; and besides, generalism was traditional.

I'm not going to get any serious work done today, she decided, and tapped the sheets back into their folders, and the folders back into the black leather carrying case. *Nor have any worthwhile conversation to pass the time; or even a mild flirtation.*

At the predinner hour the airship's starboard lounge held a third of those aboard, twoscore sitting or strolling or leaning on the rail to watch the landscape go by. She sighed inaudibly, looking at her fellow passengers. A good many were affluent older couples playing tourist on a trip to the Garden of the Empire; air travel was beyond the reach of all but the very well-to-do. The younger set included officials, men of business, military officers, MPs and their families returning now that Parliament was in recess. One handsome young Rajput looked like a maharaja's son from the rubies and emeralds on the hilt of his saber, and might be a student or a pilgrim or both. More than a few were scholars like herself, heading for Oxford; from all over India, and the Viceroyalties of Australia and the Cape, even a scattering from the farther colonies like Britain or North America.

Most were men, and she flattered herself that she was reasonably pleasant to the eye. Tall certainly, five-foot-eight. A trifle athletic, but shapely with it, eyes pale gray in a regular straight-nosed, bow-lipped face. *Quite* satisfactory, especially in the outfit she was wearing, the height of daring Delhi fashion and calculated to set off her long-limbed build. The women's-style *shalwar qamiz* had a black silk tunic embroidered with gold rosettes along the edges of its knee-length skirts, gold buckled belt, billowing sequined pantaloons, and tooled kidskin shoes with upturned toes; a transparent shawl was fastened with emerald-headed gold pins to her piled chestnut hair, and fell past it to her waist.

Plenty of men here, and every one of them convinced I'm a bluestocking freak of nature, a man-hating Sapphist, or both, and terrified of me. Another sigh; the freak of nature was debatable, but a dismally unexciting experiment had convinced her she wasn't a Sapphist. *The man-hating I* might *manage, if this nonsense continues.* Her own close colleagues were mostly more accepting; the problem was that they were also mostly decades older, married, or both. Usually both.

A white-jacketed steward came through, tapping at a xylophone. "*Sahibs, memsahibs*, dinner. Dinner is served."

"At last," she murmured sarcastically, and finished the glass of white wine that sat before her.

Count Vladimir Obromovich Ignatieff wore a patch over one eye—the blue one. Here in the Imperial territories he was passing as a trader in raw lapis from the Wakan highlands, come to sell to Oxford's numerous jewelers, with papers that included a meticulously forged border-crossing stamp and customs payment. The Wakan Tadjiks were fair enough that his Slavic complexion—much weathered by the Asian sun—was unremarkable. Blue eyes were uncommon but not outlandishly rare there, too—some said it was a legacy of Alexander's Macedonians passing through.

But the combination of light and dark would be too likely to attract attention. The patch would not; one-eyed men were many.

The persona was one that had served him a score of times and more among the teeming millions of the Raj; the Empire's sheer size could be a boon to its enemies. The loose trousers, hairy sheepskin jacket, dirty *pugaree*-turban, and truculent walk with one hand on his knife hilt were similarly nondescript.

As with any mission beyond the Czar's domains, before he left a priest had given him dispensation to remove his sigil of initiation at need and bear the defilement of eating with Deniers. Okhrana secret-police funds covered the necessary gold and gifts and sacrifices, and the rites of purification always made a pleasant homecoming. Long training altered his stance, the way he held his shoulders, the movements of his hands, and the manner of clearing his throat . . . so many things that it was easy not to spit when he saw a fain of the Traitor Christ. Or even not to lash out when some underling jostled him.

This was his first time in Oxford—even the natives did not call it Srinagar anymore—and he had to admit that it was a pleasant-looking town, worthy of its setting in the mile-high valley, surrounded by white-tipped peaks rearing into heaven. Less beastly hot than the cities of the lowland plains to the south, for a beginning; less crowded, too, and not so foul with the effluent of smokestacks and factories. The air was cool in early October; the smells were mostly of woodsmoke, humans, horses, often of the flowers that the *Anglichani* so loved.

Most of what he saw had been built in the last century or so. According to the Okhrana background files it had been very bad here in the dark years, three freezing-cold summers one after another. All who could walk had joined the desperate attempt to mass-migrate into the warmer low country, where *some* crops ripened even in the worst seasons right after the Fall; that had been part of what the histories of the Raj called the Second Mutiny, along with the Afghan invasion and general revolt. Here in Kashmir reprisals by the equally desperate *sahib-log* mostly finished what little the famine left.

Even the Anglichani *were hard then,* Ignatieff thought. *But they refused the Truth, and so their souls grew infected once more.*

Resettlement by the Raj had brought in a new population, but a few landmarks remained. Beside Nagin Lake reared the gleaming white marble dome and spires that had been the Hazratbal mosque and were now St. Kelvin's Cathedral; a rise bore the fortress of Hari Parbat, built four centuries ago by the Mughal Padishah Akbar; and atop the hill called the Throne of Solomon the great Shiva temple of Sankaracharya brooded over the valley as it had for a millennium and more, while the empires and rulers came and went.

Most of modern Oxford, however, was built in New Empire styles along a gridwork of streets, two- and three-story houses of reddish stone with carved wooden balconies and steep-pitched tile roofs. Crisp yellow leaves fell from the trees that arched overhead, to scritch under his boots on the brick sidewalk, and stone troughs full of nasturtiums separated the walkway from the street like a barrier of cool fire. Folk in the streets lacked some of the raucous intensity he remembered from other Imperial cities, street vendors and beggars were few, and beyond the end of the avenue he could see a park that gave onto the blue waters of Dal Lake and floating houseboats.

He turned past a Christian church, past a shrine with a statue of Shiva dancing creation and destruction, and into an eating house thick with cooking smells and tobacco smoke. It had amused him to set the meeting here, where wine and meat were served—the men he awaited were fiercely orthodox high-caste Hindus, Brahmins who would feel defiled even to see another touch the forbidden. His sense of humor stopped short of using a place that the *sahib-log* were likely to frequent. This catered to craftsmen, shopkeepers, upper servants; mostly Christians, and English was the commonest tongue you heard. He ordered *barra* kebabs on saffron rice—saffron was a cash crop here, less of a luxury than in most places, and Kashmiri rice was famous—and a squat flask of indifferent local red wine.

The two who came to join him were slight, fine-boned brown men, clean-shaven, dressed in fawn jackets and *dhotis* and sandals, and little boat-shaped caps on close-cut black hair; they hid their distaste for their surroundings well, even when he waved at his plate and glass:

"Plenty for you, brothers," he said, in coarse lower-caste Hindi with a strong Tadjik-Persian accent. "*Bahut acha! Bahut acha!* Very good! Very good!"

He smacked his lips over a mouthful of the garlic-laden grilled meat and rolled rice into a ball with his fingers, offering it to the others.

"No—no—" The older of the two Bengali Brahmins swallowed and visibly restrained himself from leaning backward. "*Dhanyavad*, many thanks, but it is against our religion."

"Against my religion, too!" Ignatieff said, swilling wine noisily. Fortunately, pretending to be a Muslim didn't require that you pretend to be a *pious* Muslim. "But Allah will forgive me, if I strike a blow in the Holy War."

The younger man whispered to his companion in Bengali: "How can we trust this cow-murdering wine-bibber, my teacher? Even for a Muslim and outcaste, he is vile."

The older man flicked a look at Ignatieff's face to make sure he hadn't understood—Bengali and Hindi were closely related—and the Okhrana agent beamed uncomprehending friendship.

He spoke both languages perfectly, of course.

"Peace," the older Bengali said. "The enemy of my enemy is my friend. Damascus has suffered from the aggressions of the *sahib-log*, too."

He repeated the last part in Hindi, and Ignatieff nodded sagely. *Perfectly true; a friend until the time of the knives*, he thought. In the last generation or two the *Angrezi* Raj had taken Zanzibar from the Caliph's Omani vassal-sultans, sunk and burned Arab slave-dhows in the Red Sea, and it was extending naval patrols into the Red and Arabian Seas. Against pirates and slavers, Delhi claimed . . . but where the Empire's foot trod, there it stayed.

"Here," he said, shoving a scrap of paper and a large brass key across the table under the cover of a napkin. "As we agreed; here is the address of the godown with the weapons—and the gold."

Coined in those beautifully calligraphic *dinars* minted in Baghdad. The Indians took both and left. Ignatieff smiled broadly and waved for a dish of the peach ice cream that was also a Kashmiri specialty.

We can discuss the details when we meet again in Hell, he thought. Which they would—everyone left in the Fallen world would, sooner or later—but *he* wouldn't be surprised to arrive there.

I might as well get something out of this damned chivalry nonsense, Cassandra King thought.

A gentleman gave place to an unaccompanied gentlewoman as a matter of course. Normally it annoyed her no end; a pedestal was a very bad starting place in the race of life. Today she took ruthless advantage, cutting in near the head of the line filing out of the lounge into the airship's dining room. That let her pick a single table with a window; better honest silence than strained chitchat and glances.

The décor of the dining section was light and airy in the modern style—teak and ebony tiles on the floor, sandalwood chairs carved into fanciful lacework and cushioned in white cotton, chiseled brass tables with inlay and enamel, murals of colorful jungle birds on the exterior walls between windows. It soothed her slightly as she considered the menu. The *Diana*'s kitchen had a rather Central Provinces bent, which was a pleasant change from the Mughal cuisine of Delhi: She ordered baffla wheat cakes rich with ghee and ate them with pungent lentil dal soup and sweet laddoos dumplings, followed by spicy rogan josh, shami-kebab, and sheermal bread. Waiters brought bowls of rosewater to clean the hands, and crisp fluffy towels to dry them.

Squares of iced mango and watermelon on skewers and Assamese tea came after the main courses. She nibbled, sipped, and wondered the while who had had the bad taste and sheer gall to ruin the dining room's effect by picking a reproduction of Lord Leighton's *Martyrdom of St. Disraeli* as the mural for the interior wall.

She'd seen the original at her coming-out, when she was Presented at court in Delhi twelve years ago; that one was twenty feet high and done in gold, coral, ivory, faience, and semiprecious stones. It was the backdrop to the Lion Throne, after all, staring each generation of young gentlewomen in the face as they were led up and made their curtsey to the King-Emperor and Queen-Empress.

This was an excellent rendering in oils, on the canvas partitions that made up the interior structure of the *Diana*. Leighton had taken his inspiration from the Exodus Cantos of Kipling's epic *Lament for the Lost Homeland;* the burning dome of St. Paul's looming behind, "stark flame against a sleet-filled August sky," as the poet had put it and generations of schoolchildren had memorized ever since; the red-coated Foot Guards struggling with the snarling cannibal mob in the foreground and being butchered and devoured even as they fought; Disraeli himself standing alone, draped in a fur cloak as the ice fell about him, looking southward to where the last ship of the Exodus would wait in vain. The great Martyr, dying like Moses without setting foot in the new homeland which he'd prepared for his people.

Heroic. Inspiring. Great art, no doubt. But for a dining *room? Whatever could they have been thinking of?*

Her generation was less obsessed with the Fall and the Exodus than those before it, in any case. It was ancient history, though she remembered how shocking it had been to hear her grandmother talking of actually *meeting* Kipling when she was a young girl, a man born before the Fall.

There was a slight hissing sound as the airship's heating system came on, and a rumble as water ballast valved out from the tanks along the keel. Attendants stood by discreetly with oxygen cylinders and masks, in case some lowlander was overcome. They were rising above dense pine forests now, two-hundred-foot Himalayan firs below, then over naked rock above the tree line and the saddle of the Banihar Pass. Below, the railway looked like a child's toy, a puffing locomotive disappearing into the Jawahar Tunnel—she could remember the celebrations when that was finished, not long after her sixth birthday. Snow peaks shimmered ahead and all about, floating in infinite blue and trailing banners of glittering windborne frost as the great airship went sailing silently along the roof of the world.

Cassandra smiled as they crested the heights, and gasps broke out from others at the sight of the Vale of Kashmir below. *Garden of the Empire indeed*, she thought. And the province of her own birth.

It was supposed to be like the lost Homeland—although from what she'd read, she doubted that terraced vineyards and rice fields had been all that common in pre-Fall England. Certainly this was green and lovely enough in the glowing long-shadow light of sunset; thickly forested mountain slopes surrounding a mile-high patchwork quilt of plowed land, pasture, prosperous farmsteads, the regular lines of apple and peach orchards, almonds and apricots, roads lined with great poplars and chinars and oaks. Parkland and garden surrounded the country seats of landowners and the boarding schools that were almost as numerous—the climate was famous for healthfulness. Some of those schools bore names like Eton and Winchester, United Services and Cheltenham, and they drew children from all over the Empire.

Rexin was there, the King estate near Avantipur. *Not really home anymore*, she thought, with a trace of sadness, although she was always

welcome on visits. *Athelstane's, really. I'm an Oxford girl now.* The eldest
son inherited, and the siblings had to make their own way in the
world, by marriage or career.

The city brought further murmurs from the other passengers;
Cassandra ignored the ancient monuments, the famous racecourse,
polo fields, botanic gardens, and Lord's cricket grounds, even the lakes
and the Jehelum River where Cambridge came to row against Oxford
and usually be soundly thrashed, which was a high point of the Empire's social year. Her eyes were on the mellow stone of the university's
quadrangles, glimpsed among the trees and ivy. The ships of the Exodus had borne books and instruments and scholars, as well as weapons
and machinery and hungry refugees crammed into every nook and
cranny—more of St. Disraeli's foresight. Work had begun on the university in the fourth year after the Fall, and continued even during the
terrible years when survival hung by a hair. The workaday city had
grown up around it in the generations that followed.

Now there was a considerable airship port on the lakeside as
well, with great arched sheds and another huge silvery shape curving
up from the water even as she watched, off south to Delhi and
Madras, perhaps even to Singapore and Perth. Sunlight remained on
the mountain peaks, tingeing the snow with crimson, but night was
falling on the lake and city below. Lights appeared and twinkled, the
blue-white of the airship port's electric arcs, the softer yellow and
yellow-white of lamp flame and gaslight in the streets and houses
beyond.

The Goan steward with the xylophone came through again. "Prepare for landing, *memsahibs* and *sahibs*. Prepare for landing, please."

Part of Cassandra King's stomach unclenched. Fairly soon her feet
would be on the ground, away from this flying bomb. Another part of
her nerves thrummed yet more tautly. That meant she'd have to over-
see the priceless cargo that was in her trust, as well.

Yasmini lay still on the narrow bed, for the moment simply enjoying the sensation of space around her. Most people would have considered the little attic room of the Kashmiri inn to be strait quarters.
But it was all hers; even the Master had to knock to gain entrance, for
appearance sake. None watched or spoke or shouted; there was only
the low murmur of sound from below, smells of curry and garlic from

the kitchens, wheels and feet from the street outside. Compared to the pens at home, it was a palace. Space and quiet and . . .

Her mind shied away from *freedom* with an automatic reflex, as mindless as the flinch before a Master's upraised hand. The time lines where she failed to do that were—

How are they worse than what I see? she thought suddenly.

True, they mostly ended in death. Often death by torture. But she was twenty-four years old; she had been Active for nearly ten years. Soon it would be her daughters the Master would want, not her visions.

Unbidden, a face from the dreams. An *Anglichani* face; a man, young—only a few years older than herself. Dark brown hair, brown eyes, a square jaw, and a thin scar along one cheek. The vision had a sharp outline; only a few paths led to it, then. An overtone that meant the vision was close and personal, something that might happen to *her*, yet with overtones of weight—enormous, crushing weight.

Her breath came faster, and her hands felt clammy with fear. That meant that whatever it was concerned both her and a huge number of other world lines; instinctively, she strained to see more. The lines twisted. There were glimpses of fire, of a floating sensation unlike anything she had ever known. The clash of sabers, and a body falling into infinite blue space—

No. That way lay death. A wash of no-thought went through her; she controlled her breathing, concentrating instead on an unvarying hum at the back of her mind.

Chapter Three

"**D**uty calls, *chaebli*," Athelstane King said over his shoulder to the naked woman behind him.

One of the Peshawar Club's discreet manservants had slipped the calling card under the door. As King read, he fended off the soft rounded warmth that pressed to his back, and the hands that reached teasingly around his body and tried to undo the bath towel wrapped about his waist.

The card was severely plain, printed in black-on-beige:

Sir Manfred Warburton, Bart.
Imperial Political Service
Metcalfe House, Chandi Chowk
Delhi

On the back was a scribbled: *requests the pleasure of your company at dinner, at 7:15, to discuss matters pertaining to the King-Emperor's service.*

He turned to give the young woman a kiss and then a firm smack on the backside. *Seven o'clock already, dammit!* Ganesha alone knew how long the card had lain ignored. The Club had telephones since year before last—no expense spared *here*. Why couldn't the man have called up?

He hadn't planned on going downstairs at all. In fact, he'd planned on having something sent up for dinner and spending the rest of the evening the way he'd spent the afternoon; it had been a *long* four months of involuntary celibacy on the frontier. Then when he was exhausted enough and Hasamurti was crying for mercy, there would be time to read accumulated letters from his mother and twin sister and younger siblings, and then sleep for eighteen hours. But . . .

The Political Service?

Politicals served as advisors at the courts of the Empire's client states; they supervised the Tribal Agencies beyond the frontier; they adventured far into the barbarian lands, sniffing out troubles to come and staking claims; they ran the Intelligence departments . . . and they fought the Great Game with the Czar's agents, and the Mikado's, and the Caliph's, and assorted subversives.

The Army and Navy were the Empire's sword and fist; the Political Service was its eyes and a goodly part of its brain besides.

"Not now, *chaebli*," he said again, grabbing the wrist of an exploring hand as it crept around his waist.

Hasamurti pouted despite the endearment—darling, roughly—and flounced off to sit poised beside the sunken marble tub, still full of steaming water with wisps of foam on its surface. She leaned back on one hand and tossed her hair.

"Wouldn't you rather be with me than with some moldy old bookmonger *kitub*-wallah from the capital?" she said.

He chuckled and nodded as he finished toweling himself off. *Good to be* clean *again*, he thought. And to smell slightly of rosewater and musk, rather than horse sweat and his own unwashed hide.

"If it were mine to say, I'd stay," he said. "But needs must."

Quite a change from squatting to scrub in a chatti *of ice water, waiting for an Afridi to pop out from behind a rock waving a knife*, he thought. *And Hasamurti makes a pleasant change of scenery, too.*

The troopers of the Peshawar Lancers were good lads one and all, but not much aesthetically. His mistress was a classic Kashmiri beauty of nineteen, strong-featured, with wavy raven hair falling past her full breasts to a narrow waist and hips that completed the hourglass figure. A cross on a silver chain dangled between her breasts, and tooled-leather bands sewn with silver bells were clasped about her ankles. Altogether a pleasing sight . . . She tried one more time as he tied on his loincloth and dressed.

"But *chaebli*, I want you to make my new bells ring again!" she said, shaking one long slender leg amid a sweet chiming.

"The things I do for the Sirkar," he sighed, and grinned at her. His arm was a little sore, but a gentleman always showed consideration. "Later, my sweet."

She subsided, grumbling and pulling on a robe and flouncing off to the bedroom, there to entertain herself with sweets and a trashy novel. It was the usual arrangement; she was a shopkeeper's daughter in Avantipur, a market town near Rexin, the King estate. King had met her when he dropped into her father's place to dicker over a saddle. He'd see that she got a husband and a substantial going-away present for a dowry, when his mother finally managed to shackle him to some horsy deb; in the meantime, they jogged along very well with friendship and honest mutual lust. He wasn't a harem-keeper—that sort of thing was out of fashion anyway in these enlightened times, when there was even serious talk about giving women the vote. And he wouldn't have wanted the type who adored his shadow; that would be cruelty, when he'd be bringing home a wife someday.

A thrill of a different sort gripped him as he turned to look again in the mirror, settling his indigo-colored turban and tugging at his jacket. He was in civilian mufti, high-collared tunic-jacket of midnight blue silk trimmed with silver braid at neck and cuffs, worn over a white cotton blouse; loose trousers of the same dark silk tucked into half boots; and a crimson sash under a tooled-leather belt. It set off broad shoulders, narrow waist, long legs; he smoothed down one of his sleek brown mustachios and contemplated a face tanned to oak color, high in the cheeks, straight-nosed and square-chinned, with level dark brown eyes flecked with green and a thin white scar from a sword slash along the right side of his jaw.

That had hurt like blazes when a frothing Ghazi administered it with a *chora*-knife, but it gave a certain *gravitas* and distinction to a face still a few years short of thirty, he decided. And considering that he'd blown the man's brains out with his Webley a second later, he didn't really have grounds for complaint.

The modest silver-and-enamel *aigrette* on his turban showed the family crest, pistol and pen quartered with a crown and the King motto: *Kuch dar nahin hai*—There is no such thing as fear.

Altogether the sort of outfit a well-to-do *zamindar*'s son from Kashmir might wear, or an Imperial cavalry officer on leave; since he fitted both categories precisely, it was appropriate enough. Even if he *had* also taken a double first at Oxford.

He hesitated a moment before he picked up a knife and pushed it through the sash, a seven-inch curved blade of wootz steel, with checked ebony handle and silver sheath. A formality, these days; barbarians, cannibals, bandits, and rebels were a lot less likely to swing through a window or come down the chimney than they had been in his great-grandfather's time. Even the Border country was peaceful in this Year of Grace 2025, by *those* standards.

There were other challenges and dangers, though, even if they were less physical. And he was going to meet them. It never hurt to be prepared.

"Thank you, Lakshmi, Patni," Cassandra King said.

Oxford's airship port bustled about her. One more young lady disembarking with her maids juggling the luggage behind was nothing to remark. The heavy dolly that followed, with four well-paid and extremely careful porters about it, decidedly was. So was her anxious care for the square timber box on it.

She looked about. Passengers were flooding off the *Diana* through the connecting corridor, meeting their personal attendants from the steerage deck, and those were hailing uniformed porters as luggage was brought in and placed on long tables. Turbans and head scarves and hats in a hundred different colors waved against the rows of ticket offices along the walls, and swirled through the pointed-arch doorways to waiting cabs or restaurants or shops. Families and friends greeted each other with cool reserve, or glad cries and embraces—her lip curled a little in scorn at that. Some of the servants were holding up signs with names on them, to guide arriving guests to the carriages of their hosts, or in a few cases to their motorcars.

Voices and unintelligible *clunks* and *clanks* from the machinery elsewhere filled the air along with the scent of jasmine in the man-high stone jars that stood here and there on the marble of the floor. The last light of sunset speared down from the high clerestory windows, off the bright gilding that covered the arched ceiling; then the floods came on with a *pop* and flare of brightness that turned it to a shimmering haze of gold.

Interesting, she thought, looking up as she always did here. The building was five years old, and the spiderweb complexity of gilt, groined vaulting above her was all laminated wood, the latest thing— everything from teak to bamboo, in precisely calculated gradients. With scientific tree-breeding and modern resins, it was almost as strong as steel girderwork, and much lighter. Not to mention cheaper. And the mathematics had been done here in Kashmir, at the university's own great Engine.

The rest was not much different from a railway station, even to the murals of Work and Sacrifice and Duty and other uplifting sentiments lining the upper walls. Bronzed *sahib-log* engineers in dusty turbans laying out irrigation canals, with grateful peasants invoking the gods in the background; missionaries in some godsforsaken ruin (probably Europe, by the vegetation) reclaiming hairy savages who crouched in awe at their feet; noble soldiers heroic on rearing steeds, trampling cringing enemies beneath their hooves.

She snorted slightly; they'd left out the traders with crates of gin and beads and cheap muskets, and the prospectors. Whenever her brother saw official military art, he tended to laugh. Or curse, if he'd had a gin and tonic or two, and swear at how many young subalterns got killed trying to act out nonsense like that before they learned better.

"Dr. King!" a voice called.

She craned her neck, then saw him. "Dr. Ghose!" she replied happily.

The little Bengali beamed at her, a wide white smile in the dark brown face; he was a plump man in his early forties, in white shirt and pantaloons, black waistcoat and canoe-shaped hat. He gave a nod and a word to King's two attendants; Dr. Chullunder Ghose was a kindly man as well as one of the Empire's foremost physicists and astronomer-mathematicians.

Although it didn't hurt that his family was fabulously wealthy with jute mills and shares in Orissan coal mines; he could have dropped the purchase price of the King estates across a gaming table with a laugh. Not that a Bengali *bhadralok*—respectable one—would go in for high-stakes gambling. Behind him came Lord Cherwell—Earl Cherwell of Rishikesh—looking sour, his white mustachios working and bushy brows frowning under a crisp, conservative turban of snowy linen, the tail of the *pugaree* coming almost to his belted waist in the back, and an egret plume nodding from the *aigrette* in front.

Damned old fool. I know what you're thinking, Cassandra said to herself. *First* natives, *then* women, *what's the university coming to . . . He did good work once, they say. God, that must have been in Arjuna's day! Or Victoria I's, at least.*

It was Ghose who'd shown flaws in the basis of the Kelvin-Maxwell synthesis, the existence of the luminiferous ether; and he'd won the Salisbury Chair in Theoretical Physics by sheer ability. *He should be head of the Project.*

Then, reluctantly: *Well, be fair. Lord Cherwell's still a good academic administrator. Why waste a first-rate theorist on that?*

A half dozen others followed, mostly *sahib-log* except for a Gujarati whose field was Babbage engineering, and male, apart from one painfully shy but brilliant young specialist in Darwinian Geological Catastrophes; she was a Parsi girl from Bombay with buckteeth. They all crowded around the dolly, looking at it with awed reverence. One reached out and touched the rough planks of the box gently.

"Thirty-four inches . . . what a *mirror!*"

Cassandra nodded, throwing the right end of her *dupatta*—head shawl—over her left shoulder. "Thirty-four inches and *perfect*," she said. "Smythe wasn't drawing the longbow."

"Oh, my, yes indeed," Ghose crooned. "Very much so, yes."

"Rather a feather in our caps, what?" Cherwell said, for once sounding cheerful. "Do a deuced good job at reflector-grinding, those Imperial University chappies. Pity they don't have a mountain to put a *machaan* on themselves, eh, what?"

He snorted and rubbed his hands together. "Thoms suggested the Nilgiri Hills, for God's sake—right down in the jungle country, and barely a few thousand feet. *Kiang!* I brought the chancellor's motor-wagon down for it. Ladies, gentlemen, *chalo!* Let's go!"

Cassandra paused to wave the porters forward again. There was a commotion a little way off, but she ignored it until someone shouted.

Then she did look up, frowning. Men were pushing their way in, against the flow of the crowd. Several of them, young men; Bengalis by their looks and dress. Not many wore the *dhoti* up here in the northwestern provinces, especially in the mountains; the big wraparound loincloth was just too cold for the climate, particularly in October.

One of them shouted again: *"Bande Materam!"*

Hail Motherland, she translated automatically. *Why, that's—*

Then she saw the pistols, and for a moment simply gaped. Revolvers, big and heavy and clumsy-looking, with long barrels. *Why, that's illegal!* she thought. The slogan only mildly so—she'd read Tagore's poetry herself. The pistols were *violently* illegal for anyone but the military and police; private licenses were extremely rare.

She had time for one thought before the first weapon boomed. *Assassins—*

Time slowed. The men came toward the knot of scholars, shouldering the crowd aside amid shouts and gasps of surprise and indignation. The pistols barked, deep and loud, with long spurts of smoke and flame. Cassandra saw her maid Patni turning, astonishment on her plain middle-aged face, a suitcase in either hand. Then she spun, catching at herself and crying out.

That brought the scholar out of her daze. She had been a King of Rexin, with all the responsibilities toward dependents that involved, much longer than she'd been a gentlewoman of science. Without another thought she dived, catching both her maids around the waist and throwing them to the ground, her own body over them and sickeningly conscious of blood soaking through the fabric of her clothes, wet and warm over the hands she clamped down to stop its spurting.

That gave her a view of what happened afterward. A third man carried something besides a pistol, a cloth bundle that trailed a hissing and plume of smoke . . .

Dr. Chullunder Ghose recognized it as a bomb sooner than she. It was pitched to fall under the dolly; the explosion would shatter the metal and wood into lethal shrapnel and kill everyone within a dozen yards. He grabbed the parcel out of the air with the skill of the fast-bowling cricketer he'd been, and curled himself around it. Cassandra squeezed her eyes tight, but she could not shut out the horribly muffled *thudump* of the explosion, or the feel of what spattered her, or the smell.

She forced her eyes open; there were still the men with revolvers—and men willing to set off bombs under their own feet would be horribly dangerous with firearms as well. There was one more shot, and something crashed and tinkled in the middle distance. Half the crowd was stampeding in terror, some trampling those ahead of them.

The young Rajput prince she'd seen on the promenade deck of the

Diana drew his blade and began a lunge, staggered as two lead slugs struck him, lunged again with his *scimtare*, a murderously sharp length of fine Jawahdapur steel. It rammed through coat and ribs to emerge dripping red from the gunman's back. Lord Cherwell was a step behind him, big blue-veined hands outstretched.

Then the four young men disappeared beneath a wave of men wielding swords, knives, walking sticks, fists and feet and a wrought-brass cuspidor stained with betel juice. Despite the nausea that clogged her throat, despite screams and cries and horror, Cassandra thought she saw brief bewilderment on the faces of the terrorists; and that puzzled her itself. What else would men of the martial castes do, when they saw a crowd attacked by assassins?

After the explosion and the brief deadly scrimmage things moved by in a blur; doctors, one putting a pressure bandage on Patni's wound and setting up a plasma drip, stretchers carrying away the wounded. Police came running up, men in blue-and-yellow uniforms with long *lathi* clubs. Hands helped her to the rim of a fountain, where she sat staring.

"*Memsahib.*"

The voice was firm; she looked up. A thirtyish man in plain crimson-and-green civilian clothes, but with two uniformed policemen behind him, a notebook in his hand and a pistol in a shoulder holster under his red jacket. He was too dark for a Kashmiri, with sharp, brown, clean-shaven features and weary eyes so black the pupil disappeared.

"Detective-Captain Tanaji Malusre, *memsahib*," he said gently—in good English but with a strong Marathi accent. "My apologies, but we must take statements before memories fade and change. Now—"

During the questions someone thrust a mug of hot sweet tea into her hand. She lifted it, swallowed at the sight of what was drying on her hands, then forced the porcelain to her lips. A little strength returned, enough for her to ask in her turn:

"Why? Captain Malusre, why? Who *are* these people?"

"Subversives—Bengali secessionists—enemies of the Raj. We think we know who, but this group has never operated outside Bengal province before. One may live long enough to answer questions, if we are lucky. Very strange."

"But . . . but none of us are political people! Poor Dr. Ghose—" She squeezed her eyes shut again.

I will not vomit. I am Cassandra Mary Effingham King of the Rexin Kings, and I am the sister and daughter and granddaughter of soldiers of the Empire. My ancestors rode with the Light Brigade and held Piper's Fort. There is no such thing as fear!

"Dr. Ghose was a very brave man," the detective said, looking down at his notebook. "Without him, several others might have died."

Cassandra shivered again, barely conscious of the detective muttering to himself as he made quick shorthand notes: "Very strange . . . the pistols were foreign. Damascus armory cap-and-ball make; but the Caliph's men are not so foolish, are they?"

She burst out: "*None* of us are political people! We are scholars—scientists—why would anyone come all the way from Calcutta to attack *us*?"

"I do not know, *memsahib*," the policeman said, tucking his notes away. "But I would very much like to know."

Yasmini closed her eyes as the bitter, sweet-sour taste of the *bhang lassi* slid into her mouth. Her body recognized it, like a sudden dryness in the throat and tongue that increased even as she drank. Yogurt and ice water, sugar . . . and hemp resin and poppy juice and things less common. Slowly, she set the silver cup down on the rock beside her and sat on the flat cushion, cross-legged, with each foot resting sole up on the opposite knee, her hands resting on her thighs with index finger touching thumb. Breath and heartbeat slowed, matching the thudding of a distant drum.

"See. See the Path." Ignatieff's voice boomed out like a brazen *radong*-trumpet, echoing on stone and down the corridors that burrowed more deeply into the earth. "Tell. Tell us the Path."

Her master spoke Hindi for the benefit of the men who knelt ranked before her. It was damp and chilly in the chambers beneath the ancient temple; great roots wove through the stone of the walls, writhing like snakes. Voices chanted in the background, a deep rumble that echoed off stone like the flickering light of the ghee-fed lamps that cast yellow highlights. It made the faint, faded images painted on the walls seem to move of themselves, whirling around the great room in a sinuous dance.

The drug was not needful, for ordinary purposes—for sensing where a patrol would turn, or what would come of taking one pass and not the next. When she slept, eventually, she would pay for the drink in a torrent of unasked, unsought vision. For the present, it opened the gates of the mind, letting the trained will range farther, and faster.

Her eyelids drooped over the blue-rimmed green of her eyes. Lips opened. Sight blurred, but not as an ordinary woman's might. Here the outlines shifted as she saw the *if*; this man might be here, or there, might lean forward or sit straight. He might not be here at all, or might be slightly different . . . now she saw Ignatieff with eyes of the same color and no patch, now with a steel hook in the place of a hand. Now an Ignatieff who did not command, but smiled a reptile's smile, while she answered with the same expression . . . that one was very bad, and she wrenched her mind away.

"See! Speak!"

Might-be frayed out in either direction, to pasts and futures, being and not-being all at once. A present in which buildings stood impossibly tall, sheathed in mirror; one in which nothing lived save insects and grass and only shaped stones remained of humanity; one in which dark soldiers with strange, powerful weapons and crawling metal fortresses fought here in the Vale of Kashmir.

"I see . . . I see . . ."

Forward, a part of the fan of *might-be* collapsed into a knot. She recognized it. A *thing* twisting in space, its dark pitted bulk rolling ponderous against the stars—there was no reference point to show its size, but she sensed a hugeness about it, an utter cold, a metallic tang as of iron. Like a mountain of frozen steel, falling from forever. Then a blue curve marked with the shapes of continents beneath drifting cloud; a flash of fire, night darker than night, a blizzard that blew ice like swords over seas frozen from pole to pole, a last emaciated body crouching in a ruin gnawing at a human skull.

"It comes . . . closer." The fingers of her mind stroked the webs of *might-be* and *if*. "The one slain. His death brings it closer." A small brown man's hands, reaching for a bag that twisted in the air. "Closer. But the—"

She stifled a shriek. "Their faces! I see their faces!" A man and a woman's much alike. Young. *That is the* Anglichani *soldier I saw before. The one I must not see, but the Master commands—*

"They are the ones! With them dead, death comes!"

A murmur went through the watching men, and their eyes glittered like wolves watching around a campfire at the edge of sight. Their clothes were of many kinds—saffron yellow robes and caste marks, hairy jackets, silk—but their eyes were the same.

"Kali Yuga!" one whispered. The others took it up with a hissing sibilance. "Kali Yuga! Kali Yuga! *Kali Yuga!*"

Kali Yuga: Age of Darkness. The dance of the death goddess; the triumph of Ignatieff's Peacock Angel.

Chapter Four

The dining room of the Peshawar Club dated from the Old Empire. There were many clubs in the city, down to the ones where the *chi-chi* foremen of the Indian Railways Administration gathered, but only one was *the* Peshawar Club to anyone who mattered. Dark and cool and elegant; modernization in recent years had brought newfangled overhead fans rather than punkhas. Plus a ghastly antique Georgian-era statue of St. Disraeli near the entrance, in the style of a century ago, with a look of ruptured nobility and his hand raised as if to call a waiter about a fly in his soup.

The smells made King's mustache twitch as he walked quickly through the lounge outside, reminding him that he was damned sharp-set; luncheon had been a handful of chilies and some chapatis and ghee by the side of the road, with his charger's reins looped through his belt as he sat on his heels to eat. The Club's chicken vindaloo and Khara Masala lamb were almost as good as the versions that came out of his mother's kitchen. He'd been fighting in the cause of civilization, and his stomach reminded him that he deserved some of its fruits.

"Sir Manfred?" King said, as a man stubbed out a thin cigar and rose from a divan in the waiting room. A companion stood behind him. The Lancer officer pressed palms together before his face and bowed with a formal:

"Namaste—ram-ram."

The man was a baronet, after all, and from the sound of things an eminence in the shadowy realm of the Political Service. King didn't think he was the sort to truckle, even for the chance of advancement, but a little courtesy never hurt. Being *too* disobliging might be the first step to a posting in some godsforsaken outpost on the Tibetan border, or to Singapore or even—merciful Krishna avert!—to a garrison in England.

"The same," the Political said, then extended a hand for the less punctilious greeting between equals. "Captain King, I presume, of Rexin in Kashmir and the Peshawar Lancers? Good of you to sacrifice time on leave."

And courteous of you to pretend I had a choice, King thought, studying the other man. He was slim and a few inches shorter than King's six-two, middle-aged, with a thin, pale face and gray showing in a close-clipped yellow mustache and the hair under the edge of his *pugaree*-turban. That was dazzling white, like the rest of his outfit save for black half boots. The blue eyes were sharp and appraising, and the hand in his was soft-skinned but strong.

"My apologies for the delay," King said. "Your card caught me *in media res,* as it were, Sir Manfred." *Bulling away with Hasamurti's legs wrapped around my arse, actually.*

"*Koi bat naheen,* not a problem, my dear chap. Allow me to present a friend," the Political went on.

The stranger bowed with a courtly gesture before offering his hand in turn. King's brow rose slightly. *Not an Imperial,* he decided at once, although in nondescript tunic-jacket and trousers and sash. A white man, but on the darker edge; black-eyed, olive-skinned, with raven-dark shoulder-length hair; clean-shaven, but with slightly paler patches to his face that suggested mustaches and a chin-beard not long ago. In his late twenties, a little older than King. He made a quick guess . . .

"*Enchanté, monsieur,*" he said, and continued in French. "Welcome to the Empire—the *British* Empire, that is."

The stranger's eyebrows rose. "A man of acute perception," he said, with a glance and shrug at Sir Manfred, in fairly good English with a slightly archaic book-learned flavor.

"May I present Colonel Henri de Vascogne, Vicomte of El Oudi-enne in the Duchy of Tunis, Chevalier of the Order of the Mahgreb, currently on detached duty, in the service of His Imperial Majesty Napoleon VI of Algiers and France."

"Monsieur le Vicomte," King said, and bowed. *Another Political*, he thought. *But a man of his hands as well.*

He recognized the signs, broad shoulders and thick swordsman's wrists, and a rim of callus around the index finger and thumb of the right hand. And the way he moved, light and alert, with a circle of awareness about him. *Département Secret* or *Deuxième Bureau* without a doubt; uncooperative Berber chieftains assassinated, nests of Moorish pirates on the Andalusian coasts identified, Caliphate spies tracked down on request.

"An honor," replied the Frenchman, a charming smile lighting his ugly-handsome Mediterranean face.

A silent waiter conducted them to their table; King noted that it was in a corner and far enough from any other that even the sharpest ears would have trouble picking up a conversation. De Vascogne raised his brows again as the wine was uncorked, paying tribute to an excellent Swat Valley red.

King let Sir Manfred lead casual talk while he did justice to the garlic nan, vindaloo, stuffed eggplant, cauliflower and okra cooked in aromatic yogurt with chilies, cinnamon, peppercorns, and cumin.

"I see our ancient tales about English food are not of a certainty true," de Vascogne said, eyeing the plates with the air of a pious man who had just taken the Sacrament.

"We're scarcely English," Sir Manfred said. "British, of course, by descent."

Well, mostly, King thought.

One of his great-grandmothers had been a Rajput noblewoman; he had a vague half memory of reading somewhere that there was an Afghan princess in the Warburtons' background—one of *his* ancestors had been a notable Political Officer in these parts right after the Fall. And Ganesha knew enough foreigners had been swept up in the mad three-year-long scramble to escape from the frozen charnel house of Europe. They hadn't been picky about who arrived in Bombay or Karachi in the generation of the Exodus, provided they could work, breed, and be relied on to fight on the right side.

Sir Manfred went on: "These days?" A shrug. "We're the *sahib-log*"—ruling folk—"of the *Angrezi* Raj; although it's a social distinction rather than a legal one, strictly speaking."

King nodded, recognizing an academic's precision; in strict law, the Raj didn't recognize caste—but nobody could rule India for a month if they didn't do so in fact. Much less live there for a century and a half.

It was still the *British* Raj, although usually you simply said *the Empire*; that was like referring to *the* Club in Peshawar, with no need for further qualification. Technically there was a mort of empires in today's world; the East Asian colossus that Akahito ruled from Peking as Mikado and Son of Heaven; the Czar's hell-born cesspit in Central Asia; the shadowy dominion centered on Rio de Janeiro that was reigned over by Dom Pedro and ruled by the *caudillo* of the month; Napoleon VI's own Algiers-centered imperium around the western Mediterranean. There was also the Caliph in Damascus, of course; he did rule from the Danube to Baluchistan, even if he was a wog. Kali alone knew what titles savage chiefs in the interiors of barbarian Europe and the Americas and Africa used.

But it was the Raj governed from Delhi that mattered; and John II, King-Emperor, Padishah, and Kaisar-i-Hind, his House of Lords and Commons and prime minister.

And His Royal and Imperial Majesty's Army and Navy and Political Service, King thought.

Warburton turned toward him. "How's Colonel Dammit?" he asked.

A snort of laughter forced its way through King's lips, before he schooled his expression. "You know Colonel Claiborne, sir?" he inquired.

Warburton smiled, a tight, controlled curve of the lips. "We were at school together," he said. "United Services. And I served under him in the Second Siamese War, when we had that touch-up with the Mikado's men. He was *Captain* Dammit then, of course."

King nodded respectfully. That had been as close to a major war as the Empire had had in the past two generations; closer to a draw than was pleasant to contemplate, if you read beneath the schoolbook histories. Quite disconcerting, fighting Asiatics—the Raj wasn't accustomed to enemies nearly as advanced as itself. There had been clashes since, and someday there would be another war.

"In fact, I knew your father in Siam," Warburton went on. "And later." He cleared his throat. "Monsieur de Vascogne is here to consult about the Canal project. Formally, at least."

King nodded, wary. Delhi and Algiers had both been talking about dredging out the old Suez Canal since the dying years of the twentieth century. Neither had done anything concrete; it would be devilish expensive—impossibly so for France-outre-mer, she being much smaller than the Empire and several generations behind in technique. And while the Sultanate of Egypt was a rich prize ripe for the plucking, for either to conquer it would offend the other. Not to mention the possibility of war with the Caliphate of Damascus, which would be genuinely unpleasant even from Delhi's perspective and a life-and-death struggle from that of Algiers.

"The prime minister is serious, then?"

"Quite," Sir Manfred said, flicking open a silver case and offering it to his guests. "Lord Somersby generally means what he says, even during an election. You're a Whig yourself, I suppose, Captain?"

The younger man nodded cautiously as he selected a cigarillo with a murmur of thanks; the Whigs were the King family political tradition, from Old Empire times.

"I was happy to hear that Lord Somersby would 'kiss hands,' " Athelstane said. "He'll make an excellent PM, even if he isn't a second Disraeli or Lord Salisbury or Churchill. Not that Majors and the Tories did so very badly, but the Small Tenants Rights Act was overdue for passage—should have been put through in my father's day. A quarter of the crop and two days labor-service a week is all that a good *zamindar* should expect from his *ryots*."

He paused for an instant. "And any *zamindar* or yeoman-tenant who needs a debt-bond to keep his laborers from moving away to the cities isn't fit for authority. With the way the population's growing, a decent man doesn't have problems finding workers."

Warburton nodded. "Not popular in some quarters, though. The *Kapenaars* are howling about it, from Table Bay to Mount Kenya."

King shrugged. The Cape Viceroyalty always voted two-thirds Tory; Australia went two-thirds Whig; India was the swing vote. None of the other parts of the Empire had enough MPs to matter, as yet.

De Vascogne selected a cigarillo, sniffed it appreciatively, snipped off the end with a silver clipper, and leaned forward to light it from the gas lamp in the center of the table. The staff cleared away the dishes and brought the cheese platter, cardamom-scented coffee, and snifters of brandy.

"My sovereign is also of an enlightened mind, and quite sincere," the Tunisian nobleman said. "The time has come for this affair of Suez and many another project of extreme value. Like his namesake, the third Napoleon, our ruler is possessed of a passion for *la grande mise en valeur*. So much so that he has proposed a co-dominium, a joint protection of the unhappy lands of the Nile to promote order and progress and permit the reconstruction of the Suez Canal, that product of French genius."

A talkative nation, King thought. Yet he had a feeling that the *outre-mer* Frenchman was revealing precisely what was intended, and no more.

"Well, this is capital," King said, lighting his own and taking a draught of the fragrant smoke; first-rate Zambezi, and no mistake. He followed it with a sip of the brandy. "But, if you'll pardon me asking, Sir Manfred, Monsieur le Vicomte . . . why are you discussing it with an anonymous captain in a down-country cavalry *pultan*?"

The Political Service agent and the foreign nobleman exchanged glances. Sir Manfred spoke slowly:

"For several reasons. Keeping an eye on an old friend's son, and all that. And . . . perhaps it's thought, in certain circles, that your talents are wasted in . . . hmmm, 'a down-country cavalry *pultan*.' Not that the Lancers aren't a first-rate regiment."

King nodded, feeling a tingling along his nerves, and pride at the steadiness of his hand as he held up the cigar and glanced at the glowing end.

"Mmmmh?"

"You have languages, I believe?" the baronet went on.

"Hindi, Punjabi, Pushtu, Tadjik"—which was close enough to speaking Persian for government work—"Bengali, modern French, Arabic, and Russian, some Nipponese," King admitted. "And the classics, of course." He shrugged. "Languages come easily to me; more of a sport than work."

"Double first in Moderns and Ancients—and a paper or two on philology since," the Secret Service *bimbashi* continued.

"Family tradition," King said. Rare but not unknown for an officer, and his family had a custom of combining scholarship with Imperial service. He added reluctantly: "In fact . . ."

"Yes, your sister is a Fellow of the Royal Academy and has a doctorate in mathematics and astronomy," Sir Manfred noted, reading from some file in his mind. "I read her paper . . . 'Orbital Characteristics of an Asteroid . . .' with some interest."

De Vascogne's brows headed for his hairline, demonstrating that he had more than a nodding acquaintance with the Empire. Even in these progressive times and in this progressive land and in a Whig family, *that* was unusual; Oxford had only started admitting women to the degree program fifteen years ago, when Queen-Empress Alice added her patronage to a generation's agitation by various radicals. A bare few hundred had taken advantage of it since, and far fewer in the sciences.

Not respectable, really, King acknowledged, thinking of his twin sister. But then, Cassandra had never taken convention seriously.

"Remarkable, and commendable," Warburton said. "Returning to your own record, Captain . . . you've already been poaching on the Political Service's preserves, what? That mission to the Orakzai chiefs—"

"Needs must, Sir Manfred. We had to keep those passes open, and—"

"—and you charmed them, impressed them in that dust-up with their neighbors you rode out on, and generally kept them sewed up. Passed as an Afghan yourself for several weeks. Saved us several nasty little actions."

King felt his arm twinge in remembrance. He'd gone through those weeks, disguised among aliens who hated his kind, in a state of continuous, well-controlled fear. Probably that had been what kept him alive, just.

"So you see," the older man said. "Our little *bandobast*"—organization—"has had its eye on you for some years."

He smiled and added other details, ones that left King shaken behind an impassive front. The Department had a reputation for omniscience, but it was uncomfortable to have the all-seeing eye applied to oneself.

"Am I to assume you wish me seconded to the Political Service, Sir Manfred?" King asked.

His unspoken flicker of the eyes added: *And why the devil are you doing it with a foreigner in earshot, even if it's a friendly foreigner?* Granted, there was no set application procedure; you didn't apply, they asked you. *This is pushing the boundaries of informality rather far, I would have thought.* Nor was he sure he wanted to leave the regiment—generations of Kings and their retainers had served with the Peshawar Lancers.

"Not precisely, Captain King . . . and not quite yet, in any case." Warburton paused for a moment. "Tell me, young fellow, who are the friends of progress? And who are its enemies?"

He hadn't expected *that.* "Order and Progress" was the Empire's motto, near enough.

"Enemies? Why . . . the barbarians, of course, Sir Manfred. The Russians, too, of course; well, they worship Satan, so what would you expect? A few of the wild-man fringe of the Tories, here and in the Cape. As to the friends . . . we are, of course. Mostly. And the other civilized and allied countries," he added politely, nodding to de Vascogne.

"True enough in outline, old chap," Warburton said. "But the devil's in the details, don't you know. For example, the Empire's prosperous as never before."

King nodded. "Yes, we're finally getting back to where we were before the Fall," he agreed. "Even surpassing the ancestors, in some ways; we're far more advanced in the biological sciences, for instance. Damn me if I can see how anyone would object. Except our enemies, of course."

"Ah, but in any rise, *mon capitaine,* there is a rearrangement of positions," de Vascogne said softly. "*N'est-ce pas?*"

Warburton nodded. "To name an example, more prosperity means more natives with the franchise."

"It's always been open, even in Old Empire times," King said. "Why, the Queen-Empress Victoria promised in 1858, right after the First Mutiny, when the old East India Company was wound up—"

"—that all positions would be open to every qualified subject, without consideration of religion or origin, yes," Warburton said. "However, that's been fairly theoretical until recently. Now with the cities growing so fast . . . why, I doubt there's a *sahib-log* family as wealthy as the Patnas, to name only one."

"It is of a muchness in my sovereign's dominions," de Vascogne said. "Although we have always made a place for a Moor who is, how do you say, *assimilé,* yet there are among us those who are unhappy that recently so many of our subjects desire to take up our expressed wish, and to acquire a new past, one in which their ancestors were Gauls."

He chuckled. "Not to mention the extreme misery that this causes the Caliph and his mullahs. That we rule Muslims angers them; that we *convert* them is an anguish inexpressible."

Warburton continued: "So you see there might be some of our own people who feel . . . how shall I put it? To be charitable, who feel that the Empire's gone soft since the days of our great-grandfathers."

King winced slightly behind a gentleman's impassive mask. His ancestors of the Exodus and the Second Mutiny had been heroic, no doubt of that . . . but like many of his generation, there were aspects of that period he preferred to keep in the footnotes. They'd done what they had to do, those post-Fall Victorians, to preserve the Empire and civilization and the lives of their families. It had been a time when men had no good choices; you didn't, when your children were hungry, and the only way to get them food was to take away someone else's. That didn't justify turning brutal necessity into a virtue. He forced himself to think, let smoke dribble from his nostrils, and added:

"I suppose there are others who're displeased at the course of things, too," he said.

Some of the Sikhs and their leaders, for instance, who'd been close allies of the Sirkar in both Mutinies, and had been rewarded well for it; better than a quarter of the land in the Punjab was Sikh-owned. The Rajput nobility, who had their representatives in the House of Lords; and the rulers of the Protected States like Nepal. None of them would be happier than the stiffest of the *sahib-log* at seeing Gujarati or Bengali box-wallahs making inroads on the seats of power.

"Now," Warburton said. "Consider for a moment—who would be . . . not happy . . . who would *like* to see a Third Mutiny?"

King was appalled, but he responded with slow, careful calm. "Well, the Mikado." The Far Eastern empire would be the dominant power in Asia and the world if the Raj were badly weakened. "And the Czar, of course."

Both the other men nodded. *Here's a catechism for me to go through,* King thought, with wry amusement. That brought back a sudden flicker of memories; old Father Gordon, the smell of hassocks and psalmbooks, light flickering through stained glass. King went on, feeling his way forward:

"And the various subversives, the ones who'd like to overthrow the Raj or split their home provinces away. After which the Afghans would invade. There wouldn't be a rupee or a virgin between Peshawar and Calcutta six months later; then the Czar's men would arrive to sacrifice everyone to Tchernobog and eat their hearts."

"Fanaticism does not make for a realistic or long-term political perspective," Warburton said, nodding.

"And," de Vascogne added, "some among the influential in the smaller powers would also love to see the Raj trimmed back. For fear of your power; for envy of your wealth; and to remove the disturbances of custom your trade and ideas bring."

King's eyes narrowed as he glanced at Warburton. "But even the . . . excessively conservative, shall we say . . . among our own people couldn't wish the Raj overthrown."

"No." Warburton nodded. "But you see, my young friend, that would only happen if a rebellion *succeeded*, which is most exceedingly unlikely, despite what some of our home-grown radicals think."

He sighed, tapped his cigarillo against a carved brass ashtray. "Comes of expanding the supply of graduates from second-rate universities faster than the number of bureaucratic jobs. They should remember where the Sirkar's army is recruited."

King rubbed a hand along his jaw. There were the *sahib-log*, of course; Sikhs; Marathas; high-caste Rajputs; Jats and others from the canal colonies of the Punjab; many came from client kingdoms like Nepal, or were mercenaries from beyond the Imperial frontiers. *And there's the military in the Cape and Australia, of course, and the outlying garrisons.* The Empire kept three-quarters of a million men under arms, and that was counting professional soldiers only, not reservists and militia and police and the armies of the vassal states.

Warburton went on: "But a *failed* rebellion, with reprisals and confiscations afterward . . . that could set relations with the other castes back a century. Cripple the manufacturing cities, perhaps let full-plumed neofeudalism make a comeback. Or should I say *neoneofeudalism?*"

He smiled and shrugged and leaned back. "And now, since the cricket season is coming, what do you think of Oxford's chance against the All-Australia 11?"

Narayan Singh was content. The Peshawar Club had many military members—and those officers were fighting men stationed on the most dangerous frontier of the Raj, not commanders of garrison troops or hangers-on at court. Their orderlies were not valets in uniform, but picked fighting men themselves, often born to the duty as he had been, *jajmani*-followers in a hereditary patron-client link between families.

So the quarters for those *servants* were as you would expect. Not as luxurious as those for their employers, but spacious, with soft beds and baths of water and steam; there were ample spaces where a man might throw dice or swap stories, wrestle or fence; and you did not have to go out into the bazaar to find music, clean girls, or liquor. Clad only in his drawers, the Sikh leaned back at ease in his private room, while one such combed and oiled his waist-length hair.

"Eye-wallah, Miriam, give me to drink," he said. "Chasing Pathans is thirsty work."

Then he stretched, pleasantly conscious of the ripple of muscle along his heavy shoulders and arms, and the scars that seamed white against brown skin and heavy black body hair. The girl—she was wearing considerably less than he—cast an admiring glance at him as she went to mix cane spirit with mango juice and pour them over crushed ice in a tall glass. Then she rolled her rump where she stood and winked at him over one shoulder.

Narayan grinned, with a stomach pleasantly full of rice and curried lamb and more pleasures to follow. He considered himself a man of reasonable piety, if not as much as his mother would have liked. He read the Adi Granth at times; he followed the Five K's—he kept his hair uncut, wore a soldier's drawers, carried a steel comb and wore the steel bracelet and kept a *kirpan*, a steel blade, at his side. When there was time he prayed at the *amritvela*-hour of dawn, reciting the Name; when there was a place of Sikh worship to hand, he attended a *gurudwara* to make his offerings and receive the blessed *kara-prasad*. He had even taken time on leave to visit the birthplace of Nanak Guru. Nor did he touch tobacco or *bhang* or any other narcotic.

Drink in moderation was different—or at least he thought of it so, nor did he deny himself meat or lying with loose women. He had no pretensions to being a *sant*, a holy man, nor had he the slightest desire to be an *Akali*, one of the Children of God the Immortal. When the time came he would wed himself a true Sikh *kaur*, a lioness, and sire sons, and find a guru who could lead him to the opening of the Tenth Gate.

Until then he would be true to his soldier's salt; that was his *karman* in this life.

So he pulled the girl onto his knee when she returned, tossed off a swallow of the drink, and handed it to her, scraping his beard over her full breasts as she raised it to her mouth in both hands and giggled. Sometime later she giggled again, into the thick thatch on his chest, and proclaimed that he was so fierce it was remarkable there was a Pathan left alive.

"And famous, already," she said. "You and your *sahib*."

"We made some play with steel and shot among the dogs," he said complacently. "Men see, and speak."

"So I heard," she said. "And the men who said so were Muslim themselves—*sais*-grooms here. Oh, they were anxious for word of thee, my lord with the great strong *baz-baz*." Her hand strayed. "And thy *sahib*, as well."

A chill ran down his belly, and he pushed her hand aside. "Tell me more!" he said, and the girl cowered a little at his tone. He shook his head. "I am not angry with you. But speak."

There would be no followers of Islam in the grooms or staff in *this* club; not so close to the border. That would not be safe. There had been too many raids on the frontier, too many intrigues with Muslim rulers over-border. And from what his grandfather had said of *his* grandfather's tales, too many of them had joined in when the Fist of God struck earth and a million starving Afghans poured down the passes to try and take the warm plains from the *sahib-log*.

While she spoke, he was dressing. When the last bewildered word was past he was out of the door with his sheathed saber in one hand, running down the corridor toward the stairs and the *sahib-log* section of the club with a lightness astonishing in a man of his barrel-chested heft. If he was wrong, the *sahib* would laugh at him for being an old woman. That would be as it would be. His honor was to preserve the *sahib*'s life; and it was also the life of the man who had called him *bhai*—brother—and fought by his side, and pulled him from a melee when his horse was hamstrung and the Pathan knives were out.

A phonograph disk saved Athelstane King's life. He could hear it even before he brushed unseeing past two Club servants and opened the door to his rooms; it was one of his favorites, a classic piece in the

Keralan style, with a tambura droning, drums, a vina. He didn't understand the vocalist's lyrics, Kannada wasn't one of his languages, but—

But the devil take it, Hasamurti detests Carnatic music! he thought. She'd never go to all the trouble of winding the phonograph to put one of those disks on when he wasn't there. The incongruity of it jarred him out of an abstracted brown study.

He swung the door open. "Greetings, *sahib*," Hasamurti said, standing in a pool of light from one of the gas lamps and bowing with hands palm to palm before her face.

That brought his ears up even more; his mistress *never* called him that in private—and after leaving her up here while he went to dinner on his first night back from the Frontier, and on top of that sitting late talking, he'd be lucky if it wasn't "jungle-born *pig!*" and something heavy thrown at his head and exile to the couch.

The heavy carved-teak door slammed shut and the bolt snapped home, the gaslight went out, and darkness fell. Hasamurti screamed once, a shrill sound cut off in mid-breath. Lightless colors played before his gaze. The music and the obvious falseness of his mistress's greeting had alerted him just enough to jerk his chin down and begin to turn as something swept through the air behind him. His left hand came up and caught at it, a smooth fabric that swung as if a weight pulled one end. It closed around his neck with an instant wrenching force that made him hiss with pain.

His mind was still slow with food and talk and puzzles that it worried as a dog does a bone, but his body and reflexes knew that suddenly, unbelievably, he was fighting for his life in his rooms at the Peshawar Club. A thing as unlikely as assault and battery by the Archbishop of Delhi in the High Cathedral, and to the accompaniment of the plaintive beauty of the music on the phonograph.

The cloth wrenched savagely at his neck, and the two fingers of his left hand underneath it would delay death by seconds only. A knee jammed into the small of his back, and he could feel the wiry strength in the hands that held the *rumal*, the strangler's handkerchief, and the enormous leverage of the tough cloth and crossed-wrist grip.

King heaved himself backward. The man on his back was strong but no giant; the Lancer officer stood six-foot-two and weighed a hundred ninety pounds of gristle, bone, and tough, dense muscle. They slammed into the plastered stone of the wall, and for a second the assassin slipped downward. The terrible pressure on his neck eased hardly at all, and blood hammered in his temples with spikes of pain. In that instant he snatched the ornamental knife out of his belt and slammed it back and up with all the strength his injured right arm could yield. A bubbling shriek half deafened him, and then the intolerable choking hold on his throat was gone.

Nobody, not even a trained strangler, pays attention to anything else when seven inches of razor-edged steel are rammed into his groin. The wounded man screamed again and again, then fell with a thud and lay thrashing and moaning.

King let himself fall to the carpet also and rolled, straining not to gasp as air flooded back into his lungs and blood into his brain, and light flared in his retinas, tinged with red and the shapes of veins. He was locked into a darkened room with a man—men, perhaps—deadly as cobras. Leopard-crawling in the darkness under cover of the sounds of the man he'd stabbed, he felt for the door and rose, crouching. Silence, save for the labored breath of a man dying. King made himself relax until he was waiting, lightly poised on the balls of his feet and open to every sensation his nerves could deliver, not straining. A whicker of air, and he let his knees go and crouched. Something went into the wood behind him with a *chi-thunk* of metal into wood; not a knife, but that didn't matter, as long as it hadn't hit *him*.

His crouch turned into a leap. Blind, he could only aim for where the sound *hinted* the thrower had been. He crashed into a body and they went over in the dark, falling together over a settee and knocking the phonograph to the floor with a sudden screech and crash. King found himself grappling with an unseen opponent, naked skin covered in some sort of grease. It made the smaller man's limbs impossible to pin down, for he had the speed and flexibility of a mongoose and a demonic skill. They fought in silence save for grunts and snarls, hands grappling for holds and breaking them, only occasionally able to strike with fist or elbow or bladed palm or fingertips, and hitting floor or furniture as often as flesh.

King's hands finally clamped on a wrist and elbow, but before he could break the arm, fingers came groping for his eyes. He snapped his head aside, then lunged back and sank his teeth into a wrist, but his opponent used the moment to tear his right arm free and whip the leading edge into the Lancer officer's temple. Then he pounded his fist into the side of King's own right arm, striking the half-healed stab wound with cruel luck and tearing himself free.

Lights shot before King's eyes. Yet even as he gasped in pain he pivoted on his back and kicked; luck reversed itself, and his boot struck the other man in the buttocks with tremendous force, catapulting him into a stone wall like something shot out of a hydraulic piston.

King heard the crash and flipped himself back to his feet, arms outstretched to either side—he wasn't certain where in the room he was, much less where the assassin had landed. Then he heard something from the corridor outside, muffled through thick wall and door. The clash of steel, shouts—*Allahu Akbar, God is Great,* the war cry of Islam—then a great bass bellow:

"*Rung ho! Wa Guru-ji! Rung ho!*"

"Narayan Singh—in here—more of them!" King shouted back, and made a daring leap. "*Kuch dar nahin hai!*"

That landed him at the corridor entrance; some distant corner of his mind gibbered in relief as his hand fell on the handle, twisted the dead bolt free, and threw the door open. In the same motion he flung himself aside and slitted his eyes against the flare of brightness from the gaslit corridor outside.

A man stumbled through backwards, steel flickering in his hand as he frantically parried the Sikh's saber cuts. The light showed two others in the corners of the sitting room; near-naked men with skins coated in black grease, loincloths also dyed night color. Each held a weapon in his right hand, a curious thing with a blade at right angles to the haft, like a short malignant pickax; the left hand held a cord and noose. Tucked into the loincloth of each was the *rumal*, with a corner lapped out ready to grip.

They hesitated a single instant, blinking against the pain of light in dark-adapted eyes, then skittered forward with the vicious quickness of weasels.

"*Rung ho!*" Narayan Singh shouted again. A tremendous overhand cut knocked his opponent back on his heels; the Lancer took the instant to pull a Khyber knife from his girdle and flip it through the air toward King.

"Here, *huzoor*—for you!"

It flashed through the air; a genuine Pathan *chora*, a pointed cleaver two feet long with a back as thick as a man's thumb and an edge fit to shave with. King snatched for the hilt—almost missed, with the pain and weakness in his right arm, but forced his hand to steadiness. The solid weight of the weapon was inexpressible comfort, and the assassins checked their rush. King didn't stop his own, pivoting with the momentum of his catch and attacking in the same motion. One down cut struck the haft of a pickax, and smashed it out of the smaller man's grip. The backstroke shattered and cleft his jaw, sending him staggering aside in a spray of blood and teeth; turning, King kicked the other killer in the stomach. Not too hard, because he struck in haste and the footing was awkward, but enough to keep him from interfering.

Then the last strangler was left with a short pickax to face a bigger, stronger man with twenty-four inches of straight razor in his hand and nothing but pure murder in his expression. Blood ran down King's arm from the reopened wound, but he scarcely felt the stabbing pain of it.

Narayan Singh's fight ended in the same instant. Another yell of *Rung ho!*, an unmusical *scrinnng* of steel on steel and the edge of his *tulwar* slammed into his opponent's arm. The heavy saber cut halfway through it with a thick wet sound of cloven muscle and a crack of parting bone. The Sikh shouted in exultation, brutally efficient blows reducing his enemy to something that looked more like a carcass hung in a butcher's stall than a man.

Then he screamed in fury as the blade jammed between two vertebrae, and he had to spend seconds wrenching it free with one foot on the dead man's body.

The last assassin wasted none of the time bought by his comrades' death. He threw his pickax at King in a snake-swift movement and darted for the door that led to the suite's bedroom. The windows there were covered with a lattice of iron bars, but they gave onto the street. King dodged the flying weapon; he *knew* the window bars must be cut through and that the killer could dive out and lose himself in the alleys—might have confederates waiting for him. Useless to pursue that greased speed. Instead he whipped the *chora* in an overarm throw, hard and fast.

It turned twice, glinting in the light streaming through the open door, then struck point first at the base of the fleeing man's skull, with a sound like an ax *thunking* home in seasoned hardwood. The assassin's body arched for an instant in a spastic rictus, then dropped as limp as an official explanation.

King staggered, panting and clutching at the reopened wound with his left hand, feeling blood seeping through the cloth.

"Doctor's going to hate me," he muttered, then turned the gaslights back on.

The bright yellow light showed a slaughterhouse scene of tumbled bodies and blood spreading on marble floor tiles and soaking into Sikunderam rugs. King ignored it—and the unpleasantly familiar stink of violent death—to kneel by Hasamurti's side. There was no obvious wound, but she was bleeding from nose and ears, her eyes wandering. His exploring fingers found a spot on the side of her head that gave unpleasantly as he touched it, despite the lightness of that touch and the swiftness with which he jerked his hand away. She cried out once, then rolled her head to look at him.

"I . . . tried . . ." she whispered. "Hurts . . ."

"You saved my life, *chaebli*," he said, gripping her hand and leaning close. *The* banchut *must have hit her with the hammer end of one of those pickaxes.* "Don't try to—"

Her face grimaced and went slack. He put his fingers to her neck for an instant, then swallowed past a thickness in his own throat and pulled her eyelids down over staring eyes. Bone splinters driven into the brain; he'd seen enough head wounds to recognize it.

"*Huzoor,*" came Narayan Singh's voice. "*Sahib,* you must look. *Huzoor—*"

King shook his head violently, squeezed his eyes shut for an instant, and pressed the heel of a blood-sticky hand to his forehead. There were tears pressing at the back of his eyelids, and he couldn't remember weeping since his father's death, when he was six.

She'd thought fast, and risked her own life for his . . . When he opened his eyes again they were as level and hard as agate, and he went to the Sikh's side. *Whoever was behind this is going to pay,* he thought. *And pay full measure.*

The *daffadar* had peeled back an eyelid on one of the half-naked stranglers. On the pink skin was a tattoo, a crude representation of a spider . . . or a figure with many arms.

"Thug!" the Sikh swore; he pronounced it *thaag*. "One of the brotherhood of the Deceivers."

"Krishna," King swore to himself, softly.

The cult had been nearly wiped out back in Old Empire times—there were statues to Colonel Sleeman in half a dozen cities. Then it had revived on a vastly larger scale with the Fall and the chaos and famine afterward—this time not only murdering and robbing travelers in the name of Kali, but devouring them also to the glory of the Dreadful Bride. Evidently the repressions since the Second Mutiny hadn't gotten them all.

"Surgeons cut out cancers, but there's always a little left to grow again," he said grimly.

"There will be a reckoning," the Sikh said, his face equally hard. "But *sahib*, look here also. I saw them in the corridor, lounging about as if they were nothing save idle servants—but when I sought entry they drew steel on me."

He indicated the hacked body of the swordsman he'd killed. The process had removed much of the outer clothing, and beneath it the man wore linen bands tightly wrapped around his limbs—a winding-sheet, such as some Muslims were buried in. Another body similarly clad lay outside the corridor entrance to the suite, dead eyes staring at the ceiling. Only one type of Muslim wore such *before* burial; Shia fanatics on a mission they expected to end in their own deaths. The corpse could have been Arab, Persian, Afghani, or northwest Indian—dark hair and eyes, olive-brown skin turning gray with blood loss and morbidity.

"Krishna," King muttered again. *Deceivers* and *hashasshin—that doesn't make any bloody sense at all!* Hindu fanatics in the service of the death goddess; Muslims convinced that dying while killing enemies of the Faith was a ticket to Paradise. "This is madness."

Singh grunted again. "Madness that slays, *huzoor*." He looked at the body that lay half in and half out of the bedroom door, still twitching, with the *chora* upright in his skull like a boat's mast. "A good cast, by the Guru!"

King shook his head. "My arm was weak and my aim was off," he said, with bitter self-accusation in his voice. "I was aiming for his thigh, so we could take one alive for questioning."

When all was said and done, when the police had come and gone, when a doctor had put stitches in his arm and strapped it up and strictly forbade any motion, a Club servant brought him a note on a silver tray.

It was Warburton's. This time the message read: *Meet me in Delhi on the third week after* Diwali. *In the interim, remember that official help may not be conducive to continued health.*

Slowly, Athelstane King crumpled the square of pasteboard in his hand.

Chapter Five

The gracious smile on the face of Princess Sita Mary Elizabeth Jandeen Victoria Saxe-Coburg-Gotha lasted a full fifteen seconds after the rosewood-and-ivory door of the small audience chamber closed behind the Franco-Mahgrebi emissary. Then it ran down into a snarl.

"No!" she yelled.

The scream gained force from her overarm throw as she rose from the jeweled throne and pitched the silver-framed photograph at the door panels of rare woods and ivory. One of the ladies-in-waiting hastily intercepted it with her fan, to protect the priceless carvings of scenes from the *Mahabharata*—ironically, those were of the Pandava brothers and their joint wife Draupadi.

"No, no, *no*! I will not marry the foreign pig! I'd rather marry an untouchable, a diseased pariah sweeper with no nose! *No! Never! Never!*"

She dropped from the dais and began to stride angrily back and forth across the marble floor with its inset designs of tigers, peacocks, and jungle flowers in carnelian, lapis, and tanzanite. Energy crackled from her slight form; the princess was just eighteen years, rather short, and willowy-slender in a blouse of sheer Kashmiri wool and *kanghivaram* sari of gold-shot indigo silk sewn with a tiger-stripe pattern in tiny garnets and jet. A tiara was bound around her brows, diamonds and gold with a dangling fringe of Madras pearls shimmering like polished steel. The long hair looped in an intricate pattern beneath it was raven black, and her eyes a blue almost as dark. On her the rather bony features of the Imperial dynasty were muted to delicately regular good looks trembling on the verge of beauty. The fashionable red *tikal* mark between her feathery black brows stood out vividly against the pallor of her anger.

"Why me?" she asked—just on the smooth edge of a shriek; even then the training of her high contralto showed. "Why me?"

One of the ladies-in-waiting picked up the picture. She was the sister of the Maharana of Udaipur, taller and a few years older than the one she served, with boldly handsome Rajput features that she was visibly schooling to sweet reason:

"Sita—*Kunwari*—Imperial Princess—he seems a handsome man. And you will be a queen, and your sons will be kings."

"Then *you* marry him and bear a whole *litter* of kings. I give you leave!" Sita snarled.

She kicked at the confining hem of the sari as she strode, her glittering sandals clicking on the inlaid stone beneath. "I am daughter to the Lion Throne, and they expect me to marry this . . . this . . ."

"Heir to the ruler of France-outre-mer," her brother finished for her. He looked around. "Leave us!" he said, clapping his hands together sharply.

Courtiers and ladies and servants filed out; not many, for it had been a private audience. The Rajput lady-in-waiting handed him the picture as she stalked by in affronted dignity. Gurkha guardsmen shouldered arms to a brisk order from their officer, with a smack of hands on wood and metal, then moved back to the farther walls, discreetly out of earshot for anything but a shout; only a direct order from the King-Emperor himself would have sent them out of sight.

The audience chamber was part of the summer rooms of the palace, a twenty-foot-high roof supported by tall columns of polished crimson stone with gilded capitals. The outer edge had no wall, merely a series of staggered screens of ivory carved into fretwork as fine as lace.

"Come, let's take a walk," Prince Charles said. The tone was friendly, but the glance that went with it bottled his sister's fury.

They walked between the screens, along a path that gave out onto a courtyard garden, centered on a tall fountain of dazzling white. Paths of colored stone wound between green lawns, flower beds, tall trees, manicured shrubs, man-high jars of polished stone with sprays of bougainvillea tumbling down their sides. Tiny antelope the size of cats moved fearlessly through the garden, and strutting peacocks with silver rings on their claws spread their tails and screeched; fish with fins like multicolored veils of gauze swam through pool and channel.

"Why don't you stop the hysterics, Sita? They'll probably expect *me* to marry his sister, after all, and I'm not complaining."

The eldest son of the King-Emperor was in the walking-out uniform of a colonel in the Gurkha regiment of the Imperial Foot Guards, forest green *kurta* and trousers, plumed long-tail *pugaree*-turban and polished boots. The hilt of his *tulwar* was as plain as regulations permitted, and he carried the Gurkha *kukri*-knife as well. Both showed use; the Guards had been in action on the northwestern frontier only weeks ago, and Charles Saxe-Coburg-Gotha didn't regard his colonelcy as an honorary one.

"*You* don't have to leave home," Sita said sullenly.

"Wish I could," Charles said frankly. "It isn't a life fit for a dog, the way Father's tied up in ceremony. *I'd* rather sail off to the Straits to start a rubber plantation, or go to Borneo and fight pirates."

He was a strong-featured young man in his mid-twenties, of medium height and slender, clean-shaven save for sideburns of dark glossy brown. He went on:

"In any event, you *know* the pater will get his way. Bad form to kick up such a fuss. Duty, and all that. *Rajadharma*."

Sita sighed and took the picture back. It showed a dark young man in an ornate uniform of antique cut—long-tailed buttoned blue coat, red trousers—well slathered with medals, his beard and mustaches trimmed to points. Beside him was a woman of her own age, dressed in a low-cut dress—that would be the sister.

"Is she wearing a *corset*?" Sita asked incredulously. "That dress looks like something Victoria I would have worn!"

"Well, they're old-fashioned in France-outre-mer, I grant you," her brother said. "But for Pravati's sake, Sita, you'll be the *queen*, there, soon enough. And one from the Raj—*the* Empire—at that. *You'll* set the fashions; have 'em all dressing civilized in saris or *shalwar qamiz* in no time."

"*Are* they civilized?" Sita asked, suddenly serious and quiet.

They sat on cushions piled on a marble bench beneath a pergola of autumn roses.

"Sita, Father wouldn't propose this if they weren't, diplomacy be damned, and you know it," he said persuasively, taking her hands in his.

"It's a foreign country, things will be strange, but they're pukka twice-born, believe me. And it's not as if it's the other side of the world. We'll be setting up a regular air service, it'll be only a week's travel, closer than Melbourne." His voice grew coaxing. "Come on, Sita—how many of us get to add a new province to the Empire?"

"I didn't see anything about annexation in the proposal," she answered dryly, giving his fingers a grateful squeeze and releasing them.

"Well, give it a generation or two," Charles replied. "Come on, be a brick, Sita—think about it, at least."

"I'll *think*," she said, pouting slightly. Then, slowly, considering: "The envoy was sort of interesting, at that. A cool one. I wonder what the prince is like?"

Charles left her sitting lotus-style beside the pool, propping her chin on one hand and staring at the photograph held in the other.

Henri de Vascogne looked admiringly around the interior of the motorcar that held him, the heir to the Lion Throne, and Sir Manfred Warburton. It was a big boxy vehicle, running on six wire-spoked wheels as they purred eastward; the interior was luxurious, in a quieter fashion than he'd become accustomed to in the Empire. The rear was a semicircle like the fantail of a yacht, cushioned with plain white cotton. Outside . . .

"Very pretty," he said to the prince, nodding at the palaces and administrative buildings, the Imperial University, the great museums and libraries, the statuary and monuments spaced along the broad avenues. The glories of Delhi's southern fringe showed as glimpses behind wrought-iron rails and through lush greenery only slightly sere with autumn; smooth red sandstone, marble, bulbous dome and slender tower and carved blocks. The emissary went on:

"But I would rather see more of your factories. There, my old, is the source of your power—together with your universities, I grant— and the reason for this alliance we negotiate." A smile. "Although the palaces and such are impressive enough. There are only thrice as many people in all my . . . sovereign's domains as in this one city."

"But France grows quickly," Prince Charles said diplomatically; it was true, as well. "The Political Service"—he nodded to the other man in the motor—"estimates that now that you've taken Sicily, you'll have all of Iberia and Italy and southern European France within a generation."

"If this fire-eating new Caliph al-Hussein doesn't whip his *wahabi* fanatics into a frenzy and wage a successful *jihad* to get Sicily back," Henri replied. "I fought in the conquest when we took it from his slug of a father, and it wasn't easy—by land or by sea. Al-Hussein is young, and not in the least sluggish."

Sir Manfred Warburton smiled with diplomatic silence and spread his hands slightly. If the Royal and Imperial Navy gained free access to the Mediterranean, the Caliph's clumsy steam-rams and paddle-frigates would be easy meat for modern ironclads and airships. Of course, that would require that France-outre-mer give them bases . . .

"Our two realms are the last of the seed of Europe, of the West," Prince Charles said seriously. "If you were to fall, half our heritage would be lost. We must stand together."

"Just so," de Vascogne said, nodding. "Grant that God wills it so."

The motor passed through a high stone wall topped with iron spearpoints. Beyond lay a hunting preserve that stretched over thousands of acres, an edited version of the jungle scrub that would have covered the Delhi area without irrigation canals. Waist-high grass stretched away beyond the gardens of the low-slung rustic pavilion and stables, with clumps of tall sal-trees, eucalyptus, and waist-high thorny scrub in the gullies. The hand of man had unobtrusively added rivers and pools, flowering shrubs, and cleared bush from the ruins of buildings old before the first Englishman set foot in Hindustan. It was early enough in the morning, and late enough in the year, that the air still smelled fresh green.

The party changed quickly into tough khaki riding clothes in the lodge. *Sais* led up horses; Henri nodded, unsurprised at their quality. North Africa was better horse-raising country, but he'd have expected the rulers of the Raj to have the best. He was more impressed at the knowledgeable way Prince Charles checked his mount's tack and the leather gaiters buckled around its legs, and the affection with which it nuzzled him.

"One thing puzzles me," he said aside to the Political Service

Officer who was his minder and tour guide. The man was usually alarmingly well informed:

"If this family of little *hoberaux* you are concerned with, of squires as you say it—this King family—is as obscure as you think, why do your Russian enemies expend so much effort in the attempts to kill them?"

He'd expressed a strong desire to see the Empire's Secret Service in action on his trip; Algiers *knew* the strength of the Imperial armed forces, and the wealth behind them. It behooved him to explore that which his government did *not* have on file.

"That *is* the question," Sir Manfred said. "We have evidence that this isn't the first generation of Kings the Okhrana has tried to kill. That episode in Oxford is bizarre in itself; the project Miss King is involved with has *no* military applications. No industrial ones, even; it's pure science. It *could* have been merely local terrorists, but . . ."

He shook his head. Prince Charles reined his mount around in a precise circle and took up one of the bamboo lances a groom offered; the long keen head glittered in the bright sunlight of the Gangetic plain.

"Certain you want to try this, Henri?" he said. "It can be tricky for a beginner, old chap."

"With lances I am somewhat acquainted," Henri replied. "And we also hunt the boar with spears—on foot, to be sure, in the mountains of the Kayble and the Rif Atlas, but I do not think your Indian pig is any fiercer than our wild boar. When you come to my homeland, I will show you our sport."

"Tally-ho, then!" the Empire's heir called, looking more cheerful than he had since the Frenchman first met him.

"Tally-ho!" Henri replied, swinging into the saddle.

And for a moment we have a chance to escape ceremony and formality, he thought; which explained the smile. *My old, I understand* exactly *your sentiments.*

The head *shikari* retreated, quailing before a coldly blue-eyed Imperial glare.

"I kiss feet, I kiss feet," the huntsman stammered. "Yes, *Kunwari,* immediately, *Kunwari!*"

Sita kept the stare going until the huntsman brought her a lance and a groom came leading Shri, the little Kathwari mare she rode by preference for rough work. Meanwhile she thanked the Gods it wasn't old Gunga Singh she was arguing with. He'd taught her to ride as a girl, and how to handle a spear on horseback, and tanned her bottom for her whenever she broke the rules—spankings administered with her parents' hearty approval. She couldn't come the heavy princess with *him*. But Gunga Singh was on leave in his village for the *Diwali* festival. The assistant here was a competent man, or he wouldn't be on the staff of the Delhi hunting lodge, but he was new, and she could frighten him—Gunga Singh had no son to train to take his place, only daughters, fortunately, and had had to hire a stranger.

"Thank you," she said graciously, and handed him a few coins. "For your trouble."

Intimidating the huntsman was a good deal easier than shedding her bodyguard. *Those* were troopers of one of the Guards Cavalry regiments—six men of the Bikaner Horse, under a keen-eyed young subaltern who was also a nobleman of the Guhilot clan of Ratanghar, and a polo champion to boot. His ancestors had been warrior-nobles of Rajputana when those of the Saxe-Coburg-Gotha's were pig-farming peasants in Germany, and he certainly wouldn't take any nonsense from a mere Imperial princess.

Every one of the *sowars* was born to the saddle as well. Their standing orders said they couldn't prevent her from taking a ride where she pleased, within reason; and also that she wasn't to be out of their sight under any circumstances whatsoever while out-of-doors. Unless she were relieving herself behind a bush, in which case they were to form a circle around her, facing outward.

At least I can speak to them, she thought; most of the Gurkhas who watched over her indoors didn't have six words of any language she spoke.

But . . . she thought. The cavalrymen all stood six feet or near it, and rode at near twice her weight, and they were using military saddles and carrying *tulwars* and carbines. Their horses were excellent, but not equal to her Shri, not by half a mile, not in broken ground.

"Are you planning on hunting, *Kunwari*?" their commander asked politely, in Rajasthani-accented Hindi.

"No, I'm carrying a lance to frighten the birds, Lieutenant Utirupa," she said dryly in the court dialect of that tongue. "It's useful for catching on things, too." A snort. "The Cold Lairs have leopards. I know your men are all good shots, but think of this as insurance."

He inclined his head, the shadow of his bulbous turban falling over his doubtful frown. Sita nodded back regally; there was a certain pleasure to teasing handsome wellborn young men, and she was conscious of the picture she made in her dazzling white jodhpurs and tunic and tight-wound turban, with the silver-hilted hunting knife belted at her waist. Probably he wasn't too used to court ways yet, or city customs—townsmen didn't join the Bikaner Horse.

Yes . . . She cudgeled her memory; there had been a file on his lineage when the Bikaners were assigned bodyguard duty, along with details of an impressive fighting record for a man still not twenty-five. *Family estates somewhere on the edge of the Thar Desert, where they probably still keep girls in* purdah. *Well, not quite, but I still probably shock him* . . .

"I wish to look on Safdarjan's Tomb, Lieutenant," she said more kindly, giving him a dazzling smile and letting a sidelong glance replace the glare. Being shocking was *fun.* "And the Asoka pillar there. It will be safe enough . . . with a *bahadur* such as yourself as guard."

"At your command, *Kunwari*," he said, swallowing hard and lowering his eyes in momentary confusion.

Hooves clacked on the stone paving of the stables, then plopped into the deep soft dust of the laneway; she kept her mount to a fast walk while they were within the grounds of the lodge, waving to servants and groundskeepers who made salaam as she passed; Sita had spent much of her time here since childhood and many of them would remember her on her first pony, or rolling a hoop.

Then they broke out into open meadow, and she tightened her thigh grip on the mare's flanks.

"*Chalo*, Shri!" she called. No more was necessary. "Go, Shri!"

The mare responded with jackrabbit acceleration and Sita crouched low over her neck, the light hunting lance held horizontally as they dashed through tall grass, body moving with the horse in a dance of speed. The tall chargers of the guardsmen were left behind for a hundred yards or more; she could hear them swearing artistically behind her. Their mounts' longer legs closed the gap a little after that, until she went under the branches of a grove, ducking and weaving with a dancer's grace.

More blasphemy behind, and then she pulled in and Shri sat on her haunches and slid down into a dry gully; the princess leaned back and sat the heaving saddle as easily as a cushion in a palace drawing room. Sita laughed in sheer exuberant glee as the pony kept her footing with cat agility amid the dust and rocks and clods of hard earth, conscious every moment that a slip could break her neck on that stony ground, or send eight hundred pounds of horse rolling over her.

Shri snorted and wheeled as they reached the floor of the gully— it would be a torrent in the monsoon—and sped up it with a rattle of horseshoes, striking sparks from ground that was a shifting mass of rounded brown rocks, weaving around thick clumps of bush that reached for her with long white thorns like tiger's teeth. This time the blasphemy behind her was mixed with genuine yells, and a shout of rage as someone lost his saddle; and for all that they were taking the slope more cautiously than she had. No choice, with their tall horses carrying two hundred pounds and more of man and gear on each back.

In a moment the Rajput troop commander would bring order out of chaos and think to have his men climb out and beat the sides of the ravine; she put her mare at a narrow side gully and came up it with a plunging heave.

That put her in another grove that shaded off into artificial marsh where a few migratory duck still lingered, and birds buzzed about after insects. Sita strangled a betraying whoop as she spun her light lance around her head and turned the horse to canter off toward the place she suspected was her goal.

"Vive le sport!" Henri cried.

The hunt went forward in a mad dash over rock and gravel, dry watercourses and crumbling slopes and fanged brush. Dust rose far ahead, where the beaters were hammering iron bars on brass triangles and shouting. The brush and long grass seethed with half a dozen sounders of wild pig, scores in all—big ones too, he saw from the glimpses he got, both sexes and all ages. They were ready to turn at bay—

A boar did, grunting to tell the females and young to remain behind, then leading the men off and away. The beast looked to weigh four hundred pounds at least, the long tusks on its bristling snout like curved knives. Low to the ground, it led them eel-like through the brush and then turned with snake-suddenness in a clearing.

"He's led us just where he wants us," Prince Charles cried gaily. "At him, you chaps!"

Henri whooped again and put his horse at the shallow nullah ahead; it was a superbly trained beast, and leapt the slight gully like a champion. The others reined in to give him room.

I thought these Angrezi *cold-blooded*, went through him, as he saw the boar sink back on its haunches and launch itself forward like a cannon shot of bone and gristle. *But if this is their idea of enjoyment, perhaps I was wrong!*

The weapon used for pigsticking was shorter than a war lance, with a ball on the butt end for balance. It danced in his hand as he closed with his target, leaning out . . .

. . . and his horse stepped on a round pebble lying on a glass-smooth paving block from an ancient building. It shot out from under the gelding, and the animal's head went down like a pendulum. Henri had ridden since he could walk; he kicked his feet free of the stirrups and curled himself into a ball in midair. He lost the lance, and a rock struck him an agonizing blow on the point of his elbow as he landed. Time slowed as he stared between his own feet at the wicked dished-in face of the boar, and the yellow slobber-wet daggers that curled up from its snout. For a moment it hesitated, twitching its head from side to side to look at the other riders and the horse that thrashed on the ground.

The problem with pigs was that they were intelligent—more so than a dog, much more so than a horse. The domestic breed knew why men kept them; this one knew who the real threat was, and that it wasn't the downed horse. The little cloven hooves dug into the dry clay, and it bounded forward with an enraged squeal.

Cursing, Henri tried to roll to his feet and draw his hunting knife with the same motion. He had just enough attention to spare to hear the pounding of hooves behind him, and flatten again. The thunder paused, and he saw the underside of the horse overhead as it leapt, even the tiny gold spurs on the rider's black boots. It landed in mid-gallop, and traveled exactly seven paces beyond him. The pig reared on its hind legs, trying to slash at the belly of the horse attacking it. The Frenchman blinked dirt out of his eyes; the morning sun seemed to glow on the white-and-gold clothing of the rider.

A lance dipped, couched underarm, driving down with a surgeon's precision between the beast's hunched shoulder blades. The speed and strength of horse and boar and rider combined to pin the pig to the ground beneath, dead with a cloven heart and spine. The lance snapped across with a gunshot *crack* and the rider was past the kill, swaying back erect in the saddle and flourishing the weapon's stub, guiding the horse about with superbly casual skill. It stood and tossed its head, mouthing the bit, foam streaking its sweat-dark dappled neck; above was a delicately beautiful face framed by a tight white silk turban, grinning an urchin grin, the tail of the *pugaree* fluttering in the hot wind.

More hoofbeats as the prince and Sir Manfred came up, and the attendants. Several of them were swearing in amazement; one gave an involuntary shout of "*Shabash!*" and then they were all crying it.

All but the prince. "Sita, what the devil do you think you're doing here?" he began.

"Excuse me, Your Highness," Henri said. "It appears that your sister is here saving my life. A thousand thanks," he continued, with a sweeping bow made less graceful as he winced and rubbed his elbow.

Sita looked down at him from the saddle, her eyebrows raised against a smile gone cool and considering. "You are welcome, Monsieur le Vicomte," she said. "My apologies also, if I have shocked you."

Henri grinned. "*Au contraire*, Princess Sita. Let me say at once that *my* prince will not be in the least shocked. In fact, I think I may say that he would heartily approve."

"Good spear," Sir Manfred said quietly. "And a very fortunate one, Your Highness."

The party all looked up as the file of Bikaner Horse troopers pulled up on lathered horses. Their commander saluted and took a long look at the little tableau. When he nodded to Sita again, the iron mask of control over anger had turned to wary respect.

"Good spear, *Kunwari*," he said. "And I would pay thirty gold *mohurs* for that horse! *Kunwar*," he added to Charles. "If there is fault, it is mine—I took my men in the wrong direction when the princess's horse . . . bolted."

Charles snorted, and Sita looked offended at the notion any horse could run away with *her*. Henri bent to check the legs of his own mount; uninjured, except for a bad fright and some bruises, he thought. That gave him an unobtrusive chance to study Prince

Charles's face, which was scowling as the heir to the Lion Throne saw one of the troopers gray-faced and cradling an arm.

"You, *sowar*," he said. "Are you injured?"

The trooper looked as though the attention from on high was more painful than the arm. "It is nothing, *Kunwar*," he murmured. "A clean break—my horse shied—it will heal."

Charles turned to his sister. "It might have been his neck!" he snapped.

Sita flushed. "I am sorry," she said; then repeated it in Hindi to the horse-soldier.

"It is nothing, *Kunwari*," the trooper demurred. He looked at the dead boar, and at the spot where the royal family's guest had lain. "Good spear! And the arm is nothing; I have eaten your salt; it is my *karman* to shed blood for your House."

"And *rajadharma* not to make men risk their lives without need!" Charles said crisply, and called over his shoulder for a surgeon.

Sir Manfred had dismounted; he murmured in his guest's ear: "*Rajadharma;* ruler's duty."

The prince went on: "What is your name, *sowar*?"

The man drew himself erect: "Burubu Ram, *Kunwar*."

"Where did you break that?"

He nodded when the officer described the location; he knew this hunting park as well as most knew their front gardens.

"Miles, at a gallop, with a broken arm?"

The Rajput officer coughed discreetly: "He would not return, *Kunwar*. Please forgive the indiscipline." The words were apologetic, but the tone rang with pride.

"Very well," Charles said, and looked at the trooper again. "You are given six months sick leave, with pay. Before you return to your home . . . your family hold land?"

"*Han, Kunwa.*" Yes, Imperial Prince. "Thirty acres, northwest of Bikaner on the new Es-smeet Canal—a grant to my father for twenty-five years' service. I am heir to the holding."

"The Smith Canal . . . Good. Surgeon, see to this man's arm."

His comrades helped him dismount, and the doctor began to probe it gently, then to prepare a splint. That sort of medicine was always available on the hunting field.

"*Sowar* Burubu Ram, before you go on sick leave, you may select one horse and its tack from the Imperial stud; that is my sister's gift to you." He looked up and shifted to English for a moment: "You're paying for it out of your allowance, by the way, Sita." In Hindi once more: "Also, if you have a younger brother who would care to enlist in the Guards, I will furnish his mount."

The trooper grinned despite his pain. Imperial cavalry regiments were raised on the *sillidar* system; the Raj provided weapons and ammunition, but the trooper found his own horse and its fodder and gear out of his stipend, replacing the mount as needed unless it was lost in battle. It ensured the cavalry a better class of recruit than the infantry units, but the initial expense could be heavy for a middling-prosperous yeoman, and prohibitive for more than one son.

Sita swung down out of the saddle. She unfastened the long jewel-hilted hunting knife from her belt and tucked it into the injured man's sash.

"A keepsake from your princess, *sowar*," she said. "And if you have a sister who wishes a position in the household, it will be given."

The trooper started to salute, winced, and gave a dignified salaam as he spoke his thanks. Then he walked off, accompanied by comrades who helped him toward the roadway and damned him for a lucky dog in genial whispers, swearing that they'd gladly break both arms for the favor he'd been given.

"I don't think this has to go any further, Highness," Sir Manfred said quietly. "Seeing how embarrassing it would have been if our special ambassador had been ripped up by a boar on the outskirts of Delhi."

Charles nodded. "Leave it to the rumor mill, then," he said in a clipped tone. "And Sita, isn't it about time you grew up?"

"You mean it's adult behavior to *let* ambassadors get ripped up by boars on the family's hunting grounds, brother?" she said sweetly, and remounted. "Lieutenant Utirupa," she went on. "Perhaps a gentle canter to the ruins?"

Prince Charles shook his head as the diminished bodyguard followed her. "Merciful Krishna help the French court," he muttered.

Henri de Vascogne smiled.

Chapter Six

"I do not like these *palitikal* officers," Narayan Singh said. "They will make an intriguer of thee—a *cutch-sahib*, instead of a fighting man."

He stepped back a pace and considered his handiwork. Athelstane King stood naked on the floor, looking at himself in the mirror. The stain made the rest of his body match the tan of his face and arms; only the neat new bandage on his right forearm showed what had happened a few hours ago.

"*Bhai,*" King said. "If we do not become intriguers, these swine of Deceivers and *hashasshin* daggermen will make us dead men altogether." He used the Punjabi that was the Sikh's mother tongue, and one of his own.

Narayan Singh nodded, then frowned. "We cannot say thou'rt a Sikh; it would take too long for the beard to grow." Sikhs never cut theirs, tucking the ends up under their turbans instead.

Then he snapped his fingers and grinned. "I have it, *huzoor*! I had thought to make of you a trooper in Probyn's Horse, or a *jawan* of the Rumbur Rifles. You could pass for a Punjabi Jat—perhaps—or certainly for a Kalasha. Or even a man of Sindh. But instead you shall be of the Kashmir Horse Artillery; a *naik*"—corporal—"and a learned man with a *sahib-log* or two in your bloodline, skilled in mathematics."

King nodded; the technical branches of the Army were the likeliest places to find a Eurasian, since they required more in the way of technical education. It would make a Kashmiri accent natural, too, and his was slight but noticeable in both his English and his Hindi; it would also account for the odd little slip or carelessness about caste rules. Kashmir had the most mixed population of any province in the Indian part of the Empire, and the highest proportion of *sahib-log*.

Narayan Singh went on: "A desirable position, *sahib;* twenty-five rupees a month, and *batta* field allowance! We shall call thee . . . Kiram Shaw. Nor will it be strange for you to travel to your home for the festival."

Home, King thought. *Krishna. I'll have to tell Hasamurti's parents what happened.* The thought brought sadness back, combined with shame heavy and thick like castor oil. He'd been Hasamurti's protector, and that was a duty he'd failed at—badly.

He'd have to tell her kin, and they'd want to know *why* she'd died. The worst of that was that he didn't have the faintest idea.

"Pranam," King said.

He pressed his palms together and bowed to the near-naked, tangle-haired ascetic who sat on his mat at the corner, eyes staring at emptiness, with the sacred thread across his shoulder and three lines of yellow ash drawn across his forehead to represent the three aspects of Shiva—creator, preserver, and destroyer. A bubble of space surrounded him in the thronging crowd that filled the roadway.

King would have made the reverence anyway, out of politeness, and it sat well with the character he'd assumed. The man blessed him absently, scowled a little at Narayan Singh's lordly disdain, and returned to his meditations. The two young men bought *samosas* hot from a vat of oil presided over by a vendor at the corner of the narrow, winding street and walked on, carefully munching the three-cornered savory pastries, holding pieces of corn husk beneath them to keep the oil off their uniforms. A man jostled King's elbow; he caught himself just in time to suppress his natural icy stare at the effrontery and scowled instead, letting his left hand drop to the pommel of his plain stirrup-hilted saber.

A horse-artillery *naik* couldn't expect the deference due a *sahib-log* cavalry officer. On the other hand, he wouldn't be expected to show the same restraint on his temper, either.

"Watch where you step, *hubshi*," King said, with a truculence befitting a soldier of the Sirkar.

The man—a hairy, hulking young Pathan with a *potsheen* coat hanging off his shoulders—put his hand on the hilt of his *chora* in turn, growling insults in Pushtu and asking what man expected to live after calling him a *hubshi*, a wooly-haired Negro.

"Does this misbelieving pig with hair on his liver insult thee, *bhai*?" Narayan Singh asked, turning and letting his teeth show white as he jutted his chin. "Doubtless he comes to town seeking to find who fathered the children of his wives—let him look in the pox hospital for men without discrimination. Or perhaps he tires of the embraces of goats."

The Pathan spat aside, pretending not to understand the Hindi the two men spoke, which was exceedingly unlikely—it being one of the official languages of the Empire along with English, and used more often. He looked to be a hillman come into town to trade, but ready enough to quarrel, until a shrill whistle sounded. A policeman trotted up, in blue jacket and yellow trousers and leather hat, twirling a sal-wood truncheon and looking the Pathan up and down.

"There is to be no brawling here," he said mildly. "About your business, *banchut*. I shall have an eye to you on the streets I patrol."

The policeman was stout and middle-aged—positions in the Imperial Indian Police were a common reward for military service—and armed only with the yard-long billy club. The Pathan showed some acquaintance with good sense by growling a final oath before he turned and shoved his way through the crowd; not without a last curious glance at King's face. The constable touched his hand to his cap and walked on.

One lesson King had learned in this latest frontier campaign was that confidence was most of the battle when you were trying to seem something you were not. People saw what they expected to see, and at least the effort of keeping up his disguise was distraction enough to keep away angry puzzlement at the assassins—in the Peshawar Club, of all places—and nagging guilt over Hasamurti.

"I must be a man of more importance than I thought," he said quietly. "Someone is willing to go to a great deal of trouble to kill me."

They filed through the workaday chaos of the railway station and showed their leave passes—free second-class travel on the Imperial Indian Railways was among a soldier's perquisites. A mordant flicker of humor went through him as the *babu* clerk read them; he'd signed his own ticket-of-leave permit with Captain King's name.

"It is not a desirable honor, to be thus sought after," Narayan Singh said dryly, as the railways porters stashed their duffels over the seats of their compartment. "We are like to die of it."

The compartment was dusty, and the upholstery on the seats was threadbare, but it was better than the crowded board benches of third class, and the Indian Railways' broad standard gauge of five-foot-six made for comfortable rolling stock. King had gold *mohurs* in his money belt, as well as banknotes and silver rupees and copper pieces in his pouch, but it would have been dangerously conspicuous to use them. Not that there was any law against two enlisted men buying a first-class ticket; it was just jarringly unlikely. King leaned out of the compartment window, looking at the crowd that thronged the platform under the high arched glass-and-iron roof.

Is that the Pathan we met? he thought. Then: *Probably not.* Not even a mountaineer nourishing a grievance would follow them all the way into the train station—spending money on a ticket—for so casual a quarrel.

Nobody else tried to enter their compartment; a middle-class Muslim came down the side corridor with his veiled wife and daughters, took one look at the raffish, smiling soldiers, and decided that the next section wasn't so crowded after all. So did a fat *babu*-clerk in a tussore turban with a watermelon under one arm and a valise under the other, for entirely different reasons, fearing a deficit of friendliness where the husband anticipated an excess.

The local to Rawalpindi and Oxford was no Trans-India Express; it chuffed along at a stately forty miles an hour, trailing black coal smoke. It was pulled by a Babur-class 4-6-2 built to a design standardized in the days when Edward was King-Emperor, Lord Salisbury was prime minister and the twentieth century was young. Thousands of them worked everywhere from Australia to the Cape and even beyond; some had been sent to aid in the resettlement of Britain and the still more remote colonies on the North American coasts. This one also stopped at every small town along the way, those growing more frequent as they moved out of the Northwest Frontier Province and into the richer, more densely settled Punjab.

Like most soldiers, King had long since learned to snatch sleep when he could, but today his slumber was troubled. Several times he was startled awake as the train crossed bridges in a rattle and hum of metal; a huge affair of girders over the Indus River, and dozens of smaller ones over the lesser streams and innumerable irrigation canals that diverted the Five Rivers to the fields and made the Punjab the granary of the Raj. The waterways that laced the land flashed silver and red in the setting sun, with the green line of the Muree Hills to the northeast.

The square fields were dead-flat for the most part, and would have been dull to any but a countryman's eyes—dusty where the cool-season crops of wheat and barley had been reaped, others shaggy with cotton or rustling green-gold with maize or neat with stooked sheaves of rice. *Ryots* looked up from the round-the-clock work of cutting sugar-cane, nearly as incurious as the oxen that carried the heaped stalks; at sunset a cloud of fruit bats took off from a grove of oranges and circled against the great red globe of the rising moon before heading for a mango orchard.

Narayan Singh ate a chapati and half an onion, then put up his boots and slept, snoring, with his head lolling to the rhythmic clacking of steel wheel on rail. King found sleep remained elusive, nodding drowsy far into the darkness, envying the Sikh; when his eyes slid shut he kept remembering the attack at the Peshawar Club . . . and worse, Hasamurti.

I even miss that damned annoying giggle of hers, he thought sadly. That was what *Hasamurti* meant: merriment. *Dammit, I liked that girl, and not just when she was on her back. She made me laugh. She didn't deserve to have that happen to her, and I was supposed to* protect *her.*

A chill awoke him in the middle of the night, or so he thought. The military greatcoat had slipped down from his shoulders; he reached a hand for it. Then—

Ibrahim Khan of the Dongala Kel jerked himself awake again. He couldn't afford to sleep, no matter how tired he was; the creosoted timbers and gravel bed of the railroad were flashing too close beneath his rump. If he slipped from beneath the carriage, the railroad maintenance workers would scrape him off the wood and stone and iron with brushes. He forced hands and legs to cling more tightly to the iron tie-rods under the passenger carriage, swaying amid the darkness and metal clangor and stink of coal and lubricating oil. It was maddening to one raised in the clean air of the heights above Tirah.

"There is no God but God, and Muhammad is His Prophet," he whispered to himself; prayer never hurt and the noise would be lost in the background. *Thy curse upon this te-rain, O Allah*, he added to himself.

The hard shape of the *chora*-knife slung across the small of his back was even more reassuring; unlike prayer, it had never let him down.

I must strike soon, he thought. *My muscles grow stiff, and that will make me slow.*

His father and uncles had taught him long ago that speed and stealth were first among the skills of a Pashtun fighting man. The damned-to-Eblis *sahib-log* would always win a contest of raw strength and hammerblows; there were too many of them and their hired men, and their weapons were too powerful. Even when the Raj was weakened by the Sword of Allah—and the Afghan tribes united by stark hunger—outright invasion had failed. They had driven his people back into the hills; it had been generations before the Pashtun tribes were more than a scattering of starvelings again.

So when you fought the *sahib-log* you must strike hard, but above all strike quickly and from a direction they did not expect—then vanish before they could strike back.

"Now," he muttered to himself.

The train was traveling north in the small hours of the night, cresting the first of a series of rises as it headed toward Kashmir. That slowed it, to little more than the speed of a galloping horse. Muscles cracking with the effort, he won his way to the edge, hanging upside down from its bottom like a great hairy spider. Then he inched forward, bent himself upward so that his feet twined under the rods beneath the carriage. A single heaving convulsive effort and his upper body was plastered to the exterior door of the compartment, with the half-opened window directly above his head.

He paused, panting and making himself forget the heart-stopping instant when it seemed he'd lose hold and tumble downward to the moving ground only inches beneath.

Revenge is good, he thought; he would repay the *sahib-log* for their harrying of the Tirah country; still more for keeping the riches of the plains to themselves.

But revenge is a dish best eaten cold. And as for the gold the strange fakir *with the seeress promised, gold is useless to a dead man. Carefully, Ibrahim, carefully. All things are accomplished according to the will of God, but a wise man does not tempt Him.*

He drew the *chora*, slowly, thankful that he had never indulged in extravagances like silver bells for the hilt, even if they did make a pleasant accompaniment to a fight. It was twenty inches of fine steel—forged from the saber of a dead Imperial trooper in the year of Ibrahim's birth—but severely plain. He clamped the thick back of the blade between his teeth and reached upward to plant both hands firmly.

With his hands on the sill of the window, he would have to support all his weight on his arms with his body bent into an L-shape, then chin himself and go headfirst through the opening with his legs drawn up behind him by main strength. That entry might wake those within, no matter how great his care. He must kill or disable in no more than two or three strokes; the Sikh and the *sahib-log*-pretending-to-be-halfbreed had both looked likely men of their hands when he saw them in the streets of Peshawar town.

He drew a deep breath, reminded his God that those who fell fighting the unbelievers were deserving of Paradise, and lunged upward and in.

Athelstane King blinked fully awake in less time than it took for his greatcoat to slide to the floor. Moonlight and starlight seeped past a bulky shape in the half-open window, glittered on steel. No time to reach for a weapon; the intruder's shoulders were already inside the window. If King scrabbled for blade or pistol, the hillman would be inside the compartment, or mostly; and unpleasant experience had given the Lancer a hearty respect for what that breed could do with a few lightning-quick hacking *chora*-strokes.

"*Turn out!*" he shouted.

In the same motion he struck upward with a knee, the only blow he could make from his slouched position on the couch. Cat-quick, the Pathan twisted his head. That meant his jaw wasn't broken against the unyielding steel he gripped between his teeth, but the knee glanced painfully off his temple instead and the long heavy knife dropped to the floorboards rather than into a waiting hand.

For an instant the Pathan was dazed. King's scrabbling left hand found the hem of his opponent's sheepskin coat and wrenched it forward, pinning his arms and covering his head for a crucial moment. The same movement also pulled the hillman three-quarters of the way into the compartment, shins across the windowsill and head down between the seats.

Narayan Singh woke cursing, confused but throwing himself into the fight. For a minute and a half the darkness of the railcar compartment was a confusion of grappling, punching, kicking, gripping, wrenching combat. There was no science to it, scarcely even much comprehension; half the blows of the two Imperial soldiers landed on each other or the wood and horsehair upholstery of the train. At one point King found himself wrestling with the Pathan's filthy *pugaree*-turban rather than the head he thought he'd been grappling, even as the man tried to tear out his collarbone with his teeth.

This is like trying to fight a tiger hand-to-hand in a closet, he thought, snarling in pain and heaving the mountaineer off; there was no breath to spare for yells, only hisses and grunts and the dry hard sound of blows delivered point-blank.

Narayan Singh gave a strangled roar as the Pathan tried to wrench out a handful of his beard and throw himself backward out of the open window at the same time. That move put a little distance between the combatants, and let in some light. Sparing his aching and still-healing right arm, King kicked once more and managed to connect with his enemy's stomach. There wasn't much space to swing his foot, and the target was armored in hard muscle—he'd been aiming the reinforced toe of his riding boot at the other man's crotch, and missed by a foot—but breath went out of him with an *ooof*.

Narayan Singh had kept a grip on the hand that tried to rip out his beard. He jerked it forward; King grabbed the other, the one trying to drive ragged dirty fingernails into his nose again. Together they twisted both arms behind the hillman's back. That took two hands for King; unwounded, Narayan Singh had a hamlike fist free to pound over and over again into the back of the pinioned man's neck. Eventually the Pathan went mostly limp.

Thank the ten thousand faces of God for that, King thought, winded, every one of his bruises aching again and some new ones added. The Pathan had added another to a short list of men he'd met who were as strong as he was.

Of course, I'm not at my best, he reassured himself.

The Sikh orderly reached for the short utility knife at his own belt and jerked the prisoner's head back to bare the throat. King shook his head:

"No. He must answer questions."

Just then someone thumped against the other wall of the compartment and called for quiet. King grinned despite the pain of a split lip and pulled out a linen handkerchief to wipe at the blood pouring from his nose. Ganesha alone knew what they thought had been going on: despite the way the nightmare fight had felt like forever, it had taken less than two minutes.

"*Han, sahib*—I mean, Kiram Shaw," Narayan Singh said, grinning harshly as he bound the man's arms behind his back with his own *pugaree* and pushed him roughly into the seat opposite. "Questioned with things sharp, or heavy, or hot—or all three, *huzoor?*"

"We'll see," King said, not sharing the Sikh's bloodthirsty enthusiasm, despite the fact that they'd both lost friends to the prisoner's kinsmen.

If you faced capture by Pathans, rolling to your rifle and blowing out your brains was infinitely preferable to letting them turn you over to their wives. Torture was women's work across the Border, although men would do well enough if they were put to it. And there were times when you had to get information to save your own men's lives, or the mission, no matter how—although an officer walked around a rock when that was necessary.

He still didn't like tormenting helpless men, even ones who'd be glad enough to kill him by inches; and he remembered things Narayan Singh's father had taught him.

"Turn up the light," he said, before the groggy Pathan could do more than mumble. "And search him."

The Sikh did so, and also blocked the door to the corridor when a train attendant came by to ask if anything was wrong, snarling something that sent the man scurrying off again.

And scurrying off is exactly what he'd have done if he'd found our bledout bodies instead, King thought sardonically. There were times when he thought it would do the sheltered folk of the inner provinces good to be exposed to frontier conditions, a little, now and then. On the other hand, protecting them from that was precisely his duty . . .

The gaslight had a yellow tinge, even when the incandescent mantle around it started to glow. It showed the hillman's face with merciless clarity, nose and lips and both eyes starting to swell, a sheen of sweat, and blood clotting in the dense silky black beard. King judged the other man's age to be a little less than his own—somewhere around twenty—and they were about of a size, which made the other a tall man even among Afghans. His skin was an olive color only slightly darker than King's, his nose a hawk beak in a long, high-cheeked, full-lipped face; without his turban, his head showed only cropped stubble apart from a love-lock on one side.

King bent carefully—keeping the other man's feet pinioned with one boot—and picked up the *chora*. It was a fine example of the blade-smith's art, and cruelly sharp. The Lancer officer laid it across his knees and waited.

"Here, Kiram Shaw," Narayan Singh said. "This purse—six rupees, a dozen piece, one silver *dinar* of Kabul. Two small knives—good knives. And this piece of paper; nothing else upon him but lice. Though if we could train up the stink of this savage to obedience, it would cleave teakwood."

King unfolded the paper. It was heavy and rather rough, yellowish, a hand-made product of some little town beyond the Imperial frontier. Sketched on it in charcoal was a face, done rather skillfully but in a style he knew by instinct had never been taught within the Raj . . . and a woman's hand as well, he thought.

A man's face framed by a turban, clean-shaven save for close-clipped sideburns and mustaches. A young man: one he saw every morning in the mirror, and an arrow carefully marked out the scar on his jaw. The words below were written in Pushtu and Hindi, using the *Angrezi*—Roman—script; they were succinct and to the point: *two hundred gold* mohurs *for this man's head.*

King grunted, although he knew well enough that *someone* was trying to kill him, not that someone was evidently willing to pay a very considerable sum—a gold *mohur* would buy four good horses, or pay a year's wages for a noncom such as he was pretending to be. Five *mohurs* were a year's rent from a yeoman-farm.

Two hundred were a small fortune, or a not-so-small one across the Border.

"So," King said, tapping the paper against the blade of the *chora*.

"What would you do with two hundred gold *mohurs*, man of the hills? Give him water," he added to Narayan Singh.

The Sikh grumbled but obeyed. The Pathan's eyes flickered between the two men, and then he sucked at the waterskin and grinned—painfully.

"Istrafugallah!" he said. "What would I not do with your head and so much gold, *gora-log*?"

That was the less complementary term for the *Angrezi*, and Narayan Sikh raised a hand. King waved him back.

"With the gold and the fame of slaying you I would build a fort—raise a *lashkar* such as Iskander of the Silver Hand commanded—become an emir—"

The hillman spoke good Hindi, with the rough accent of the Border country. "But instead I shall hang with the filthy pig."

He shrugged, pretending indifference to dying sewn into a raw pigskin and with a piece of pork thrust down his throat.

The officer and the Sikh exchanged the slightest of glances. "Perhaps," King said casually. "Who gave you this picture of me, O Pathan?" He considered the man closely. "If you were to tell me, perhaps the pigskin could be spared."

The hillman grinned. "You will not trick Ibrahim Khan son of Ali that easily, unbeliever," he said. "A *fakir* gave it me—a holy man. But his name I never knew, nor his home. Nor could you make me tell, even if I knew. Such is against your law."

"I have leather for a knotted cord, *huzoor*," Narayan Singh said eagerly. "Give me leave—betake yourself to the dining car—he will talk. Easily, if he is so stupid he cannot tell the difference between us and a judge, or the distance between this place and a law court."

"A cobra spits, a Sikh speaks—who will know the difference?" the Pathan said, and there was real anger in the orderly's answering growl.

King raised a calming hand. "Peace, brother. This is a Yusufazi Pathan, I would say—of the Chagarzi sept; perhaps of the Nasrat Khel, perhaps of the Dongala."

The Pathan gave a slight start; at the knowledge, and at the accentless Pushtu in which King spoke for a moment. The Lancer officer went on:

"You met a *fakir* who had two hundred gold *mohurs*? Two hundred, to spend on one officer of the Empire, among so many?"

"It was you who suborned the Orakzai chiefs with silver and smooth words, until they stood aside from the war and left my folk alone to face your army, the pig-eating sons of whores," the Pathan growled. "You are no ordinary unbeliever. Perhaps the *fakir* had the gold of Damascus, where the Caliph of the Faithful dwells in might."

King took the handkerchief from his injured nose. His frown and slight sneer made dried blood crackle in his mustache. "Two men wearing their own winding-sheets tried to kill me in Peshawar. Waited outside the door of my dwelling to meet me."

Narayan Singh grinned, too, an unpleasant expression. "Instead they met me. I disturbed their winding-sheets with bloodstains, and in them they were buried—if the *konstabeels* did not throw them to the pi-dogs."

The Pathan's eyes narrowed, suspecting a trap. "Should I weep for them?" he asked rhetorically. "Such men would be Shia, near as worthless as you Nasrani dogs, or this Hindu idol worshiper."

The Shia branch of Islam was common in Persia, although persecuted by the Caliph's men; and common among the Empire's Muslims, where the Raj enforced toleration. Pathans were fiercely orthodox Sunni, though. The Sikh growled; *his* faith was an offshoot of the Hindu stock, but ostentatiously monotheistic.

"Would your *fakir* have bought *hashasshin* killers?" King said. "If he was a Sunni *fakir*, that is."

Narayan Singh pulled something from the neck of his tunic. The Pathan's eyes went wide. The *rumal* of the stranglers was unmistakable. The Sikh undid the fold at the end and showed the coin there—gold, also an Imperial *mohur*, new-stamped, fresh from the Lahore mint.

"While I slew the *hashasshin*, my *sahib* slew others who waited for him within—Deceivers, followers of Kali," he said. "Would your *fakir* have dealt with worshipers of the Dreadful Bride?"

Doubt showed on the Pathan's face. "The tale of Deceivers who sought the life of a *sahib* was in the bazaars of Peshawar town," he muttered.

King nodded. "They sought to slay me." His mouth thinned with remembered anger. "And then did kill my woman."

The Pathan shrugged indifferently at that. *Beastly lot*, King thought. Pathans saw women as fit only for work and breeding; many didn't even think they were worthwhile for pleasure. An old Pathan song went:

> *"There's a boy across the river*
> *With a bottom like a peach*
> *But alas, I cannot swim . . ."*

"This *fakir*, was he of your people?" King said. He lifted the knife. "Speak. If you do, I promise you—on my honor as an *Angrezi* officer—that you will die clean and your body be buried by the rites of your faith."

The Pathan licked his lips. "I am Ibrahim Khan of the Dongala Khel," he said. "My father is a *malik*, a great chief. He and my brothers and kindred will avenge me, however I die."

Another long moment's silence, then: "No, the *fakir*—the man who called himself such—was not *Pashtun*. Not Pathan, you would say. He was Tadjik—Tadjik of the Wakan uplands. A tall man, who moved like a swordsman, fair of skin. One eye was covered in a patch."

Now, who . . . A sudden thought sent a chill crawling up from King's groin to his gut. *Who would be posing as a Tadjik, who wasn't one? A white man, at that?* Tadjiks were common in northern Afghanistan . . . and farther north still, among the human cattle of the Czar. Easy enough to acquire their language there.

"He called himself a Tadjik," he said softly. "But was he? Was he even a Muslim?"

Ibrahim snorted. "He spoke Arabic—more than I ever learned in the medrassa school of my father's village. He could quote from the holy Book."

King lifted the Khyber knife and tapped the flat against his knuckles. "A knife speaks truth, but men lie," he said, quoting an old Border saying. "I also speak Arabic, and have read the Koran, but that does not make me a Muslim, much less a *fakir* or *mullah*."

"You do not say that this man was of your people!" Ibrahim sneered.

"By no means. When he spoke your tongue, did he speak it thus? With this sound?"

Languages were among King's hobbies; his own Pushtu was idiomatic, to the point of having a slight Kabuli tinge like a courtier of the Emir. With an effort, he gave it another accent; one lisping and purling at the same time. Narayan Singh started, and stared at his commander in surprise.

"Yes," Ibrahim said, shrugging. "He used Pushtu much like that. What of it?"

"That is not how a Tadjik would speak Pushtu," King said grimly. "That would be *thus*." He demonstrated, and the Afghan nodded, puzzled. "As I speak now, that is the mark of a different folk." He paused for a long moment. "*Russki*, they call themselves. In your tongue, *E-rus*."

The Pathan froze for an instant, then heaved against the bonds that held him. "You lie! None of the Eaters of Men, the worshipers of Shaitan, would dare walk among us!"

King shrugged. "Who else? A true *fakir* from the Caliphate would not consort with Shia—or worse, worshipers of Kali. Who else besides the Commander of the Faithful hates the Raj, and borders on the land of the Afghans, and has gold and guns to buy men?"

Ibrahim's face twisted with anger and disgust. The Pathans hated the *Angrezi* Raj; because the *sahib-log* were infidels; because they had taken the foothill country and Peshawar from the Afghans long ago and ruled it still; because expeditions punishing raiders had left smoking ruin in the upland villages time after time.

But they hated the Russians and the Czar who ruled in Samarkand with a frenzied loathing that made their anger toward the Empire a pale and tepid thing.

"You lie!" Ibrahim said again, but doubt had crept into his tone. "What proof have you?"

"None," King said promptly. "Any more than I know why the *E-rus* should seek my death more than any other *Angrezi* fighting man's. But nothing else makes any sense at all, does it?"

"The only gold I will take from Shaitan's bum-boys is the gold I take from their lifeless bodies," Ibrahim growled. "That does not make me love you like a brother, unbeliever—even if your tale be true."

"Good," Narayan Singh said sardonically. "Since you have undoubtedly stabbed all your brothers in the back, over the love of the comeliest sheep in the Border country."

Ibrahim glared at him, but restrained his impulse to spit as the Sikh raised a sledgehammer fist.

King frowned in thought for a long minute. "Listen to me, man of the hills," he said at last. "For reasons I know not, this *E-rus*-who-passes-for-a-Tadjik seeks my life in secret *razziah*. And he has made of you and your kin his dogs and slaves, tricking you to be the servants of abomination. So it seems we both have blood feud with him."

"Aye," Ibrahim said, his eyes kindling. "That is *Pukhtunwali*, the way of the Pathans. Death for an insult. He has broken the bond of hospitality, lied and deceived his hosts—lied to *me*. I would aid you in your revenge on him, even though you will soon hand me to the slayers. But why do you tell a dead man all this?"

King kept his face grave; a smile at the wrong moment could turn the highlander sullen again. They were the most sensitive of men to mockery, although they made an art form of inflicting it on their enemies. Instead he went on solemnly:

"Because we have an enemy in common, I will forgive—once— that you tried to take my head. I give you your life. You may take it and go, or you may seek this *E-rus* out with me."

Ibrahim's eyes went wide for a moment; then he snorted. "You would call a Pathan blood brother?"

"No!" King said. "If you come with me, you will come as my servant and sworn man. Or you may go your way, and if I see you again, I will slay you out of hand."

Now the Pathan put on an impassive face of his own. "Will you give me back my knife, if I choose to go?"

"By Nanak Guru!" Narayan Singh swore. "This is insolence past all belief, even in an Afghan thief; he seeks to cut our throats, and asks for the return of the blade!"

Ibrahim snorted. "A man who does not try never conquers," he said, and turned back to King. "If I am thy man, what wage will you pay?"

"None! You shall have your food and keep, and a horse," King said promptly. "And when we take the head of the *E-rus*, two hundred gold *mohurs* and freedom to ride back to the hills. If we fail . . . dead men need no gold. Turn."

The Pathan did; King freed him from the Sikh's tight knots. "We will leave the compartment for the space of ten heartbeats," he said. "If you are still here, you will swear. If you are gone, I will throw the knife out of the window."

"That I may slay thee with it later?" Ibrahim Khan asked, grinning.

"Nay. You have come closer to slaying me than ever you will again. Think, O Ibrahim—but do it quickly! I have no need of sluggards in my service!"

In the corridor outside, Narayan Singh began to expostulate in frantic whispers. King smiled in the swaying darkness and held out a hand.

"That onion, *bhai*," he said. "Lend it me for a moment."

The burly Sikh stopped in mid-word, then smiled. "*Han, sahib*," he said, pulling a half-eaten one from a pocket of his *kurta*-tunic.

King scrubbed the onion up and down the blade of the *chora* several times, and then lifted it to his nose. He could smell it—just barely. Which meant that the Pathan couldn't take the scent at all; his nose was far more swollen and damaged than King's.

"Stay here for a moment, *bhai*," King said, and cut off complaint by heading back into the carriage compartment.

The Pathan was still there; he'd wet one end of his *pugaree* from the canteen and used it to wipe some of the blood from his face, and was in the process of rewinding it in the loose manner fashionable beyond the Border.

"I will swear," he said. "Although I warn you, I am likely to be a poor servant, and if you pay me in food, know that I can eat a great deal. And the horse had better be a good one."

King nodded, familiar with the manners of the Afghan highlands, where insolence was a way of life. "Swear, then," he said, and laid the Khyber knife on one cushion.

Then, carefully casual, he turned his back. He *might* be able to dodge if he detected the movement of the hillman snatching up the blade and hacking for his spine. Or he might not. The prickling up his back was wholly natural; the wild man was as dangerous as a wounded leopard in these cramped quarters. Still, it was courtesy, showing he trusted the other man to take the oath fairly.

Behind him there was rap of knuckles and a flat smack, as the hillman tapped the grip and then slapped his palm down on the broad blade. "On the hilt and the steel, before the face of God and by my father's head, so long as you keep faith with him, Ibrahim Khan is thy man and thy soldier, unto death or until you release me as you have pledged."

King turned and took the Pathan's extended hand, which had a grip like a mechanical grab in a steel mill. When he released it, Ibrahim was smiling a shark's smile. He rubbed one finger on his eyelid. Tears flowed; then he swore and rubbed it on the sleeve of his tunic before using his fingers to blow his nose free of blood clots. He did it outside the window, though, knowing the finicky nature of the *sahib-log*.

"The old trick, lord," he said, laughing in a surprisingly high-pitched giggle. "You will smell the onion juice on your fingers, even if I do not."

Reflexively, King brought his hand to his face. A Pathan who intended to break that oath wouldn't touch the steel, a trick as old as the hills—but the dodge to detect that was an old one, too.

"Come back in, Narayan Singh. We have much to discuss."

The Sikh pushed through the door and slammed it shut behind him. His glance told how he'd prefer to discuss things with Ibrahim Khan, but he held his anger to a scowl. The Pathan smiled back, perfectly aware of how the Sikh felt and just as obviously relishing every moment. After a moment, Narayan Singh nodded with a grudging respect.

"Set a bandit to catch a *banchut*," he said gruffly. "So, child of misbelief—where did you first see this *E-rus*?"

"*Veno vat*, Excellency," Yasmini said. "It is my fault, my very great fault."

"Oh, stop sniveling," Count Ignatieff snapped, and cuffed her out of his way.

He continued his pacing, throwing a glance the girl's way now and then. Inconvenient, that only the girls of the select line showed the precious talent; it meant he had to drag a whining female about with him. The males went mad at puberty, when the girls first started dreaming the dreams—it was tricky and difficult to get the males to breed at all, and the girls were prone to madness as well, if you waited too long to put them to breeding. Ten years was about the limit. Doubly aggravating, that the girls only dreamed true while they were virgins—some nonsense about the world lines tangling after that.

He'd have dismissed the tale as priestly play with words, except that no amount of torture could produce a useful word from any of the bitches once they'd been broken in.

A pity, he thought, looking at Yasmini. *She would be . . . interesting.* Docile enough on the surface, but he suspected some unbroken spirit beneath.

The Dreamers all had a family likeness, pointed chins and high cheeks, ice green eyes rimmed with blue, and flax-colored hair. Not surprising, when dam was bred to son and sibling to sibling over generations; that kept each line pure, although it meant you had to cull vigorously to get rid of the idiots and cripples. This one would have to be returned to the breeding pens soon, for all that she was the best Dreamer of them all. That was *precisely* the reason it was essential. It would still put a major crimp in his plans, and the Supreme Autocrat's schemes. Perhaps it would even delay the Third Coming, the Secret Reign that was to come.

The girl was shrinking from him, holding a hand before her eyes. "Go," he barked. "Sleep, eat. We have work tomorrow."

She scurried off to the room that gave on this. Somewhere close by in the tangle of If, there must be an Ignatieff who had less control of his anger or his lust. The Okhrana agent scowled at the thought and threw himself into a chair by the narrow window; it looked down on a teeming street in Old Delhi, dusty and hot even in October. The cheap wood creaked beneath his solid weight; the only other furniture was a low table, and a cotton pallet in one corner of the whitewashed room. It was surprisingly clean, and cheap enough to suit his cover persona, although hiding the girl was difficult—women in strict *purdah* did not travel, even with their "father."

He reached into his baggage sack and drew out a bottle of *arrack*, pulled the cork with his teeth, and spat it out and took a long swallow of the rough spirits distilled from dates. Cold fire traced down his gullet, and he hissed with satisfaction as it exploded in his stomach. The Peacock Angel bid men satisfy their lusts—but drink and comely flesh were commonplace needs, next to power; the sort of thing an ordinary Cossack or lesser nobleman wallowed in. For power, he would renounce any amount of pleasures such as that.

The spirits helped him control his imagination, too. It was unnerving, even after all these years of working with the Dreamers, to think of every moment as a fan of probabilities, flickering into and out of existence—his very atoms a blurred mass of might-be. When you thought about that too much, *you* might go mad; thinking of the world where on an impulse you stepped out the window and laughed as you plunged toward the pavement . . .

With a complex shudder he took another swallow of the arrack, then corked the bottle with a decisive tap on the heel of his hand.

Time to work, Ignatieff, he told himself, taking out his writing set. The ciphers were mostly in his head, but he still had to think hard as he filled two pages with the tiny crabbed script . . .

Chapter Seven

"Magnificent," Cassandra King breathed.

The Engine at Oxford was that—the largest Analytical Engine in the Empire, or it would be until the new one at the Imperial University was finished, and that was already six years behind schedule. She never failed to feel a prickle of awe, however familiar the thing became, at how it had grown over the generations, from notes and descriptions brought out during the Exodus, through the first small beginnings to . . . this.

Directly ahead of her was the Primary Control Center, a great semicircle of levers and keys and activating-pulls, the handles glittering with smooth-worn ivory and turned wood. Technicians scurried about, feeding in streams of the brass instruction cards—derived from the Jacquard principle, about twice the length of playing cards and covered in patterns of holes. They clattered and vanished down the slots, amid a clicking and ticking as the brushes read the gaps; the output rondels delivered a stream of numbers in return, to be noted down by the Exemplars or automatically printed on rolls of paper that were constantly renewed. Supervisors in old-fashioned black coats and tall stovepipe hats sat in their swivel chairs, barking an occasional order, or touching a control.

All around them stretched the actual workings of the Engine, shafts and bevel joints and pulleys, steel and polished brass and cast-iron pillars, gears and cams and rods moving in an endless regression that made you dizzy if you looked too long. More technicians crawled through the maze on narrow catwalks, inspecting and oiling. There was a constant groaning, querning rumble of metal meshing with precisely machined metal; a sough of ventilation fans; the rattle of rail carts passing by with spare parts, or tubs of mineral oil. Sight vanished into distance in either direction, into subsidiary bays that branched off to either side from the main building.

Under the working of the Engine could be heard a rumble of waters: Unlike the smaller Engines in use elsewhere, Oxford's was driven by water-powered turbines, rather than steam or Stirling-cycle engines. The same dams and spillways provided the coolant that coursed through hollow steel and bored-out alloy; not so long ago a disastrous series of errors had crept in when heat softened crucial gears. Far overhead sunlight poured through an arched ceiling of yellow glass; the quiver of the giant mechanical mind came up through the metal latticework and shivered from her feet through her bones to her teeth, the same eternal motion that made dust motes dance in the golden rays of light.

Some thought the Engine even grander by night, under the harsh blue-white glare of the arc lamps. She preferred practical daylight. This might be the most complex machine ever made by the hands of man, and certainly the largest—although it was half-underground, the Engine Works were about the same size as the main train station in Delhi, or the Imperial Palace. It was still a machine, a tool, and she tried to keep that in mind.

Far too many tended to worship it as if it were an oracle like Delphi of the ancients. Her maid, Patni—present because of the absurd convention of chaperonage; did anyone think she was going to burst into a fit of fornication *here*?—was frankly terrified, and making gestures of aversion while she silently mouthed prayers.

"What's going through now?" Cassandra asked in a whisper.

"Biochemical analysis," Saukar Patel said; the Gujarati was an Assistant Executor in his own right. "Part of the malaria vaccine program."

Cassandra snorted—quietly. That had been in the works for decades, and she considered it a waste of time. Artemisinin drugs cured the disease handily enough. But biology was all the rage these days, had been since Angleton's discovery of the molecular structure of genes a generation ago.

One of the men in frock coats came up and bowed.

"Dr. King," he said. "I will take your entries, if you please. You will receive the output within no more than two months."

For a moment shock held her speechless. "Two *months?*" she said, her voice clipped. "I was assured by the dean that it would be two *weeks.*"

The alloy-steel gearwheels of the Analytical Engine showed more feeling than the face of the Engine's functionary. "I regret, Dr. King, that an Imperial request has downgraded your priority."

"What sort of an Imperial request?" Cassandra snapped.

Imperial request could cover a multitude of bureaucratic sins. It was probably some idiotic shuffling of the census data, or someone wanting to know trends in the tonnage of shipping clearing Melbourne for the South American ports. Whereas *her* project was something which affected the whole future of the Empire, of humankind for that matter.

The Executor unbent a little to a specialist in his own field. "From the Political Service. A matter directly from the Lion Throne."

"Oh," Cassandra said. Some of her colleagues looked a little daunted: Her Whig backbone stiffened at the sight.

"This is a country ruled by law, not some benighted despotism," she said firmly. "I require that you furnish me the name, rank, and department of whoever it was who *dared* to interfere in academic affairs, in order that I may register a complaint!"

"Very well," the Executor said, and handed her a card.

Cassandra studied it before tucking the square of pasteboard into her reticule. *Whoever this Sir Manfred is, he'll be getting a piece of my mind, and soon!*

"Magnificent," Henri de Vascogne said, the cams and gears moving still in his mind's eye. "I thank you for the opportunity to see it— and the Engine in Kashmir is greater still, you say? *Magnifique.*"

Sir Manfred Warburton laughed as he leaned back in his swivel chair. A tea-wallah brought in a pot and left it on the curve-legged stand by the window. He went through the small ceremony of pouring, offering a lump of sugar; his guest managed the whole thing very well for a non-Imperial, even to the casual gesture with which he produced his handkerchief and snapped it out to drape over his knee.

"The Engine—Engines, now that we have more than one—*are* magnificent," he said. "With them, we can do things that were only theoretical potentials before. Unfortunately, they're not quite the Delphic oracles"—he paused, and his guest nodded, showing that he caught the reference—"that popular superstition believe." He scowled slightly. "In fact, whatever the Russians use seems to work as well, or better."

De Vascogne's eyebrows rose. "Forgive me, but I thought that they were relatively primitive." A slight grimace. "From those reports you showed me, of a certainty their customs are. Barbaric."

Warburton sighed slightly and sipped at the tea. "No doubt, old chap—although espionage has always been one of their strong points. Some of my colleagues think I'm a bit of an old woman where the Czar's men are concerned. However, *I* don't think so in the least—and the Oxford Engine itself agrees with me."

He tapped the printout. "The thing is, they *should* be exactly what you said, a gang of primitives whose forebears were driven mad by the Fall, and what they did to survive it."

The other man nodded. That was one of the fundamental distinctions of the modern world, the gap between those whose ancestors had come through the great famines by eating men, and those who hadn't. Perhaps it was a trifle hypocritical; taking away other men's food killed them just as much as eating the flesh from their bones directly. A prejudice didn't have to be rational, of course; even today, after a century of recivilizing missions, natives of Britain were looked on a little askance by the descendants of the Exodus.

The Russians were different. Like many of the tribes of Europe, the Muscovite refugees in Central Asia had made virtue of necessity, and developed a religion of abominations that continued cannibalism as ritual long after it ceased to be necessity. De Vascogne supposed that back in the terrible years of universal death it had even seemed reasonable that Satan was loose in a world seized from a defeated God.

But most groups who'd taken that route were bone-through-the-nose savages, beyond the Stone Age only insofar as they pounded pre-Fall metal into crude knives rather than chipping them from flint. Poetic justice, in a way; when men hunted each other to eat for a generation or two, it destroyed even the memory and concept of trust—and mutual trust was what let human beings live at a level beyond skulking misery. Perhaps the Russians who'd set up around Samarkand were a special case, because they hadn't eaten each other—they'd survived by culling their Asian subjects, until the great cold relaxed its grip. They still did, for ceremony's sake, and to maintain the terror of their rule.

"But they are not savages," Warburton went on. "Or rather they are very sophisticated barbarians indeed. In fact, they have matched many of our technical advances. The question is, how? According to our best intelligence, they have no real community of scholars—a few engineers of sorts from the beginning, and more of late, but no real science. They shouldn't be able even to *copy* what we do these days. Yet according to this statistical study from the Engine, they've been *anticipating* our developments, as often as not. More and more over the past two generations."

De Vascogne sipped at his tea in turn, the little finger of his right hand delicately curled—he *had* been given a thorough briefing on upper-caste *Angrezi* manners. He suspected that Warburton knew, and found that amusing. He also suspected that Sir Manfred knew several other things about him, including a few he would have preferred remain his possessions alone.

"Did you not mention that the Dragon Throne of Dai-Nippon has aided them?"

Warburton poured another cup. "Biscuit?" he said. Then: "Yes, and that's also a bit of a puzzle. The Mikado's men aren't charitably inclined. Much of what they've shipped to Samarkand and Tashkent over the last generation is both expensive and of a quality that the Russians could not possibly have made it themselves—precision gauges, jigs, machine tools, catalysts for chemical plants. The sheer *expense*! A good deal of that had to go by camelback across the Talimakan Desert."

"Camels can be surprisingly efficient," de Vascogne pointed out.

"They have to be, there. Talimakan means *You go in, you don't come out.* And as I said, very expensive indeed. The Czar must be giving them *something* in return. The Nipponese aren't what you would call humanitarian chaps, but they're nearly as disgusted with the Russki as we are."

Warburton shook his head and sighed. "I'm afraid that if you thought the Political Service was omniscient, this must be a sad disillusionment."

De Vascogne laughed. "On the contrary. The scale of affairs is intimidating, here. Our little Mediterranean world seems very provincial."

"Quality and quantity," the Political Service agent said, stirring a spoonful of sugar into his tea with a sad chuckle. "The Russians . . . their acumen seems almost supernatural at times. Why, I've had reports that their Black Church maintains a cult of seeresses who can foretell the future, or at least the possible consequences of an action."

De Vascogne laughed. "Of a certainty, *that* would be an asset for any Intelligence service! Just imagine being able to tell which man can be suborned or threatened, how he will react to—"

He paused; Warburton's face had gone entirely blank. "You don't believe these rumors, Sir Manfred?"

"I would be well-advised not to," Warburton replied. "Officers who babble of occult reasons behind the failures of their departments don't tend to have very successful careers—at least, not in our Empire."

"Nor in ours," de Vascogne answered. "We have a phrase—*le cafard*. The . . . bug, you would say."

"Equivalent to our *doolalli*," the *Angrezi* officer said. "Named for an insane asylum of former days." He sighed. "Moving on to other matters, what do you think of our princess? More to the point, what will your ruler and his son think of her?"

"Enchanting. Personally, I find her enchanting," Henri de Vascogne said.

Then he shrugged expressively and spread his hands in a purely Gallic gesture. "His Majesty Napoleon VI is . . . shall we say, somewhat more stiff and given to extreme decorum than your humble servant? I venture to say the prince will be more of my opinion . . . and . . ." A momentary sadness showed on his face. ". . . in any case, this is a political matter, *n'est-ce pas?*"

Sir Manfred sipped his tea. "Indubitably. However, the point of a dynastic measure is to improve relations between the two nations. If the marriage is an unhappy one—"

He shrugged. "For purely political negotiations, your Ambassador Fleury would have done well enough—very well indeed. He gave us fits over the trade treaty back in '20; for a man with a losing hand, he fought like a mongoose. He *did* handle the preliminaries for this, and extremely competently."

Henri made an extravagant gesture. "But for negotiations with a beautiful young princess, Ambassador Fleury is . . . perhaps . . ."

"Too fat?" Warburton asked. "Too old? Too obsessed with food and drink? Too testy when his dyspepsia strikes?"

"Most exactly." Henri caught himself stroking a vanished mustache. "Whereas I . . ."

"Are young, handsome, dashing, and charming," Warburton said with a slight smile. "And your Imperial prince trusts you with this delicate mission?"

Henri nodded. "I think I may say with pride that our prince, and his father, trust me as they would no other man. The prince and I are of an age, and we have been close since birth—very close."

"Home," Athelstane King breathed, looking up through the terraced fields to the blue fir forests on the hills and the white peaks above.

"And not before time, *huzoor*," Narayan Singh said.

He felt the same sense of relief as he filled his lungs with the cool crisp highland air. The rice was in and stooked, sheaves resting in tripods; maize rustled dryly ripe; tobacco spread its broad green leaves and rippled in the wind. A team of oxen pulled a plow, and from the steel share furrows turned in crumbling red-brown earth through the stubble. The plowman raised a hand from the grips and waved to the riders passing by; in a meadow beyond sheep wandered with their muzzles down amid the green of pasture; everything breathed peace amid the musty dampness and autumn smell of woodsmoke and fresh-turned earth.

Narayan knew it was foolishness to feel easy here; if enemies of the Raj and his lord could steal into the Peshawar Club, could they not crawl unseen into Kashmir? Yet these mountains and fields were the framework of his life; on these trees he had climbed as a boy, in these fields he had labored beside his kin. Soldiering was a man's life, honorable and well paid, and adventure in far lands fed his soul, so that he did not walk forever in the same rut like an ox. But a man needed a home— which barracks could never be. Here as nowhere else he felt secure.

"Fat land," Ibrahim Khan put in from behind them, unasked. "Fat and rich." He smacked his lips. "What a countryside to loot!" He met the scowls cast over the other men's shoulders with an innocent smile.

Border wolf indeed, Narayan thought, before he shrugged and turned forward once more.

The familiar road up from the river was lined with Chinar trees, some of them left over from Old Empire times and all of them enormous—many were twenty or thirty feet thick at the base and a hundred high. They met overhead, and the shade they cast was densely umbrageous, with only an occasional flicker of sun; when the three men crossed an irrigation channel on a wooden bridge the light was an explosion that made them squint against the glare. The broad flat leaves shone in autumn purple, claret red and burnt gold, making the roadway ahead into a tunnel of fire for a moment amid the hollow clopping sound of hoof on plank.

Rexin manor was half a mile away southwestward on a low hilltop, surrounded by park and garden; some of the great trees that shaded it were English oaks, descendants of a basket of acorns the *sahib*'s many-times-grandfather had brought out from England—some place called Yorkshire—during the Exodus. Narayan's own ancestors had been in the Kings' fighting tail even then, and had followed them to Kashmir.

A fortunate thing, he thought: He'd seen the Sikh homeland in the Punjab often, and while the Seven Rivers country was fertile enough— abundantly so, near the irrigation canals—it was far too flat and harshly dry for his taste.

And you cannot find good fruit or good mutton there; summer is like a bake oven; only the dust you eat is of note.

"Shall we go to the manor, *sahib*?" Narayan asked, nodding his chin in that direction.

"Not directly," King replied. "Best we lie up and sniff the winds first."

"My home, then," Narayan said. "I'll ride ahead and give the *pitaji* warning."

"A good thought. *Namaste* from me to Ranjit Singh, and we'll follow when you signal us."

Narayan grinned to himself with anticipation as he pressed his thighs against the horse's flanks and turned up the rutted side lane that ran through his family's steading toward his home. The house was set in the middle of their farm, for there was no need to huddle close for protection amid the long peace of the Empire's inner provinces. Nor was the holding small; it covered a hundred acres, many times that of a *ryot*, a common peasant. By Mahatma Disraeli's wise law every *zamindar's* estate had ten such yeoman-tenant farms let at half rent to families of the loyal martial castes; a garrison in the terrible years, recruiting grounds for the Imperial armies now.

A countryman's eye showed the farm in good heart as he rode, ready for the wet cold and occasional snow of a Kashmiri winter. The hedges of multiflora rose were neatly trimmed, the yellow-coated dairy herds plump and contented amid the clover, with thatched hayricks here and there. The low brick-built farmhouse itself was hidden by orchards until he rode close enough to hear voices; there were apples, peaches, pears, grapes raised on trellises, hops twining up tall poles, quinces, apricots, and walnuts and cherries. Kashmiri fruit was famous, and latterly some produce was even air-freighted from Oxford to the great cities of the southern plains. The *sahib's* mother had been debating buying a motorwagon for years now; more expensive than horses, but there was always a premium price in town for the freshest fruit.

Narayan drew rein outside the courtyard gate—the buildings of the homestead were grouped around it, barns and sheds about a yard cobbled with round stones from the river. He could hear his father's voice now, raised in a stentorian bellow:

"*So!*"

The young man's grin grew wider; he could well imagine the scene within. His father was nearer fifty than forty, with a rolling limp to his stride, legacy of a left knee that had never worked well after it stopped the lead slug of an Afridi *jezail*, long years ago. Despite that, despite the iron gray of his beard and the solid fat that overlay hard muscle, he looked to be exactly what he was; a long-service saddle-and-lance man, a retired cavalry noncom with a voice that could still flay the hide from an ox. His bellow had an edge of rough good nature to it, but only the very foolish would ignore the words:

"Slugabeds! Lazy idlers! Good-for-nothings! Do I feed you fat and fill your pockets with rupees so that you may sleep? The rice is in, but is the tobacco all cut? Is there no dung to be carted to make the wheatfields ready for plowing? Is there no—"

Right now he'd be slapping his considerable belly and belching contentedly as he strode through the rear doorway of his farmhouse, full of *Gogji Shabdegh*—good Kashmiri mutton and turnips, served with fragrant *buzhbattah* rice from their own fields. Narayan's mother cooked better mutton and turnips than anyone else on the King lands; he could smell it now, and his mouth spurted saliva after months away.

Narayan dismounted and led his horse through the gates in time to see dust smoke off his father's rough jacket and cummerbund as he slapped his belly again, it being working dress and the rice harvest just in. His mouth opened for another bellow, before he saw his son. That turned into a great shout:

"Narayan!"

The dozen or so folk within the courtyard froze—two of Narayan's younger brothers' sons had been wrestling, stripped to their waists; a gang of day laborers was hitching the oxen to a heaped cart of pungent, well-rotted manure and straw; his aunt and a maidservant gripped the handles of a great wicker basket loaded with laundry, on their way to the washhouse.

The younger Sikh heard his name repeated a dozen times; by his brothers, his aunt, the housemaid, his mother come out of her kitchen with a ladle still in her hand. His sister Neerja—how *she'd* grown, she was a maiden now and no gawky schoolgirl!—fairly shrieked it as she dropped a shallow basket full of cracked maize. The hens she'd been scattering handfuls to descended on it in squawking ecstasy as she dashed over and hovered about, jumping from one foot to the other in excitement and letting the shawl slip from her braided black hair.

"*Pitaji!*" Narayan said, putting his palms together and making the reverence due one's sire. "Father! I have returned."

"So I see," Ranjit Singh growled, putting his fists on his hips and mock-scowling. "And late, as usual—wasting your leave time carousing among the gambling dens and loose women of Peshawar town, when we could have used an extra pair of hands with the harvest!"

His scowl broke into a roar of laughter as he gave his son the gesture of blessing, then folded him into his arms and danced the young Lancer around in a circle.

"And grown to be a *burra-sowar*, a real horse-soldier, I see!" he said, releasing him. "Perhaps the Sirkar will make a *rissaldar* of thee before thy hanging, boy! And where is thy *sahib*? We heard news that he was wounded—but not badly?"

"No," Narayan said, feeling the joy of homecoming wash out of him at the reminder of their peril. "Not badly; he is indeed well."

He leaned close to his father again, whispered in his ear: *"And he is with me, disguised, at the corner where the laneway meets the Manor Road. But he must not be seen—can you make it so?"*

Ranjit Singh's face changed for an instant, then put on pleasure again. Narayan felt another rush of relief. He might be a man grown and a *daffadar* of the Peshawar Lancers himself, but he knew the value of his father's shrewdness—he was old enough now to put aside a youth's resentment of age. The older Sikh turned to the folk of his holding:

"About your tasks! Donkal, slaughter a lamb—no, two yearlings. Wife, set about preparing a welcoming feast for our son. Let nothing be spared in preparation, and let no ordinary work go undone between now and sunset either!" He clapped his hands, and the throng began to scatter. "And young Atkins, my thanks to your father for the repair of the bridle—tell him he and his are bid to the feasting."

Young Thomas blushed; it was fairly obvious, for his pathetically downy attempt at a mustache was the color of saffron, his eyes pale blue, and his pink skin showed his feelings nakedly, flushing up to the edge of his plain dark brown turban. Narayan knew him well; among the yeoman-tenants of the Kings were five lesser *sahib-log* families like the Atkins family, four of Sikhs including his own, and two Rajputs. He remembered Thomas as a spotty-faced youth two years behind him in the village school, but the boy—young man—had put on inches and broadened in the shoulders of late. He exchanged a glance with Neerja as he left; she let her eyes fall, and hurried in to help her mother.

"Oh, so?" Narayan said to his father.

The older Sikh's chin jutted and his mouth set. "That is in hand. He must leave for his military service soon—we will arrange a good match for Neerja while he is gone. The memory of youth is short, and any nonsense will be forgotten. I will have no half-caste grandchildren."

"It would be a good match, if he were a Sikh," Narayan pointed out—caste barriers were less strong in Kashmir than most provinces, and the population more mixed.

And if Neerja's look was as I thought, there will be a battle like elephants battering their heads together, he mused. Stubbornness ran in the family on both sides.

"But he is not a Sikh," Ranjit said, and shook his head. "Now, come, we have business of real weight to discuss. I will say that two friends of yours have come to visit your home on leave—but that will not hold for long. I must hear what has happened, from the young captain-*sahib*'s own lips."

Athelstane King sat his horse quietly, smiling as he looked at his home once more; the beast twitched its ears, shifted weight from hoof to hoof, swished its tail at flies, opened nostrils, and swung its head toward the water that pooled in the roadside ditch.

The rider's gaze was on the manor where the shadows of afternoon were falling mellow across brick and tile and garden. The house itself was a rambling structure of wings and annexes added over the years, comfortable and homey rather than grand. Below the hilltop was the complex of barns, stables, and workshops that were the business side of the estate, and Kingsby village strung along the road. There were small brick houses for the hired laborers who did what work the Home Farm needed beyond the labor-service of the *ryots*; more homes for house servants and grooms and gardeners; and the shop-residences of the craftsmen—blacksmith, tailor, wheelwright, estate carpenter, and more.

Among them stood larger homes for the bailiff, accountant, parson, doctor; a teahouse-cum-tavern; a shop or two; a church, a Sikh *gurudwara*, a miniature temple for orthodox Hindus, and a small mosque; a stone-built mill beside its clacking waterwheel; a school, bakery, fruit-packing sheds, a small jam factory. The whole complex was silhouetted against the Pir Panjal range to the southwest, slopes where cloud-shadow slid across huge folds of earth. Those heights rose blue with deodar-cedar forest varied with crimson maple, until they reached the tree line. There birches were gold-leafed splashes, before they gave way to crags white and pale rose with sun-splashed snow.

"It's well that you are rich," Ibrahim Khan said, jarring him out of his reverie. "This horse is a sorry nag, if it's the one you meant me to keep."

"You'll get a good one from my stables here," King said, amused.

"That is well. Although a wealthy man could surely afford to pay his sworn man a decent wage—so far, even the food hasn't been very good, nor overmuch at a serving."

King snorted laughter; the Pathan hadn't stopped trying to whee-dle money out of him yet, and probably wouldn't.

"You'll be well fed while we're here," he said. "For gold, you'll have to hope we find the *E-rus*."

"Or they will find us," Ibrahim said. "Ah, thy Sikh calls us."

King nodded, and they heeled their horses into a canter up the laneway that led to the farm—the mounts showing an eagerness that probably came of the scents of fodder and stable. Ranjit Singh greeted them, his arms folded over his barrel chest.

"Come," the yeoman said curtly—when he saw Ibrahim's Pathan features, his hand made an unconscious move to the hilt of a *tulwar* that hung by his bedside now. "We will talk in the stables; that is nat-ural enough. Go thence, and I will join you in moments."

In the stables there was none of the comfortable, functional clutter that the rest of the farm showed; the brick floors between straw-bedded stalls were scoured clean, the tack and saddles stowed just so, tools racked, the boards and rails of the pens and loose-boxes painted and neat, just as they would have been in the horse lines of the Peshawar Lancers. Three of the horses were elderly cavalry mounts, with the lion's-head military brand; the rest cobby dual-purpose farm stock. Narayan Singh shooed the stableboy out, and the three young men spent a moment unsaddling and rubbing down the horses before turning them in to empty stalls. It was a chore as automatic as breathing to horsemen, and Narayan reached for the pitchfork on the wall without looking, hand guided by the un-conscious familiarity of a lifetime. He tossed shredded maize-fodder and clover into the mangers, and wet chewing sounds followed.

Ranjit Singh appeared in the doorway, noted what had been done, nodded approval.

"A troop of monkeys in a ruined temple has less curiosity than the folk of this farm," he grumbled. "And better manners; at least the monkeys will run away when you shout. *Sahib*," the elder Sikh went on, with a courteous bow. "Captain King."

"*Rissaldar* Singh," King replied, inclining his head.

Under his calm facade—and the damned itchy new beard—King felt a rush of relief as he watched the brown, broken-nosed face with its gray whiskers, coarse-pored wrinkled skin, and shrewd dark eyes. His own father had died in action when he was six, in the same Bor-der skirmish that gave Ranjit Singh a lifelong limp.

It had been Narayan's father who taught him how to hunt, the finer tricks of horsemanship, trained him to handle a rifle and a blade with merciless perfectionism, and set him and Narayan running up the hills beyond Rexin several thousand times over the years, each youth with a heavy sack of wet sand across his shoulders. Every morning from his fourteenth birthday on, along with much else in the way of discipline and preparation.

Not to mention covering up for me with Mother in that embarrassing little matter of the nautch-girl, he thought.

If there was anyone on Rexin who could help him make sense of all this, it was Ranjit Singh. And he certainly trusted the older man far more than he did the Political Service.

The Sikh cast a pawky eye at Ibrahim Khan, who squatted on his hams a little to the rear; an eyebrow rose to see the *chora*-knife hanging from the Pathan's belt. It was not illegal to carry a blade, strictly speaking, at least outside city boundaries. Only firearms were closely controlled by law. It was certainly *unusual* to see an armed Pathan this far from the Border, though.

"I presume this one"—he jerked a thumb at the Muslim—"is part of the tale?"

"He is," King said. "Listen, then . . ."

"It is a bad business," Ranjit said at last, slowly. With a brief, grim smile: "Except that thou, Narayan, have played the man at the young *sahib*'s side past all expectation. You are now comrades who owe each other a life; that is good."

He shook his head. "I do not like this matter of the *E-rus fakir*."

He sat on an upturned bucket, rubbing absently at the knee that had never quite healed properly, staring off into times long gone. Then, abruptly, he began to speak.

"Young *sahib*, there are things of which I have never spoken to you. Things concerning your father."

King blinked in surprise; he hadn't expected *that*. Half his boyhood that he remembered was sitting at Ranjit Singh's knee, hearing tales of his father and the Sikh, wild adventures together across half the Empire and beyond. Border skirmishes, raids on slave-traders' nests in the Gulf; the terrible campaign in Siam; an expedition against the Masai in the African highlands behind Mombasa; hunts for tiger and elephant in the jungles of the Terai country on the lowland edges of Nepal.

Even faring to Europe, when a detachment was sent to guard scientists probing the bush-grown, savage-haunted ruins of the pre-Fall cities. Armed nights spent listening to the drums of the cannibal tribes throbbing in the dark valley of the Rhine while the archaeologists dug among the stones and bones of Essen; trekking through the endless forests and steppes to the east . . .

"You know that your father fell in an Afridi ambush in the Border country," the older man said. "What I have never told you is why we were on that patrol. Oh, the records say it was a routine matter—to question a village headman over a trifle of cattle-lifting from an estate near the frontier, perhaps to levy a fine or take back the loose-wallahs who did it. Question the headman of a tributary tribe, safe and law-abiding, or so the *kitubs* say in the books in Delhi."

King nodded warily. After years of service in the same lands, he could fill in the rest himself. Hooves clattering up a rough track amid huge man-empty hillsides scored by gulley and ravine, rearing into rock piles that cut off heaven. The sudden volley of slugs from long-barreled *jezails*, and of bullets from stolen rifles, the harsh war cries, a rumble of boulders tipped downslope. Then a sudden screaming wave of men in dirty brown coats and *pugarees*, their fists filled with bright steel, rising out of the very earth. In among the horses too quickly for the lancers to react, a wild, hacking, stabbing melee . . .

"The report is honest, in that it does not lie," Ranjit Singh said softly. "But it does not tell all the truth. Nor could I, under my military oath; we were all cautioned by the colonel-*sahib*, later; Colonel Haighton that was, long retired and dead these ten years. Yet I was—am—thy father's man before I am the Sirkar's. I ate his salt when still a lad; *my* father bequeathed to me the task of being his shield-on-shoulder; and now my duty is to you."

He leaned forward. "The patrol was not just a patrol. It was a *palitikal* matter. With us rode Warburton *sahib* . . . ah, I see you know him."

"A man of middling height, slender, yellow-haired? About my father's age he would have been then, or a little younger. With a face that shows nothing save what he wishes. One who moves well, very still at rest, and I would think swift in action."

"*Han, sahib,* that is him—to the inch."

The Sikh held up a hand, scarred and gnarled and with one joint of the little finger missing:

"I do not say that Warburton *sahib* is not a true man, and a brave one. He fought very well; not a man to smash down a foeman with heavy blows, but skilled—and quick, quick. But he had a mind as twisted as the path of the little silver viper, the *kerait,* as it circles through tall grass. I could tell my *sahib* was troubled by our mission and what the *palitikal* officer said, although it was not fitting for me to listen to their private speech.

"What I do know is that there were rumors also of guns among the Afridis—not their own rubbish, nor a few stolen from our men, but many. Breech-loading rifles. Berdans."

King shaped a silent whistle. That was the Russian weapon—had been, rather, in his father's time; they used a magazine rifle now. Even single-shot Berdans were much better than what the Afghan tribes usually carried, though. They were bad enough with their native weaponry, and pure murder with stolen arms—even though those were few, and ammunition for them even scarcer. If they were to get modern or even semimodern guns en masse . . .

He shuddered slightly. The things they came up with on their own were bad enough. Some of the Border clans had started making imitation mortars, for instance; cursed good imitations, too. The western tribes, over by Herat, had even taken to experimenting with crude airships, this past generation.

Ibrahim Khan hissed between his teeth. "We raid and rob the worshipers of Shaitan, too," he pointed out, speaking for the first time. There was an edge of doubt in his voice. "And we fight them when they come among the hills in reprisal, or on *razziah* for sacrificial victims to slay on the altars of the Peacock Angel and devour in their devil feasts." He spat. "We steal their guns, too, when we can. My father has a Cossack saber that *his* grandfather took from one such."

"You do not raid them for hundreds of new Berdans—still packed in the grease, in their crates, with the writing of the *E-rus* burned into the planks, and the double-headed eagle," said Ranjit Singh. "Silence, child of misbelief. Silence is the beginning of wisdom."

His eyes went back to King. "Yet, young *sahib,* I think that somehow these rifles were a lure, a trap. We tracked down the cave where they lay too easily; aye, and smashed and burned them, with their ammunition. Then we set ourselves to cut our way back to the frontier forts, but the paths which were easy going in became a hornet's nest when we sought to leave.

"The pursuers dogged our track like hounds upon that of a jackal, and pushed ahead to cut us off—as if they could read our intentions, although your father led us with cunning skill. And when they ambushed us at the last, the cliffs fell—those were blasting charges that brought the mountain down on our heads, laid with skill, no mere pile of rocks. Yes, perhaps it was some such as this"—he nodded to Ibrahim—"who served a term in the Sappers, and was false to his salt, and took his training back to his kin."

The Sikh set both big hands on his knees and leaned forward over his kettle belly.

"But I do not think so, *sahib*. While we were among the Afridi villages, there was a woman, and she and I . . . no matter; it was long ago, and the wench is dead. She spoke of a *fakir* who preached *jihad* against the Raj; that it was lawful to take any aid against the *Angrezi*, even that of the servants of Shaitan, for the Raj was closer and a greater threat than the *E-rus*. This *fakir* gained great credence among the hill people, because he had a seeress with him, a seeress who could pierce the minds of men and tell things that were secret and make true prophecies. The *fakir* himself claimed to be a Kurd—a servant of the Caliph from the Zagros Mountains far to the west. He had one eye that was brown, another blue . . ."

Ibrahim stirred, like a boulder moving under the tent of the sheepskin coat he wore loose from his shoulders. "The *fakir* I told of was one-eyed," he pointed out. Then: "Bismillah! If—"

Narayan Singh snorted. "This is a Pathan who can see a millstone and cry out on it for a cheap looking glass that shows not his ugliness," he said. "Yes, a man with eyes of different colors would be easy to mark. But a man who lost one eye in a fight, or to some illness—you will see some such in any crowd. An eye patch can hide many things. So that none would think back a generation. And Ibrahim, what age was this *fakir*?"

The Pathan frowned. "Hard to say. Not young—but still strong. Perhaps . . ." He shrugged. "Thirty years at least? Perhaps forty;

perhaps even fifty. You plainsdwellers age slowly. The woman? Young, but she wore the *burqua* always."

"That walks too well with thy story, *pitaji*," the young Sikh said.

Ranjit nodded. "So, there is more between those bat ears of thine than bone, Narayan," he said. "Yes, there are too many similarities in the tales for comfort—a *fakir* who claims to be Persian or Kurd or Tadjik, accompanied by a woman who sees visions . . . The man spoken of by this Pathan who runs at the *sahib*'s tail would be the right age. For the *fakir* of my day was young; a man in years, but in his earliest prime."

He looked at King again. "The fall of the cliff killed many of our squadron. After that, *sahib*, they broke us and harried us through the hills; we ran, and fought, and twisted back upon our path, and it seemed we had our blades out every second step of the way. Little battles to win past the fording of a river, or for food and water or fresh horses, traveling by night and hiding by day. Always they were ahead and turned us back farther into the hills just when we thought we had broken past their cordon. Warburton *sahib* rubbed stain upon his skin and hair, and donned the clothes of a dead Afghan, and said he would go for help.

"And by the Guru, he lied not! For am I not here, alive, today? But when help came—*sahib*, I saw strong men weep with joy when they heard the bugles blowing down the defile, the place where the hillmen had the last of us cornered. I wept myself; partly for relief, partly because my knee was broken and I knew I would never back a horse in battle again. Mostly I wept for your father, Captain Eric King of the Peshawar Lancers, for without him we would assuredly have all died, and he was a man in a hundred, a thousand, a true *bahadur*. By then he was raving much of the time, for the wound in his side had mortified—a wound he took as he dragged me free from the fight where I got this—"

Ranjit Singh slapped his crippled leg. ". . . and that he did when every moment was precious, with me useless, howling like a dying dog and blind with pain. On that last day I sat beside him. I had given him what water we had, so he strengthened for some moments, enough to hear the bugles and the shots, I think. I told him we were victorious, that the regiment had come for us, and soon the learned doctors would cure his hurts. He smiled. He knew me and heard my words, and spoke a little—things for the *memsahib* your mother, and nothing to repeat—and gave me letters. And he gave me this."

The Sikh fumbled within his coat. He brought something out, and held it upon his broad leathery palm. The silver chain was incongruously delicate on the callused hand of a farmer and soldier. The chain led through a loop and a narrow band that clenched one end of an ivory rod the thickness of a man's thumb. The ivory was old, slightly yellow, carved in a simple pattern of bamboo stalks and leaves. About three inches from the band it ended, in a jagged broken surface—as if a longer piece had been snapped in half.

King's breath caught. The bit of broken ivory was a *tessera hospitalis*—a mark of obligation—between his family and whoever held the other half. It wasn't a common thing and never had been, although perhaps a little less rare in generations past.

"He gave me this," Ranjit Singh continued. "And he said . . . *sahib*, I do not know if his mind was still clear, for afterward he raved once more, calling out orders as if we were in battle, then talking to his lady mother, who was long dead. But when he gave me this, I think he still had command of himself. He closed my hand around it and said *For the boy*—meaning you, *sahib*—and then, *I should have listened to the Jew.* Then he was silent a few moments, and his eyes opened and looked into mine.

"*You will know when the time is,* he told me. *When he stands in danger from the* E-rus. *Or if it does not come, then when he weds. Give him this, and say . . . say that he should seek out Elias the Jew, in the Chandi Chowk in Delhi. Ask Elias . . .*"

Silence fell in the rustling dimness of the stable. Ranjit Singh's face was still, as if he looked through the veil of years and was once more young himself. Crouched beside a dying man, his leg a mass of agony and blood, straining to hear the faint whispers amid the screams and clamor of battle.

"Yes, *rissaldar*?" King prompted gently.

"*Sahib*, those were his last words for a long time. Then he called out to *Daffadar* Bucks—who was a week dead—and told him to reinforce the pickets. He no longer knew where he was."

He held out his hand, and King extended his. The weight of the silver-bound ivory toppled into his palm, and he closed his hands around the cool smoothness of it, felt the jagged broken portion cutting into his skin.

Ranjit nodded and sighed, like a man who has carried a weight for a long time, and feels it taken from his back. "I hope it may help you, *sahib*. This is an evil matter, this thing of assassins in the dark. Perhaps it is even somehow linked to what happened to your sister, the young *memsahib* Cassandra."

King sat bolt upright. "What?" he said. "Something happened to Cass?"

Chapter Eight

*T*hunk-chink.

The hammer on the reverse of her climbing ax drove the piton into the crack in the cliff face. Cassandra King used the best equipment she could buy out of a modest salary and a generous inheritance; this type had an interior screw, and when you put the handle of the ax through the loop at the end and turned it, it drove the sides of the piton out, gripping the rock with unbreakable force. She twisted until the rock creaked, then snapped the support of her harness onto it and let herself sag back a little while she put in two more and reeved the main rope through their eyelets.

The cold wind blew a flush into her cheeks. She pushed the goggles up onto her forehead, squinting a little against it, let her quick breath subside.

Odd, she thought. *If this view were from an airship, I'd have a knot in my stomach.*

Hanging from a steel wedge hammered into the living rock, she was conscious of nothing but the sheer beauty of it. She was a little under ten thousand feet above sea level; that put her a thousand feet up on a rock face over the Ferozepur nulla—a side valley cut into the ranges on the south side of the Vale of Kashmir.

Not far away to the right a streamlet bawled and leapt down the crags, the spray wetting the cliff to within a hundred yards of her position. It dissolved in rainbow mist not far below, then became a small river winding through naturally terraced steps of brilliant green meadow starred with white cosmos, flowing down into the woods on the lower slopes. The spurs below were clad in dark green spikes of silver fir, forest opened here and there by sunlit patches of grassland or a crimson explosion of maple, hills turning a deeper and deeper purple as they receded from sight. Across the Vale itself—eighty miles or more distant—hung the great peak of Nanga Parbat, soft pure white in a gauzelike haze of delicate blue.

Times like this, you feel as if you could float free. Away like thistledown, into an infinite sky.

It was like the passion of numbers, somehow; on a more emotional plane, but with much of the same eerie transcendence. At last she sighed and willed herself back into the light of common day. It was like turning from the wilder speculations of Ghose—she pushed away a shocking rush of memory—to the solidities of Newton. And that was one reason she'd specialized in astronomy; there, at least, the modern uncertainties had not yet crept in.

And now it was time to return. The way down was easy after the muscle-cracking effort of the climb; she rappelled down the last hundred yards in a smooth swift rush, then unclipped the harness and skipped over talus and rock to her starting point. That was a stretch of meadow shaded by a big deodar, enough for the horses and two servants and a small canvas enclosure she used to change her garb—even Cassandra King wasn't unconventional enough to wear climbing overalls anywhere but on a mountainside. Her retainers were there, but her eyes widened slightly to see others as well. Two horses—very good ones, though not showy—and two men, one a groom and one—

These days she carried a small revolver tucked into a pocket; a permit wasn't too difficult to come by, for a *zamindar*'s daughter and university professor, especially one with her recent history. Her hand went to the checkered butt of the Adams, finding reassurance in the solid ebony and blued-steel weight of the weapon. Her brother and an old retainer of her father's had taught her to handle firearms. The hand dropped away in puzzlement; certainly the eminently respectable-looking *sahib-log* gentleman wasn't a terrorist. . . .

"Permit me the liberty of self-introduction, Dr. King," the man said; he was short, fair and wiry. "Sir Manfred Warburton, Bart. IPS."

He handed her a card, and her brows rose as she read it. *Well, when*

I sent in that memorial of complaint, I didn't expect a response so early—or *one in person.*

"Is this concerning the Analytical Engine assignments?" she asked. "Or the assassination? I was told that my statements were sufficient."

The questioners at the sessions after the attack had taken her through the whole business over and over again. A frosty edge came into her voice:

"The process was long, and unpleasant, and I had assumed that it was over."

"Oh, indeed," the baronet said. "Captain Malusre gave a most complete redaction, and is pursuing the rather meager leads with commendable efficiency. No, I was hoping to speak with you on another matter—related, to be sure, but distinct from both that and the, ah, commandeering of the Engine."

"Here?" she said, her brows still high.

"Discretion," the IPS agent said. "A matter of political importance. And to your family, Dr. King. I knew your father, by the way. Before you were born—at United Services School, and in the service."

"By all means, then, Sir Manfred. Any assistance I can give to the Sirkar, of course; or to a friend of Father's."

The servants laid out blankets and seating cushions on the thick green turf, while Cassandra used the tent to change into a plain country gentlewoman's riding habit. The two Imperials sank down naturally into a cross-legged posture.

"Tea, Sir Manfred?"

As she poured, Cassandra composed herself. There was no use in pretending that the . . . incident . . . hadn't happened. Or that it wouldn't continue to affect her life, and in ways more obvious than the fading nightmares.

They exchanged polite nothings—not quite an empty social ritual, when he mentioned King family matters that nobody who *hadn't* known her father would know. Not that there was any real possibility of someone impersonating a Political Service Officer, of course. And it set her a little at ease, enough to react calmly when he went on:

"You had a priority problem consulting the Oxford Engine recently, did you not, Dr. King? You and your colleagues on the Project."

"Yes, and none of us were overly happy about it," she said. "I

presume, since your name was attached, that you were the author of
our woes?"

Sir Manfred spread his hands in a placating gesture. "I understand
your impatience, Dr. King," he said; oddly, she felt it was sincere. "In
the long run, your work—the Project's work—is vital to the future of
the whole human race. We cannot afford another Fall, and the Project
has already proven that such impacts are a recurrent part of Earth's
history. Of course, in the light of those studies . . . even if we knew it
was coming, perhaps we could not do much. Adding only the terror of
anticipation, as it were."

"That's nonsense," Cassandra snapped. "If the Old Empire had
had several years warning, most of the worst of the Fall could have
been avoided easily enough. Simply maintaining large food stockpiles
and having plans to evacuate coastal areas would have preserved civilization in Europe and North America. We *do* maintain famine reserves, and that's partly the reason."

"Ah, forgive me . . . I had in mind the research on far worse impacts, ones which Oxford's students of Darwinian Geological Catastrophes have demonstrated to be responsible for mass extinctions."

"Oh." Cassandra blushed; she knew her temper overcame such
social graces as she possessed all too often. "I am sorry, Sir Manfred.
Yes, a much larger impact—one such as ended the dinosaurian era
sixty-odd million years ago—yes, that would be deadly even with all
possible precautions. Perhaps enough so that the survival of the
human race would be endangered, not merely civilization. Even
there, though, theoretically there are countermeasures; very large
cannon, for instance, capable of throwing shells beyond the atmosphere, or possibly rockets. Nothing we could do now, but science
is progressive. In a century, who knows what we will be able to accomplish?"

She leaned forward, earnest. "Yet who knows if we have a century?
Or if a century will be enough? Another Fall could occur *at any moment*. Our network of observatories is pathetically inadequate—much
of the sky is uncovered, particularly in the northern hemisphere. Ide-
ally we need—"

Sir Manfred made another gesture, exquisitely polite. "Yes, Dr.
King. I fully and completely agree with everything you say . . . which
is *why* the Political Service was forced to interrupt your work."

"I don't understand," she said in honest puzzlement. "Could you explain, please?"

Sir Manfred smiled. "Dr. King, if only you knew how refreshing a request for an *explanation* is . . . yes. What could be more important than the Project? Determining how and why someone—some powerful agency—is attempting to *destroy* the Project."

Cassandra felt her lips begin to shape *that's ridiculous*, and then fall silent; she'd always despised anyone who rejected a hypothesis merely because it jarred on their set notions. She set her teacup down with a slight clink of stoneware—no sense in taking anything fancy on a mountaineering trip.

"Why on earth . . . the Project benefits *everyone*. It's not as if it . . . oh, increases the strength of the Empire relative to some other country, the way some military or commercial endeavor might. We spend the resources, and everyone else benefits as much as we!"

Warburton cleared his throat. "Yes. However, the fact remains that someone did attempt to destroy the mirror for the new telescope—and had the attempt succeeded fully, many of our foremost scientists would have died at the same time. They *did* succeed in killing one of our finest physicists."

"I thought . . . was that not, mmm, Bengali secessionists?"

"Yes. Captain Malusre has developed several very promising lines of evidence which lead in that direction. However, while the evidence is satisfactory, the motivation is not. Malusre—a man wasted in his present post and due for promotion—has also uncovered some evidence indicating that money and arms have been flowing to the secessionists and other subversives from the *diwan* of the Caliph of Damascus."

Cassandra frowned. "But doesn't that just push the problem further back?" she pointed out. "The Caliph and his people can't want another Fall, surely!"

Sir Manfred raised a brow. Cassandra flushed; she *had* studied history, even if it wasn't her specialty. The Fall hadn't been a complete catastrophe everywhere; in the low-lying deserts of the Middle East for example. They had suffered wild weather and floods and unseasonable cold, but nothing like the devastation to the north. And afterward, the Arab peoples had seen their Turkish oppressors and Christian enemies struck down—by the very hand of God, or so it seemed. These days the Caliph in Damascus ruled from Hungary to the Baluchi frontier of the Raj in what had once been Persia.

"Well, they were lucky," she said. "Given the location of the strike. They might not be, again."

Sir Manfred nodded. "I know that, Dr. King. You know that. It's quite likely the Caliph and his advisors don't. They have some extremely shrewd men among their number, as we've found to our cost. They *don't* have a scientific tradition. Not a living one; they have only some rote-learned engineering tricks they picked up before the Fall, or during it from refugees; no theoretical framework. Even if a few of them are familiar with the physical explanation for the Fall, it isn't emotionally real to them."

Cassandra bowed her head in thought, running one finger meditatively over her upper lip. "Your pardon, Sir Manfred," she said. "I don't want to encroach on your specialty . . . but that's no reason for them to actively *hinder* the Project, is it? And they wouldn't dare to provoke the Raj."

"They might dare," the man said. "A major war with them is looking increasingly likely—" He waved a hand at her shock. "Your pardon; another matter entirely. No, you're right. They have no reason to aim specifically at the Project, even if they were indeed supplying subversives with arms and money. Nor do the subversives themselves—they gain nothing but public dislike. Yet *someone* gave them money and arms; and I must assume that that *someone* also made the aid conditional on this attack against the Project. And against you specifically, Dr. King. You and your family."

She put a hand to her throat and swallowed. "My family?" she said faintly.

"Indeed. This is a business whose roots seem to follow a twisted path—"

When he finished, Cassandra blinked, her mind racing. "I'm not altogether sure your suspicions are totally credible," she said. "And if they *are*, you certainly haven't done me any favors by telling me."

He smiled bleakly. "No, I haven't . . . but I may have done the Empire a favor; and the human race, for that matter. You see, going through the records of the Service, I've found evidence that several other agents have come to the same conclusion that I did . . . but only hints."

"Why on earth?"

"Because . . . things . . . happened to them. They were killed in duels; in hunting accidents; run over by motorcars, of all unlikely chances—and that a generation ago, when the damned things were rare as hen's teeth. Records were lost in fires, misfiled—"

"Oh, come now, Sir Manfred!" Cassandra said. "This *is* the twenty-first century; we don't believe in curses and witches."

"No," he said grimly. "I don't believe in coincidences, either, my dear, not on that scale."

He pulled a manila envelope out of his saddlebags, one secured by string and a wax seal. "You said you were willing to do anything for the King-Emperor, Dr. King," he said. "Apart from doing your best to remain alive, what I'd most like you to do is keep this; it's a duplicate of my research."

"Keep it?" Cassandra said, taking the heavy envelope reluctantly.

It crinkled slightly under her hand, and she felt as if she should be wrapped in lead, like one of the researchers on radiant materials after Dr. Currant's mysterious burns.

"Keep it. Open it when you need to."

"But . . . how would I know?"

"Believe me, Dr. King, when—if—the time comes, you *will* know. And if you think what I've told you strains credibility . . . then you'll know why I left the rest in there."

Aedelia King watched her son ride up the road to the manor, as a cool autumn wind blew wine red leaves like flecks of fire through the rain-washed air. She'd been trimming roses when one of Ranjit's younger sons pounded up the road with the news, and she'd clipped right through the stem of her best Ranipur Delight. A small sigh escaped her; the days had been long, with no word since the news of the attack on Athelstane in Peshawar. Colonel Claiborne's bare word that her son was safe had been little comfort.

They ride away, our men, she thought. *Husbands, brothers, sons . . . and until they return all you have left is the memory of the sound the hooves make, falling hollow on the earth, and the rattle of scabbards against the stirrup iron. Until they return. Or they don't—only their swords and their ashes.*

With an effort, she buried the thought. *No need to blight a happy occasion with amateur philosophy.*

Instead she murmured to the man standing two steps down from her on the front terrace of the house:

"He shapes well."

"*Han, memsahib,*" Ranjit Singh said, equally quietly. "He is become a man to reckon with, these last years, and a *burra sahib* indeed; though I would not say so to his face, lest the boy suffer from a swelling of the head. His father would be proud."

"Narayan won't disgrace his father, either."

She smiled to herself as the elder Sikh expanded a little with pride; she knew exactly how he felt. Not that *that* was a new experience. *Ranjit's been a godsend, ever since Eric died. I couldn't have carried on without him.* Well, perhaps—but it would have been hard, hard. Hard for Athelstane, too, without his honorary uncle.

Besides the family—herself, Cassandra, her youngest two standing in a twin-set of freckles and happy smiles—the manor staff were waiting, and some from the village. The notice had been short—doubly so, with everyone in the middle of the pre-*Diwali* bouts of housecleaning and preparation. Of course everyone had also been expecting the young lord's return from the frontier, and puzzled when no day was set for homecoming.

He rode up to the gates at the entrance to the gardens proper— the area beyond was parkland—and then dismounted. A *sais* ran to take his horse and those of his two followers, and he walked up the curving, crushed-rock surface of the drive, nodding to the salaams that greeted him. The schoolmistress from the village led two of her pupils forward to curtsy and present him with a bouquet.

At least I managed to keep Father Gordon from having the choir sing, she thought.

That would have started up the perennial feud between the village's four religious specialists. Nobody expected the Kings to be neutral when a matter of faith and caste came up, but they did expect fairness. Herself, she found the modern upper-caste *Angrezi* belief—that God had ten thousand faces, all true, and that any road truly followed led to the Unknowable at last—comforting enough. She kept up the forms of the Established Church, however; and Father Gordon was old-fashioned.

Which reminded her, along with the unmistakable Pathan countenance and dress of the man behind her son. She murmured a name aside:

"Hamadu."

The *khansama*—butler—acknowledged it with an inclination of his head so subtle only twenty-three years of his service enabled her to see it.

"My son has brought an Afghan in his service home to Rexin. Make sure that there is food in the kitchens ritually pure for a Muslim to eat; also . . ."

Hamadu made the same infinitesimal gesture. He'd see that a couple of the manor's veterans—there were dozens—were always unobtrusively about, to make sure that the man stayed well behaved. That was not entirely a matter of suspicion. With the best will in the world—not something you could take for granted with an Afghan, even a tame one—he'd be at sea among alien customs. It wouldn't do to have some kitchen maid's idea of a little harmless flirtation be misunderstood. If the man had eaten Athelstane's salt, it would be extremely awkward to hang him.

At last her son stood grinning at the foot of the stairs, one booted foot resting on a step, gauntlets in his left hand—the hand that rested on the hilt of his saber to steady it as he walked. Her heart clenched at how much he looked like his father, when he tossed his head like that. His old *ayah* Damayanta waddled forward with her arms spread, calling his name and getting a hefty buss and hug that hoisted all two hundred twenty pounds of her into the air; well, a nursemaid was allowed such displays. When he put her down again she was smiling and weeping into a fold of her sari at the same time.

Athelstane mounted the steps, his spurs jingling quietly on the marble. "Mother," he said, raising her hand to his lips.

"Athelstane," she replied, offering her cheek for his kiss; Cassandra did likewise; the younger sisters got a rumpling of russet locks that left them squealing with dismay at the ruin of carefully arranged coiffures.

"Do remember they're not nine anymore, Athelstane," she said.

Sixteen, in fact—she'd been pregnant with them when the news of their father's death came. "Now run along, girls. There are adult matters to discuss."

"Haven't got the *rangolis* done yet," he said whimsically, looking down as they crossed the threshold. It wasn't marked with the colorful, intricate chalk patterns whose drawing marked the beginning of *Diwali*.

"You know that's supposed to be bad luck, starting early," she said, leading the way down the great hallway. "And the head of the house should do it."

Ancestral portraits of Kings and their relatives looked down from the high pale plastered walls under an inscription that read *Kuch Dar Nahin Hai!*

She'd learned all their stories when she came here as a bride, half her lifetime ago. She suspected some of those stories were as much fiction as anything Kipling or Hardy or Tagore had written. Take that stalwart dark-haired man with the cavalry whiskers and the ribbons of the Victoria Cross and the Military Medal; a collateral of the Kings and the Padgets.

If half the official stories about him were true, he'd have been the greatest paladin since Galahad—and she doubted that even a tenth were, because that was a rogue's face if she'd ever seen one. The sort who died old, honored, and rich.

But people live by stories, she thought, looking back over her shoulder at her tall son. *Athelstane grew up with these . . . and he'll make them real by living them.*

"It's good for the people to do the festival properly," Aedelia went on aloud. "We were waiting for you."

"Yes, of course I knew," Aedelia King said twenty minutes later. "Ranjit told me when he brought your father's sword back from the frontier."

Little had changed in the study that had once been Eric King's; his wife had left the dark-wood décor, the heads of tiger and sambhur on the walls between the bookcases, the souvenirs ranging from a Nipponese screen to a rusty battle-ax hammered out of a chunk of railway iron by some European barbarian. It had been just short of seventeen years since Ranjit Singh rode up the road to Rexin Manor with a plain funeral urn balanced on his saddlebow beside a sheathed saber wrapped in its scabbard belt. Still, only the flowers and a basket with balls of wool and knitting were hers.

Those years had dealt kindly with the lady of Rexin; at fifty her face had a pink-cheeked prettiness that a woman ten years younger might have envied—although the Kashmiri climate was itself commonly supposed to stretch out youth. She wore a plain maroon sari trimmed in green with a fold over her graying black hair, and sensible flat-heeled sandals. The gray eyes behind the wire-rimmed spectacles were warm but shrewd as she looked across the desk at her eldest children.

"Do drink your tea, Athelstane," she went on. "And try to look a little less like a carp. And of course Ranjit also gave me the gist of what was going on when he came up to get your uniform."

Athelstane King hauled his jaw closed and sipped politely. *Well, that's the mater,* he thought. *The Sirkar may think I'm a cavalry captain, and the Political Service may think I'm a devil of a fellow, but she can always make me feel like a six-year-old again.*

Nearly two decades of acting as *zamindar,* Justice of the Peace, and, for all practical purposes, ruler of several hundred souls might have something to do with it, but Athelstane suspected that she'd had the same force of character the day his father brought her back from Kandy. The years alone had probably let it show more plainly, just as they'd worn away a Ceylonese accent until it was no more than a trace of hardness in the vowels.

Cassandra cleared her throat. "Then why did you never *tell* us, Mother?"

Aedelia sipped at her own cup. "Because you didn't need to know, dears, and it would have done nothing except worry you unnecessarily."

Cassandra made a choking sound. "Someone's been trying to kill off the whole *family,* for *generations,* and we didn't need to know!" Her voice took on a rising note, more of anger than of fear.

"Control yourself, dear," her mother said sharply.

"Sorry."

"Very well. No, we don't *know* that. Your father suspected it, from things *his* father said and wrote. It's not as if assassins were waiting around every corner. And . . . there's the matter of Elias. He's been the King man of business in the capital since your grandfather's time."

They both nodded; it was customary for any *zamindari* family to have an agent in Delhi, and convenient in any number of ways.

"And Elias's father was our agent in your great-grandfather's time. Evidently Eric"—a faint shadow of pain flitted over the calm of her face—"consulted with him in this matter, just before he died. Elias disclaims any knowledge of it to me, of course . . . but there *is* the *tessera.*

Presumably your father instructed him to speak only to you, and Elias, I gather, is a gentleman of an exceedingly literal turn of mind."

"The question is, what should we do about it?" King said. "Attempts on both our lives in the space of two weeks—that's da . . . er, dashed unlikely to be coincidence. Nor is Sir Manfred turning up again—now that I know he was involved with Father, as well."

"Well, as head of the family, you'll be the one to make any decision, of course," Aedelia said.

Ha, Athelstane thought. *Ha.*

And was that a slight snort of incredulity from his sister as well? His mother went on briskly:

"But the first thing you must do is stay here and celebrate *Diwali*. The people"—by which she meant the inhabitants of the estate, high and low—"have a right to see you, and that wound has had entirely too much activity. You'll be better for a few weeks' rest. Then, I think, it would be best if you were to travel to Delhi, as Sir Manfred suggested, but . . . incognito. You as well, Cassandra."

Cassandra blinked in surprise. "In disguise? How on earth . . . I can scarcely pass myself off as a wandering *sannyassin*, Mother."

Athelstane grinned, the first expression of honest enjoyment he'd had since listening to the tale told in Ranjit Singh's stables. Imagining his haughty, bluestocking sister with a shaven head, rags, staff, and begging bowl, meditating on some mountaintop or trudging along dusty roadsides in search of enlightenment . . .

"No, that wouldn't do, Cassandra," their mother said. "But what point is there in being wellborn, or going to Cheltenham Ladies College as a girl, if you can't rely on your connections?"

She smiled indulgently at Cassandra's bewilderment. Perhaps it went with a scientific education, but her offspring had a touching faith in official channels as opposed to the subterranean network of kin and friendship and clientage that meant as much or more.

"Connections at court, daughter of mine. You'll find them a good deal more useful than a fellowship in the Royal Society, in this matter at least."

And it's the best I can do. You had to keep up a brave face before the children, of course—before the world, if it came to that. That didn't make the cold trickle of fear in her stomach go away, worse than the gnawing worry she'd known when Athelstane took up his commission and the regiment was posted to active duty. *That* was a worry a gentlewoman had to learn to live with, or go mad. This . . .

For twenty years, worry meant wondering whether a ryot's roof needed replacing, or if I should buy that damned motortruck, or getting a scholarship for some village lad, or if Cassandra would ever marry, or . . . Now I have real worries again. It's something I haven't missed.

"I find the whole business . . . irritating," Cassandra King said. "Profoundly. A *dikhdari*, an annoyance. These—these *people* are interfering with my *work*."

She and her brother walked in the gardens in back of the manor. They were less mannered than the formal area in front of the building; less likely to be seen by guests, of course. There was a broad stretch of lawn, green with that peculiar brightness that comes just before frost; an ancient gardener moved in slow motion, raking up leaves that fluttered down dull gold from the oaks above, and they nodded polite response to his salaam. A low brick wall overgrown with rambling rose and a line of poplars marked the rear; single-story brick buildings showed beyond it, stables and sheds.

There were swings dangling from the branches of a few of the trees, gravel walks, flower beds now mostly mulch and bound-up vines, their younger sisters and a few servants' children playing with a dog. Wisteria overgrew the rear of the house, with trunks thick as peach trees and branches writhing over the stone.

"You may be merely irritated," Athelstane began, and paused, holding up one finger.

Oddly enough, I believe you, he thought in the same instant, serious beneath the banter. Cassandra had always been bossy; back when they were both tots, she'd always been the general or raja in the children's games. She was more likely to react with outraged indignation than fear.

He went on aloud, using the finger to tap himself on the chest.

"I, on the other hand, am bloody terrified."

She had her hands tucked through the crook of his left arm. He worked his right a bit as they walked. The stab wound was only a faint catch now; he was lucky enough to have quick-healing flesh. It ran in the family on his father's side, from what he'd heard, along with a talent for horses and languages—all assets for a soldier.

"I thought," Cassandra said, "that whoever attacked us—the university people—must somehow want to destroy the Project. But then, why would they attack *you*? You are, ah—"

"Just another brainless cavalry officer?" Athelstane said, with a chuckle in his voice.

There was a joke nearly as old as the Raj about an intellectually inclined artillery lieutenant who'd named his tomcat *Imperial Cavalry*, because all it did was sleep, drink, eat, groom itself, play games, and fornicate.

"No, of course not," she said. "You could have made an academic career, if you wanted to . . . but in the arts, to be sure. Still, it's puzzling. Attacking me; attacking the Project; trying to kill *you*. There's no *pattern* to it. That's irritating too."

"There's a pattern," Athelstane said. "Perhaps even Sir Manfred doesn't see it all. But someone does."

"Ah, yes," Cassandra said, her brows drawing together. "Sir Manfred. I have a few more questions I'd like to ask him—in light of what you've told me."

"After me, sister dear, after me," Athelstane said.

Cassandra's head jerked up in slight surprise at the tone and expression; then she squeezed his arm. "Perhaps I *will* let you go first," she said.

"I'll soften him up," Athelstane said. "You can finish him off, Cass."

He was surprised at how pleasant it was to see Cassandra again. They'd been affectionate enough siblings, but not what you'd call extremely close, not since they passed thirteen at least. Perhaps it was the news about the attack; he still had to throttle down a reflex of cold fury when he thought about that. People trying to kill him—well, that went with the uniform, even if this was unorthodox. People trying to kill his sister, that was a violation of what he wore the uniform *for*.

And Hasamurti. I haven't forgotten her either. He wished he *could* forget how her parents had sat in stunned grief.

Because there was no point in thinking about that—not right now, at least—he nodded ahead to where the setting sun was staining the peaks crimson.

"About time," he said.

They walked around the last wing of the rambling E-shaped manor, and under an open colonnade covered with dormant rosebushes. That connected the main building to a summerhouse, where the family often ate in June or July—though only beneath netting. Kashmir's climate might seem perfect right now; for about six months of the year it *was* perfect, or longer if you liked cold and snow. In high summer it could be insufferably muggy and bug-ridden.

The last light faded from the mountaintops as they came down the steps. At once they were in the midst of a laughing, chattering crowd—the mood at *Diwali* was always good, not least because it was settling-up day, and traditionally any small arrears of rent were forgiven. The two Kings dug into their pockets for the also-traditional small candies and distributed them to squealing children; *Diwali* was devoted to the worship of Laxmi, consort of Vishnu, among many other things, and she was goddess of wealth and prosperity. Eager hands were hanging lines of lanterns covered in colored paper along walls and in windows, and from the boughs of trees; others were set atop the clipped tops of hedges all the way down to the village, twinkling up into a sea of stars crimson and blue and yellow to mark cottage and shop. The air carried a tang of the fruity odor of lamp oil and jasmine-scented candles.

"About time," their mother said.

She handed a small brush and a pot of pigment to Cassandra. Athelstane bent forward, and felt the brief momentary coolness as she painted the *tikal* between his brows—always done by a sister on this day of the festival, if you had one. A cheer went up as he turned and showed it; now the Kings would walk down to the village square, to preside at the play, where a local boy would act out the appropriate deeds of Krishna as he battled the demon lord Ravana. Then he'd start the fireworks display. It always felt a little odd doing this himself; one of his few memories of his father was of Eric King bending to light the first touch-paper and a rocket soaring up.

Mother and sister brought a fold of their saris up over their heads against the evening chill. Athelstane offered an arm to each, and the whole assemblage moved off down the hill.

"The Sikh with the big feet is gone," a man whispered in the bush ahead. "The idolaters are about their festival and notice nothing."

"It is time indeed, brother," another answered.

Ibrahim Khan smiled as he listened to the voices whispering in his own tongue. With a different accent, of course; Maxdan Pathans, from the upper valley of the Kabul River. Utmanazi sept, and probably Bihzad Khel, to judge by the embroidered skullcaps they wore in place of turbans and the golden hoop earrings one sported. At a guess, they were Kabulis by residence, townsmen—the Maxdan were the Emir's tribe, and many of them dwelt in the houses about his fort. The way they moved off through the shrubs beside the laneway in the wake of the *gora-log* family was an indication; not bad, he doubted any of the locals would spot them, but they didn't have quite the ease in moving about the countryside at night he would have expected from his own people. And neither of them showed the least awareness of the countryman ghosting along at their back.

True, this wasn't like his tribe's home territory or theirs; much more thickly grown than anything in the Border hills. It smelled wrong, too green and rank, full of chirps and clicks and small rustling sounds. Still, if you kept keenly aware of your surroundings and made no hasty move, you couldn't go far wrong. He moved after them at a leopard's stalking pace, leisurely and certain but not slow.

Once he let them draw a little ahead; enough to let Ibrahim safely grab a small boy running about with some sparkling firework and growl a message in his ear.

One thing he couldn't fault the Kabulis on was patience. They marked their target's movement and waited with commendable lack of motion in the shadow of a grain store; waited until the night grew cold and the last revelers—or the devotees in the little temple and the church—had gone home. The brown of their sheepskin coats and baggy trousers blended into the shadows along the side of a house as they crossed the laneway. A few lanterns still guttered from windows and walls, and the moon was three-quarters full in a sky only half cloud; plenty of light for him to mark their weapons. He followed as they vaulted a wooden fence and went through a cottager's farmyard at the edge of the village.

Sheep baaed sleepily in a pen; not even a watchdog barked, though. Hay was rustling in the shed ahead—more than the two cows tethered inside could account for—and he heard a rhythmic feminine squeal. Then silence, and then a woman came out, pulling the skirts of her sari back down over the sleek curve of her hips and smiling over her shoulder as she tucked in her blouse and rearranged the upper folds of the wraparound garment.

Ibrahim grinned at the sight, with half appreciation—she was a plump moon-breasted beauty, one worth the trouble of stealing as they said back home—and half envy; he'd had no luck here in that line himself, despite the notorious looseness of women in lands ruled by the *gora-log*. Athelstane King came out behind her, brushing straw off his jacket and giving her a swat on the rump.

"Run along home, oh daughter of delight, before anyone notices you're not in bed yet," he said. "I wouldn't want to return trouble for the transports of Paradise."

The girl giggled and snuggled up against him, murmuring something about one of the gods of the idolaters; Krishna, he thought, and the milkmaids he was supposed to have sported with. Just then there was a slight *click-chack* from behind the water trough that stood ten yards from the shed door.

Ibrahim blinked, impressed: He'd rarely seen a man move as swiftly as King did then, although it was a waste of time to sling the girl squawking backward into the hay. Still, the sword was out and the man moving like a charging tiger before the hidden assassin had the double-barreled shotgun halfway to his shoulder. Whether that would have been swift enough only the Most High could say, because Ibrahim took three paces forward and slammed the point of his *chora* through the gunman's liver. The Khyber knife pinned him writhing to the ground, his shriek strangled as he bit the packed earth of the farmyard in uncontrollable reflex. Ibrahim twisted the blade with professional competence as he withdrew it, and the body went slack almost instantly; there were many large blood vessels in a man's liver.

Narayan Singh charged in from the far side of the farmyard in the same instant that Ibrahim drew his blade. As the other assassin had said, he had big feet; Ibrahim frowned at the amount of noise he made. And he nearly collided with King, as the *zamindar* leapt the water trough. The second Afghan was already coiling up from the ground, his own blade out and striking upward toward the *Angrezi* landowner's belly with the sudden licking viciousness of a striking cobra. That was where a *chora* was more useful than a saber, at close quarters. King met it with a slamming punch of his sword's brass guard, striking at the Afghan's wrist rather than the steel.

Ibrahim giggled in delight at the crunch of bone. *Shabash!* he thought in delight—it would have been a blow upon his honor, if the one he'd sworn to wasn't a good man of his hands as well. Narayan was carrying a three-foot oak cudgel. He cracked it across the Afghan's other elbow, smashing it; then rammed the blunt point under his ribs and kicked the legs from beneath him in the same motion. One heavy-booted foot came down to pin the injured man to the dirt.

"There never was a Maxdan worth the powder and ball it took to blow him home to Shaitan," Ibrahim said with satisfaction, going through the clothes of both men with practiced skill and slicing the gold rings out of the dead man's ears with a double flick of his *chora*'s point. "Bazaar bullies, not real warriors."

Several good knives, a length of fine chain with a spiked weight on the end in one man's sleeve, fastened to his wrist with a leather bracer—*Kabuli bazaar rufflers for certain*—and two fat purses that held gold as well as silver from the weight. Reluctantly, he flipped one of those to the Sikh and tucked the other into his sash. To King he handed a folded sheet of paper, twin to the one he'd had from the *fakir*-who-was-not.

"More seeking the two hundred *mohurs*," he said cheerfully. "Although these had not the manhood to do it alone." He spat into the glaring hawk-nosed bearded face of the man beneath Narayan Singh's boot. "And even for the Maxdan, the Utmanazi are the worst of a bad lot—sons of noseless whores and fifty fathers each."

"Do you wish to question him, *sahib*?" Narayan asked.

King shook his head, bending to examine the weapon the dead man had been planning to kill him with. The Sikh grunted satisfaction, transferred his boot to the living Afghan's neck, reached down to grab a fistful of beard, heaved sharply upward. There was a sound like a green branch snapping, the man's legs flailed once to drum on the ground, and then he went limp.

"Look," King said. "This shotgun is a hunter's weapon; see, the Sirkar's licensing stamp and the serial number. They must have bought it in the black bazaar, or more likely killed the owner and stole it."

"Men of some resource, then," Ibrahim said. "Still, for that much gold even a Maxdan will show spirit, I suppose."

Narayan snorted. "Their horses were where Ibrahim said, *sahib*. Two horses. Good ones—Kashmir breed, geldings."

"And why didn't you tell me a bit earlier that I had them sniffing on my trail?" King said sharply, looking at the Pathan. "Or Narayan?"

"You would not have thanked me for interrupting your sport, *huzoor*," Ibrahim pointed out reasonably. "The Sikh? He is a good enough fighter, but he has big feet."

The Lancer officer didn't look convinced. King was not a bad master, but inclined to be . . . what was the *Angrezi* phrase? Ah: *picky*. The Afghan went on:

"And it was a small matter."

Narayan snorted again. "A small matter among the Border hills, child of misbelief," he said. "Not here in the lands of law."

"You folk of the Raj talk much of law, idolater," Ibrahim said. "So far, I don't see much in it."

"From your own mouth," Narayan said dryly. "Note well: I did not call thee *fool*." He looked at King. "Shall we call the *chowdikar*, *sahib*?"

The Lancer officer shook his head. "This is not a matter for the *polis*; certainly not for a village constable." He paused, thinking for a long moment. "It is time that I became Kiram Shaw once again. To remain here longer would be to endanger our people. Two horses, you said?"

"Geldings; four years and six, by their teeth," the Sikh confirmed.

"Undoubtedly stolen, but doubtless their owner is dead. Meet me by the bridge at dawn tomorrow, and bring them with you. One is yours, Narayan; one to Ibrahim here; bring two remounts also—we buy no more tickets for the trains. The stations are too easy to watch."

"*Han*," Ibrahim said, grinning widely.

He'd had a good night's sport, and was the richer by several valuable weapons, a purse of rupees, and a good horse. Perhaps he'd stay by King's side for a little longer—there was much to be said for his service.

"What shall I tell my father, *sahib*?" the Sikh asked.

"All that you know, and that he's to meet me at the bridge also—there are matters of watch and ward to be set. I'll discuss the details with him then. We will know our homes and kindred safe, with Ranjit Singh guarding them."

"*Han, sahib*," Narayan Singh said; his eyes glowed, at the honor done his father and the prospects before himself as well.

King went on: "And I'd better see that Vrinda isn't frightened, and doesn't speak out of school," he finished, giving them both a nod and heading back toward the shed.

"He certainly doesn't lack for stones, the *gora-log*," Ibrahim said, slitting the dead men's belts and sashes and bootheels to find any last-resort money.

Ah. No money, but some lengths of silver wire, and a set of lock-picks. That wasn't one of his skills, but they were good tools. He rolled them back into their cloth, tied the thong around them, and tucked them into an inner pocket in the cloth lining of his *potsheen.*

Narayan nodded at the Pathan's remark; he'd given up any hope of the hillman ever showing proper respect. "Brave to recklessness, is Captain King *sahib,*" he said. "It would be well if he married soon; they are not a long-lived breed, the Kings. Help me with the bodies."

Ibrahim looked at him in surprise. "Why, will you give burial to enemies, then? Are there no hungry pi-dogs in this village, or children to play kickball with the heads?"

The Sikh snorted once more. "Child of misbelief, there are places in this world where dead men arouse questions, even if a hacked corpse or two is of no moment up in the Tirah hills. Come, we have work to do before dawn. I know you can use a *chora.* Now we shall see how well you dig."

Chapter Nine

The embassy of Dai-Nippon—Greater Japan—was one of the notable sights of Delhi. One of the few embassies of any size, Dai-Nippon not only used its own ancestral architecture, but did so with ostentatious pride; the Russian compound was fairly spacious, but it presented a blank whitewashed stone wall to the outside. Ignatieff nodded with approval as he craned his neck to the soaring height of the stepped pagoda tower—let the arrogant *Anglichani* see that not all the world bowed its neck to Imperial fashion. Of course, Dai-Nippon was the only state which rivaled the *Angrezi* Raj in numbers and wealth and power, too. He swallowed envy, a taste as sour as vomit, and studied the grounds carefully.

Half an acre of garden, rocks, and miniature trees and pools separated the low street wall from the great dragon-guarded entrance to the inner complex. The guard was being changed as he watched; two platoons marched and countermarched to shouted orders. They had long pigtails, and wore uniforms of black silk trousers and jacket with a red sun on the breast, and steel coolie-hat helmets polished to a high gloss. Butterfly longswords hung at their waists, for show, but the bayoneted firearms on their shoulders were excellent copies of the *Anglichani* magazine rifles, Metfords.

The officers who exchanged low bows as the ceremony concluded were in black as well—military kimonos, in their case, with long *katana* and short *wakizashi* thrust through their sashes; the front half of their scalps were shaven and the rear hair pulled up in a roll, marking them out as of Dai-Nippon's ruling caste. The infantrymen taking the guard stood at an easy parade rest, as motionless as statues. The samurai officer knelt on a low platform, even more still as he sat with his left hand resting on the long hilt of his sword—Ignatieff saw a fly crawl across his face and one eyelid, and the blink that followed was slow and wholly controlled.

He nodded approval, always pleased at seeing flesh driven to do more than its nature intended. The flesh came from the traitor Christ, but Malik Nous gave them the will to turn the flesh to His service. Ignatieff thought of that for a moment, smiling as the Black God might smile at souls new-risen in Hell.

The man beside him looked at his face, blinked, stepped back a pace despite being the straw boss of the labor gang. The Ohkrana agent cursed himself silently, schooled his expression to meekness. He imagined how the foreman would look on the altar, would scream as he saw the tools prepared and the braziers heated. The taste . . .

The foreman cleared his throat and waved his gang forward as the street cleared for a moment. The ox wagon creaked into motion; it was like a hundred thousand others in Delhi's streets; wooden frame and spoked wooden wheels rimmed in rubber, steel bearings. The cargo was anonymous bales covered in jute sacking, held down with sisal rope; the beasts that pulled it were hornless and floppy of dewlap. Ignatieff walked alongside, one more laborer among many in ragged shirt and *dhoti* and turban shuffling bare-legged over the hot dusty pavement. The sentry at the final gate slung his rifle and examined the bill of lading that the driver handed down, sitting with the tails of the oxen twisted around his toes.

"All correct, sir," he said over his shoulder to the officer, in accented Nipponese. "Pass, then," he went on to the driver, in bad Hindi.

Under the tremendous black-and-red-lacquered multiroofed tower of the pagoda the other buildings of Dai-Nippon's embassy were low-slung and scattered amid gardens, pools, and graveled paths, tile roofs rising in swooping curves over walls mostly of paper; within lights were beginning to gleam. The wagon went directly to the rear of the compound, where storage sheds of plain brick formed the rear wall. Inside the godown all was dim and noisy, piles of bales and boxes making corridors and rising nearly to the teak rafters; a Chinese overseer with a long cane whacked Ignatieff across the shoulders with it by way of encouragement. He grunted to himself, remembering the man's face, and worked at the same slow but steady pace as his fellows.

After twenty minutes a servant came and gestured to Ignatieff from between two stacks of boxes. Ignatieff followed, shoulders bent—every movement of his body signaling a life of beaten-down submission. It was not *quite* perfect; he was too tall, and too well fed. It was still good enough that nobody spared him a second glance, as he passed down the corridor between rows of clerks sitting cross-legged before low desks and flicking at abacuses. A staircase gave onto a landing; the sliding paper-paneled door revealed another office. This one had a spare elegance of decoration—several bonsai trees on lacquered stands, a wall hanging that showed a single willow branch, and the window looking out over a rock garden.

Two men waited, motionless while he slid the paper door panel shut behind him. One was an elderly bureaucrat in a long, embroidered robe, wearing a round cap with a jade button over his brows; his skin was the color of old ivory, and the wispy hair of his beard and mustache snow-white. He folded his hands in the full sleeves of his robe and bowed his head slightly to the newcomer. The man beside him was younger—Ignatieff's own age or a little less. He was also shorter, stockier, his skin a little browner, with a face like a hawk's and cold black eyes; his plain dark kimono rustled slightly as he matched the minimal bow; doubtless the two swords on the wall stand behind were his.

The ambassador formally in charge of Dai-Nippon's legation here in Delhi was an Edo aristocrat of ancient lineage and exquisite manners, famous for his calligraphy and the troop of Noh actors he maintained. These two were the men who did the real work.

"Honored Li Tsu-Ma," Ignatieff said. "Colonel Nakamura."

"*Hai,*" Nakamura said.

Which could mean yes, *or so* or what have you to say? *or half a dozen other things.* The Russian noted that neither used the formulas of hospitality, or offered him tea. *It is better to be feared than loved,* he reminded himself; and if they didn't fear—and need—him, then he wouldn't be here.

"I am grieved," he said, in Mandarin, "to hear of the Son of Heaven's reverses near the Fragrant Isles."

"An unfortunate incident, no doubt due to overzealous underlings on both sides," the Chinese said smoothly. "Even now my *yamen* engages the Raj's foreign ministry in talks on the matter, seeking a mutually satisfactory resolution."

"Horse shit," Nakamura said, in his own language—he knew Ignatieff was fluent in both of Dai-Nippon's official tongues. "We tried probing their defenses and they kicked us in the balls. That new torpedo of theirs is fearsome. The defeated admiral has already made the final apology to the Emperor."

Ignatieff allowed himself an inner smile at the glance Li shot his colleague. As a Chinese and good Confucian, he probably despised Nakamura twice over, for being a barbarian "eastern dwarf" and again for being a warrior—his people had a saying that you didn't use the best iron for nails, or the best men for soldiers. The Mikado was still dependent on the Home Islands for fighters and engineers, but he spent more time in Peking than Edo these days. Li probably also thought the custom of *seppuku* about on a par with Russian massacre-sacrifices and cannibal feasts.

Of course, a lot of Japanese had settled in China as well, landlords and merchants, industrialists and technicians. Not unlike the *Anglichani* and India, save that the Nipponese homela d survived, too.

Li's voice was smooth as he went on: "Doubtless the will of Heaven was otherwise."

"Our ignorance and overconfidence were otherwise," Nakamura said. "We're not ready for a final showdown with the Raj . . . yet. Which is why we agreed to this meeting, Ignatieff. Your ruler's Intelligence service has been demon-powerful before. We're willing to use it again."

Ignatieff reached up and took off his turban. Unwinding it, he produced a sheaf of papers and slid them across the low table. They lay neatly spread across the writhing dragons beneath the lacquer. Nakamura seized them eagerly, his blunt callused fingers flipping the thin, half-transparent leaves of rice paper. After a moment he gave a grunt of satisfaction.

"If these are genuine, we should be able to duplicate their oxygen fuel system quickly enough," he said. "Or the engineers will account for it. Back before the Fortunate Event, we were weak because the Hairy Stinkers had better machines. That isn't going to happen again, by the kami!"

Li nodded; there was no disagreement *there*. The Fall had been gruesome enough in East Asia, but both the main groups of Dai-Nippon still called it *fortunate*. The Japanese were brutally pragmatic; the disaster had catapulted them from impoverished obscurity to second place among the world's powers, which made any number of dead peasants a trifle. And China's scholar-gentry had an unbelievably long memory for slights and humiliations. The British of the Old Empire had burned the Summer Palace and made the Son of Heaven flee in terror, and put up signs in the public gardens of the Treaty Ports that had read *No dogs or Chinese allowed*. It was unforgotten.

"The plans are genuine," the Russian said. "We have our . . . sources."

What Yasmini and her sisters could do wasn't exactly clairvoyance. They *could* generally tell you the consequences of an action to a high degree of likelihood—what would come of trying to bribe or blackmail an *Anglichani* official, for instance. Sometimes the unlikely happened and things fell out otherwise, but those were the exceptions. It was like gambling with loaded dice, for the most part.

"And now," Ignatieff said. "We've found some aspects of *your* Intelligence service more than useful . . ."

"Well," Sita said dubiously. "If you *insist*, Aunt Jane . . . I rather thought the regular studies were enough . . ."

"I'm sure you and Miss Rexin will get along famously," the sister of the King-Emperor said. "After all, you *did* want to go to Oxford, didn't you? Before you . . . well . . ."

She glanced aside. Cassandra King sat in a posture that would have been prim if it hadn't been graceful as well, with her hands folded in her lap. A plucked brow rose a fraction of an inch, showing that she'd heard the implied *matters not discussed before outsiders* and filed it.

She reminds me of Aedelia, Sita's aunt thought; they'd been at Cheltenham together, back longer than she liked to remember, when the world was a simpler place. *Or when we simply knew less about it, perhaps.*

"And if you think I or your father will see you in without passing your Finals, you may think again," she went on to her niece.

"Oh, I know *that*, Aunt Jane," Sita said.

"Very good. Then I'll leave you two to get acquainted."

* * *

This girl is trouble, Cassandra King thought, as she smiled and made a polite salaam after the King-Emperor's sister left—it seemed a little incongruous to think of her as a princess, while the word fit Sita like a glove. She hadn't done much teaching—mostly graduate students—but she could recognize the vibrations. Not spoiled exactly, but—

Willful, she thought. *Willful, headstrong, brilliant*. "What field were you thinking of going into, *Kunwari*?" she said aloud. Presumably the sciences, or Mother and the King-Emperor's sister—so strange to think of them being friends!—would have thought up some other cover for her besides cramming-tutor.

"Oh, do call me Sita," the princess said, with a charming smile. "Formality is such a bore. Physics, I thought, eventually—Dr. Ghose's work is *so* exciting!" A frown. "I cried when I heard about him—what a *despicable* thing for those wicked goondahs to do, to attack a man of his . . . his brilliance!"

"Yes," Cassandra said, choking down memory. "It was."

She'd wept in private, and would not again. Instead she looked around. She'd never seen more than the semipublic parts of the palace before, at her coming-out as a debutante and more recently at official receptions—the King-Emperor was officially head of the Royal Society, of course, and patron of more academic organizations than you could count with an Analytical Engine, so scholars from Oxford came down to Delhi fairly regularly, visits to the Imperial University aside.

The private quarters were grand, but in a lighter and more graceful style than the overpowering magnificence of the public rooms. Generations more recent, as well—not being national treasures, there was no need to preserve the décor as if it were a museum. This upper-story day room was typical, all light tile and stone and wood, with glass clearer than air between tall alabaster pillars and making up half the domed ceiling above. The furniture was similarly light, in pale pastel colors save for the bright fabrics of pillows, and the equally bright sweet-scented jasmine and honeysuckle and bougainvillea twining about the columns and foaming from planters.

One could get used to this, Cassandra thought wryly; although at heart she preferred the homey comfort of Rexin Manor, or the plain privacy of her rooms at the university.

But for sheer reassurance, the Gurkha sentries discreetly posed at the entrances and outside on the flat rooftop garden would be hard to match. Their uniforms were splendid—rifle green trimmed with silver and faced scarlet, all their metalwork and leather polished to mirror brightness—but the flat brown Mongol faces were intent and their eyes never ceased moving; the rifles over their shoulders were entirely functional.

Athelstane had told her that Gurkhas were a cheerful breed as a rule, given to chattering and laughter. These might have been statues except for those ever-moving eyes and the coiled readiness to move she sensed about them. A number of the servants who moved about had suspicious bulges under the left armpits of their jackets, too; hard-faced, broad-shouldered men of the martial castes.

If there's anyplace in the Empire that I'm safe from assassins, it's here, she thought. Reassuring, and frustrating as well. *How am I supposed to get any* work *done, though?* Oh, she could use paper and pencil and slide rule well enough here, but she needed her books and references, her colleagues, the Engine. Scholars worked together as a community for a reason.

"Physics then," she said briskly; not her own specialty, but she knew the basics and a bit more. "I presume you've been through the D Levels?"

"Two months ago," the princess said, reclining on a settee and nibbling a candied almond. "Tea? Juice?"

"Thank you, *Kunw*—, ah, Sita," Cassandra said.

Truth be told, I'm a little flustered, she thought, accepting a glass of chilled pomegranate juice from a servant. She'd been born to the upper-middling-gentry class, untitled squires of solid but modest wealth; there were nobles at Oxford—Earl Cherwell, for instance—but such things mattered less in scholarly circles. Here she'd probably be tripping over duchesses and rahnis and maharajas' sisters at every turn.

Well, at least Cassandra King has done something besides *pick her ancestors wisely,* she told herself. *Not that the Kings are anything to be ashamed of. Families like ours are the backbone of the Empire.* Kuch dar nahin hai, *and get on with it.*

"Tell me then," she said. "What did you think of Dr. Ghose's hypothesis concerning the unexpected results of the Jawaheer-Morley experiment?"

"The one that they tried in 2011, to determine the absolute velocity of the earth by splitting two beams of light?" the princess said, her face lighting with interest.

Twenty minutes later a fine film of sweat had broken out on the Imperial brow, and Cassandra nodded thoughtfully.

Not bad at all. Well up to undergraduate admissions level, and her mathematics are adequate.

She doubted the young woman would ever be anything of special note in the field; physicists tended to make their mark early, as opposed to astronomers like herself. Still, if this little charade continued for any length of time, at least she wouldn't be totally wasting her days. She didn't suppose that the Imperial princess would actually be headed for the scholar's life, but it was just as well to give some of the Empire's reigning family a real knowledge of what was going on in the sciences. Their education usually tended to the military side of things, or engineering at best.

"I have to agree with Her Grace, though," she said. "Your instruction has been quite good . . . tutors?"

"For the last year. Cheltenham until then—Aunt Jane thought it would do me good to mix." She smiled again at Cassandra. "I hate it when people go easy on me, though. I can tell you won't."

"No, Sita, I most certainly won't," Cassandra agreed. "And—"

A crisp smack of hands on wood and steel sounded as the guards came to attention.

Well, well, Cassandra thought. *Sir Manfred. But I doubt I'm going to badger him in* this *company. The heir to the throne, no less . . . and who's that with him?*

A moment later Prince Charles was kissing her hand. Their eyes met for a moment. *Why, he isn't nearly as horse-faced as his pictures,* she thought in astonishment.

"Charles!" Sita said enthusiastically. "Miss . . . Dr. Rexin is going to be giving me some advanced training. She's from Oxford."

The prince shot her a sudden look; then his face went carefully blank. "I'm glad to hear it," he said.

Oh, no. Not another *male intimidated by a woman with a degree!* Cassandra thought.

Sir Manfred coughed discreetly. "The lady and I are acquainted," he said. "But if I may present my friend—"

It was Cassandra's turn to blink. *A foreigner, here?* A nobleman, of course; and a soldier, if she'd ever met one. Still, he seemed to be in Sir Manfred's company. An uneasy feeling stirred in the pit of her stomach. One reason she'd gone into astronomy was that it was—not simple, but *straightforward*, for all its complexity. It didn't have the bending, confused *squishiness* of human affairs.

She was getting that squishy feeling now. Things were going on, and she didn't know quite what.

"Oh, I'm sorry, Your Highness," she said to Charles, realizing with a start that she'd ignored something he said.

"*Koi bat naheen*, not a problem," the heir to the Lion Throne said. "I was merely asking if you rode or hunted, Dr. Rexin."

"To hounds," she said. "Actually my sport of choice is rock-climbing; I'm an alpinist."

She waited with resignation for the baffled aversion. Instead, Charles smiled: The expression sat a little uneasily on his naturally solemn face, but it was oddly charming.

"I've done a little myself," he said. "I envy you the opportunities in Oxford, so close to the mountains. There's little sport near the capital, but there *is* one place—"

"It sounds a little like Kashmir, or the Hunza Valley," Sita said thoughtfully, arms around one knee.

Henri de Vascogne still wasn't comfortable sprawled on pillows, but that was the Imperial idea of moderate informality. *As one penetrates the public veneer, the less* English *these* Angrezi *seem*, he thought—and caught himself thinking in Hindi rather than French.

"Perhaps. It is a valley inland from Algiers, yes, and a rich one. In the spring, the villages are like the red-tiled centers of flowers, for then the almond and cherry orchards blossom about them, and the flower plantations for the perfumeries—the scent alone can make youths and maidens drunk with love, an old song says. The prince has a small country palace there—not more than a great farmhouse, really, though the gardens are very lovely—between Blida and Boufarik. In the winter, you can see the white peaks of the Tell Atlas to the south; nothing compared to the Himalayas, but grand enough—and there is excellent hunting. Peaceful lands besides, being so near to the capital; and the inhabitants nearly all French and Christian."

He shaped the air with his hands: "But in season, the Veiled Men come north to trade—"

Sita clapped her hands. "The Veiled *Men?*"

"Yes, so they call themselves. The Tuareg—or as some others say, the Forsaken of God; also the Blue Men, for their veils are dyed with indigo, and it stains their skin. Among them men are veiled and women not; curious, for Muslims. They are nomads of the deep Sahara, camel-riders of the sand seas; fierce warriors, too, who fight with great broadswords and lances. We trade with them, but always there is skirmishing at the edge of the desert, raid and foray and *razziah.*"

"Like us with the Afghans," Sita said.

"Even so. The Tuareg caravans cross the desert from oasis to oasis, down to the *Bilaud-as-Sudan*, the Land of the Blacks, where they trade dates from their own groves, salt, and our manufactures for gold and cattle, grain and slaves and kola nuts. Thousands of miles between there and the northernmost outposts of your Empire, of course."

"Could I see the Sahara?" Sita asked.

"Of a certainty," Henri smiled. *Suitably escorted*, he thought. Aloud: "The prince himself was stationed there for a time at Fort Zinderneuf—it is customary for the heir of our ruler to follow a military career, as a young man."

The daughter of the King-Emperor nodded, unsurprised; the Raj had the same tradition. "Were you there?"

"I was stationed with that regiment of the Legion, yes," Henri said. "As I said, the prince and I are close comrades."

He smiled wryly to himself at memories of sand and monotony, winds drying your skin to leather, hardtack and jerky and constant longing thoughts of the orange groves and vineyards and tinkling fountains of the north. And men going mad with *le cafard*, running berserk through the barracks until their comrades roped them and left them raving in the punishment cells . . . Places like Zinderneuf were extremely romantic, contemplated at a distance, or between the covers of a book.

Since his task was courtship, rather than disillusionment—and courtship was far more enjoyable, in any case—he went on: "And the prince bears a scar from a Tuareg lance."

"Where?" Sita asked curiously.

Henri grinned, teeth white against the ugly-handsome Mediterranean face, blue-black with incipient stubble despite twice-daily shaving:

"In an indelicate position, I am afraid, for the nomad surprised him while he answered a call of nature."

Sita giggled; it made her look much younger than her just-turned-eighteen years. He launched into a story of newspapers in Algiers and the duels their editors fought—with words and swords—and that had her laughing aloud.

It also awoke the chaperone—de Vascogne's mind thought of her as a *duenna*; there was a good deal of Spanish in the bloodlines of France-outre-mer, and in their tongue. That lady was an elderly noblewoman of impeccable breeding, and nearly stone-deaf herself; they were alone save for her, the princess having dismissed reluctant ladies-in-waiting some time ago.

They shared a divan in a dayroom of Sita's private quarters, raised on a dais beneath a dome of almond-shaped alabaster panes. Columns of ruddy rose quartz stood around the rest of the room, their capitals gilded flowers; the smooth pale marble of the floor bore a red-and-blue Fatipur carpet. There was a huge arched window on one side of the room with the curtains drawn back to reveal a view of the Palace of the Lion Throne, a fantasy of dome and spire, tile and marble and mosaic, of ruddy stone and green garden and brilliant flowers hardly brighter than the crowds who thronged over causeway and gate. In the aching blue sky above it floated a great whale shape of silver, the Union Jack on its fins and the lion-and-unicorn sigil of the Saxe-Coburg-Gothas on its side as the silent air engines drove it above the city.

It was hard to notice the surroundings, when the laughing face of the girl was so close. She wore some light perfume, and her dark hair fell like a jewel-bound wave across the creamy white silk of her gown.

Henri rose, clearing his throat; the neck of his blue uniform tunic suddenly seemed a little tight. He walked around a great golden ewer of iced sherbet, and a truly hideous Old Empire walnut table holding a clock of equally elaborate bad taste. The clock was an heirloom from the reign of Victoria I, stopped at precisely 2 P.M.; the hour of the evacuation of Buckingham Palace—June 21, 1879, a day of sleet and freezing rain. Nodding toward the window, he said:

"That airship; it is the yacht, is it not?"

Sita swung up and came to stand beside him; he could feel the slight pleasant warmth of her body. "Yes, the *Garuda*. It's named after—"

"But yes, the mount of Indra," Henri said. "My homework was most thorough."

"Oh, ogrelike Brahmin tutors made you memorize the Vedas, too? I know *exactly* how you feel," she said sympathetically, and then laughed. "Yes, the *Garuda*'s been in the yards, getting an overhaul. We're going down to Rajputana, Charles and I. Political; keeping the rajas sweet—everyone with three goats and his own well is a king in Rajputana—but they didn't want Father to make an Imperial progress out of it. Can you come along, Henri? There'll be a lot of fun, too."

"I would be delighted," he said sincerely. "But I fear duty may intrude—Sir Manfred wished me to go over some material with him."

Sita pouted slightly. "I thought *I* was your duty," she said.

"Only the most pleasant part of it," Henri said; which was true enough. "And the only pleasant part."

Which was a minor lie. Most of the rest was fascinating, if strenuous.

"*Rajadharma,*" Sita sighed. *Ruler's duty.*

"But . . ."

"But?"

"But yes, there may be a cruise in the offing. It was thought . . ." He hesitated.

"Leave it at that and I'll throttle you like a Thug, you . . . you . . . you *diplomat!*"

The Frenchman laughed aloud. "Well, any actual marriage would be years away," he said. "But a state visit by you and your brother . . . possibly even your father . . . a cementing of ties, a little touring of interesting places in our modest country . . ."

Sita glowed. Henri shook himself mentally. *Keep your heart whole, de Vascogne,* he scolded himself. *This is, unfortunately, an affair of politics and interest, not the heart.*

"*Rajadharma,*" he said in turn. "Yet it need not always be a burden."

Chapter Ten

Yasmini stopped her pacing and splashed water on her face from the basin. It was lukewarm and tasted faintly of some chemical. Heat stifled her, noise beat around her, until she pressed her fists against her temples and panted.

No. She told herself the simple word again and again, like what the people of these lands called a *mantra*. More and more of late, the visions of her *own* future had come.

The count will not send me to the breeding pens yet. I am too valuable. The very best of all.

But that was *why* he would, in the hope of daughters who would be her equals, or superior. And she was old for a functioning Dreamer, ever closer to the madness that was the price of the talent.

The lines lay very close together there, bunching and knotting, all ending with a face above hers—a jerking idiot face, tearing pain, and then blackness. Not death; her own personal world line did not terminate. What ended was her ability to use the talent itself; it was terrifying in a way mere nonexistence was not. As if she could see the loss of her own eyes, ears, tongue—see it approaching closer and closer.

At least then I would not see the death of all the world. The other vision would not leave her either. The mountain, the mountain of steel falling from forever.

"*Pajalsta,*" she murmured to herself, her tongue feeling dry in a mouth gone gritty. "*Pajalsta . . .* mercy, Excellence; mercy, your pardon . . ."

But there would be no mercy from Ignatieff. Not in any of the lines that she could reach, even under the drugs. Not in any line that held close analogues of herself and her master at all.

Yasmini stopped, lowered the hands from her head, took a deep breath, closed her eyes. Other eyes opened within, deep and brown, clever and infinitely sad.

There were some things you could only decide to do if you did *not* think of them. She knew where Ignatieff kept the *bhang lassi;* in a little portable icebox—another one of those astonishing Imperial luxuries. A wave of vision overwhelmed her as she touched the smooth lacquered surface of the teak; again and again, the touch of the steel on her neck, and then—

No. Yes. No. Her hand quivered. A deep breath. Yasmini hummed softly, the sound in her throat growing inside her until it filled the ears of her inner self. *Mind becomes no-mind,* she thought; then she was acting in a waking trance.

Open. Startling cold on her skin, in the close heat of the room. Beads of moisture on the pebbled glass of the jar, a slight sticky resistance as she pulled the glass-topped cork free. Sour-tart taste on her tongue.

A silent explosion went off behind her eyes. Yasmini's own eyes were keen, but she had spoken with those who needed corrective lenses and heard them tell of how they turned blurred outlines into shapes hard and definite. This was something similar, but it was a clarity so sharp that it cut.

So clear that there was no *need* to think. Turn. A thousand thousand Yasminis turned in her mind, receding in an infinite series as if she were trapped between two mirrors—but the images stretched on every side, backward and forward in time, blurring into the *her* that saw. Now there was no need for choice. Only one action in any second could lead to the best result, after all. Strange to be using it for *herself . . .*

Turn. Walk three steps toward the window. Ignatief's chest was there. Look down. A piece of wire . . . pick it up. Bend. Bend. Kneel by the chest. Push the wire into the keyhole. Turn . . . *so.* And *so.*

When the *click* came it startled her for a second. She took another deep breath, another, faded back into the multiplex now. Ignatieff's weapons were inside—she took a light double-bladed *khindjal* knife, tucked the sheath into her belt, and a revolver. Imperial make, an Adams, the only one small enough to easily suit her hand. It was empty; she went through the slow process of swinging down the gate beside the cylinder and slipping a round into each chamber. Money. Papers. Close the chest, twist the wire again until the *click* sound came.

"Why?" she murmured, then tried to drown the thought. A glimpse of Ignatieff; seeing the open chest, his face flashing through puzzlement, thought, dawning rage, turning on his heel. A flash of pain, an iron hand gripping the back of her neck and a slamming impact as it rammed her head forward into a wall of dusty brick, then nothing.

Ignatieff, walking through the door; the chest closed. Throwing himself down on the bed, sleeping, waking to call for her—

Shivering, she repeated the breathing exercises. So easy to lose control, under the drug. So easy to stand here lost in the visions for hours.

The *burqua* came next, the all-covering tentlike black garment of orthodox Islam. Not common among modern Delhi-born Muslims, but you saw enough of the garments on the streets—the Imperial capital was a magnet that sucked in travelers from the remotest regions and spat them forth again.

The stairs creaked beneath her feet. She stood aside, in a patch of shadow; a man came around the bend of the stairs, muttering in some Dravidian dialect, passed her without seeing. Out into the savage brightness of the street . . .

"I'm getting used to being anonymous," King murmured. "I may take it up full-time. Tempting."

I'm joking, of course, he thought. *But only half-joking.*

It had been a pleasant enough ride down from the mountains; even Ibrahim Khan was good company, if an acquired taste. Nobody looked twice at the three young men riding south from the high country, except to examine their horses, try to sell them something, or to pick their pockets. There had been a fair bit of that, since they were well dressed and rode excellent mounts. Nobody tried to kill him— well, not counting an innocent brawl here and there in a wayside caravanserai—and he wasn't *responsible* for anyone except his two followers, both of whom were well able to take care of themselves most of the time.

Now the villages were thickening, merging gradually until you could say you'd been riding in the outer fringes of Delhi for half a day, through slums and warehouses and factories and worksteads and streets of shops, until the buildings reared three or four stories and shut out the horizon. The crowds were just as varied; all of India's races and castes and classes, Hindu and Muslim and *sahib-log*, everything from Imperial University savants down to a group of Bhil bowmen from the Vindhaya jungles who were probably headhunters, staring about them in amazement as deep as Ibrahim's.

And more, from all over the Empire and beyond; a train of yellow-robed lamas spinning their prayer wheels; Lesser Vehicle Buddhist monks from Ceylon glaring at their Nepalese rivals; flat-faced Malays in sarongs with wavy-bladed knives thrust through their sashes; a Brazilian nobleman in billowing pantaloons and broad-brimmed plumed hat and rapier; an Australian station-holder in a motorcar with a ram's head emblazoned on the door; a man from one of the weird theocratic city-states on the west coast of America earnestly talking about the First Men and the Tree of Life to a Jain who wore a scarf across his mouth lest he commit murder by inadvertently inhaling a fly . . .

They said that to be tired of Delhi was to be tired of life, because sooner or later here you'd meet every variety of human being in the whole wide world.

A singsong voice from above broke into his reverie: *"Hamare ghal ana, acha din!"*

He grinned and waved to the tart who'd called the invitation as she leaned from her balcony, displaying smooth brown breasts.

Hello, and come into our street, big boy, he translated to himself, chuckling. Her face wasn't much, but two weeks of involuntary celibacy focused his attention considerably lower. Probably poxed, to be sure. Not that that was any great matter these days—modern medicine could clear it up in a week—but he was a fastidious man, in some respects.

A different voice cut through the swarm in the street. A man chanting as he walked, old and thin and tough as rawhide, vastly bearded and with a mane of gray-white hair falling past his waist, naked save for a meager loincloth, carrying nothing save for begging bowl and staff:

"Utterly quiet
Made clean of passion
The mind of the yogi
Knows that Brahman,
His bliss is the highest.

Released from evil
His mind is constant
In contemplation:
The way is easy,
Brahman has touched him,
That bliss is boundless—"

The *sannyassin* scowled angrily as he had to step aside for the riders, and saw the two horsemen behind King looking up and jesting with the harlot as they blocked his path. He raised his staff in admonishment:

"Those who wallow in foulness in this life court foul rebirth," he said, shaking his tangled white hair. "Renounce desire! Seek escape from the grip of the senses, which turn the spirit to gross and worldly things. Fear desire for worldly pleasures like fire, for the wind is no wilder!"

King laughed. "Pranam, heaven-born," he said, making the gesture of respect—in this crush it was easy to drop your reins on your horse's neck. The man wore the sacred thread across his shoulder.

Better say something. If Ibrahim spat on a Brahmin ascetic, there might be a riot, and the Pathan was fully capable of it.

"Your blessing, heaven-born," he went on.

"Shall I bless mockers and fornicators?" the wandering ascetic said.

Whatever other sins he's shed, pride isn't one of them, King thought, meeting the fierce dark eyes. Instead of replying directly, he chanted himself:

"Action rightly renounced brings freedom:
Action rightly performed brings freedom:
Both are better
Than mere shunning of action."

In a normal voice he went on: "We are men who act, holy one; better to act as our *karman* in this turn of the Wheel demands, than to try a path beyond our merit, and fail. Bless us!"

He tossed a silver rupee into the man's begging bowl; the ascetic looked as if he was seriously considering throwing it out, or arguing further—King's theology was exceedingly weak, if you knew the next section of that *gita*—but he scowled and made the gesture of blessing before he strode on, chanting again:

> *"Who burns with the bliss*
> *And suffers the sorrow*
> *Of every creature*
> *Within his own heart,*
> *Making his own*
> *Each bliss and each sorrow:*
> *Him I hold highest*
> *Of all the yogis—"*

"Maybe he isn't such an old sourpuss as I thought," King said, raising a brow in surprise.

"Idolater." Ibrahim Khan shrugged.

"Polytheist," Narayan Singh agreed, then caught himself with a frown.

Narrow-minded, the pair of you, King thought, looking about and taking his bearings.

He was familiar enough with Delhi, though not the northern outskirts they'd spent most of the day crossing. The central districts, Old Town, he knew a little, but he'd spent most of his time there in the Red Fort—a Moghul work which was still formally the headquarters of the Imperial armed forces. Most of the real work of governance—and upper-caste social life—happened in the southern zone, in buildings no older than the New Empire; the tide of commerce flowed through the great factory districts and workers' housing of the East End. In those parts of the Raj's capital it was easy to forget that there had been a city here before Victoria the First arrived in Calcutta in the forefront of the Exodus.

And spent one month among the Bengali bogs, before she shook the mud of the Ganges delta from her feet and commanded that the capital be moved to Delhi, King thought sardonically. *Which is abominably hot in summer but at least not a total swamp.*

But coming in from the north, up the Rohtack Road and past the Kashmir Gate; there you rode past the memorial to the heroes who'd fought the First Mutiny, standing near an ancient lion-headed pillar the Maurya ruler Ashoka had erected Gods-knew-where not long after Alexander the Great. The pillar itself had been moved here by Feroz Shah Tughlaq in the days of the Slave Dynasty, around the time of Richard the Lionheart . . .

If you came that way you were reminded that when London was founded as a trading post among head-hunting savages, Delhi was already a great metropolis attracting scholars and merchants from half the world.

Which it still is, and London's a trading post among savages again, King thought whimsically, reining his horse over to the side of the road at the ring of a silvery bell.

That let him avoid the silent smooth rush of a motorcar; there were enough in the environs of Delhi that there were special laws governing them, one being the bell. Fewer of them came into their destination, the narrow ways of Old Delhi. That was the walled city that Shah Jahan had refounded in the days when the pride and pomp and power of the Mughals was the wonder of the world, and she whom the Taj Mahal would enfold forever still lived amid the pleasures of the Padishah's court.

And in Shah Jahan's day the Chandi Chowk—the Square of Silver Moonlight—had been a stately, tree-lined processional way running down to his seat of power in the Red Fort, flanked by the mansions of Jahan's courtiers and poets and adorned with a canal down its middle.

Here and now it was a shoving, chattering mass of folk on foot, riders or rickshaws, oxcarts, now and then a wandering dewlapped cow given space for its sacredness. Gathering evening made the crush even greater than in full day, as those who worked regular hours headed home. As the huge red ball of the sun sank westward the streetlights came on with a sharp *pop*, electric sparks lighting gas. The light was warm and yellow, shading a little brighter as the mantles of the gas jets began to glow, throwing a hectic mass of moving shadow on the walls. Ibrahim started at the sound and wash of light.

Narayan Singh grinned. "There, it is time for prayer," he said.

The muezzins were calling from their minarets. "Shall we stop while you unfold a rug, child of misbelief?"

"Are you mad? In this crush?" Ibrahim said, then scowled as he realized he was being teased—or mocked, depending on how you chose to look at it. "Chaff not at the All-Powerful, the Beneficent, the Merciful," he growled.

"The Stupid, the Nonexistent, the Pimp of the houris," Narayan said.

"He will turn thee into a worm in Hell!"

"And I shall gnaw the stupid thing's entrails!"

King looked over his shoulder, and the two young men grinned sheepishly and subsided; he knew the Sikh had used anger to drive out the Pathan's gathering unease at his surroundings. When they passed the Fatehpuri Masjid—a mosque built by one of Shah Jahan's wives—they were on the Chandi Chowk proper, the ancient Street of the Silversmiths, and the roaring turmoil of the packed pavement made the country-bred horses snort and roll their eyes, tossing their heads with a champing of teeth and a spray of foam. The street was broad by Old Delhi standards even after it left the square, perhaps forty feet, flanked on both sides by buildings of stone or brick four or five stories high; shop windows and entrances below, slit-windowed dwellings or blank-walled warehouse or workshop above. Temples and churches and mosques were exclamation points of chanting and incense amid the swarming, sweating throngs of commerce.

Signs in half a dozen scripts advertised wares as various as the languages vendors used to scream out the superb quality and infinitesimal prices available within. They made wedges of brightness spilling out onto the sidewalks, many glinting as light shone on the piled goods— metalwork of a hundred kinds, from brass trays to kitchen knives to swords and samovars and hookahs, glass, piled silk bright with dyes, trays of colored spice-powders . . .

By then it was full night, and the horses weren't the only ones who felt out of place amid the endless throngs. Narayan Singh was smiling a little at the Pathan's discomfort as Ibrahim turned gray and fingered a string of worry beads. They rode on at a slow walk, past the Digamber, the Jain temple, with its attached hospital for sick birds; past the clanging bells and shrill cries of vendors selling flowers and vermilion powder around the Gauri Shankar temple dedicated to Shiva and Parvati with its thousand-year-old sacred *lignam*. The Sikh made a gesture of reverence at the great marble-and-gold *gurudwara* of Sisganj, where Tegh Bahadur, the ninth of the Gurus, had been martyred by Aurangzeb, the last of the great Moghuls.

A little farther, near the spice market of Khari Baoli, was the Kotwali police station. King and Narayan both saluted: there had been a battle there and a great killing in the First Mutiny, when the troops of the Old Empire reconquered Delhi—and an even greater one a century before, when the Persian warlord Nadir Shah watched his men behead thirty thousand townsmen. The people of the modern city swarmed by like ants, claiming the stage for a moment until they became one with the dust they raised.

Ibrahim shoved his beads away at last, straightened in the saddle, and spat eloquently on the bare feet of a street vendor who took one look at the Border countenance and decided to push his handcart heaped with silk slippers elsewhere.

"Istrafugallah!" the Pathan burst out. "This city is a lie! There are not so many folk in all the world!"

He glared about him, his gaze not even stopping when it passed over the display in a jeweler's window. It was behind a latticework of steel bars that covered the glass, but the black velvet behind flashed and glittered. Inside the proprietor bowed and smiled as a woman in a silver-shot sari and her maids picked over trays temptingly lain out. This was not only the largest city in the world, but the richest; even most of the porters and rickshaw men were healthy-looking. There was a dense smell of dust, packed sweating humanity, of curry and ghee, but little sewer stink.

"Not the place I'd choose to live myself," King admitted, hiding a smile. "But quite real, I assure you."

The Pathan grunted again, then seemed to take himself in hand by main force. "Sheep are many," he said. "Wolves care not."

Narayan Singh grinned; he'd been born a farmer himself, but in a civilized province with many towns, and the city of Oxford—small, but definitely urban—no more than a day's travel away.

"Many sheep mean many guardians," he pointed out. "And the wolf cares much for those . . . if he be a wise wolf."

"From thy own mouth. Note well: I did not call thee *dog*," Ibrahim said with poisonous politeness, and grinned in his turn at the Sikh's flush. "Not even a dog who guards sheep."

"Peace," King said. "We're all of the same pack, for now." *And I'm the head wolf*, his tone added without words. The two younger men subsided.

The buildings had numbers, as required by law, but they were small, often faded or obscured. *Time to make up your ruddy mind*, he thought. Elias's address was just up the side street ahead. Sir Manfred's was at Metcalfe House, which was a bit farther east, toward the Red Fort. *Duty calls, and official business takes precedence.*

The crowds thinned a little, enough so that walkers didn't have to use their elbows continuously. There were still a few government bureaus close to the fort, and many small trading firms had their head offices here; some were less small than old-established and discreet. One building held a modest brass plaque that read *Metcalfe House*. There were also a few bays with hitching posts. You could hire a watcher to water and guard your horse for a few *piece*, and would get exactly what you paid for. King had a better trick than that.

"Ibrahim," he said, as he reined in. "Watch the horses. And *watch*. Someone looking for me might think to lie in wait here."

To do that would mean weeks of surveillance on an office of the Political Service, whose members generally *would* notice and take action. Still, people had been trying to kill him—and his sister, by Krishna!—since Peshawar. Better not to take chances.

Ibrahim nodded. "*Han, huzoor.* You know the call?"

"Are we weaned?" Narayan Singh said. "Do *you* know the place of refuge?"

"Did your lord not point it out?" the Pathan said, insulted. "Four buildings back, on the far side of the alley, the entrance marked with the Seal of Solomon."

Ibrahim's eyes were already scanning shadowed rooftops and balconies as they dismounted, much as he might have boulders and ravines in his native hills. Frustration shone from him with an almost palpable heat; there were just too many here for him to see plain intent among the crowds. His left hand gripped the hilt of his *chora* with a force that made the skin turn pale under the grime embedded in his knuckles. King himself was pricklingly conscious of the weight of the *tulwar* at his side, and the pistol riding at the small of his back under the thigh-length *kurta* he wore. The tunic was split behind and before, horseman's fashion; his hand could sweep in quickly to get at the weapon. If there was a fight, though, he preferred cold steel; he was a good shot, but the sword was his weapon, and with that he was very good indeed.

"—*po-russki?*" a voice asked, and a small hand tapped him on the elbow. The question was repeated, louder, to cut through the white noise of the crowds. "*Govorite-li vy po-russki?*"

He spun, reaching for his hilt, then relaxed; it was a woman, slight-built under a black *burqua*, and very short—no higher than his breastbone, like a blacker shadow in the dimness of the street. Then he tensed again as the words made sense. *Do you speak Russian?* The question was *in* Russian, and in the old High Formal mode, at that. An aristocrat's dialect, the type they spoke at the Czar's court.

"*Da*," he said reflexively. "*Govoryu. Kto vy* takoy?"

Yes, I understand Russian. And who are you?

"There is no time," the woman said.

Her voice had a high, slightly singsong note; all he could see of her as she spoke again was a hint of eyes through a slit in the chador.

"You are going in there. Men will try to kill you. You must kill them, and bring away the other man they seek to kill, or you die. The whole world will die."

Charles Saxe-Coburg-Gotha levered his fingers into the crumbling rock and swung himself up onto the summit plateau with a grunt of effort. For a moment he lay panting, letting the warm wind dry his sweat, then sat up and unbuckled his harness.

The rock face beneath him was an upthrust ridge of granite and rose-colored quartz, an outlier of the Aravali Range on the border of Rajputana, where central India heaved itself out of the flat clay plains of the Ganges and Indus. The view northward was familiar but beloved; this area and several thousand square miles surrounding it were Imperial Forest land, theoretically property of the ruling dynasty, although much of it was open to anyone who paid a modest fee and didn't try to poach. The wind blew mild and clean from the north, over leagues of grassland dotted with brush and trees. There was a teak and sal and rosewood forest at the foot of the hills, crowding around the clearing that held the little lodge where the court party was staying, and the tall mooring post for the *Garuda*, the royal family's air yacht.

Clouds towered into the sky northward, like mountains that grew from black through clotted cream to rose-tipped pearl.

Good hunting country, too, he thought. Black buck, boar, tiger, and leopard in thickets and along the watercourses, and lion on the open plains. Bustard if you were in the mood for hawking. *And, of course, fine climbing.*

Odd how it upset his guardians; they didn't object to pigsticking or polo, which broke hundreds of necks a year, or even to his seeing combat with the Guards regiment of which he was colonel-in-chief. Though the ten thousand faces of God all realized that even the frontier Pathans knew better than to risk killing the heir to the Lion Throne.

But let me climb a little way up a cliff, and the security detail all react like a bunch of nervous women clucking and squawking.

The thought made him grin a little; from below he could hear panting, and a quiet curse. *Now Dr. King is not nervous at all. Not about climbing, at least. Extraordinary woman!*

Her head appeared over the edge, and he restrained the impulse to extend a helping hand, which she would *not* appreciate. A fierce grin of concentration split her unfashionably tanned face; a movement, the slap of her hand on a knob of rock, and she hauled herself onto her belly on the edge.

"*Shabash*, Dr. King," he said, holding up his hand and snapping his fingers.

There were already guards and servants—and two of Sita's ladies-in-waiting, for chaperonage—on the little plateau. Several scurried forward with a bright silk umbrella, a picnic basket, and carafes of iced water and juices; there would have been an orchestra and a pavilion, if he hadn't put his foot down.

And I can never really get away from them. Not without climbing a much more inaccessible cliff; this one had a footpath, steep but doable, up the southern slope. Most of the time he didn't think about it much; the attendants were part of his life and had been since infancy. It wasn't until he went to the Sandhurst, the military academy up near the old hot-season capital at Simla in the lower Himalayas, that he appreciated what *privacy* could mean. Cadets weren't allowed to have more than a batman and a groom; and the security detail were discreet about it, their presence far in the background.

But back at the palace, or even at a country lodge like this . . .

There's no escaping them; prying, peering, hovering—all for my own good, of course, lest I lack anything I want or be endangered or stub a toe. May their dear loyal souls be reborn as termites!

He didn't mind the Gurkhas, really; most of them were as relieved to get out of the palace as he was. They stayed well back, covering the approaches.

"That *is* an interesting climb," the young scholar said. "Not particularly strenuous, but interesting, and the view is superb." She sat lotus-style on the rock and accepted a tall glass of ice water lightly flavored with citron. "Ah, that *is* pleasant, too. Yes, a good climb; you took it at a very brisk clip, too, although I suppose you're familiar with it."

Charles nodded. There was praise and praise—most people around court still abided by St. Disraeli's unfortunate maxim about laying it on with a trowel when dealing with royalty. He didn't think Cassandra King was one of them, though.

He nodded. "I have to speed-climb it to get anything worthwhile out of it," he went on. "Now, I understand that the south approach to Nanga Parbat—"

They talked rock-climbing for a while; after a moment he opened the picnic basket and offered a sandwich.

"Ham," he said. "Or there's mutton, or watercress."

"Ham will be fine, Charles," she replied, then raised a brow as he chuckled.

"A moment ago I was thinking of how a surplus of servants is as inconvenient as a deficit," he explained. "No privacy, and you're always tripping over someone trying to be useful. But then again, when you have to have food that's pure to guests of any caste, several sets of kitchen staff are *very* handy."

"That *would* be a problem," she said, taking a bite of the sandwich, and obviously mentally listing the varieties: strict vegetarian and prepared only by Brahmin cooks for the more picky high-caste Hindus; no pork and all the other meat slaughtered in *hallal* fashion for Muslims; and then there were the Jains, who considered even some plants to have souls and so be on the forbidden list—

She gave a slight snort. "These food taboos are all absurd, of course. Superstitious nonsense."

Charles raised a brow in turn. "Would you prefer a roast beef sandwich, then?" he said, with a sly grin.

Cassandra choked slightly. "Touché," she admitted. "My Whig intellect says *why not?* My *sahib-log* stomach would rebel, I'm afraid."

India had thousands of *jati*-castes, many associated with some specific trade or neighborhood, and each with its own weird complexity of rules about food, ritual purity, and marriage. Since the days of the Vedas they had been grouped in four rough categories called *varnas*—colors. There were the Brahmins on top, at least in their own opinion; they were the priest-scholars. Next the Kyashtrias, the warrior-rulers; in the middle the Vaisyas, merchant-artisan-farmers. Those three were the twice-born castes. On the bottom—not counting casteless untouchables, sweepers and pariahs—were the Sudras, the common laborers.

Most Hindus—all but the stiffest purists—had long ago accepted the *sahib-log* immigrants as a caste of the Kyashtria *varna*, since they were men of governance and war, just as they had come to see Christ as yet another avatar of Vishnu, like the Buddha.

The influence went both ways, of course; objectively, Charles knew his great-grandfather *had* eaten cow meat with innocent calm—Australians and *Kapenaars* still did, although more and more of their upper crusts followed Delhi fashion. But emotionally . . . emotionally, the land of his birth had laid bonds on him. And on Cassandra as well, it appeared.

Once a group settled in the land, that all-absorbing acceptance was the natural course, and fighting it was like trying to slash a cloud with a sword. Only the fierce monotheism of Islam had even tried, and not altogether successfully. For all their claims of descent from Sun and Moon and Fire in ancient Vedic times, he suspected that the noble Rajput clans had ridden down the Khyber from Central Asia fairly recently as history went, and bullied their way into the Kyashtria category at spearpoint just as his own *Angrezi* ancestors had shot their way in.

A faint tinkle of music came through the warm breeze. They both shifted and looked down over the cliff face; there *was* a pavilion there at its foot, open-sided and with flaps on one side to shade a broad area covered with rugs that glowed wine red, gold, indigo, and crimson. Sita and a group of young women—some ladies-in-waiting, some the daughters of local Rajput nobles—were dancing on the carpets, to the sound of a one-sided drum and plangent flutes, their own voices, the skip-and-stamp of feet bare except for anklets and toe rings. They were all in Rajasthani dress, tight bodices and gauzy shawls and long wine-red-and-spangles skirts that flared to the slow twirls and swift gliding steps. The princess turned in the middle of the circle, laughing, her arms moving through graceful curves to the sweet *ting-ting* of the finger cymbals she clashed.

"Is that the *ghoomal*?" Cassandra asked.

She knew most of the Kashmiri dances from her childhood, but Rajputana was a long way from her native province.

"No, it's the *panihari*," Charles said after a moment's thought. "The Water-Carrier Dance . . . there are two; for the other one you have to put a jug on your head and it's much slower. Sita prefers lively dances."

"I'd noticed," Cassandra said.

"Sita seems in a better mood lately," Charles said. "I'm glad you two are getting on so well."

"Yes. She's very intelligent and a likable girl, if a bit of a handful." Cassandra coughed discreetly and hesitated. "Ah . . . Highness . . ."

"Charles, I thought?" he said.

"Charles . . . I understand arrangements for a marriage are in progress?" He nodded. "Well," she continued, "while in theory I disapprove of arranged matches . . . though I suppose they're inevitable for the dynasty . . . let's put it this way: That girl needs a man. And in the *worst* way."

Charles blinked. *Well*, that's *blunt enough*, he thought. One reason he liked the young woman from Oxford was that she was forthright, but it was a bit startling at times.

"Has she been doing the thousand-hands-of-Pravati thing again?" he asked. Usually only a problem when she was bored, but . . .

"No, not at all, but I'd say she definitely has an, ah, ardent nature."

Charles chuckled. "She's going to be a handful wherever she goes," he said. "I'm just relieved that de Vascogne isn't more alarmed. The French court is quite stiff about decorum and appearances, I understand."

"Where is the Vicomte de Vascogne, in any case? He and Sir Manfred were here yesterday."

"Business in Delhi called Sir Manfred back to the capital, I understand," Charles said. He sighed slightly. "Real business."

The young woman looked up, slightly startled, and turned her head to one side in inquiry.

"Cassandra . . . this sort of thing"—he waved a hand—"is all very well. But it's not a substitute for *work*."

"You do have a fairly busy schedule of official business," she pointed out.

"Makework, most of it. Or ceremony—like this damned camel-judging festival in Udipur I'm supposed to go to next. And there you have the story of my life; complimenting camels and cutting ribbons."

She blinked, surprised at his bitterness. "Well, may the current King-Emperor live forever, but even John II won't, and ruling the Empire . . . *that's* a life's work, surely?"

"Of a sort," he said, looking out over the plains with his elbows braced on his knees. "Father isn't quite the figurehead that Old Empire monarchs were—he doesn't have to accept a prime minister he disapproves of; whatever PM Parliament does send to 'kiss hands' would think three times before crossing him; and he really does set most foreign policy, and—but at seventh and last, the politicians run the Empire. The Whigs tend to exaggerate the powers of the throne, so they can whittle them down; the Tories do the same thing, so they can use the King-Emperor as a combination totem and bombproof shelter."

A wry quirk of the mouth. "I can be a genuine patron of the arts and sciences, of course—that *is* within the throne's power."

"And *that* is an important job," Cassandra said with quiet conviction. "Believe me."

Slowly, Charles nodded. "I grant you that. It's been . . . educational listening to you, Dr. King."

"Cassandra," the young woman reminded him. Smiling: "And if you knew how *refreshing* it is to meet a man who *isn't* an academic and who *does* listen, instead of getting a look of glazed desperation—"

Charles snorted. "Give me some credit, Cassandra. I can't follow the mathematics you use, but I *can* take them on faith and then consider the *implications* of what you and your colleagues have discovered."

The young woman glowed back at him. It was oddly satisfying. There had never been a shortage of women, as such—the matter had been taken care of with quiet competence by the household major-domo when he turned thirteen. And of course as soon as he came to man's estate there had been something like a normal young aristocrat's social life, with a huge golden advantage.

But I've never flirted with a girl who got that *look when I complimented her* mind *before*, he thought.

It was a relief from the giggling highborn debutantes court was full of, and the even larger legion of wives who'd done their repro-ductive duty to their spouses young and were taking full advantage of the traditional unspoken liberty to do a little discreet wandering after-ward.

For that matter, the conversation itself was a relief. He'd done a little to expand the company acceptable at court, or at least his portion of it. Not that he had anything *against* the martial-caste noblemen, generals, and administrators—often the same people—who made up the traditional inner circle. Still, he'd created a little scandal now and then by bringing in others; wealthy commoner industrialists and mer-chants, scholars, even artists.

But not many attractive women in any of those groups, and ones with a taste for sport as well, he thought happily. *For once, let* rajadharma *wait for a bit.*

The sun was declining in the west, turning the rose quartz of the cliffs around them to the color of its namesake flower. The com-mander of the guard contingent coughed.

"My thanks for a very pleasant afternoon," Charles said half-formally. "Unfortunately, I have to dine with a selection of Rajput lordlings here, and . . ."

". . . and while they don't exactly practice *purdah* anymore, they'd be scandalized at a mixed banquet, yes," Cassandra said, smiling.

"Father wants me to talk them around to passing an equivalent of the Ryot's Protection Act in the client kingdoms here in Rajputana," Charles said apologetically. "Real work, if you like—the maharajas aren't subordinates of some abstract thing called the Empire, they're vassals of the King-Emperor, the real breathing man who sired me. If we *don't* talk them 'round, questions will be asked in Parliament. It's damned difficult real work, at that."

"Not as difficult as my task, Charles," Cassandra said demurely, lowering her eyes for a second.

Was that a glint in her eye? "Well, I *said* that I grasped what you were saying about the observatories for—"

"No, no. I have to go to the women's dinner with Sita, and convince the lordlings' wives and daughters and sisters that I spent the entire afternoon with you talking about science and politics."

His laugh joined hers as he bowed over her hand and strode away. The banquet would be damned dull—Vishnu knew he liked to talk polo and horses, but there were limits—yet suddenly it didn't seem so utterly wearisome.

Chapter Eleven

Sir Manfred Warburton looked up from his desk. The punkha was doing its best—the punkha-wallah outside was an agent under punishment, doing *his* best to earn forgiveness—but the air in this office was always a little close, except in January, when it was chilly. For now he undid the high collar of his tunic and sighed. Nevertheless, he'd kept refusing offers of better quarters for his subdivision of the Service. It was his considered opinion that staying too long down among the splendors of South Delhi tended to isolate you from reality and promote delusions of omnipotence.

"Just look at what it does to Parliament," he muttered, and reached a hand to turn up the desk gas lamp; night was falling, and the narrow slit windows didn't let in much light even at noonday.

The staff were leaving for the evening, as usual; as usual, he was staying—the telephone, that instrument of the *rakashas*, would leave him alone if he worked through the dinner hour. His own meal came in on a covered thali platter, catered from Nizzamudin, his favorite Delhi-style eatery; spiced lentil-and-tamarind mulligatawny soup, kahari chicken, with a salad of pickled tandoor-grilled cauliflower, onions, okra, and capsicum; flat bakarkhani bread and papads to accompany it, sandalwood-flavored sherbet to drink and melon to finish off.

One advantage of eating at your desk was that you could comfortably use fingers and flatbread on the food, rather than the archaic formality of knife and fork.

His executive assistant came in as the tray was being cleared away; Rabindra Das was a short, fat Gujarati who looked exactly like a moderately prosperous trader in ghee and cottonseed from Bombay. He also looked very much like his brother, who *was* a moderately prosperous trader in ghee and cottonseed, in Ratnagiri, which was a port just down the coast from Bombay. The utter ordinariness of his appearance had been a considerable asset over the years. He gave a fastidious shudder at the remains of the meal—being like many from his Jain-influenced province a vegetarian so strict that even onions and garlic were taboo—and spoke:

"Allenby *sahib* will be here for his appointment in two hours twenty minutes," he said, sliding a stack of paper bound with a length of red tape onto Warburton's desk. "Here is the Madagascar file."

The baronet snorted. "He's trying to distract me again," he said, reading and making an occasional note for the meeting.

The perennial question of adding Madagascar to the Empire could wait; it had waited generations. The *Kapenaars* wanted annexation, from sheer greed; Australia was against, on general principle and because the island was ruled by a friendly, progressive, and three-quarters-civilized dynasty. The natives and their rulers were even Anglicans, converted by missionaries back in Old Empire times and accepting the Archbishop of Delhi's ecclesiastical authority ever since; on the whole, the present free-trade-and-alliance treaty gave both sides all the benefits of official Imperial overlordship with few of the drawbacks.

The central government was going to go on doing what it did best, ignoring the issue in the hope it would solve itself with time. That often worked. Sometime later he murmured to himself:

"Why is he trying to distract me? It's not just that he doesn't believe me about the Russians." Warburton snubbed out his cheroot with a savage gesture and lit another.

"Self, being mere failed B.A. of Bombay University, not even of martial caste, and not being confidant of *sahib-log* upper-rogers, could hardly be expected to know inner recesses of Allenby *sahib*'s mind," Das said unctuously. "Have therefore succeeded in suborning guardians of his *bibi khana*."

"Ah?" Warburton's ears pricked up. *Hell to pay if that's ever discovered*, he thought.

Allenby was old-fashioned enough to keep both his mistresses on the premises and semisecluded; the Gods knew how he got his wife to go along with it, these days. *Bibi khana* meant *women's quarters*. It wouldn't do to be found interfering in a fellow-Political's personal arrangements.

Unless Das had dug up some very, very good dirt, in which case all would be forgiven. The Service was decentralized, and its actual pathways of authority were obscure even to someone at his level. One thing he could say for certain was that its ultimate masters didn't quarrel with success.

"Have found that strangers—male strangers—are in practice of visiting Allenby *sahib* there," Das said, a trace of smugness on his fat features. "Would venture perhaps to say that Allenby *sahib* wished these visitors to remain secret . . . from the Service."

Warburton shaped a silent whistle. That would be the best place; sacrosanct even from spies, usually. "Well done, Das," he said. "Find out more if you can. Precisely who, why, and what discussions."

Rabindra Das made the salaam, began to turn . . . and dropped silently to the floor like a puppet with cut strings. Warburton rose, his hand darting under his jacket, then slumped across his desk as something struck a massive blow to his side. He gasped as the pain slammed home like a chill blade in the flesh, trying to turn and see what had crept up behind him. Another blow struck, this time with a length of fine sharp-edged chain that cut through cloth and flesh as it wrapped around his right forearm. The same pull that savaged his arm twisted him around to face the door.

"*Zdravstvuyte, gospodin* Warburton," said the tall man with the eye patch. "*Radsvamee poznakomit'sya.*"

Allenby stood beside him, his face sallow and expressionless save for a sheen of sweat that he licked at nervously as it stung chewed lips.

"I have been looking forward to this conversation for some time, Sir Manfred," the big man said in excellent Imperial English. "More than twenty years, since you escaped me in the Border country and ruined my little ambush. I am sure it will be a pleasure."

He smiled, and pushed the eye patch up from one blue eye. "For me, at least."

"It is the *E-rus fakir*'s seeress!" Narayan Singh said.

His hand went to his hilt. King's hand went out to touch him on the arm. "Be still, *bhai*," he said.

For a moment he seemed to be apart from the milling crush on the nighted street, from the city and the world. His skin prickled, as it might when he felt a sniper's gaze behind a rock five hundred yards away.

The slight woman swayed on her feet. "You must go in," she said. "You must go in *now*."

"A trap, *huzoor*!"

King hesitated, but only for an instant; if there was one thing being a cavalry commander on the Border taught you, it was that a second-rate decision made in time was usually better than a perfect one made too late. Ganesha, god of luck, had an elephant's head—you couldn't grab his trunk once he'd passed by.

"No," he said. "We were going in here anyway—she merely tells us to be wary, and she *makes* us wary, herself. Only a madman would make such a trap. Quickly, now—but keep the woman between us. She must be questioned, later. And no weapons yet! The gatekeepers won't let us through if we look like we're on *razziah*."

Metcalfe House didn't look much different from the rest of the buildings on the Chandi Chowk, apart from not having its ground-level frontage broken up into small shops. Instead there was a simple teak door with a knocker. King took a long deep breath to center himself and swung it with a *clack-clack-clack*.

The *khansama* was a tall thin man dressed from turban to toes in shades of beige, set off only by the scarlet of his cummerbund. His face stayed a mask of politely expressionless inquiry as he salaamed and asked:

"May I help you, sirs, madam?"

Not even a blink at whoever-she-is, King thought. *Well, Sir Manfred's butler has probably seen everything, at one time or another.*

King was still in disguise, in that he'd allowed his beard to grow out to a neat spade shape and was dressed in civilian clothes four or five steps below his station—jodhpurs and *kurta*, sash and sword belt and plain turban without an *aigrette*. He might have been a prosperous yeoman-tenant, or from some sort of middling rural business family; dealers in grain or hides or wool, something of that nature. He did keep a supply of his own cards in his sleeve pocket, and now he flicked one out between the first two fingers of his right hand:

Athelstane King, Esq.
Rexin Manor, Kashmir
Captain, Peshawar Lancers
Peshawar Cantonment

"Sir Manfred is expecting me," he added, and dropped it onto the silver tray the *khansama* extended.

The man's eyes flicked downward; King wouldn't have thought that was enough time to read the small print, but the butler's manner underwent a subtle but unmistakable shift.

"Follow me, please, *sahib*," he said, bowing. "I am sure Sir Manfred will see you directly. Your man and this woman—"

"They come with me," King said curtly. "Imperial business."

"As you wish, *sahib*. Sir Manfred Warburton *sahib*'s office is on the second floor. If you will wait here—"

He led them down a dark corridor. Nobody else seemed to be about, which wasn't surprising given the hour. The waiting room was either very formal, or very old: carved teak paneling below a painted dado and high, thickly cushioned furniture, plus little tables littered with knicknacks. King perched on a horsehair settee; Narayan Singh squatted comfortably on his hams; the woman—

"I can't very well just call you 'woman,'" King said. "Who are you?"

"My name is Yasmini," she replied, in excellent but accented Hindi. At his surprise, she went on: "I spoke Russian so that you would not dismiss me quickly."

Now that they were out of the noise of the street and in better lighting he could tell that she was young, quite young—the fingers that showed beneath the long sleeves bore that out. Pale skin, neatly tended almond-shaped nails; hands as small as those of a child of ten years, but the voice wasn't *that* young and when her movements pushed the fabric of the *burqua* against her there were fleeting hints of curves. Either she was around eighteen, or—he had a momentary flash of childhood fairy tales; her voice had a sweetness like silver chimes, and there was something more eerie still in the tone and cadence—as if she were speaking in a trance.

"I am of the Sisterhood of True Dreamers. I have fled from my master, Count Ignatieff, to warn you."

The Sikh pricked up his ears at the sound of the Russian name; King did himself, with a chill feeling in his gut.

"The *fakir*!" the *daffadar* said. "Her master must be the *fakir* who set the Deceivers on thee, *sahib*. The one who killed thy father and crippled mine!"

King nodded, but extended a hand palm down for silence.

"Go on," he said to the woman.

"They are trying to kill the man you came to see—trying now. They must not succeed, because if he dies, very likely you will as well. You will believe me when the door opens—"

Not bloody likely, King thought to himself.

This was getting stranger and stranger, and he desperately wanted Sir Manfred to appear and make sense of it. He felt like the mental equivalent of a man running at full speed downhill in the middle of an avalanche. The effort was enough to crack your skull, but if you hesitated you'd be swept under and ground into sausage meat.

The door opened. The impassive *khansama* stood there. King waited for an instant for him to open his mouth and speak, then realized what was about to happen. The man did open his mouth, slightly, but it was blood that welled out rather than words. He pitched forward like a toppling tree, and hit with a sodden thump, lying slack. There was blood on his hands as well, and several short, finned metal darts stood out from his back. The Lancer officer didn't recognize the darts, or know what sort of weapon threw them except that it was probably very quiet. The butler was extremely dead nonetheless.

Narayan Singh came smoothly to his feet, the blade of his *tulwar* flicking out with a snap. He thrust his left hand into the pocket of his tunic; the cloth writhed for a moment, and when he pulled the hand out again he was wearing a skeletal metal gauntlet with long, curved blades over the fingers—what those who used it called *tiger claws*. King reached under the skirt of his *kurta*, pulled out the heavy pistol, and tossed it into his left hand, and drew the sword with his right. His eyes met the Sikh's, and they gave identical slight nods.

The open door showed a stretch of hallway and a stair leading upward, dim and dark under the light of ceiling lamps covered in lacy brass fretwork. King stepped to the entrance and took a deep breath.

Kuch dar nahin hai, he thought as he bent slightly—you were a little less likely to attract the eye that way—and moved his head out into the open, looking both ways to scan the corridor. *There is no such thing as fear.*

"Clear," he said.

This was nothing like mounted combat, and not much like skirmishing on foot. It *was* quite a bit like street fighting—through the jumbled, close-packed, stone-built houses of a big Afghan village, for instance.

Narayan Singh went first, running lightly—he might have heavy feet by Pathan standards, but not by anyone else's. King followed, putting his back to the doorless wall and coming along behind crabwise, covering their rear. He was aware of the woman following them—the Russian woman? Yasmini was an Indian name, or Persian. The knowledge was pushed to a corner of his mind, lost in the total focus of the moment. Narayan went up the stairs in four swift bounds, crouching as he rose where an upright man would have shown above the floor of the second story. Then, very cautiously, he raised his head—

Crack.

The robed woman had pulled a light pistol from her garment and fired. Acrid smoke jetted from the muzzle. Narayan dropped; for a frozen instant King thought that she had shot him. Then a black-clad body toppled down toward the Sikh, thrashing. He had just enough time for a fleeting moment of astonishment; the woman was holding the pistol in a clumsy two-handed grip, and she'd fired *with her eyes closed.*

Then there was no time for anything at all. A stubby gunlike thing slithered down the steps, dropped by the dying man who'd been about to shoot Narayan. Another black-clad figure vaulted the railing beside the stairwell on the second floor, dropping down toward the Sikh and slashing with a straight one-edged sword.

"*Rung ho!*" Narayan Singh shouted.

There was an unmusical *skrinngg* as the Sikh caught the sword on his saber and punched the tiger claws into the man's belly, turning and throwing him down toward King. The Lancer stamped down hard on the man's neck as he passed it going upward, using it as a fulcrum to swing himself backward. That put his back to the risers of the stairs, looking up to the rear of the stairwell—where a third black-clad figure was raising his hand to throw something, something round that glittered.

CRACK!

The big Webley bucked against the muscles of his left hand; his right caught his own weight. He fired twice more; the range was no more than fifteen feet. The last bullet clipped the top of the man's head and flipped him backward as if he'd been kicked in the face by a horse. King still grimaced—he'd been aiming for the center of mass. Nothing more moved, nothing but the heels of the man he'd shot drumming for a moment on the floor, muffled by the carpet. The woman in the *burqua* was coming up the stairs behind him; he could hear her panting slightly as she climbed, lifting the long skirts of the tentlike garment in both hands—one of them still gripping the little Adams revolver.

She can dress how she likes, he thought with some splinter of his mind. Her shot had saved both their lives. *Not to mention doing it with eyes wide shut.*

King flipped himself back to his feet and passed Narayan Singh. The upper corridor had windows that showed an interior courtyard or light well; from the looks of it, the passageway went around all four sides, with a series of doors opening onto rooms spaced against the outer wall of the building. A quick glance through a window showed that the courtyard was empty save for a few benches set on the stone pavement, shadowed and still in the dim light that shone through a few windows.

One of the iron-framed glass panels was missing. King bent to take a quick look while Narayan Singh poised behind him, keeping the whole corridor in view as far as the corners at either end. Someone had cut a circle through the glass, removed it, and opened the simple lever-latch that held the window closed. King's eyebrows went up; he leaned out the opened window and saw a long slender cord dangling down from the roof.

"Well, is it the stranglers or the *hashasshin*, *huzoor*?" Narayan Singh murmured, a hint of harsh amusement in his gravelly voice.

"Neither," King said.

His mind played back the brief deadly scrimmage now past, despite the tearing need for haste—it was a wonder that the shots hadn't already brought attention; perhaps all the regular occupants of this building had gone home. They *were* civil servants, after all.

Their dead enemies had been dressed in black cloth jackets and breeches, with hooded masks that covered all of their faces save for a slit across the eyes. He didn't recognize their gear or weapons, either.

Yet another team in on the kill-the-Kings-and-their-friends tournament, he thought. *Now, which of these doors gives on Warburton's—*

"Here," Yasmini said. She wavered a little. "Here, quickly!"

The door was closed, and thick; there was a chance that nobody within had noticed the sounds from outside, that they were relying on their trio of killers to guard the entrance.

King hesitated for a second. *There's a time to be subtle, and a time to bloody well smash things up,* he decided. If Warburton was alive, he needed to be kept that way, and there was no known method of bringing a dead man back to life. *This is the latter sort of occasion—speed and impetus, Athelstane, like a good Lancer.*

Narayan Singh braced himself against the wall opposite the door, and King put his hand to the latch.

"Wait a second . . . a second more—" Yasmini's voice was a half chant. "Now!"

"*Chalo!*" King said. *Go!*

In the same motion he flung the heavy teakwood portal inward, throwing his shoulder against it with all the power of his legs and weight behind it. There had been a man standing on the other side, waiting where the opening door would hide him and let him strike at the back of anyone innocently coming through. That would have been the plan; in fact, he wasn't going to be doing anything of the kind. The door had struck like a giant flyswatter, slamming him into the plastered stone of the office wall and rebounding.

King followed the door with smooth speed, stepping in and to the right with his sword poised across his chest ready to parry, thrust, or make a backhand cut. The door guarded his back, and his pistol fanned across the room, looking for targets. Narayan Singh followed on his heels, breaking left and poised to attack.

The outer part of the office had been separated from the interior by a carved screen; from the two desks, it had served as working space for secretaries or assistants. The screen was lying across one of the desks now, giving an excellent view of the inner room. One man was kneeling there, right hand pressed to his right side where blood leaked onto his white high-collared jacket; his turban had been knocked off, and there was more blood on his face.

Above him on the wall a painting—it was either a very good copy
of Alma-Tadema's last work, *Sita and Ravanna*, or the priceless original—had been swung back to reveal a safe.

Two other men stood beside him, one holding his collar—an Imperial by his looks, *sahib-log*, in expensive civilian clothes, including a
natty cloth-of-gold turban. The other man was big but nondescript—
until you saw his face, and the eye patch turned up above his blue left
eye. Three more of the black-clad men stood closer to the door, already wheeling and bringing up short thick-bodied weapons vaguely
like shotguns.

"Go!" King said crisply.

Narayan Singh obeyed like a sprinter coming up out of the starting blocks. King leveled his revolver and fired, working the stiff
double-action, letting the weight of the weapon bring the muzzle
down again to aim. His second shot hit the dart-throwing weapon one
of the black-clads held and ricocheted away with a murderous wasp-
buzz, spinning the man around; the third punched into his throat.

The Sikh was on the other before he could shoot; the enemy
blocked a *tulwar* slash with the dart-thrower, skipped backward, and
drew the sword slung across his back with both hands. King fired twice
more before the Webley clicked empty. Neither bullet struck the
black-clad bringing his dart gun to his shoulder and taking careful
aim.

Damn all pistols! he thought, beginning a doomed charge. *Morituri
te salutamas.*

Another, lighter pistol went *crack-crack-crack!* And then *click!*

The *burqua*-clad woman was just behind him, firing two-handed
and blind again. All three shots punched into the man who'd been
about to kill King, and all three struck his chest within palm's width of
each other. He fell limply forward, like a sack of grain thrown from a
wagon.

The two men who'd been standing over Warburton threw him
aside. One—the Imperial—drew himself up and spoke:

"Stop this immediately, in the King-Emperor's name! I am
Richard Allenby of the Political Service, and I require you to lay down
your arms at once!"

"You sodding *traitor!*" King roared.

Allenby—if that was his name—skipped back just in time to avoid a backhand chop that would probably have lifted his head from his shoulders, and would most certainly have killed him. He drew his own sword, but it was a flash out of the corner of his eye that drew King around. Training for the melee saved him, the sort of engagement where you had to watch all around or take a blade in the back of the neck. Steel rasped on steel as he made a frantic parry and gave ground across carpet littered with fallen papers and bodies and inkwells.

It was the man with the turned-up eye patch—the eye it would have covered was a cold light blue in a high-cheeked, snub-nosed face. It lit as the man recognized King.

"So," he said. "*Spacebo* for the gift of your presence. My name is Count Vladimir Obromovich Ignatieff, Captain King. Now I will kill you myself—and save the Czar much gold!"

This is the man who killed my father, King realized with a sudden thrill. And killed poor brave little Hasamurti, and threatened his sister, and sent hired murderers to invade his home. Rage flashed through him, not hot but cold and chill.

It calmed him, and he met the whirlwind attack with an economical set of parries. He backed, careful on the cramped uncertain footing, taking the man's measure as the blades swung and glittered in the lamplight. Feeling for him through the ringing impacts of steel on steel, and the way the blows shivered up through the hilt and into his wrist. The Czar's agent was a good aggressive swordsman, experienced, fearless, very strong, and quick—but King was at least twenty years younger, a little taller, with an edge in reach and speed.

Right, you swine, he thought, and went in to kill.

The Russian's eyes went a little wider as King cut right and left from the wrist, the blade of his curved *tulwar* a horizontal silver-blue blur. Ignatieff parried with a *ting . . . tang* of steel, backing as King came in foot and hand, lunging to take advantage of his reach. That parry turned into a corps-à-corps, the hilts of the sabers locked as they strained against each other. Ignatieff combined it with a knee to the groin and a left-handed punch to the face, but Ranjit Singh and the master-at-arms of the Peshawar Lancers had been well up to those tricks—neither had been concerned with academic niceties. King caught the knee on his thigh and the fist in his left hand, gripping and squeezing as he pushed back.

The locked blades bent back toward the fixed snarl on the Russian's sweat-slick face, and King could smell the vodka on his breath as the two men pushed against each other like rams in rutting season, feet skidding and churning. His own breath came in long gasps; his enemy was horse-strong, and their straining was exerting enough force to uproot young trees. Then Ignatieff gave way all at once, pitching himself backward in an acrobat's roll. King launched off the coiled spring of his left leg, forward to run him through as he recovered . . . and had to turn that into a cat-agile upward leap as the Russian came to one knee and slashed horizontally in a hocking stroke. The steel hissed beneath the soles of his boots; he cut downward at the older man's head as he landed.

Ignatieff caught the sword on his, but the backs of the crossed blades struck his head glancingly, knocking off his *pugaree*. Close-cropped gray-blond hair showed beneath as the Russian leapt back again, landing in a crouch, then lunging forward immediately with a running thrust.

King pirouetted like a dancer, knocking the sword aside with his own blade and looping the motion over into a cut at his enemy's spine as he went by. Ignatieff turned it with a sweep of his blade behind himself as he passed, then pivoting and backing—content to defend for now. The Lancer saw Allenby behind him. Somehow Warburton had grabbed the traitor around the legs, hanging on doggedly as the other man pounded at him with fist and sword hilt, only releasing his grip when the saber slashed at him.

Warburton slumped to the floor. Allenby ran out, heedlessly pushing Yasmini aside; she fell also, bonelessly limp. Ignatieff hadn't seen her until that moment; he started when he did, almost dropping his guard and taking a slash on his forearm as he recovered.

"Bitch!" he hissed in Russian.

Outside, Allenby's voice rose to a bawling yell, calling for a *daffadar* and his squad, which must mean for police or troops; that was an official rank. *They* wouldn't know who was the honest man here; Allenby could have told them anything.

Ignatieff heard, and smiled despite the panting effort of the fight. "I will eat your liver while you still live to see it," he bit out. "And the bitch's, too. Here, and then again forever in Hell."

"You go first," King replied, and attacked again.

That nearly left him dead on a stop-thrust. Ignatieff followed it up with a flurry of cuts, rocking the Lancer back on his heels, then spat into his eyes and flung the sword. King batted it out of the air with his, but that gave the Russian time enough to dodge out the door.

With a wrenching effort of will, King stopped himself from following. Instead he wheeled, just in time to see Narayan Singh's opponent spin away with half his face flayed off by a backhand cut.

"Wa Guru-ji ko futteh!" the Sikh roared and lunged; his point tented out through the cloth on the man's back. His foe's long straight-bladed sword—it looked like a Nipponese *katana* save for the lack of curve—dropped from nerveless hands. Silence fell, echoing in ears still ringing with the discordant music of steel on steel.

"Here," a weak voice said.

King knelt by Warburton's side. The older man had a deep wound in the flank, rib deep or worse; a long shallow slash on his back, and enough bruises and cuts about the face and arms to concern a hospital. Both eyes were swelling shut, and half the fingernails were missing from his left hand, their places raw and oozing red.

"Merciful Krishna!" King swore.

Warburton managed a smile, although his eyes were wandering. "Tried to make me tell them . . . combination of the safe." A shake of his head. "Nothing there since . . . couldn't say that, or they'd have finished me." Another shake, harder, and a wince. "Get us out—Allenby'll see us dead . . . explain it all later, blame it on you or me or Ignatieff . . . *quickly.*"

Narayan Singh limped up, and King raised his head in quick alarm.

"Stab in the leg, *sahib*," the Sikh said. "And I would not have thought a sword could be well wielded with two hands, so."

"Must get . . . out," Warburton said again; he was gray, and his eyes wandered.

There was noise growing in the street, men's voices shouting. The Sikh crouched—carefully, for the cloth tied around his leg was sodden red—and gave the Political's wounds rough field treatment. King ripped a scrap of black cloth off one of the dead men and cleaned his sword, sheathing it with a snap and a feeling of enormous frustration. The face beneath the mask was amber-colored, with slanted eyes.

Oh, bloody hell, he thought, spilling the spent brass from his pistol round by round and reloading. *Nipponese. Who's next? Dom Pedro's gaucho cavalry trying to run me down with bolas? How the hell did that Russian* banchut *get all these different badmashes on my trail?*

"Damn, I *had* the bugger," he whispered savagely. Then: "Let's be going then. Over the roofs, it'll have to be. Until this devil's mess is sorted out, we can—"

"*Sahib.*" Narayan's voice was flat. "Let there be no foolishness. I cannot run with this wound; in a few minutes it will stiffen, and I will not be able to stand. You can perhaps bear one wounded man along the way, if he be a small man and slight. You cannot bear me, who weighs more than you. Me they will not kill; I am merely a *daffadar,* an orderly who can say he followed orders. And if they do slay me, that is my *karman;* and more hangs on this matter than either of our lives— more even than revenge for our fathers. There is treason at work here, and traitors within the Raj. They must be rooted out. You know this as well as I, *bhai.* Go. Go *now.*"

"Krishna, you have a bad habit of being right," King said. His eyes fell on Yasmini. "You, woman. Take off that blasted tent. Are you coming, or not?"

Because much as I'd like to make sure you're properly questioned, I can't carry you. Not if I'm going to fetch along this damned Political.

"Yes." A nod of the head. "I did not know the Master would be here. I did not see that—"

"Get moving, you stupid bint!" To Narayan Singh: "*Bhai,* I swear that you'll either be rescued, or avenged."

The Sikh nodded, managed a grim smile, and sank back into a chair. King bent, lifted the semiconscious Warburton over his shoulder, and headed out into the corridor with his pistol ready. Behind him, scarcely noticed, Yasmini followed.

Chapter Twelve

Narayan Singh limped over to the door that gave on the corridor and slammed it closed, bracing it with several pieces of furniture. He was grinning slightly by the time he finished; partly with pain, partly at satisfaction at having gotten the *sahib* and his precious cargo on their way. He looked around at the bodies.

And partly at my own part, he thought, noting the bodies gashed by his saber or tiger claws. *May God grant the* pitaji *hears of this!* He had *some* hope of telling it himself, if not much.

Heavy feet sounded on the staircase; booted feet, official feet. Having led parties after defaulters and rounded up men lost in the stews in Peshawar town often enough, he recognized the sound. The barking of orders was familiar enough as well, and then from the sudden oath there was someone outside who understood the smell of violent death.

"You inside!" a voice bawled, in Punjabi-accented Hindi. "Open up, in the King-Emperor's name!"

"All honor to the Padishah," Narayan bawled back. "And if you want us, you'll have to come in and take us! *Sahib*, lie quiet or your wound will begin to bleed again! Woman, be silent!"

He grinned again at that, the more so when he recognized Allenby's voice raised in command. Let the traitor think he'd caught them all here. The Sikh limped over to the window, risked a quick glimpse outside. The street had emptied—it was amazing how the news of an official raid could spread—but there was a line of men cordoning off the entrance, men in blue uniforms armed with old-style Martini-Metford rifles . . . no, with a modified type that threw soft round balls. They handled them clumsily. *Polis* then, of the Delhi City force. More accustomed to clubs than firearms, and issued guns only in rare emergencies. One loosed off a shot at the movement in the window. The soft metal went *wtinggg* off the stone as he jerked his head back, and he heard an underofficer screaming abuse at the luckless *konstabeel*.

Light brightened—they had brought floods, then. More tramping on the stairs, and several heavy shoulders thudded against the boards, repeating the process amid cries of pain and blasphemies and assurances to the Political Service agent *sahib* that the pox-ridden door was indeed both strong, and locked. Narayan Singh stifled a chuckle and limped to the desk to find water and drink it in great gulps, lest loss of blood make him light-headed. More shouts and clamor arose from outside in the street, and a ladder thudded against the window.

He waited until trembles and jerks told him it was full of climbing *polis*, then crouched—wounded leg stiffly outstretched—put the point of his sword against the left-hand pole of the ladder, and pushed hard. Sideways, so as not to fight the weight of half a dozen men; the outside stonework of Metcalfe House was smooth. A chorus of yells ended in a crash and screaming; this time he chuckled aloud. He had been clubbed over the head once or twice by city *polis*, when seeking amusement outside the cantonment of Peshawar town.

Next someone tried to fire a stink bomb through the window. Hopping agilely over, the Sikh scooped it up on a piece of broken board and threw it back out, bringing more yells. At last the sound of heavy panting came from the inner corridor, and a voice shouting:

"As close as you can to this wall, brothers, then all together."

Ah, Narayan thought. *A doorknocker.*

A billet of cast iron, with attached handles, and just the thing for breaking down doors—the Army used them occasionally; they were handy in street fighting. He thoughtfully turned up a lamp and waited in the center of the room, laying his saber at his feet. The door shuddered under the rhythmic hammer of the metal ram, although there could not be much room to swing it—only six feet or so between the outer panels of the door and the inner wall of the building. That was enough, with strong men and determination, but every moment was another for Captain King *sahib* to make his escape.

When the hinges came loose there was another confused shoving, as men tried to push the furniture clear without exposing their hands to steel; they knew a dangerous Sikh and a saber were within, at the least, and they had seen the bodies and bullet marks without. When it fell down at last three men crowded through, all of them leveling guns. Those *polis* longarms were designed to be as nonlethal as a firearm could be, used mostly for guarding prisoners or occasionally to put down a riot between faiths or castes. Narayan Singh still didn't care to be shot by several of them, if he could avoid it.

"Do not shoot!" he said crisply. "I make no resistance to arrest!"

The *konstabeels* fanned out to let more of their men into the room, looking about in awe at the tumbled destruction and dead black-clad bodies. One youngster with only the beginnings of a beard gulped noisily and turned to vomit—Narayan felt an abstract sympathy, for the *polis* were only obeying what they thought were lawful orders, and upholding the city's peace. Allenby came through far from the first, with two men in plainclothes behind him—Narayan could sense that they were *his* men, not commandeered from the city force—and more police behind.

Before the *Angrezi* traitor could speak, Narayan said in a loud, carrying voice:

"I am *Daffadar* Narayan Singh, Second Squadron, Peshawar Lancers—a soldier of the Raj! I demand that I be taken to the military prison in the Red Fort for examination by the Imperial Army's own police. You civil *konstabeels* have no jurisdiction over me!"

There was nobody of the *polis* here higher in rank than a non-commissioned man that he could see. Head-butting—what in English they called a pissing match—between the civil and military police was an old story in any town with a substantial garrison, and nowhere more so than in Delhi, from what he had heard. The policemen would hesitate to get involved in such, without orders.

Unfortunately, Allenby had thought of that—and they would be even less likely to defy orders from a *sahib* of the Political Service.

"This man is a spy and a traitor," he snapped, drawing his pistol.

He didn't train it at the Sikh, but Narayan could sense a trembling willingness to kill, even before witnesses. He narrowed his eyes: Was it worthwhile to court that, to discredit the traitor? *Not quite. There is the* E-rus, *and he may have more tools within the Raj. I must live as long as I can.*

"Take him," Allenby went on.

The two men in plainclothes grabbed Narayan's hands and twisted them behind him for the lockbars as Allenby's eyes checked over the room.

"Where is King, and the girl?" he snapped.

"Where is the *E-rus* spy who is your master?" Narayan said in response—and loudly.

Allenby did strike then; a skillful blow alongside the head with the butt of his pistol, aiming below the turban that would have cushioned a clumsy strike. Narayan sagged as the world went gray; he was barely conscious as he was hustled outside into a closed *gharri*—two-wheeled horse cart—and the hooves clopped away on the pavement.

Warburton was still mumbling as King jogged up the stairs to the fourth floor and the flat roof; trying to tell him important details, the Lancer supposed, but it was a bloody nuisance. The Russian woman was staggering a bit now, despite being free of the *burqua;* underneath it she wore a perfectly ordinary *shalwar qamiz,* tunic-and-pjamy-trousers suit, like a third of the women in Delhi. She'd retained the hood and face veil though, merely wrapping them tighter and taking a turn of the fabric around her neck. When she leaned close to help him with the trapdoor he caught a glimpse of eyes pale green rimmed in silver-gilt blue . . . and a green, musky scent he recognized.

Bhang lassi, potent and only marginally legal—slipping it onto the menu and then robbing the blissfully helpless customer was a standard trick of the shadier establishments in the red-light district.

Merciful Krishna, he thought. *She's drugged to the gills!*

No wonder she staggered now and then . . . although he'd never known *bhang* in any form to improve the user's shooting.

The worst of it was that Warburton was still bleeding, and gray with shock. King had seen far too many badly wounded men to doubt that the Political would die unless he had expert care soon; the baronet wasn't a young man, either. That left exactly one choice. He looked up at the moon reflexively, then at the silhouette of the buildings to the west. That left only one matter unsettled—

He crept to the edge of the roof, where the low parapet gave him a bit of shelter. *Yes, the* polis, *behind the game as usual,* he thought; constables were pushing their way through the throng. There he carefully cleared his throat, filled his chest, and made a sound between his teeth that Ranjit Singh had taught him—one the old Sikh had learned on the frontier, long ago. Not loud, more of a sigh than a whistle; the sort of sound a nightjar might make, settling down to rest in a nest of cypress trees by a spring. It wasn't a sound that belonged here in Delhi, with the crowds and the glare of the gaslight, but it still carried. Not as far as it would have amid the crags and dry nullahs and stony slopes of the Border, under the bright frosting of mountain stars, but far enough; Ibrahim Khan was only a hundred yards away.

King saw a *pugaree*-clad head rise from where the Pathan squatted next to the horses by the mouth of an ally. Then it dropped again, and he looked away. A second later the same moaning sigh came drifting up to him; one of the handy things about the signal was that you could make it without seeming to move your lips, and pitch your voice so that it didn't sound as if it came from anywhere near you. If you had the knack; he'd never mastered that particular trick himself, but he knew about it.

Ibrahim Khan rose casually, spat, scratched himself, and set about tightening the girths on the horses' saddles before he ambled off—the picture of some *sais*-groom on a harmless errand.

"Quickly," Yasmini said, steady again but with that otherworldly note still in her voice. "Quickly; they come. The men from Nippon. They must not see us, nor the armsmen of your Czar."

That was easier said than done, especially with a bleeding, semiconscious man dressed in white draped over your shoulder. King checked the width; doable, but only just. Easy by himself, but he wasn't alone. He backed up, carefully blanked every thought from his mind—thoughts of whether the police or the Nipponese whatever-they-were would get to Narayan Singh first—controlled his breathing. *Now.*

He ran lightly despite the weight of a middle-sized man draped across his back; Athelstane King had been awarded half a dozen ribbons for track and field at United Services, and he mentally blessed Ranjit Singh and those detested fifty-pound sacks of wet sand he'd borne on his back as he ran up mountainsides. Faster, faster—throw your weight forward, like a swinging ball on a chain out across the chasm. And *leap.*

In the air, Warburton seemed to turn to a boneless bag of lead shot, crushing him down. The penalty for failing the long jump at school hadn't been a four-story fall and a broken spine, either. For a long moment he hung suspended in the darkness over the alleyway, and then the opposite roof was rushing at him. His feet touched; for a long second he was certain the load on his back was going to throw him backward to his death, and then his crouch brought the weight back over the balls of his feet. He hopped down from the parapet, thanking the Gods that it was too late in the year for people to be sleeping on their roofs, and laid the Political down.

Now, we see whether the Woman of Mystery can jump even in the midst of hempen bliss, King thought grimly. He owed her a debt—but there were still far too many questions.

"The first of which is whether she gets here or strikes the pavement with a wet smacking sound," he muttered, turning and bracing himself against the parapet with one knee. That way he could reach a hand far out and grab—

Yasmini was a blur of taupe fabric against the blackness of Metcalfe House's roof. Then she ran toward him. *Moving fairly quickly, but she's small—those short legs—*

His hand stretched out over the dark abyss of the alley. Yasmini flew straight past it, checked herself on the parapet with a cat-light touch of the feet, then rolled forward and to her feet. King blinked.

"My master wished me to be able to accompany him in hard places," she whispered. "Being valuable to him, you see. So I was trained. This way."

King nodded numbly, took up his burden, and followed. The other side of this building proved to have an iron staircase down to the alleyway. King followed Yasmini down it, and found her swaying and wide-eyed again at the exit.

"Right," he said. The way she was porpoising in and out of full consciousness meant they had to use another trick to get to refuge.

King removed his turban. His own hair was cropped, but not to the inch-length fuzz of Warburton's, and he wasn't blond—that was rare enough even among *sahib-log* to attract at least casual attention. He put the length of tight-wound cotton on the smaller man's head, tugged at it artistically to give it an air of sleazy disarray, and then pulled out a flask from a hip pocket.

"Got to get the smell right," he muttered, and poured a generous slug over the older man's head and shoulders. "You . . . Yasmini, isn't it? Get on his other side and help prop him up."

Warburton woke a little at the sting of the liquor. Yasmini put his left arm over her shoulders, but the slight man was still so much taller than she that it was her own arm around his waist that helped with the weight. King led them out into the nighttime crowd, singing a love ballad in a slurred voice. The trio drew stares as they staggered down the sidewalk, but those eyes were amused or disapproving; most were too casual to notice the state of Warburton's face, the more so as his head hung down limply. Night helped, and the flickering of the gas lamps, and the fact that they had only a block and a half to go.

Still, the darkness of the alleyway was like a wash of relief—rather like getting into the gateway of a fort, when you were being sniped at from the hills around. The safety might be illusory—he'd seen a commanding officer go down with a slug in the brain while saluting the flag as the trumpets sounded evening retreat on a parade ground—but the *feeling* was real.

He found Ibrahim Khan there, too, snarling and with his *chora* half-drawn as he argued with someone behind a stout door with a small grilled opening and a tiny silver scroll mounted on the wall beside it. The Pathan wheeled as King and Yasmini came up, his eyes going wide in the gloom.

"The Sikh?" he said.

"Taken," King answered shortly. A brief flicker of dismay went across the Muslim's face, to be hidden by a shrug. "And so we will be, if we do not find shelter soon."

"These Sons of Mortality will not open," Ibrahim said. "I should break down the door, and show the dogs and sons of owls how the Dongala Khel repay discourtesy!"

"Peace," King said. Then to the door: "I am Captain Athelstane King; this Pathan is my follower. I have an injured man here, and I am pursued. Will Elias bar-Binyamin give me shelter, or not?"

The Lancer could see a flicker of movement behind the door, and a beam of light stabbed out, for an instant bright enough to hurt eyes that had adapted to the alleyway's murk. Then he heard a bar being shot back and breathed a silent sigh of relief. The light dimmed, and the door swung open.

"Quickly," a backlit figure said.

I'm getting a little sick of being told to do things quickly, King thought, with a hint of whimsical amusement. Although this was a man's voice, in Hindi with a trace of an odd nasal accent.

"Quickly," the figure repeated. "My man will take the horses. In!"

A figure darted out of the door as King edged in, scooping Warburton up again. Yasmini and Ibrahim Khan followed, the Pathan looking about him with interest and taking in the woman out of the corner of his eye. The light turned up again as the door *thunked* shut and a hand shot the bar home again.

King raised a brow in surprise. The man confronting him was no more than middle-aged, burly and thick-shouldered in an expensive striped kaftan, with a skullcap on the back of his balding head and side curls framing a square-cut beard of black with gray streaks running down from the corners of his mouth. One hand held a kerosene lantern. The other had a heavy pistol, held with a practiced steadiness on King's midriff. Ibrahim's hand flashed toward his hilt, then froze as he saw two other men step out of the shadows—younger, and with double-barreled shotguns in their hands, but with a strong family resemblance to the man with the lamp.

That one held the light high, then nodded slowly. "You are King," he said, setting the gun down on a counter. "Mordekai—Binyamin— see to the wounded man. *Chalo!*"

"You know me, sir?" King asked courteously, as the two . . . sons?—vanished into the gloom and returned seconds later with a canvas-and-poles stretcher.

"I knew your father, quite well; and you are his image." The older man's face cocked to one side. "A little taller, a little less narrow in the face."

"Ah . . . surely you aren't Mr. Bar-Binyamin?"

The man laughed. "My name is David; Elias is *my* father. Who will be anxious to meet you. Come."

"Confess, spy bastard! Confess!"

A hand gripped the back of Narayan Singh's neck and forced his face into the tub of water. He didn't bother to struggle; the bonds clamping his wrists behind his back were iron, those that held him to the stool were strong, and the stool itself was bolted to the brick floor of the cellar. This time he merely waited a minute until the strength of his will had gathered, and then drew the water deliberately into his lungs.

The liquid was like cold itching fire in his chest. When the man behind him realized what he was doing he pulled the Sikh's head out of the water instantly, backing off as the young man spewed liquid and went into a racking coughing fit that lasted for minutes. When his head hung gasping above the tub the other interrogator came forward and wiped his face with a towel, speaking soothingly in Punjabi:

"Why do you suffer so for this *sahib-log* traitor who left you to die? Don't you realize that he is the one who causes you pain? We could give you some time to think about things—perhaps food, and a cigarette? We already have the traitor, and he has told us everything. We merely need you to corroborate what we already know."

Narayan Singh was naked save for a loincloth; his thick-muscled limbs were heavily matted with a furze almost like fur, and his long black hair lay in a sodden mass across his shoulders and chest. His beard was similarly tangled. That gave the white teeth of his sneer even more the appearance of a bear's snarl.

"Are you a Sikh, then?" he said to the man who'd been assigned to play the sympathetic part in the interrogation.

Did the fools not realize that he'd conducted questioning of captives himself? he thought. That trick was older than the hills. So was trying to convince a man his comrades had already betrayed him. He'd seen it done better.

"Aye," the man said in reply to his prisoner's question. He might well be one, from the uncut beard and the shape of his turban. "I, too, am of the *khasla*, the Pure, for six generations."

Narayan managed a harsh laugh. "Then if you must be the dog of a traitor, could you not pick a traitor who is also a man? I saw your Allenby *sahib*"—he loaded the term of respect with bottomless scorn—"cringe like a whipped dog himself when the steel was out, and my officer and I fought the *E-rus* and his minions."

"Where did your officer go, when he abandoned *you*?" the man said.

"Ask him, if he has told you all," Narayan Singh said.

"We need to check the stories."

"You need to find him, and you will not," Narayan Singh sneered. "And I would not know where he went, even if I *wished* to tell you."

The Sikh interrogator stepped back from him with a sigh. "If you persist with these lies," he said calmly, "there is nothing I can do to help you."

The other man came forward eagerly, stripped to the waist. He was massively built, heavier than Narayan, and only a stone or two of it was fat. His skin and shaven head glistened a gunmetal blue-black; from somewhere in the Dravidian south, the Sikh Lancer thought, for his features were sharp-cut, without the bluntness of an African. He had that accent in his Hindi, too.

"The pins?" the black man said. "Or the bed could be made ready for a guest."

He nodded to the iron bedstead in a corner: the one with the shackles at the corners, and a layer of charcoal beneath ready for lighting.

"No," the other replied. "Allenby *sahib* was most particular—no serious marks. Nothing that could not be accounted for by his wound. Not yet. Perhaps later, if he proves obdurate."

The Dravidian gave a grunt of frustration. The back of one meaty hand lashed across Narayan Singh's face, cutting the inside of his mouth against his teeth. The Lancer spat blood and saliva on the man's boots, bringing a curse and another blow.

"Confess, spy bastard! Where are the documents your master stole?"

"I know nothing of any *kitubs*," Narayan said stolidly. *They cannot break my will quickly*, he thought with grim patience. *Not in time to catch the* sahib.

The Dravidian grabbed a handful of flesh over the bandaged stab wound in the Sikh's thigh and twisted. Despite his clenched jaw a raw grunt of agony forced its way between his lips; the flesh there was puffy and inflamed from lack of proper treatment. Colors danced before his eyes, and it was a minute before he could feel the hand slapping his face.

"Confess, spy bastard! Confess! The law will have no mercy if you do not confess!"

Narayan raised his head. "I am a *daffadar* of the Imperial Army," he said thickly—his lips were swelling, and the pain in his leg distracted him like a shrilling behind the eyes. "I know the law; you could not treat even a sweeper thus without breaking it! And a soldier may be held only in a military prison, tried only by court-martial. This is not even a den of the civilian *polis.*"

He jerked his head in a gesture of contempt. The place of his imprisonment was a brick-lined cellar, big and dim but low-built; there were small iron-barred windows with thick dusty glass at one side along the ceiling giving out onto street level, and an iron door built into one wall. It smelled of damp brick, and faintly of drains. Besides the instruments of pain it held a wall rack of crisscrossed boards, a type he recognized from a juvenile adventure at Rexin Manor—one used to store wine bottles on their sides. He and King had stolen in there one *Holi* festival when they were eleven, and drunk themselves silly. How the *pitaji* had beaten him! Punishment came separately for Athelstane King, of course, but he'd noted a caution in the young lord's sitting down or backing a horse for a week afterward.

"This is some place of your master's," Narayan Singh said. "You dare not take me before the *polis* or a court."

The Sikh interrogator sighed again. "You are held under the Defense of the Realm Act," he said. "Regular procedures do not apply—I'm afraid you are alone, quite alone."

"And this will be the place of your death, if you do not confess!" the Dravidian said. Then to his companion: "If he loves to swim"—a nod toward the half-barrel tub of water—"perhaps he will enjoy a dance upon air less."

The Sikh interrogator shrugged. "I wish we could spare him. But if he will not listen to reason . . ."

The two men unbound him from the stool—cautiously. They were both strong, though, and the clamp of their hands on his arms was like living metal. The Dravidian ran an eyelock on the end of a rope through the bar-and-loop that held his wrists, and then both heaved on the other end. It ran over a hook set into one of the teak rafters that spanned the ceiling; weight came onto the arms and the already tight-stretched muscles of his shoulders. He clenched his teeth against it; the pain was not so bad all at once . . . but he knew he might hang there forever, as far as these two or their master were concerned.

"Narayan Singh will remember your face," he said to the dark man.

"He will have to take a *tikut* and wait in line," the man replied, laughing, and slammed his fist into the sopping red bandage on the Sikh's leg, laughing again as Narayan twisted in midair. Then he bent and set a thing like a pointed candlestick on the floor beneath the prisoner. "Perhaps you wish to stand," he said. "Stand on this, then, and relieve your pain. Come, *bhai*, let us leave the spy bastard to his thoughts."

The two men opened the iron door, giving him a glimpse of nothing but a stone-walled corridor. The door slammed with a hollow thud, taking the room's single lantern with them.

Bad, Narayan Singh thought, as darkness like hot felt fell across his eyes. *Without light, I cannot tell how time has passed.*

Then he strained his eyes to see the windows—surely that meant that it must be dark outside, also? It was hard to tell; jags of vivid color shot before his eyes anyway, and he was turning slowly. Water ran off him to drip on the floor, an added torment as his throat grew dry and the slow burning in his arms and joints swelled.

Without time, there was no ending.

King looked about him alertly as David bar-Elias led him into the building. This outer portion was drab enough—deliberately so, he thought. A man who was a Delhi agent for at least six Kashmiri *zamindars* that he knew of must be able to afford better than this. *This* was a simple long room with a counter, and shelves behind it bearing mysterious bundles and sacks. No different from a thousand or ten thousand other minor *banian*-merchant houses in Delhi.

There was a faint smell that didn't go with it, though. Something . . . *Yes, by Ganesha god of wisdom*, King thought. He recognized it from Ibrahim, when they first met—and from the bazaars of Peshawar and half a dozen places on or over the Border. Dried camel sweat soaked into cloth. And spices, and leather, and brass polish . . .

David cocked an eye at him. "A Jew learns not to make a show," he said. "It attracts the eye of tax collectors and bandits." He gave a massively expressive shrug. "If there is a difference."

The middle-aged man swung up a section of the counter and led King and Ibrahim through another door. That gave on a short corridor that ended in a staircase on one side and a space curtained with heavy ebony beads on the other.

"A room for you later," he said, nodding to the staircase. "For now, through here."

The ebony beads were cunningly carved, fitting together like a wooden jigsaw puzzle turned upright to make a wall. Light glinted through them, and they fell heavy and smooth around King as he pushed through. For a moment he stopped, shocked. Light came from several lanterns planted here and there, but they were lost in the vast shadowy dimness beyond, a warehouse that must extend clear from the Chandi Chowk to the Mukherji Marg just inside the Old City wall. And several blocks to either side, as well. A balcony ran around the inside, giving on to rooms behind. Before him was a maze, bales and bundles piled three times the height of a man's head snaking back beyond sight.

There were piles of carpets—not just Agra and Jaipur, but the unmistakable wine reds and blues of Isfahan and Tabriz in the Caliphate, and even some with the markings of Bohkhara and Samarkand in the Czar's dominions. Bundles of swords, plain Imperial-issue stirrup-hilted sabers and fantastic jeweled hilts that must be worth a fortune each, if they were genuine, and wavy-edged *kris*-blades from the Pirate Isles. Books, some modern, others scrolls made of palm leaves. Boxes of dried fruit—he saw one with the King brand on the rough poplar wood. Saddles, for horse and camel; the dusty finery of what must have been some maharaja's ceremonial elephant howdah. Tiger skins, leopard, a superb clouded leopard from the Himalayas. Tibetan devil masks; Chin silks—

And sitting cross-legged before a low table, a man. Old, the flesh grown stringy and gaunt, the long beard and side curls white. He wore a dark robe and a blue silk turban, and his face was like an ancient eagle's save for the eyes—deep, dark brown, clever and penetrating.

"Do you play chess, Captain King?" the old man said.

"Now and then," King replied.

"I played with your father," Elias bar-Binyamin said. "Sound, sound—a sound player. But too hasty."

Everyone on earth knew my father except me! King thought; but he nodded gravely and sank down on the cushion opposite the Jew. The old man's son sat beside him, silent and attentive, with a slight secret smile on his lips.

"I believe you also exchanged one of these with him," King said, fishing out the *tessera* and laying it down on the table with the inset chessboard, careful not to upset any of the pieces. Even then his gaze lingered on them for an instant—they appeared to be carved from white and black jade, and he'd never heard of the latter.

"Heh-yey, heh-yey," Elias sighed.

He reached into the neck of his robe and produced another rod of ivory. The fingers that fitted them together were gnarled, the knuckles standing out like walnuts; at some time several of them had been broken and healed crookedly. The shattered ends of the ivory fitted perfectly, and he pushed them toward King.

"Yes," he said. "Yes, I remember that—that day in the Khyber mouth—and my promise." The sharp brown eyes in the wrinkled face looked up at him. "Do you think a Jew keeps faith, then, like an *Angrezi* gentleman?"

King kept his face impassive. "I think that my father knew when a man was trustworthy," he said. "And so does my mother . . . and Ranjit Singh."

"Heh, keyh!" Elias chuckled suddenly, and his face became a child's for an instant. "Put me in my place, did you? Heh?"

"Not at all, sir," King said. As an afterthought: "St. Disraeli was a Jew, if I recall correctly."

"Poh. An *apikiros*," Elias said dismissively. "Heretic—apostate, you would say." Still, the remark seemed to have amused and pleased him at the same time. He went on: "A Pathan with you, I see," he said. "And a woman?"

"The Pathan is my man," King said. "On the hilt and the steel. The woman . . . her name is Yasmini. And I was hoping you could tell me about her."

Yasmini sank to her knees on the piled carpets. That put her face about on a level with King as he sat. Her hands came up, slowly, slowly, and unwrapped the hood and veil of the *burqua* from her face.

King watched closely. He'd been expecting something unusual, but even so his breath drew in a little in shock. *Elf, indeed,* was his first thought—something from the Rackham-illustrated book of *Legends from Lost Homeland* he'd read as a boy, an ancient heirloom a century and more old. Delicately triangular face, hair like palest gold, tiny nose, huge blue-rimmed green eyes—

Ibrahim Khan scrabbled backward in frank terror, forgetting for an instant that a warrior of the Dongala Khel feared nothing. Elias gasped aloud, and his son swore in a language unfamiliar and guttural. Yasmini seemed as startled herself, leaning forward to look at Elias.

"You have his eyes," she murmured in Russian. "Disraeli's eyes." Then she slumped bonelessly to the carpet. King leaned forward in alarm, touching fingers to her neck. The pulse was there, regular but a little faint, and slow.

"*Bhang lassi,*" he said in explanation. "She accosted me in the street just as I was about to enter . . ."

He went on to outline the events at Metcalfe House; no point in holding back, if he was going to trust these people at all. Several times during the story the younger Jew seemed about to interrupt, only to be checked by a wave of his father's hand. King brought the tale back to Yasmini at the end:

"Gave me a warning that saved my life, and saved it again several times over. By Krishna, though, she's strange!"

"Yey," Elias said. "Stranger than you think!"

Just then a woman came out with a tray; middle-aged and plump, dressed in Hindu fashion but not, King thought, of that people. Elias nodded in confirmation:

"My daughter-in-law, Rebekka," he said. "You must be hungry." He looked over at Ibrahim and spoke in the Pathan's tongue: "The food is clean for Muslims, if that concerns you." He turned his face back to King. "Eat, then. Be my guest, as your father was, and listen."

King obeyed; he felt the emptiness in his middle now, after the tension of combat and pursuit. The food was excellent, though not elaborate: minced lamb cooked with garlic, turmeric, and coriander, mixed with peas and tomatoes and served on basmati rice with naan for scooping, hot tea, and fruit to follow.

"The *tessera* . . . have you wondered why your father would exchange such a token with me, or I with him?"

King nodded cautiously.

"Heh. When your grandfather was alive, he made some investments. Not through me! But they nearly ruined him, ruined your family. Now . . . now I suspect that there were those who arranged it so. So be it, but he was on the verge of losing his land."

King concealed his shock, but not quite well enough. *Lose the land?*

That was . . . well, obviously not *impossible*, because it happened. *Disastrous* or *horrible to contemplate* came a lot closer. Rexin wasn't just an investment, or a source of income. It was the source of the Kings' *being*, and had been since the Exodus. Not least, it was a responsibility—who would look after the people of the manor, if not the Kings?

The old man laughed in a breathy chuckle: "Te-he-yay, that makes you jump, eh? We Jews have learned that the only safe wealth is the wealth you can take with you when you have to run."

He tapped a long finger to his forehead. "Best of all, what you keep here. But you *Angrezi*, you need to be rooted in a spot like a tree, even after you fled here to India. It took the very Sword of God to move you! So. I bought your grandfather's notes from the men who would have foreclosed on him, consolidated them . . . you would not be interested in the details. He paid me—he was an honest man. I made the conditions so that he *could* pay, with effort—I am an honest man, too, and your grandfather had always dealt fairly with me, and his father with my father. He swore that if ever he could return the favor, he would, or his kin after him."

The old man's son coughed and looked aside. "I'm afraid, Captain King," he said—in Imperial English, without the accent his father had, "that it was my own foolishness that compelled my father to ask for that favor of yours."

"Hey-ye-tai," Elias said, making a flapping gesture with his hands. "Foolishness is not wickedness—it was wickedness that took you."

He looked at King. "My son, my David here—my only son—was in Bokhara on business."

"*Bokhara?*" King said incredulously, looking at the younger Jew and raising his brows. "You're a braver man than I am, to dare going *there*."

Bokhara was the second city of the Czar's domains, after Samarkand; and while Samarkand was the seat of the court, Bokhara housed the head priests of the cult of Malik Nous. The name of the Black God's city was one to make men fear, from Damascus to the Yellow Sea.

"Heh!" Elias chuckled. "What will a Jew not risk—for trade—for knowledge—for family? David went for all three. The Russian *boyars* let us trade in their domains, or manage mines or collect rents for them—should they dirty their hands with ledgers? And some of us they let live there, free—free after a fashion—because we are useful if left to ourselves. They have learned that we Jews make poor slaves—as Pharaoh learned—and that we cross all borders; France-outre-mer, the Caliphate, the Empire, Dai-Nippon . . . even the Americas.

"And so some of us dwell in Bokhara. Of those some are of my family. They learned matters that the priests of Malik Nous, the Eaters of Men, the followers of Tchernobog, wished to keep secret. I offered ransom—sent David to bargain. And they seized him too—should they bother to keep faith with a dirty Jew, a *zhid* dog? They thought to squeeze me—to make me their tool here. Not merely by the threats of death or torment for my son. Other threats, to take my son's soul. They can change a man; that is their devils' skill. A Jew can face death when he must; how many of us have died for the Sanctification of the Name? But the Black God . . . that is another matter."

David spoke: "Your father rescued me," he said. "From the dungeons of the House of the Fallen. I lived, and I kept my mind. My self."

King shaped a silent whistle, and even in the press of present need felt a glow of pride. *That* was something he had to get the details on, someday. To go into the empire of evil, and the very heart of darkness . . .

I knew my father was a man of honor, he thought. He'd never doubted it, not when the track his life had made in the lives of others was plain to see. *But if he could do* that, *he was a man indeed!*

Elias nodded. "I was desperate. I went to him. And he agreed, knowing what his father had promised. When we crossed the border again, your father and I, I said that there was no more debt between us—that now I was in his, forever. He laughed, as he had laughed at death and worse, and said that now each was in the other's debt forever. So we broke the *tessera*."

The older man looked down at the table before him again. "Not long after, we learned of your father's death on the Border. Chess . . . young lordling, someone is playing chess indeed. A game against your family, and by a master player." His finger tipped over a knight. "A game across more than one generation."

"But why *us*?" King cried out, then flushed with embarrassment. "I mean . . . well, we're just . . . how many tens of thousand of others like us are there, in the Empire?"

Elias brooded silently for a moment. "There are things which can only be told to those who already have the knowledge," he said. "Because otherwise, they will not be believed."

He raised his eyes to meet King's; the contact sent a slight shock through King, like a drip of cold water on the back of the neck.

"In that city of evil we learned much—my son, and I, and your father. The priests of Malik Nous—you think that what they do, it is mere degeneracy, mere evil, mere superstition? Would that it were! There is a core of truth to their claims of power, hidden among the diabolism and sickness. Whether the Evil Councilor who tormented Job aids them, or it is knowledge of science bent to their wicked purposes, I do *not* know. What we learned is this: that there is a . . . group of women. The Sisterhood of the True Dreamers, they are called. In visions they foresee—not simply the future, but what *may* be the future."

"I don't understand—" King began.

His mind tried to shape the word *twaddle;* it would be comforting. Then he remembered.

"In the fight," he whispered. "At Sir Manfred's office. She pointed the gun and squeezed the trigger, but she wasn't *aiming*. Yet she hit every time, with every round."

"Yes. Visions they see—in dreams, we heard—of things that were, or might have been; of things that will be, or might be."

King looked down on the woman sleeping under the spell of the narcotic. Her mouth was open, slightly; he swallowed a sudden revulsion at the thought of the sacrificial feasts.

"Priestesses?"

"Hey-vey," Elias said. He held out a hand and waggled it. "Perhaps—perhaps to say slaves would be more just. Of course, in the lands under the Double Eagle, who is not a slave? Even the mightiest *boyar;* and the Czar himself is a slave to the cult of the Black God. The True Dreamers—think of the *power* that they give!"

King did, pushing aside squeamishness. To know what the consequences of an action would be, or even the likely consequences . . .

"There must be limits to it," he said. "Or the Czar would rule the world."

Elias nodded. "Limits beyond the goodness of Him who forbids necromancy, yes. The dreams are hard to command, we heard; only a few of the Sisters could call them at will, and even then the price is high; they do not live long, the Sisters, nor are there ever many of them. Only the mightiest lords and High Priests of the Czar's domain are given their services. Most important of all, they must dread the revealing of their secret, and so use the power sparingly. If it were known that it was possible, we heard, the skein of what might be would grow tangled and hard to see."

King nodded; it would be like having an agent in place. You'd have to be very careful using the intelligence you got, or you'd reveal the source and ruin its usefulness.

"Why didn't you inform the authorities?" he said.

Elias shook with laughter. "Heh-yey! A mad Jew and a mad officer, with no proof? No proof at all? Your father, he only half believed himself; and less so as time went on. Too much *Angrezi* common sense. And he had the *Angrezi* weakness—brave to madness before anything but *embarrassment.*"

King winced slightly, trying to imagine reporting something like that to Colonel Claiborne. Or to a committee of scholars like his sister, and standing while the icy scalpels of their reason flayed him alive. On the whole, he'd rather be shot, himself.

"But again, why are the Czar's men after the *Kings*?" he said.

Elias smiled crookedly and moved a chess piece with the tip of one finger. "Is it not obvious?" he said patiently. "The Sisters have told them that there is some great thing you Kings will do—or will prevent—*if* you live, some great thing against the Czar or the priesthood of Malik Nous. Perhaps something that you could not know until you do it, perhaps something whose weight can only be seen in hindsight . . . You know the poem about the horseshoe and the kingdom? Yes?"

The Lancer nodded slowly. It made your head hurt, to imagine planning strategy with that sort of foresight—you could go after the *father* of the man who was going to save the life of the commander who was going to beat your army a generation from now. They needn't be after him or Cass at all—it might be their children or their children's children.

Elias pointed a bony finger at Yasmini. "And now, seeking to track you down and kill you—they have left their greatest treasure in your hands!"

A sudden thought struck the young lord of Rexin; the meal he'd wolfed so eagerly suddenly sat like lead in his belly.

"Wait a minute . . ." He nodded at Yasmini. "She said, when she stopped me in the street—she said that if I died, the whole *world* would die."

"*Cus emok,*" David bar-Elias whispered—King recognized that as an Arabic curse. Elias went gray and pulled at his beard, muttering prayers.

King's mouth quirked. "I hope that doesn't mean I have to live forever," he said. "While I'm willing to do my bit for King-Emperor and Raj, that's rather more than I'd care to promise." More soberly: "Particularly considering the events of the last few months."

Chapter Thirteen

Henri de Vascogne raised a brow. "There is a problem, my old?"

"No entry, *sahib*," the patrolman said.

"What occurs?"

"I may not speak, *sahib*. Orders."

"Take my card to your superior," de Vascogne said, and offered it. "Now, if you please."

Police had set up barricades around Metcalfe House and constables stood behind it, some leaning on *lathi*-sticks, long quarterstave-batons, as a reminder to the morning crowds not to come too close.

After a moment the patrolman took the card and disappeared into the building. The Frenchman lit a cigarette and waited patiently amid the stares and chatter. After a half hour had passed he bought a *samosa* and ate it, enjoying the spicy deep-fried vegetables, but wishing the while for a real breakfast. A plate of *petit pain* and a decent cup of coffee, neither of which he'd had since he'd passed the borders of the *Angrezi* Raj. One heard that the *Kapenaar* could make good coffee—France-outre-mer bought most of its raw beans from the Viceroyalty of the Cape, or in Madagascar—but the Indian parts of the Empire had no conception of how to brew it, and forever drowned the taste with spices. Tea they could make, yes: coffee, no.

Presently a plainclothes officer came to the edge of the prohibited area. Henri recognized him; Tanaji Malusre, something of a protégé of Sir Manfred. *As I am myself,* he thought with amusement, throwing the cigarette to the ground and crushing it out. For the occasion he was dressed like an Imperial, and the turban felt odd. It was excellent protective coloration, though: Now he could be mistaken for a million others.

"*Sahib*," the policeman said.

"*Namaste*, Detective-Captain," Henri replied politely. "Sir Manfred has returned none of my calls."

The detective was a brave man; Henri frowned to see the nervous sideways glance he gave. Then he ducked under the barricade and jerked his head slightly. The two men walked a few steps, losing themselves in the crowd.

"*Sahib*, this is very strange," Malusre said. "Sir Manfred is . . . missing."

Henri's eyebrows climbed. "Missing?" he said, hiding his appalled start in calmness. "Name of a dog, how?"

"And presumed either kidnapped or dead," Malusre said, speaking in a low, hurried tone. "I was first on the scene—an appointment early this morning. Evidence of violence, yes; many bloodstains, wrecked furniture. Also gunshots; we found spent rounds, and the forensics people here are digging rounds from the walls. Evidence of forced entry, too. Sir Manfred's safe had been forced open and papers taken. But no bodies. Three people are missing: Sir Manfred, his assistant, and the *khansama*."

He hesitated. "And witnesses say the whole affair took place late last night. One has identified Captain King as entering the building at the same time. I think a warrant for his arrest as a material witness, possibly a suspect, is in preparation."

"*Merde*," Henri said quietly. "I do not find that particularly credible, given the circumstances, Detective."

"No indeed. However, the case is now in the hands of the Political Service. Allenby *sahib*, a colleague of Sir Manfred's, has taken it over." He went on in a neutral tone: "I am informed that I shall be rejoining the Kashmir Division of the Imperial Indian Police soon."

"*Merde*," Henri said.

Malusre nodded, smiling slightly. "I speak little French, but I think that may be appropriate, *sahib*," he said. He looked up at the facade of Metcalfe House. "I regret leaving Delhi for many reasons . . . among which, I indubitably wish that I knew what happened here last night."

"So do I, my old, so do I," Henri said.

His diplomatic mission suddenly looked a good deal more complicated. Alone, he could do nothing—Warburton had been his link to the Political Service. Luckily, he'd made other friends during his stay here, and some of them were very influential indeed.

Back to court, he thought.

Two young men and two women sat on a circle of cushions near the portside gallery of an airship, talking quietly. The *Garuda* sailed silently northward, cruising at eight hundred feet for the sake of the view. The Imperial family's air yacht was built on the same hull class as the *Diana*, the airship Cassandra King had taken to Oxford.

Pravati, was that only a few months ago? she asked herself.

Of course, the layout of the two-deck gondola was entirely different, built to accommodate the dynasty and their guests and servants, rather than scores of passengers; this section spanned a thousand square feet, with broad slanting windows along both sides, and railings around wells cut through the keel to let passengers look directly down. It was broad enough to hold the dancers for a small ball, with the main dining room to the rear and a lovely circular staircase twisting upward in a fantasy of gilt and rosewood. The conversation was not in the least festive, though.

"I cannot interfere with the civil service or police," Charles Saxe-Coberg-Gotha said, a troubled frown on his face. "For one thing, the Empire lives by law; for another, I'm heir to the throne, not the King-Emperor."

Cassandra flushed, and kept silent with an effort of will. Henri de Vascogne smiled and shrugged, a gesture subtly unlike anything a man of the *sahib-log* would have used.

"Your Imperial Highness, I was not suggesting anything so blatant."

Be damned if you weren't, Cassandra thought, as Sita snapped open a contraption of ivory fretwork from Dai-Nippon and fanned herself.

"After all the trouble we've taken to get Henri here," Sita pointed out, "it doesn't make much sense not to listen to him." She paused, and smiled. "And if *you* don't listen to him, brother dear, why should *I* do so?"

Charles winced, a slight narrowing of the eyes. *That girl is trouble,*

Cassandra thought. It was a good point, in terms of getting her brother to do what she wanted; he'd been given the task of persuading her to agree to the diplomatic marriage with the heir to the throne of France-outre-mer. If she decided to start kicking up a fuss again, Charles would have to go to his father and report failure; they could scarcely stage a wedding with a guardsman standing behind the bride twisting her arm.

And Sita would let them twist her arm right off rather than do something she really *decided she didn't want to do. So, effective.*

It was also ruthless, a bit unethical, and generally a low blow—very much like the princess at her worst. From what she knew of Charles, it might well just put his back up; and if he decided that it was his duty to do things according to the rule book, he might take a dourly dismal satisfaction in the personal trouble it caused him. Stubbornness ran in the Imperial dynasty's blood.

Henri de Vascogne seemed to sense all that in the same instant she did, and went on:

"If Your Highness feels he cannot intervene at all in this matter, well"—another supremely Gallic shrug—"I am merely a guest here, and you must conduct the affairs of your home as you see fit. Still, Sir Manfred chose to confide in me . . ."

"And *you've* always said that Sir Manfred was the smartest man in the Political Service," Sita pointed out.

". . . and Sir Manfred was convinced that this Captain King—and of course his sister—were the objects of a conspiracy by persons hostile to the Empire. Many different persons, in fact."

Cassandra spoke, her voice quiet but firm. "Charles. My brother could no more betray the Empire than he could walk on water."

His eyes met hers. "Cass . . . Dr. King . . . *you* know your brother, but I do not. All *I* have to go on is the papers that my advisors give me—and Agent Allenby strongly, *vehemently*, claims that your brother should be at least regarded as a suspect."

"That's not quite all you have to go on, Your Highness," Cassandra said. "You haven't met Athelstane, but you have met me. You have to take into account what you think of *my* judgment."

"Damnation." Charles sighed.

He rose, paced, reached for a cigarette and then stopped, looking up—smoking was, of course, strictly prohibited here. At last he returned and sank back to his cushion.

"All right," he said. "I'll see what I can do. The regional assistant commissioner of the Imperial Police for the Delhi area is a friend of mine—classmates at Sandhurst. But I make no promises. Is that understood?"

Cassandra met his eyes and nodded, forcing herself not to slump with relief. The packet of papers that Warburton had given her still rested safely in her quarters in the palace, but that was a counsel of desperation. What they contained was so wild that she wasn't sure whether it would sway Charles, or convince him that the baronet had gone completely *doolalli*.

"Mmmmm," Henri de Vascogne said. "I . . . ah . . . do not *quite* understand . . ."

"Why my brother sent me, rather than coming himself?" Sita inquired, with the slightest hint of a slyly mischievous grin.

"Yes," Henri said.

Cassandra King smiled to herself; watching Henri and Sita circle around each other was more amusing than anything else she'd seen at court—rather like two asteroids with the ability to modify their own orbits.

The motorcar traveled silently through the streets of South Delhi, with only the hum of its rubber tires on the granite paving blocks to mark its passage. At the broad circular intersections blue-jacketed policemen did double takes at the lion-and-unicorn flags fluttering from little staffs above the headlamps and set to holding up their wands and blowing whistles. Nobody could doubt that someone very close to the Lion Throne was going by behind the darkened glass.

"Well, it's obvious," Sita went on. "Father couldn't do anything like this. It would cause a political uproar and questions in Parliament. Charles couldn't—that would be almost as bad. *They* have to be careful and law-abiding and responsible and consult some politician every time they wipe their noses. But if Charles sent some aide-de-camp or courtier, that wouldn't carry the same blood prestige."

"Ah, the *baraka*," Henri said, nodding.

"Odd—we use the same word," Sita said, and continued: "That's how the politicians keep the throne in line; we have the power in theory, but the unwritten rules mean we can't use it very often. It's sort of like a tug-of-war."

Cassandra smiled again. You could see the Maghrebi-Frenchman's mind working: *Not just pretty and charming and reckless. This petite jolie femme has also a head on her shoulders.*

"But yourself?" he said.

"Well, I'm the *daughter* of the Lion Throne," Sita explained. "I can be as irresponsible as I want to be. But the bureaucrats have to be *nearly* as frightened of me as they would of my brother. After all, it's known we're close. Who knows what sort of career-wrecking words I could whisper in his ear?"

None of the bodyguards who piled out of the second motorcar were in uniform—most of them were dressed like any gentleman in town and out for a morning stroll. That didn't leave anyone in much doubt as to what they were; *sahib-log*, Sikh or Malay or castes more obscure, they all had a certain rough-hewn similarity. Sita sat like a carved image in a temple until one guard opened a door, her form glittering where the sun struck metal thread and jewels. Then she extended a slender arm and let another hand her out. De Vascogne fell in a pace to the rear and to the right; Cassandra took up a similar position on the left, and they swept forward behind the young princess's regal presence and the shell of hard-faced men whose eyes never stopped moving.

The building was smooth red sandstone, its boxy outline and rows of windows broken by columns of pale granite with gilded lotus-leaf capitals, their bases resting on cast-bronze bulls. Within they passed by the salaaming custodian, up a flight of stairs, and into a maze of corridors flanked by the little cubicle-offices of the bureaucrats.

"Familiar," Henri whispered aside to Cassandra. She glanced a question at him.

"Clerks in France-outre-mer don't sit on cushions, and they clack abacus beads instead of these clanking mechanical adding machines, and there are far more telephones and typewriters here, and it smells of tea instead of strong coffee. But for the rest—"

His slight gesture indicated the piles of folders and papers, and the thump of rubber stamps hitting ink pads and documents, the scritch of steel pen-nibs on paper, and the general air of self-important busyness glimpsed everywhere.

That shattered as the princess and her entourage plunged into the midst of the civil servants, like gaudy-feathered birds of prey into an aviary of drab sparrows. Men striding along with files beneath their arms and weighty frowns sprang aside, bending in the salaam; some of them dropped their burdens, and one broke its binding of red tape and showered the corridor with a snowfall of pages. Secretaries squeaked in dismay, jaws dropped, once a teacup dropped from nerveless fingers to shatter and spill on the tiles.

"Never let them know you're coming, either," Sita whispered.

Henri nodded. Cassandra surprised him by nodding herself. At his glance, she said:

"This is on a much larger scale than Oxford, but I assure you, we have our little interdepartmental feuds there, too."

Richard Allenby had a corner office on the third floor with two large windows, which was a mark of status. So was the polished appearance of the secretary in the anteroom without, as glossy as the marble tiles of the floor and as expensive as the trail of incense rising from a fretwork censer standing before a four-foot statue of a dancing Shiva. She rose silently from behind her low desk and salaamed, letting them into the office proper.

Someone had phoned ahead to Allenby, and he was ready with a deep salaam of his own, kissing the princess's hand and Cassandra's before shaking with Henri. Cassandra endured the courtesy with cold control; her face was set, but the Political Service agent gave a very slight start when he rose and met her eyes.

"*Kunwari,*" he said. "My lord." Then he paused, baffled for a moment.

"Dr. Cassandra King," she said, taking a small vicious stab of pleasure at his start.

"Dr. King. I confess you catch me at a disadvantage, *Kunwari,* but if I could call for a chair, or offer—"

"No tea, thank you. And this cushion will do very nicely. It isn't a formal occasion, after all, *Mr.* Allenby," Sita said—apparently with malice aforethought.

Excellent, Cassandra thought. *If he's like any senior civil servant I've ever known, a knighthood is the summit of his life's ambitions.* And alienating a member of the dynasty was an excellent way to make sure you were never on the Honors List, no matter how often the ministry suggested you.

"I'm here on behalf of my tutor—my friend—Dr. King," the princess continued. "This ridiculous matter of her brother."

"And I as a friend of Sir Manfred," Henri said.

By now he looked as easy sitting cross-legged on a cushion as he did in a chair.

"Ridiculous is hardly expressive enough," Cassandra snapped.

Allenby looked at her. *Something's wrong*, she thought. The man ought to be frightened. Not of her, but of her connections—with a daughter of the Lion Throne beside her and a foreign dignitary sent to negotiate a dynastic marriage, you might as well be holding up a sign reading: HURRAH, I'M IMPORTANT! Instead . . .

Yes, he is frightened. But not of us . . . no, he's frightened of us, but more frightened of someone or something else. More frightened than of Sita, who can wreck his career and his hopes.

"*Kunwari*," he said smoothly. "I'm sure you realize that I couldn't discuss a matter under investigation with you—your pardon, but it would be most irregular. Not to mention before this lady, who, after all, is liable to be partial, and this gentleman, who is not even an Imperial subject."

Cassandra had learned a good deal about her charge in a month as a tutor. She cleared her throat warningly. Throwing something at the man wasn't going to help at all, appealing though the thought was.

Not nearly as appealing as kicking him off a cliff, she thought. *Or perhaps nailing his head to a table with a railroad spike. Or perhaps nailing his head to a table, setting it on fire and* then *kicking him off a cliff. But one must be self-controlled.* Sita was perfectly capable of that—when she remembered.

"Sir Manfred did not feel that my origins were any bar to cooperation," Henri pointed out, pulling out a silver case. "Cheroot? No?" He lit his own and snapped the case shut.

"Sir Manfred has disappeared, in most suspicious circumstances," Allenby said. "I have reason to believe that Captain King—no offense intended, Dr. King—may have been involved."

"Poppycock," Sita said flatly.

"As I said, *Kunwari*, and with all respect—"

"You're not showing any respect at all, Mr. Allenby," Sita said—with the same flat tone in her voice. "Considering the importance of the Vicomte de Vascogne's mission to the Empire. You *are* aware of his mission? You are aware of how my father, and Prime Minister Lord Somersby, would react to any *lower-level* civil service interference in it."

"But I don't have the slightest intention of interfering—"

"That's not how it will sound after I'm through," Sita went on. Her smile was slow and cruel. "Gratuitous insults to France-outre-mer's envoy would be considered interference of the most malignant kind. And consider who here has better access to the highest quarters," she went on.

A slight sheen of sweat had broken out on Allenby's face. It was common knowledge that both the King-Emperor and the heir, not to mention Lord Somersby, doted on Princess Sita.

"I must conduct the affairs of this office as I see best, *Kunwari*."

"You will not make any official statements indicating that suspicion rests on Captain King," Sita said. "Nor will you pass such statements along the informal routes—rest assured I would know. You will issue no warrants for Captain King's arrest, either to the Political Service or the regular police under the Interior Ministry or to the military police or Intelligence agencies. And you will keep me, and through me the vicomte and Dr. King, fully informed if there are any indications of Captain King's whereabouts, or Sir Manfred's. If you disobey me in any particular in this matter, I will see you broken and dismissed. Possibly imprisoned. *Do—you—understand?*"

"*Kunwari*—"

"Shall we make a telephone call?" Sita said, nodding to the instrument on his desk. "I have the pass-code for the palace. No? *Do—you—understand?*"

"Yes, *Kunwari*," the man ground out.

Cassandra frowned. There was a slight tremor in his hands, and the beads of sweat along the edge of his turban were noticeable. *He looks like a man whose nerve has been shattered,* she realized. She'd seen that before; an experienced climber who suddenly started screaming and didn't stop until they had him on level ground again. *But Sita hasn't put him under* that *much pressure!* There was something going on, something more than the bewildering events of the past week.

Sita gave a single nod and extended her hand to one side, fingers elegantly drooping. Henri rose smoothly and put his hand beneath it, with her fingers just touching the back; she came to her feet with slow, elegant grace and transferred her hand to his arm. Cassandra fell in behind; as they left, so did the bodyguards. They weren't quite marching in step, but somehow they gave the impression of hobnails pounding along in unison.

And everyone will have noticed, she thought with satisfaction. She didn't have the slightest idea what sort of crooked game Allenby was playing, but from this moment on he'd have to do it under the interested gaze of dozens of his colleagues.

"That was a frightened man, is it not so?" Henri said thoughtfully. "A very frightened man."

"I can have that effect," Sita said with a trace of smugness.

"No, *chérie*—Highness," Henri said, correcting himself absently. Cassandra fought her brows to stillness. "Not the fear of a man who thinks his position endangered. If it were only that, he would have also been somewhat angry—angry at the interference in his, what is it which you say for the work territory, his balliwick. That man was showing the fear of a man afraid for his life."

There was a single bodyguard in the rear of the motorcar with them; he had remained there while the party went inside. He leaned forward slightly as they returned.

"Detective-Captain Malusre," Henri said.

"*Sahib, memsahib, Kunwari,*" he said. "Could you please recall for me *exactly* what passed within?"

They did, and the Marathi detective frowned. "Vascogne *sahib* is correct. That was not the response one might have awaited." He thought for a long moment. "Blackmail."

The others looked at him. "The indications are that someone is blackmailing Allenby *sahib*. With some information strong enough to make him risk the Imperial princess's anger. That would require a very heavy hold."

"And it would explain a good deal," Henri said thoughtfully.

"The same people who tried to kill Athelstane, and me, and did kill Dr. Ghose!" Cassandra burst out.

"That would be logical, *memsahib*," Malusre said. "Unfortunately, we have no proof. Nor an indication of who."

Cassandra thought of the folder of documents Warburton had left with her. A chill went down her spine, like blizzard snow melting on her scarf above the tree line and trickling inside her clothes. A chill, and a name: *Vladimir Obromovich Ignatieff.*

"I have to talk to Charles . . . to His Highness," she said. At the inquiring looks of the others: "No, there's nothing I can say right now. But Detective-Captain Malusre should report to him as well."

The man nodded. "Thank you," he said.

Sita reached out and touched him briefly on the forehead. "Thank *you*, Detective-Captain, for not just going back to Kashmir," she said. "That would have been the easiest and safest thing to do."

He grinned. "*Kunwari*, my curiosity would have tormented me all my days—and curiosity was the reason I became a detective, rather than a lawyer, as my mother so much desired."

"You won't be the loser for it," Sita declared. Her eyes sparkled. "My first conspiracy!"

Cassandra's brows tried to climb again as she caught the smile the princess exchanged with the envoy of France-outre-mer. Then concern of another sort washed the thought from her mind.

Athelstane, she thought. *My brother, where are you? Are you even alive?*

Athelstane King used a piece of warm fresh flatbread to scoop up the last of the *kefir*—milk curd with honey—and finished a mango, feeling more like a human being after a night's rest, a bath, and a shave. He felt slightly guilty about it; Narayan Singh was probably sitting in some roach-infested police cell, or the military jail in the Red Fort. On the other hand, punishing himself would do Narayan no good at all. The thing to do was to get him out as soon as possible.

Capital kefir, *and that damned beard never stopped itching*, he thought. Then, with a touch of mordant irony: *At that, I think I'm feeling considerably better than our representative from the Political Service here.*

Sir Manfred Warburton sat across from him; or *lay*, propped up as he was in soft pillows. A mummy swath of bandages covered his head, and from the way he moved the stitches in the wound on his back were paining him considerably. They were in a house that Elias's son and grandsons and several close-mouthed retainers had brought them to, after a trip through night-dark Delhi streets that King knew he couldn't have retraced himself. Wherever it was, they sat in a room with pointed arches of whitewashed stone, looking out over a small brown-tiled courtyard where a fountain tinkled. The house was obviously old—possibly older than the Old Empire—and well furnished in a good plain style not at all what he would have expected from someone of Elias's wealth. Sunlight streamed in, throwing dust motes into slow gold-lit motion.

Sir Manfred was concentrating on work, despite a hectic flush to his cheeks:

"That's usually the way," he said harshly, "when you put the squeeze on a man. If he once gives you something, you've got him for good and all, regardless of the initial hook. God knows how long Allenby has been working for them—I thought he was simply incompetent. But you never know who's a mole; that's one reason why the Political Service is so decentralized. That minimizes the damage."

King hid a grimace. *Filthy work*, he thought. *I'd prefer honest soldiering any day.*

Yasmini nodded; she ate delicately, like a cat, and there was a catlike air to the way she cleaned herself with the damp towels handed round afterward. King looked at the red lips and shuddered again. She'd come over to his side, sure enough; but what she must have done *before* . . .

Almost enough to make me forget she's the most beautiful creature I've ever seen. Nothing at all like his usual taste in women, of course. That ran to ones who looked like they'd stepped off one of the Vishvanatha temple friezes at Khajuraho, all curves.

Not exactly attractive, really—more like fascinating and exotic. I wonder what . . . get your mind back on business, you fool!

"I was not the Sister who gave the information on Allenby," she said. Her Imperial English had grown better, as if she was rusty and practice was bringing back old memory. "Count Ignatieff handled the matter before I was allowed from the training school. He only hinted at it, that I overheard."

Warburton looked at her, and his pale eyes fairly burned; not with ordinary lust, King thought, but with the fanaticism of an expert seeing the ultimate possible tool of his profession. Yasmini seemed to recognize it, and lowered her eyes in submission.

"At last," the baronet breathed. "*Proof.* That alone—and now we'll have the—"

"Sir Manfred," King said, coming to a decision.

"Captain King?" the injured man said. He might be in pain, but there was nothing wrong with his ear for a nuance.

"This, ah, young lady went to a considerable amount of personal risk to save me and Narayan Singh. And did the Empire a considerable service in the bargain. I think it only right that she be . . . treated accordingly."

Sir Manfred made an impatient gesture. "Yes, yes, my dear Captain King. Of course." To Yasmini: "Pardon me if I was a little abrupt."

Yasmini raised her eyes again, fastening them on King. Tears welled, dripping down the pale cheeks.

"I say," he said in alarm. "Are you all right?"

"*Da*," she whispered. "But nobody has ever asked before—except my mother, before she went mad."

King blinked, feeling a flush stealing up his cheeks. When you thought about it, that was extremely sad. He coughed and shrugged.

"Well, I don't claim to be a saint. Can't be many decent chaps around where, ah, where you come from."

"*Nyet*. It is forbidden. I have seen such—Seen them—in my visions, here, and in the past. Seen you all. That is why I left the count. Most of the paths that branch from that choice lead to death, but I must take the chance."

Poor little bitch, he thought. Aloud, he went on: "Well, now we can go to the authorities."

Yasmini and Warburton looked at him with identical expressions of alarm.

"No!"

"*Nyet!*"

"Why not?" he asked.

Warburton sighed, moving slightly and wincing. "Not as young as I was . . . my dear young chap, you don't believe that Allenby was the *only* traitor Count Ignatieff—and the Okhrana—had working for them? With a . . . source of information like this young lady and her . . . ah, relatives . . . they would have an unparalleled means of identifying our weak links, and exploiting them. How would we know that anyone we went to wasn't on the other side? And would have us killed, quickly and quietly, to shut our mouths. *Shot while resisting arrest* has covered a multitude of sins over the years."

"Or captured," Yasmini said. She shivered and rubbed her hands up and down her arms. "I have Seen"—the capital letter was clear in her voice—"what comes after that."

"Oh," King said, feeling a little deflated. "Well, dammit—" He stopped, grinned. "There I am, sounding like Colonel Claiborne. But dammit, I *am* just a soldier."

"You weren't with the Orakzai chiefs," Warburton said. "Don't think you can relax just because we're back within the Imperial borders."

"I've come to the same conclusion," King said with dry irony, thinking hard. "All right. I take it the Okhrana don't risk you . . . Sisters . . . inside the Imperial frontiers very often?"

Yasmini nodded. "I may be the only one since the founding of our Order," she said. "The priests of Malik Nous—Tchernobog, the Black God, He whom you call Satan—control the breeding of us." A shadow flickered over her face; she swallowed and went on: "Not half a dozen times have any of us left the Czar's domains; it is very rare for us even to leave Bohkara, apart from one or two who dwell in Samarkand for consultation with the Czar and his closest advisors. So I may indeed be the first ever brought across your frontier—though my mother was brought near, in the time of your father, Captain King. Ours is the strongest line of the Sisters, and with less deformity and crippling. Count Ignatieff was the Master for that mission also."

When my father died, she means, King thought, nodding curtly.

"Why send you, then?" Sir Manfred cut in.

She nodded to him, a little uncertain. "Count Ignatieff . . . he is very powerful. Very highborn, as well. And for this mission, he had the dreams of several Sisters showing a chance of success. Blurred visions—they often are, when we must deal with each other and the, the *consequences* of each other's own dreams. The—"

She dropped into Russian. Surprised, King realized that he wasn't catching more than every second or third word, and wasn't certain that he was right about the meanings of the ones he *did* catch. Sir Manfred looked equally baffled.

"Smudging the lines of the worlds?" he said after a moment. "Damn all technical jargon."

"In your English, there are no words, nor in Hindi." Yasmini's brows knitted in thought. "I can dream . . . I can See . . . how things *might* be. When another does also, and influences men's actions . . . the possibilities become so many that—" She threw up her hands. "As well might I describe color to a man whose eyes had been gouged out at birth!"

King winced inwardly. Modern Russian was full of similes like that; he'd had to make himself learn it, when a new language was usually a pleasure for him.

She pointed at the beam of light coming through the archway. "Like the dust motes there. Each moves; each motion stirs the others. You see the pattern of what is, in this instant, and this of-all-possible-instants. I See more, in my dreams . . . forward, backward, and, oh, how shall I say . . . *sideways*."

"Well, then," King said, concentrating on practicalities. "What success was promised?"

"Your death," Yasmini said bleakly. "That of your sister."

He thumped his forehead. "But *why us?*"

"If you, Captain King, if you die, your Czar . . . your King-Emperor will die. His heir will die. There will be no union of your crowns with the country of the far west . . . France? Yes, France. In time to come, there will be much war, and your Empire will be divided and rendered weaker because of inward . . . internal? revolts. That the Czar greatly desires . . ."

The two Imperials grew very quiet. King swallowed. *I'll bet he does,* he thought. Aloud: "How? How does the King-Emperor's life depend on us?"

"I do not know *how!*" A slight flush warmed Yasmini's cheeks; even then King noted how it made the statue perfection of her face come to life. "I do not see the future—the futures—like a book. In dreams I see glimpses, pieces. I must interpret. That is why we are educated, taught reading, drawing, science and history, unlike other cattle, so that we can *understand* what we See and explain it."

"That would certainly interest the Okhrana," Sir Warburton mused. "A chance at seriously dividing the Empire. And it's their style to the inch; subvert, get people mistrusting each other, disinform." Then: "See here, miss; what about Dr. King? Captain King's sister?"

Yasmini was silent for a long moment. "That was also why I ran from the count," she whispered. "That dream he and the priests kept secret from the Czar, from the Okhrana. If she dies—if the son of your ruler dies—then the world will die." She raised a hand. "I have Seen it! A great thing of death from the heavens—fire, and then ice—"

Shuddering, she buried her face in her hands. "Not for much time.

Perhaps a century? Perhaps a little more. But it will come. Without her, it will strike home."

"Great Scott," Warburton said quietly.

"Merciful Krishna," King answered him, his own voice hoarse. He gulped more tea. "Cassandra's bloody *Project*."

"Another Fall," Warburton agreed. "If the Project goes ahead with Cassandra working on it—somehow something she discovers, or does, or influences someone to do—it'll stop this. Another Fall—"

"Worse," Yasmini said through her fingers. "I have Seen the Fall. This will be . . . if it happens, it will be much worse. Nothing of human life will survive. Only the rats."

"Bloody *hell*," King said, vigor back in his voice. "Why would this Ignatieff bug—bounder want *that*? However mad or bad he is—"

"Count Ignatieff is a man of much faith," Yasmini said, raising her head and pulling a handkerchief from her sleeve. She smiled a shaky smile. "It is so good, not to be struck for weeping . . . Yes, he is a man of much faith, very pious."

At their look of incomprehension: "The death of all that lives . . . what could be more pleasing to the Peacock Angel, to Tchernobog, the Black God?"

Chapter Fourteen

*W*ell, *here I am, dealing with an unlicensed doctor and hiding from evil conspirators in a safe house. In a book, this would be romantic, instead of nerve-wracking,* King thought, as Elias showed him through the door to Warburton's room.

The doctor Elias had procured was of a type who could be absolutely relied on to give care of a reasonable quality and to say nothing whatsoever about his patients to anybody. Conrad McAndrews was from the Viceroyalty of the Cape; about one-half *Kapenaar*, the other half a mixture of Zulu and Cape Malay, and all three showed in his accent, at once clipped, guttural, and singsong. He had worked as an apothecary's apprentice in Durban, then stowed away on a ship—worked as a stoker when found out—bound for other parts of the Empire, where ancestry didn't play such a part in determining a man's destiny. Somehow he'd scrambled his way to an MD from the University of Columbo, which was not usually accounted among the best of the Empire's medical schools. The adventures which had resulted in the revoking of his license had also given him an air of lantern-jawed silence which did not invite either conversation or confidences.

"My fee will be fifty rupees per visit. In advance," the doctor said.

The Jew paid from a roll of Imperial Bank of India notes tucked into one sleeve of his striped robe. Then and only then did the doctor look at the man in the bed.

"Hmmmp. Injuries?"

"Bruises, cuts, a blow to the head," King answered crisply. "There seems to be some fever."

The doctor shook his head, shone a light into Warburton's eyes, investigated the contusions and cuts, took his temperature with a long glass thermometer. King helped the injured man move; Warburton bore the pain well, but there was no denying he wasn't fit for action yet.

"Whoever did this stitching on the cut running down from the right shoulder blade has a neat hand," the doctor said dryly. "He seems to be recovering from the blood loss. There's an infection, but not a bad one; I presume you used iodine? This ointment on that and the other cuts, twice a day. These pills, three times a day—on an empty stomach. There is also a concussion. Headaches? Nausea? Blurred vision?"

Warburton nodded to each, and the doctor made a sound in his throat, with the same air as a mechanic who'd found a cracked ceramic heat exchanger in a gas engine.

"No physical activity or excitement for a week. Bed rest; light diet; plenty of water or juices, broth would be excellent, no coffee, tea, or alcohol. Pay me now for the next visit."

He turned on his heel and walked out again. Yasmini threw back the scarf she'd been wearing over her hair and held across her face as if in modesty—something credible enough in Old Delhi. Elias seated himself on a cushion, perching like an ancient, highly intelligent and benevolent vulture.

"So. With his True Dreamer gone, is this Ignatieff a threat?"

"Yes," Warburton said, and Yasmini nodded emphatically. "He's one of the Czar's best political agents; and the very devil himself in person. *Him* we knew about officially, if not the, ah, Sisterhood of the True Dreamers. We suspect he's been into the Empire dozens of times in the past two decades."

"Not a bad swordsman, either," King said. "What will his next move be?"

Yasmini looked troubled. "He did not consult me—only inquired of me what the results of this or that would be. I know he met often with men of the Raj—"

She went on to describe them. Warburton sighed and lay back with a damp cloth over his eyes.

"Damn this head; my thoughts feel fuzzy . . . yes, I'd say that list included two separate groups of secessionists, and a couple of subversive cults. The Muslim Brotherhood, the worst sort of Shia—we get along well with the Aga Khan's people, but some of the other sects are long-running trials—and the Deceivers . . ."

Elias sighed and produced a copy of the *Imperial Court Gazette*; it looked a little incongruous in his hands, since the usual reader was a social-climbing matron.

"If he is trying to attack the King-Emperor . . ." he said, and began to read the main story.

King walked over to read across the old Jew's shoulder. That put him near Yasmini, and he was aware of a faint scent of jasmine and clean feminine flesh underneath Elias's sandalwood-camphor-and-old-man. He dismissed it from his mind as the printed headlines sank in:

"*The Royal Family to Visit France-outre-mer.* Well, that doesn't mean much. If this bounder Ignatieff is trying to do Cass an injury—"

Warburton groaned. At first King thought it was pain; then he realized the man was cursing himself.

"We thought we were so clever. Ganesha spare us . . ." He sighed. "Your mother called in a favor with an old school chum of hers. Cassandra is at court—tutor to the Imperial princess, supposedly. To keep her *safe*."

"Oh, *damn*," King said feelingly, and tore the paper out of Elias's hands. He scanned down. "Dr. Rexin?"

"An alias," Warburton said.

"Not much of one."

"She picked it herself," the Political Service agent said defensively. "In any case, they won't be leaving for two weeks according to what you read. Ample time to get us to Bombay, if that's where they're leaving from. Once at sea, they should be safe enough—"

"They're not going by sea," King said. "They're flying. In the *Garuda*, the Imperial air yacht, with two Air Service cruisers as escort—the *Clive* and the *Raffles*. Departing from Bombay, though."

"Oh, bloody damnation!" Warburton said. "Must be trying to impress the Egyptians—they've granted transit rights—but . . ."

He sank back. "Notifying the court of the conspiracy must be the first priority, then. Damn this head. Twenty years ago, I'd have been on my feet already. And we can't use any of the Political Service routes or safe houses or drop-offs, they might be compromised—"

"Heh-yeh," Elias said, a little smugly. "There are other ways to travel secretly and quietly than those. In India, there always have been. Many branches on the Middle Way."

At that, Warburton's intelligence-agent ears pricked up; King could almost see the effort it took to restrain his curiosity.

"Well, as soon as we've located Narayan, we can be on our way, then," the young Lancer said.

There was a frozen silence. He looked from face to face. "See here, he's my *daffadar*—and my man. I have to at least be sure he's all right. All we have to do is check the military lockup's register, surely? It won't hurt him to cool his heels in the guardhouse for a few weeks; that'll give his wound time to heal. Then we can expose these ruddy bastards, and—"

"This Allenby could not send him *there*," Elias pointed out, ignoring Warburton's shushing gesture. "A soldier would have a right of appeal to his commanding officer, or the colonel of his regiment, within—"

"Yes, within seven days," King said; the length of time the civil police could hold a soldier was something an officer had to know. And so—

"Colonel Claiborne would have him out in double-quick time," King said, nodding. "As soon as I heard his body wasn't found there, I knew they must have taken him prisoner. After all, *Allenby* might be a traitor, but all the men he was calling in couldn't all have been, surely. They were in uniform—regular police, dozens of them."

"You are so concerned?" Yasmini asked, looking at him oddly.

"Well, of course," King said, glancing at her.

"Why?" she said, with obviously genuine curiosity.

"He's one of my command, he's the son of my father's *rissaldar*, he's one of my family's tenants, he's saved *my* life half a dozen times, he's my comrade-in-arms, we grew up together—take your pick," King answered impatiently. "Any would do."

He turned back to Warburton: "The civil police, then?"

The Political Service agent sighed, laid a hand on the cloth that covered his eyes, and spoke in a resigned tone.

"Unlikely. He couldn't be held incommunicado there, either. But . . ."

"But?"

"But Allenby could have told everyone he was arresting him under the Defense of the Realm Act. Under *that*, he could be held without recourse for a week—and the regular police could be told to keep quiet about it, whatever they'd heard. A week, or longer if Allenby made up some cock-and-bull story about his cooperating with an investigation and needing protection. Suspected terrorists, assassins, foreign agents—and by the ten thousand faces of God, everyone in the Service will know that *those* are abroad in the land right now, so his claim might well look credible. Particularly since I've disappeared under *extremely* suspicious circumstances."

"Then—"

"There has been no raid on my house," Elias noted, stroking his white beard. "Your man would know that you sought help there? Yes? It was because of that that I moved you here, of course."

"Narayan Singh wouldn't—" King caught himself. *Wouldn't talk* was nonsense; everyone did, eventually, if the torture was skillfully and ruthlessly applied. "Narayan Singh wouldn't talk quickly. And he'd have them running around chasing false leads for a while first."

Warburton nodded. "And we can hope that Allenby wouldn't dare do anything too, ah, strenuous to an Imperial soldier. He was *seen* to arrest the man, after all. That will come to official attention eventually; men talk, even when they've been cautioned not to. He'll have to produce him, or a body, eventually, or face charges."

"Unless he planned to kill him and *dispose* of the body and claim he escaped," King said grimly. "And Allenby is under Ignatieff's thumb. I don't imagine the good count has many scruples."

"What does that word mean?" Yasmini asked, as King rose and paced like a caged leopard. "Something like a taboo? I have never quite understood it." She recoiled a little at his glare, bewildered.

"Captain King, I know what you're considering," Warburton snapped. "You have no right to endanger yourself. Think, man! The King-Emperor's life may depend on you."

King stopped, grunting as if punched in the belly. Then, after a moment, he spoke slowly and quietly; only someone who knew him very well could have detected the emotion quivering under the calm voice.

"The King-Emperor doesn't need the sort of officer who'd abandon a loyal man to torture and death."

"I forbid it!"

King relaxed suddenly, with a shrug and a smile. "Well, Sir Manfred, it's debatable whether you have the authority to forbid me anything at all, since you're not in my chain of command. In any case, we'll take it up with the proper authorities—Colonel Claiborne, perhaps, or the C-in-C Northwest Frontier Force—after this is all over, shall we? You can demand that they court-martial me for insubordination."

He caught Elias's eye and held up the *tessera*. The old Jew nodded, rocking himself back and forth slightly.

"Madness. But a *predictable* madness." He cackled, swaying a little. "Just such madness as his father showed, risking life and soul for a debt of honor to a Jew *banian*. Heh-vey!"

Warburton started to force himself up. Yasmini walked over to his side, kneeling by his bed, and lifted the cloth from his eyes. Leaning forward, she caught his with her moon-pale gaze and put a hand to either side of his head.

"I, too, would forbid him, if I could," she said, smiling slightly. "But I cannot, and you cannot, and we must aid him whether we will or no. But you forget something, *boyar*."

"What?" Warburton said helplessly.

"He—you—have a Sister of the True Dreaming now. And Ignatieff does not." She nodded, looking up at King and Elias. "I will dream for you, and I will dream truly."

Warburton shrugged—not a young man's gesture. Half a lifetime of making the best of the cards malignant fate handed him were behind it.

"If you're going to neglect your duty this way," he said, "I suppose I have to do my best to see you come out of it with a whole skin."

"I . . . can't believe it," Prince Charles said.

"I couldn't either, at first," Cassandra answered. "I still don't *want* to believe it. But it fits—fits all too well."

"I can certainly see why Warburton didn't reveal his suspicions," the heir said.

The two of them—and one of the elderly, near-deaf impoverished noblewomen who made a living out of chaperonage—were sitting atop one of the towers that lifted from the mass of the Palace of the

Lion Throne, the Tower of Stars. Unlike most, it didn't have a bulbous onion-dome top, but instead a hemisphere of glass in sections that ran on tracks. Back in the mid twentieth century it had been an amateur observatory for a favorite of Victoria II, until the city glow of Delhi grew too great.

Now it was a good place for a private conversation, since even the Guards officers tasked with the heir's protection admitted nothing overlooked it and there was only one way up. The sides were a smooth, fluted, marble-and-granite column over a hundred feet high, high enough that the air bore only a faint generalized urban smell of smoke, no hint of the gardens and fountains that surrounded the tower.

Charles looked down at the documents in his lap; rumors, reports from agents in Samarkand and Bokhara, Warburton's own experiences and analysis.

"What's that saying?" he said, smiling crookedly. "When you've eliminated the impossible, whatever remains—"

"—however improbable, must be the truth. Yes; the problem is, the man who wrote that believed in faeries, himself, and that he could photograph them."

"I remember," the prince said. "Old Empire born, wasn't he?"

"Yes. Came out with the Exodus, but he was never quite sane afterward."

"I've always liked the detective stories," Charles said. "Even if they were a bit escapist."

Fiction set in a paradisiacal world where the Fall had never happened had been very popular among the survivors of the Exodus and their children. Later generations tended to regard that as unhealthy.

Charles cleared his throat. "Still, the principle is sound. So tell me, Dr. Watson." That with a smile. "What *is* impossible here?"

"Honestly . . ." She squeezed her eyes shut. "I *think* I can be objective . . . I am a scientist, as much as a sister . . . I don't know. There are some hints in very recent physics, speculations of Dr. Ghose and some of his colleagues, that at a very fundamental level, reality may be probabilistic rather than determinist, and even that all probabilities may actually happen . . . somewhere or—when. So . . . there's so much about the brain that we don't understand . . . but it must operate at or around that level to be as complex as it is and yet so compact. The

Analytical Engine is hopelessly coarse and crude by comparison. A strain of human beings bred to be able to sense the shifts of—"

She threw up her hands. "Charles, I went into astronomy because I loved *certainty*. All I can say is that there is some faint shred of a possibility."

Charles shifted on his cushion, one elbow on a knee, the other toying with the hilt of the saber that lay across his lap. "Of course, the problem is that—like Sir Manfred—we have no *proof*. If we can't really convince ourselves, what chance would we have of being taken seriously by anyone else? Not to mention that if he was right, there are highly placed traitors who'd do their best to make us a laughingstock as well."

"He was afraid that the Service would think he'd gone *doolalli*," she said.

"They'd think the same of me, they'd just be much more polite about it," Charles said bluntly. "I don't think they'd call for sedatives and a straitjacket, but any real influence I had—with my father, not least—would vanish."

"And yet—"

"And yet it *is* about as good an explanation for all this as anything else!"

Cassandra sighed, collecting the documents and returning them to their folder, tying it off neatly with the attached tag of crimson tape.

"It makes sense knowing what I do of the people involved," she said. "You can't convey that, not really. People can trust you and believe your judgment of someone, but there's no way of demonstrating it. People . . . it's all so *squishy*."

"One thing it has convinced me of," Charles said decisively. "There's a lot more going on here than Mr. Allenby's reports indicate. They're misleading; either through stupidity, or something worse. A loyal officer is missing, an important Political Service agent is missing, and there was an attempt to slander them both. Things were swept under the rug—or would have been, if it weren't for you, the vicomte, and my sister. I'm going to get to the bottom of it, and I'm going to do my best to see that your brother is either saved, vindicated, or both."

"Thank you," Cassandra said quietly.

"And I'll have a watch-and-arrest put out for this Russian that Warburton speaks of, this Ignatieff. I can do that, quietly."

Their eyes met for a long moment, and Charles looked away with a slight flush, clearing his throat. "It might be best if I didn't know absolutely everything you're doing," he said. "If, for example, you were to try and find your brother in . . . unorthodox ways. But I will notify some people that you're not to be hindered."

"Thank you again," she said, and leaned over to touch his hand.

"*Rajadharma*," he said roughly, rising, obviously half-mad with frustration that his position would keep him pinned to the palace. "Duty."

"If you insist," she replied, taking his hand and rising as well. They stood for a moment so, before Cassandra squeezed his fingers and gently went to wake the chaperone.

"So," Ibrahim Khan said. "You will truly go on *razziah* to rescue the Sikh?"

"He is my sworn man," King said patiently.

Ibrahim giggled. "Would you do as much for me, then?" When King nodded, he looked into the Lancer's eyes for a long moment. "Bismillah, perhaps you would, being *gora-log* and so utterly mad. Well."

He looked down at the plan of Allenby's house. "It is not so difficult, *huzoor*."

King controlled an impulse to snort. Apart from a little rote-learned Arabic, the Pathan was as innocent of literacy as he was of court etiquette, but he had grown up in a very hard school of raid and ambush, and he understood maps extremely well. Better than any of the men Elias had gathered, waiting tonight around a kitchen table, although they looked formidable enough. One of them was David bar-Elias, dressed in rough dark clothes and a turban with an end that could be drawn across the face. A plain curved sword hung at his side, a dagger went in one boot, and a revolver of curious make rode his right hip under the fold of his jacket.

The others were caravan guards employed by Elias and Son; it seemed that David had shepherded caravans through some very rough places indeed. They ranged from a thick-shouldered, bandy-legged Mongol with a quiver and recurved bow over his shoulder—very good for quiet work, he said—through a very black African with no tongue and hideous scars on his back to a man with tattooed cheeks and red hair who was of no race or tribe King could recognize and who carried what looked like a jointed iron flail.

"The gate is heavily guarded," King pointed out. "And we must be quick, and make little noise."

Ibrahim grinned; he seemed cheerful enough, as long as his glance didn't stray to Yasmini too often. *She* put his hackles up, and made him more aggressive from shame at his own fear.

"I am not such a fool as to attempt a fortress by the front door," he said. "Yet these windows, they give onto the dungeon?"

"The basement, yes. Four of them, really, in sort of a cross arrangement under the whole house and the court. Iron doors between them."

"Dried meat and prisoners are best hung underground," Ibrahim said. "That is where they will have him—depend upon it, *huzoor*. So, let us go *in* here, at the second level of windows, or from the top of this tower. *Out* from the dungeon itself. Horses waiting—swift departure—-cut throats and confusion behind."

Warburton chuckled; he was still alternating between sweats and chills, but he had been able to draw the map plain enough.

"Not a bad general concept for the housebreaking. The gods know the Afghans have used it against us, often enough."

Ibrahim Khan grinned whitely in his downy black beard at that, bowing and making a mock-salute by touching brow and lips and heart. The Political Service Officer continued:

"I wish Rabindra Das was here," he said. "A good man—he got most of this information for me."

"Hmmm," King said, giving the plans a final check. "The tower does seem the best bet. All right, what's this room here, Sir Manfred?"

"This is not respectable," the ambassador of France-outre-mer said.

Andre Fleury carefully did *not* look at the bundle of explosives his military attaché had procured, and which lay on a chaise-longue by the door, as he went on:

"It is not remotely respectable for an accredited diplomat to engage in such . . . such an affair of danger."

"No," Henri de Vascogne agreed, puffing on a cheroot, and offering one to the other two men sitting at dinner with him.

"If this comes to light . . ."

The ambassador was a short, plump man with wide black whiskers and blue eyes; he shuddered and shrugged at once, a gesture which made his several chins shake.

"If it comes to light," he said with ghoulish relish, "we will of a certainty be exposed to the *dérision anglais*. Your—the Emperor will recall me, and I shall be sent to negotiate with savage chiefs in the pestilential swamps of Senegal or the frozen north. And you yourself will—"

"Have some brandy," Henri said. "You may plead force majeur; after all, my old, you know the authority under which I operate—direct from Algiers."

"Authority of the highest," the man said sourly.

"*Précisément*. And who can say? Perhaps all will go well. You must have another of this wonderful brandy, of a certainty, and perhaps a little of the Crème Anglese. Or perhaps this excellent *marron glacée?*"

Some of the ambassador's sourness might be his digestion. They were seated around a small table littered with the remains of lobster thermidor, a salad with goat cheese, an excellent *kefta*—minced lamb cakes baked with a pepper sauce—and a superb *poulet aux truffes*, all accompanied by several bottles of very creditable Sidi Bouhai. They had moved on to the desserts and cheeses with (at last!) decent unspiced coffee, and brandy—the latter from the ambassador's own family estates near Méknes. Henri had eaten and drunk with great appreciation but calculated restraint. The embassy's military attaché had stuffed himself with methodical enjoyment, but he was a tall and cadaverous sort. The ambassador had matched the soldier, without his frame or capacity, nervousness enhancing a natural gluttony.

Henri felt relaxed, sitting at his ease and toying with a morsel of cake. It had been a pleasure to eat proper French food again, good though Imperial cooking often was, and to speak his own language.

A suitable preparation for a risky evening which may end all such pleasures forever, he thought, and made a few companionable inquiries as to the state of the ambassador's liver—there was no sense in dwelling on details now that he'd won his point. It was the military man who insisted on bringing the conversation back around to business.

"If the vicomte wishes a few strong arms who may be relied upon most absolutely," the military attaché said, "I can provide four or five who have occupation about the embassy."

"Who have all in their time woken to *au jus* and marched to *Tiens, voilà du boudin*, no doubt," Henri joked.

The attaché nodded, with a remarkably evil and reminiscent smile. He was a *vielle moustache* himself, with a long white scar across his sun-bronzed face ending in a ruined eye socket covered by a patch and an equally white bristling head of hair. Just the sort to hold a commission not in the Regulars but in the Legion, a mercenary command with its ranks full of converted cannibals from Europe and other barbarian foreigners. The institution was supposed to spare precious French lives and yield, after a decade or so, suitable new citizens from the survivors, to be settled as military colonists on troubled frontiers. Unfortunately, sometimes the assimilative process worked the other way, as well. Henri remembered reading about that scar, in his briefing files—courtesy of an Iberian-Berber corsair's scimitar, during the campaigns up the Valencian coast a generation or so ago.

What had happened to the corsair afterward had made him wince, even in the antiseptic language of an official report.

That had been a worthwhile war, though; once recivilized, colonized, pacified, and settled, the region yielded both useful revenues and several formidable regiments. Henri had seen them in operation during the war against the Caliphate in Sicily, and had been thankful for their élan and discipline.

"But no," Henri went on; the man plainly longed to come along himself, years and wounds or no. "I regret infinitely, but we cannot risk having anyone so obviously French involved. My local friends will make the arrangements. Or . . . wait. I have one task for which I need a completely reliable man, but in a position of relative safety. Unlikely to be captured, as one of my Imperial friends might be in the event of a catastrophe."

"They could still implicate us if they were caught," the ambassador said, patting his lips with a handkerchief to hide a belch.

Or if you were caught, wellborn cretin, impeccably connected imbecile, powerful fool, went unspoken and unspeakable. The diplomat continued:

"And where, by the Merciful, the Compassionate Lord Jesus, would we be then? Where the alliance? Where the Imperial marriage?

You know as well as I, Vicomte, how badly we need that alliance against the Caliphate."

"The marriage will be in better suit than it would be if I did *not* fall in with my . . . new friends . . . in this matter," Henri explained patiently.

"Yes, it will delight the heart of the young princess," the ambassador grumbled. "Such dashing and romantic gestures do. But this is an alliance between two states, *n'est-ce pas?*"

"In the person of the princess," Henri said. It was worthwhile to soothe the man; and he *had* done his best to help, whether or not he thought the move wise. "The safe house is only a thing of concern if it can be traced to the embassy. I assume it cannot."

"Not easily," the ambassador said. "I handled the paperwork myself, through suitable intermediaries—these Imperials are charmingly naive in some respects."

"Just so; perhaps because they have not had until recently a power of comparable strength on their very frontiers, as we have had for generations. My most humble thanks for your esteemed assistance. And now, if you gentlemen will forgive me? Major, a moment?"

He rose, the military attaché coming with him, leaving the ambassador sitting and brooding over the remains of dinner—he plunged his fork into the remains of the *marron glacée* with morbid relish even as the other two men left the chamber.

"Only one man, Vicomte?" the attaché said, hinting broadly at an invitation.

"Only," Henri said firmly. *You are past sixty, my friend, and to bring you would be to emplace a sign reading MADE IN FRANCE above my head.* "Someone reliable, taciturn, and a good shot with a pistol."

"I have just the man."

The attaché went to the door of the antechamber, spoke through it, waited a second. When he turned, another man was with him, somewhat younger but still middle-aged, in the local dress of sashed jacket and loose trousers and soft boots. He had a stringy muscularity, a tuft of graying chin-beard, and very bad teeth when he smiled and saluted with fingers to brow. His eyes were a pale blue; noticeable, but by no means outlandish in Delhi.

"Marcel Dutourd," the attaché said. "*Sous-officier,* second battalion RE. Detached duty with me in Provence. Speaks good Hindi, as well."

"*Un peu,*" Marcel said, and switched to that language: "As the vicomte commands."

He had an accent in both languages, a little nasal and sharp. From the resettled provinces near Marseilles, or the port city itself—France-outre-mer had kept an outpost there even in the immediate aftermath of the Fall. At the attaché's gesture he opened his jacket to show a holster against his belly holding an Imperial-made revolver, then twitched his right hand. A slim-bladed knife appeared in it for a moment, then disappeared.

"Good enough," Henri said, and signed the man to follow.

They left by a side door; Henri swirled a hooded cloak about his shoulders. Luckily a November evening in Delhi was cool enough to make that credible, and the variety of types in the street—even here in a respectable quarter not far from the governmental enclave—made the garment unremarkable, despite its origin in a Berber village of the High Atlas. His timing was good; the little band was just assembling in the safe house when he arrived. For once, that term of craft was literally true; the building was large, and turned a blank wall to the outside world. From the quality of the floors and mosaics and floridly ornate gas lamps, Henri suspected it had been some previous ambassador's *pied-à-terre* for his mistress, slipped onto the official budget for secret-service work.

The dark-skinned captain of detectives greeted him at the door, commendably cool, giving Marcel's silent form only a single glance and asking no questions. Evidently the *sang-froid anglais* was catching.

"*Apache,*" Henri said quietly, looking over the crew that Malusre had assembled.

Cassandra King made an equally soft interrogative sound, and the Frenchman went on: "Criminals."

"*Dacoits,*" she agreed. *Bandits.* "Absolute goondahs, in fact."

Certainly they had a villainous enough look, coarse, scarred, feral faces and dusty-gaudy clothes, there and there a bit of tattered flamboyance, an ostrich plume in a turban or a hoop earring; and he could see she did not like the way they leered at her out of the corners of their eyes. Doubtless they would have done more, if they dared. Cassandra spread the plans of Allenby's house on the table, and the three principals bent over them.

"*Merci,*" Henri said. "Ah, these are most detailed. Our friend in the second-highest place?"

"A friend of our friend," Cassandra explained. "Plans for buildings have to be filed with the Delhi City planning office. These plans themselves are fifty years old, though. There may well have been changes since."

"Much better than nothing," Henri said. "Hmmm. Of storming houses I had some experience in Sicily with the Prince Imperial's army—the Caliph's men fought most stubbornly for Palermo. This here is a public park?"

"I drove by it in a *tiki-ghari*," she said. "Yes, and it faces the side away from the tower."

"Which will still have a view of us," Henri said. "That cannot be helped. We will—"

When Malusre returned from briefing the men he'd hired he made a gesture of apology:

"*Sahib, memsahib*—you realize that . . ."

"You have to operate with what's available, yes," Henri said, watching a number of their hirelings thumbing knives, thumping knuckleduster-clad fists into an opposite palm or putting on tiger claws. One rat-faced little Bengali was pulling small tools of wire and steel and brass—rather like a watchmaker's tools combined with those of a dentist—out of the folds of his turban and holding them up to the lamp, while a thickset hairy brute in a *dhoti* and impressive collection of gold chains sat beside him and stropped a curved dagger on the horny, callused sole of one foot.

"I have shown them the gold," the detective said. "They know they will be paid if we succeed, and that they will receive pardons."

That was an Imperial prerogative, and the Lion Throne didn't need to ask permission of or explain to anyone when they were granted.

Although what good it will do this gang one can only speculate, Henri thought. They'd undoubtedly commit new crimes immediately, not looking to be the sort of men who'd put the windfall into a safe investment and live off the proceeds. *Although one or two may set up as fences, or open thieves' dens.* It would be enough if they served their purpose, creating chaos and distraction while Henri and Malusre went for Allenby's documents or, failing that, his person.

Malusre went on: "*Sahib*, I am concerned that there may be injury to innocent bystanders. These goondahs I was forced to hire—if this were Kashmir I could have gotten secret volunteers from the IIP, but I am too recently transferred here to know which honest men I could ask such a thing."

"My friend, we have no time for subtlety," Henri said soothingly. "Grave matters of state are at issue here. We must be ruthless; it is needful."

This is a brave man, and able, but he is a policeman, not a soldier, he thought at the other's doubtful nod, reaching over to clap the Marathi detective on the shoulder. *Used to summoning his enemies to surrender to arrest, not throwing a shell in their general direction, or shooting them in the back from ambush.*

He didn't like collateral damage himself, but it was unavoidable if you were going to fight to win. The way to keep it to a minimum was to go in fast and rough, avoid dragging things out. With the people he had to work with tonight, that was unavoidable anyway. They weren't soldiers either, and they had all the cohesion of a handful of lead shot poured into a bucket of camel spit; they'd be useless at anything that required planning or teamwork.

"I shall make every effort to tell the bad people from the good people, and act accordingly."

The *dacoits* filed out ahead of Malusre, eagerly taking extra weapons from a table near the entrance. Those included revolvers, instruments almost impossible to secure without official license; buying them on the black market would take money in quantities most of these bravos would never see. Plus any crime committed while carrying a firearm was classified as attempted murder, even if there were no injuries. That sent you straight to the gallows; the judge put on the black ribbon to pass sentence, and you died at sunrise the next day.

The *gharis* which would carry them were in the courtyard itself, an expanse of stone-block paving dimly lit by two covered lanterns. They were larger vehicles than most, drawn by a pair of horses each, with room for six, or rather more if the passengers didn't mind crowding. The beasts were restive; they snorted and tossed their heads as men piled into them and the drivers brought their heads around.

Henri relaxed and let his eyes adjust to the darkness, ignoring the smells of sweat, unwashed feet, and bad breath. Cassandra King had insisted on coming, although she'd agreed to wait outside when they actually got to Allenby's house, and he thought he detected a trifle of nausea in her swallow and cough. Malusre was in the other *ghari*, to control the bulk of the *dacoit*-mercenaries. Which left him with Marcel, three of the same unsavory crew, and—

The fourth man looked more like a soldier in mufti than a street-bravo. Short but broad-shouldered and muscular, his features difficult to make out in the crowded darkness of the cab, but crowned with a twist of cloth that looked more like a headband than a turban. The one beside him was short and slight, a youth perhaps—

A glint of light came through the curtains over the windows, the vagrant gleam of a streetlamp. Henri de Vascogne began cursing, shifting with effortless fluency between French and Moghrabi-Arabic dialect.

". . . beshitted chicken-brained imbecilic—name of a name—expectorations of a syphilitic she-camel—"

"*Chup!*" Sita said, a rather rude word for *shut up!* Then she dropped into French herself: "Do you want these"—she nodded at the *dacoits*—"to know who I am?"

That stopped him cold, and he contented himself with glaring and grinding his teeth. Before he could call to the driver, she went on:

"You can't turn back. That would ruin everything."

"And if you are killed, *petite cretin*, that won't?"

"Why should you be able to hedge your bets, Henri? I can't, after all."

The sheer effrontery of that took his breath away for a second. Then she stuck her hands under her jacket—she was dressed in trousers and high-collared coat of some plain dark fabric, perhaps something worn for sport, and a close-fitting turban—and snapped them out in a blur of motion. One hand held a light revolver, the other a little two-barreled derringer.

"Don't worry," she said, as the rubber wheels ran silently on the granite pavement. "I've been very well trained; Father insists on it for all of us. And I have the *jawan* here—he's a Gurkha, Imperial Guards, seconded to the bodyguard detail."

"*Han*, that me," the man beside her said, in very bad Hindi, opening his jacket and exposing leather harness over his shirt. A *kukri* hung under one arm, and a pistol under the other. He grinned, and several gold teeth shone in the gloom.

"How on earth did you get him to go along with this . . . this beshitted imbecility?"

"I didn't," she said. "I gave them the slip while I was supposedly shopping—climbed through the window in the ladies' loo and lost them in the alleys. This one was the only one who managed to catch up with me, and I threatened to shoot him if he tried to take me back by force."

"Work with two. One not enough, unless hit her on head," the soldier-bodyguard said, grinning again. "Not safe, hit on head. Have to go along, keep her safe."

A shrug. "My oath, my salt, keep *Kunwari* safe. Not to make *Kunwari* be good girl." His grin grew wider. "Whole regiment not enough for that."

Henri groaned and pummeled his temples. "What would I tell your father? Or *my* Emperor?" he said.

"What would you tell the prince I'm supposed to marry?" she asked him, an edge of taunting mischief in her voice.

"That he is a man not to be envied and will know no peace," Henri said leadenly, ignoring Sita's hurt look. "But that he knows already. The, how do you say, the hue and cry will be up for you by now!"

"Not if I know the officer in charge of that detail," she said. "I left a note for him in the loo—said I'd be back before morning, and if he kept quiet about it, I wouldn't say anything about his losing me and earning a one-way trip to prison-guard detail in a camp on the Andaman Islands."

Henri stared at her. "You will stay by me and obey *every* order, or I will turn back now—on my honor, I swear it."

Sita ducked her head. "Yes," she said, sounding abashed.

A tense silence fell in the *ghari*; Cassandra was glaring at Sita with a venom nearly a match for Henri's own. He forced himself to ignore it, controlling his breathing and bringing his mind back to focus—he couldn't go into deadly action distracted. That would be a certain way of getting *everyone* with him killed.

Try another time? he thought. Then: *No. There will be no other opportunity.*

If it were merely a matter of King's life, it might be best simply to call things off—King was a brave man and a good soldier, but the Empire he served was not de Vascogne's. The ambassador was right that weighty interests of state were involved.

Yet this mysterious canker must be plumbed, he mused. *For the alliance we need, the Raj must be strong.*

And—he admitted to himself, suppressing a smile—he hadn't had this much fun since Sicily.

Yasmini prodded curiously at the skewer of grilled meat.

"That is lamb," Elias said reassuringly.

"I have never eaten meat before," the tiny blond girl said. "The Sisters are not permitted, so, ever."

King raised his brows as she took a dubious bite or two and then confined herself to the vegetable curry and rice, washed down with draughts of fruit juice. Something within him relaxed. If he had to trust his life—perhaps even the life of the Empire—to this weird little being . . . well, he was reassured by the fact that she'd never dined on fresh human hearts and livers.

The others in the arched courtyard ate as he did, sparely, watching the stars shift in the clear night air, talking quietly among themselves in an array of languages. It was a good idea to eat an hour or two before going into action, if you could, but lightly. King made himself gnaw down a few strips of chicken, swallow a little of the curry, and eat a flaky sweet pastry for the energy. Then he checked over his weapons again, and saw David doing the same. The middle-aged Jew flashed a smile and tossed his head, setting the curls on either side of his face bobbing; his dark baggy pants and long jacket looked dusty, as if they had come out of storage.

"I have been respectable too long," he said. "Too settled here in Delhi. It is not that I am foolish enough to enjoy this breech of the laws, but—"

He shrugged with enormous expressiveness, flipping up his hands—one of them full of pistol cartridges. His father looked at him sourly and spoke in a language King didn't recognize—there was a haunting tint of familiarity to it—a kinship to French, which he did speak, and Latin, which he'd studied—but not enough to catch more than a word here and there.

The older man caught King's puzzlement: "Ladino," he said. "Our family lived in Tiberias, once—and in Sepharad, long before that, before the Inquisition. In Spain, you would say. Come," he went on to David. "If you must, I must. At least you have sons of your own, now."

The son came and knelt before his father.

"*Abba,*" he said.

The older man put a hand on his head and spoke in still another language, guttural and Semitic-sounding but not Arabic:

"*Baruch ator Adonoi, Eloheinu melech hor-olam . . .*" he began. When he was finished he sighed and rose.

Hebrew. King thought. *Let's see:* Adonoi *and* elohim, *that would be* God, *and* Lord. *A prayer of blessing.*

The sight gave him a small pang of sadness; he'd never really had a chance to know his father, the memories few and fleeting. For an instant he wondered what it would be like to have a son himself—he'd always assumed he would, someday, but abstractly. Another King to carry on the family name, serve in the Peshawar Lancers, hold Rexin manor. The thought of a boy that was *his,* looking down into a small face that bore his stamp, playing in the fields where he had, laughing with delight as his father lifted him onto his first pony . . . it was a little odd. There was nothing like the prospect of death to put a hand on your shoulder and say: Hurry. He'd been thinking more and more of that these last few years.

"May the strength of Him who smote the hosts of Nineveh be with you, who go to fight wickedness," Elias said quietly in Hindi—the common tongue of most there—and left.

King shook off thoughtfulness and looked at the tall antique clock. "Time?" he said.

"Nearly," David said. He inclined his head to the doorway his father had taken. "Before that, the Ladino? Father told me I was too old and had too much gray in my beard to keep playing silly *goy* games."

Another shrug. "When I'm his age, I'll spend six days a week reading Torah and sitting in the synagogue—which I notice he doesn't himself, usually three at most. Until then, fighting the Eaters of Men is a *mitzvah,* too."

"I've heard yogis say the same," King observed. "More or less, with a few differences in the terminology."

"Details, He is in the details," David said, grinning and raising his eyes to heaven. "And He is confounded jealous about them, too."

Damn, but I rather like this chap, King thought.

A blacksmith's hammer had been sounding in the background for some time. It stopped, more conspicuous now that it was gone, and presently a servant came out with a contraption of linked, swiveling iron bars and chains, bowing as he handed it to David bar-Elias. Ibrahim Khan rose from his crouch; he'd been putting a new edge on his *chora*, working with quiet competence as he stroked it with a small hone he kept in a pouch by the scabbard, and whistling a song.

King knew the tune: it had a chorus that went—

"My blade upholds the Afghan fame
And Kushul Khattuck is my name—"

When the Pathan was satisfied—knife-sharp, but not a thin razor edge that would turn on bone—he tucked the sharpening stone away and wiped the surplus oil off the steel with the dangling tail of his *pugaree*.

"So," he said, standing and flipping the weapon up into a blurring circle. His hand darted into the silver disk like a hairy spider striking, and the hilt smacked into his callused palm. "Let us go pay a call on Shaitan's bum-boys."

They all glanced at Yasmini. She rose as well, a glass of the yellow-white *bhang lassi* in her hand. She closed her eyes for a moment, exhaled, and then drank it off in a long draught. Her throat worked, and when she opened her eyes the pupils had already begun to dilate.

"It is begun," she said quietly. "We go . . . *now*."

Chapter Fifteen

King found Allenby's house more intimidating as a squat black bulk across the road than as plans on a well-lit table. It had been built in the 1920s, when the need to design your dwelling place for defense was past in the settled provinces around Delhi, but the memory of the terrible years remained fresh. In appearance it was rather like a fortified frontier manor, a hollow rectangle with a square three-story tower at one corner and two-story walls all around, and a single gate at the front leading into a court. Trees showed over the top of that, hinting at gardens within.

Unlike the homes of the Border *zamindars* that were its model, it had exterior windows, genuine square ones with glass panes instead of narrow firing slits, in wall and tower both. They were small, though, and their outsides were covered by checkerboard grillwork of wrought-iron bars. The neighborhood was affluent, middling-wealthy and up, businessmen and lawyers of several castes with a solid sprinkling of Imperial Civil Service upper-rogers.

Broad streets were lined with trees, acacia and jacaranda, and there were brick sidewalks with planters and occasional stone benches, but no gas lamps save an occasional domestic model over a gate. The light was enough for outdoorsmen's eyes, even though the moon was a silver sliver of a boat on the horizon; the sky was very bright with stars in the clear air of winter, and the houses were neither tall enough nor close-built enough to turn the streets into canyons of darkness.

The neighborhood's respectability meant it was mostly quiet on an ordinary weekday toward midnight, although several blocks to the north the glow and noise of a large evening party or ball provided a background hum of sound and gaiety, with carriages and a few motorcars parked by the sides of the street. After that there was little traffic to dispute the road with the covered mule-drawn goods wagon Elias had furnished for the night's work.

They passed by the front gate that gave onto the courtyard, formidable-looking doors of teak taller than a man, strapped and studded with iron, then turned the corner to plod along beside the outer wall toward the tower. King found himself starting slightly as Yasmini laid her hand on his arm in the gloom, her face a pale shadow.

"Now. Now is the best . . . the least-bad time," she said, her voice a breathy whisper.

He nodded silently and made a broad gesture with hand across mouth to remind everyone that silence was absolutely necessary. Ibrahim sneered slightly as he rolled out of the back of the wagon and fell prone against the wall of Allenby's house, near-invisible in his earth-colored clothes. King went next, the whisper of his soft leather boots on the brick of the sidewalk only slightly louder. The rest of the crew followed, at intervals just great enough to give each man time to clear the next. A shadow skittered across the road and took cover behind a planter. The wagon continued on its way, the shod hooves of the mules loud enough to cover a multitude of sins; far more noise than the party made, certainly.

Ibrahim gave a jerk of surprise when Yasmini murmured *now* once more, close to his ear. What he muttered in turn were curses, or propitiary prayers against djinn and effreet. King smiled tautly to himself in the darkness; that Ibrahim Khan of the Dongala Khel saw the woman as a spirit made it possible for him to obey her in a way unthinkable for a Pathan if she had been a mere female.

Ibrahim rose and unslung the coil of strong, thin, knotted rope he'd been wearing like a bandoleer, and began to swing the small grapnel fastened to its end. That had three arched prongs, the steel covered in chevron-printed rubber, a refinement that had won his enthusiastic praise at Elias's house and a visibly hidden decision to steal the marvelous contrivance.

Now it cut the air in a whirling circle half a dozen times as the Afghan paid out cord between his fingers; and then a quiet *huff!* of effort as he flung it upward. It sailed up like a bat through the night, trailing the dark-colored rope, and vanished between two crenellations. Ibrahim stood back and pulled it in cautiously, ready in case the hooks did not catch and the little weight of forged steel came down again. When it did catch he increased the tension steadily, setting the hooks in whatever they'd caught with a steady pull before testing his weight on it.

"*Bhisti-sawad,*" he murmured; *excellent.* "The wolves are in the fold tonight!"

Then he drew his *chora*, clamped it between his teeth, and swarmed up the rope like a giant rock spider, only the occasional soft rutching of his curl-toed boots against the plastered stone blocks of Allenby's house disturbing the silence of the night. King waited below, holding the rope steady but keeping his eyes locked on the tower top. When Ibrahim was halfway to the heights there was a flicker of movement; he froze, and a man appeared at the top of the tower above, reaching for the rope.

Across the street the Mongol caravan guard rose from where he had squatted behind a planter. His recurved bow came up, four feet of glossy laminated wood and horn and sinew with gazelle-horn tips for the nocks. King had noticed the bowman's shoulders before, broad enough to make him seem squat despite being of middle height—the man had seemed an awkward waddling *yaksha*-troll in Elias's house, but David had vouched for him.

Now those shoulders bent the hundred-thirty-pound pull of the nomad bow in a single effortless twist of arm and torso, the string resting on the bone ring that protected the Mongol's thumb as he locked it around the base of the shaft. The arrowhead flashed once, then became a streak that echoed to the eyes the flat snap of the string releasing and the *vvvzzipp* of cloven air. There was a muffled thump from above, and the Mongol drew, aimed, and loosed again in another movement of stark grace.

Ibrahim swarmed up the rest of the way to the rooftop of the tower, swung over, then flicked a hand into view for a moment to show that all was clear.

"Good for you, Genghis," King whispered to himself; although actually the man's name was something like *Togrul.* A rifle with a telescopic sight could have done no better, and they couldn't afford the noise of a shot—certainly not outside the muffling stone walls of the house.

He went up next, followed by David—puffing and wheezing a little—and all but the rear guard of the crew, each man helping the next over the parapet. The tower top was a featureless rectangle fifteen feet by twenty, with nothing but a stone pavement and the crenellations 'round about. The only other feature was an iron trapdoor set into the floor, and two bodies. One had a broad-bladed arrowhead sticking out the back of his skull, and the shaft and fletching through his nose like a black exclamation point. The other was lying beside him, shot through the base of the throat just above the breastbone; *he* was still bleeding copiously, but for all practical purposes was as much dead mutton as his friend.

King glanced over his shoulder at the street. Forty yards if it was an inch, uphill, and in the dark. With no more sound or fuss than a night owl might make fluttering back to its nest.

"Useful fellow."

David bar-Elias smiled in the darkness. "Someday ask me of the girl from Kirkuk, and how Moishe saved us when we were nearly taken by her father's men at the caravanserai by the Tigris," he said reminiscently.

"*Moishe?*"

"Moishe Togrul. Long story. I promised him then that he'd have food at my table for the rest of his life."

"He's earned it," King said sincerely. "Seven courses, dessert, brandy, and a cigar."

The five men—and one dark-clad woman, her head wrapped so that only pale eyes showed—grouped around the door with weapons poised. Ibrahim gripped the ring and lifted . . .

. . . and the trapdoor shifted not an inch. He dropped to his knees, swearing expressively and softly in Pashtun, and felt around the edges and across the surface with incongruously delicate fingers.

"Locked!" he snarled. "As the plan said it was not. It must be new. See, *huzoor*, the keyhole is here under a little cover. But the blind sons of owls have put the hinges on the outside and we can knock—"

"Too much noise," King said. *We'll have to go down a story and try to get one of the window grilles—*

"Give me your lockpicks," Yasmini said, kneeling soundlessly beside Ibrahim.

The Pathan reared back, as if a cobra had suddenly inflated its hood beside him, and then groped in his sash-bound coat, handing her a cloth bundle with gingerly caution. She took it—her motions uncannily precise in the darkness—and unrolled it beside the door. She went to work at once, without even looking at what her two small hands in their black silk gloves were doing. King blinked again, and Ibrahim backed up, spitting to one side and making the sign of the Horns with his left hand. His right clasped quivering-tight on the hilt of his *chora*.

She looked at King instead, her eyes pools of darkness with only a rim of blue around the pupils. "I can tell which exact motion will work best, of all possible ones," she said, without halting for an instant the steady smooth movements.

That must be how she aimed her pistol at Warburton's, King thought, caught between fascination and terror. *Just pointed it and pulled the trigger when she saw the right moment.*

"I cannot work so for long," she said, her voice as calm as if she was discussing dinner. "The strain is too great. Much more, and my mind will break—the dreams will swallow me—many of us die so."

Click. Yasmini rose, stepping back wordlessly.

Ibrahim overcame his fear of the seeress and threw the iron door back with casual strength, dropping through immediately without bothering with the ladder that showed beneath the trapdoor. King followed, sliding down the ladder with his back to the rungs instead of leaping. When his feet touched the boards of the floor he unhooked a small bull's-eye lantern from his belt and squeezed the grip lightly, opening the shutter a crack. A quick glance showed only a storeroom, shadows dancing across old furniture and boxes and bales and heaps of dusty files, plus a staircase leading downward.

The others followed. King went to the head of the stairs—there was another door, wooden this time and unlocked—and signaled again for silence. He put his hand to the knob—

THUDUMP.

The ringing crash of the explosion slammed at his ears and the thick beams and planks of the tower floor shuddered and flexed under

his feet. Dust shot out from the walls, making him sneeze and bringing multilingual curses from others of David's retainers.

"That's torn it," he snarled. "Someone's blown in the bloody front
gate while we were sneaking in the rear! *Chalo!* Go, go, *go!*"

He tore the door open and lunged through.

The target, Henri thought. He leaned out and put the night glass
to his eye for a moment.

"No movement on the tower," he said, and drew a deep breath.
"Marcel. You will stay with this lady and guard the vehicles." *Meaning,
kill the drivers if they try to run away.* "Give me the satchel."

He took it in his hand, a rough jute sack with straps, the sort of
thing poor men used to carry their goods on their backs as they traveled. Inside was a toggle fuse, and a set of linen tubes of blasting powder lashed together around it to make a twenty-five-pound bundle.
The *ghari* slowed, and Sita—might the all-powerful and eternal God
and His son smite her with hemorrhoids—leaned over to open the
door. He jerked his left hand, and the toggle came away as the cord
pulled the igniter free.

A low hissing and bitter smell came from the satchel as the time
fuse began to burn, along with a thin haze of blue smoke. This one was
industrial make, not an armory product; his lack of faith in its accuracy
showed as he pitched it to lie against the base of Allenby's teak doors.

"*Allez! Chalo!*" Henri shouted, and the driver snapped his whip at
the horses' rumps.

They were swaybacked and somnolent beasts, but the unaccustomed *pop* made them break into a shambling gallop, nearly losing
their footing on the sharp turn, then sinking almost to their haunches
as the driver stood on the seat to haul on the reins. Henri piled out of
the dim, ill-smelling interior; his eyes saw the faint light of the street
as almost day-bright. He squeezed them tight and shielded them with
a hand as the clock in his head counted down the seconds. There was a
delay; just enough for him to wonder if the fuse the attaché had found
was going to work, then an ear-shattering crash and roar. The charge
was much bigger than he'd thought was really needed—but it was an
open-air explosion, and very few military operations had ever failed
because too much force was used.

"*Chalo!*" he shouted again.

And reached out to grab Sita's shoulder as she tried to dash past him and draw a light saber at the same time. The Gurkha grabbed her by the other. Bandits pelted past them, yelling their glee at the chance to loot a rich *sahib*'s house and get pardons in advance, and good gold coin as well. This wasn't an operation where there was any sense in trying to lead from the front—trying to inspire these gallows-bait would be more likely to get you shot in the back. The only one left with them was the rat-faced little Bengali who was an expert at opening things, and that because he had no appetite for fighting and the prospect of a very fat reward. The Frenchman took the scabbard of his own sword in his left hand and drew his pistol with his right, conscious of Malusre and the Gurkha arming themselves as well.

"Now," he said.

They trotted around the corner, into the light of gas lamps on cast-iron pillars within the house grounds, and into a choking cloud of powder smoke. One leaf of the gates had been torn loose and was lying in the road; the other leaned drunkenly, held only by the upper hinge. There was less damage within, but a man lay moaning with a great splinter through his thigh, a servant from his looks. One of the *dacoits* was bending over him with a knife in hand, rifling his pockets. Henri kicked him in the buttocks before he could cut the man's throat.

"The servant is one of the Good People, perhaps," he said tightly, as the *dacoit* gave them a glare and ran off. The servant moaned again and clutched his thigh as if trying to squeeze the flesh back together. Henri could hear Sita gulp slightly as she took in the blood and the whimpers of pain.

The formal garden and fountain were Mughal-style, with water running down a marble channel in the center, geometric flower beds now mostly bare for winter, and clipped trees. The house proper surrounded it on three sides, an arched gallery of pillars on either side and an upper story with balconies; the main entrance was at the rear of the enclosure, tall glass doors and Classical pillars flanking them. The bandits were already breaking the glass panes down, scattering through the formal entertaining hall. He could hear shots and screams and the clash of steel from within, as he led them by the shattered glass. The memory of the plans came back to him easily; memorizing maps had been part of his trade since he was a boy.

"This way."

Up a broad staircase at the rear of the hall that led to a landing, the burnt-sulfur smell of the powder mingling with incense and wax and polish. Right there, up more stairs, and down a long corridor that led back around the central court, colorful with tile on the walls and the arched ceiling, lit gas lamps caged in brass arabesques. It ended in another door, teak covered in ivory inlay, but looking formidably stout. The little rat-faced burglar went to work on the lock.

"Open, *sahi*—"

He threw the door back triumphantly, and the words cut off in the beginning of a squeal and an unpleasant crunching *thock* sound as an ironbound sal-wood club slammed into his face, square in the center of the prominent nose. The man behind was huge, muscular under his blubber, and very dark. Henri shot him, and Malusre and the Gurkha followed in less than half a second, the sound of their pistols blending into a single long crackle. Sita's gun was out and pointed well, but she hadn't fired, and her eyes were wide as the man toppled backward with three red dots blossoming on his chest. He twisted as he fell, showing craters the size of a young girl's fist in his back, full of torn flesh and blood and splintered bone. Sita gulped again at the sight, and wrinkled her nose at the smell.

"Not much like hunting," she said.

"Good," Henri said. At her inquiring look: "I've known men, and a few women, who never made that distinction. None of them persons you would be happy to associate with. But next time—shoot anyway. This was one of Detective Malusre's Bad People."

"It's dirty work, but someone has to do it?" Sita said, with a flash of spirit.

"Exactly."

The décor within was in the Imperial fashion, and looked of good quality but old—inherited, perhaps. One piece in a niche was new; a goddess dancing on a gashed corpse. She was dark-faced, with hair of snakes and a long, lolling red tongue, a necklace of skulls across her breasts, a belt of severed hands about her waist, clutching weapons and dripping heads in her many hands. A third eye flamed in her forehead, winking red—a ruby.

"The Dreadful Bride," Sita whispered behind him. "Kali—the dark aspect of Durga."

"A demon?" he asked, moving forward.

Yes, a desk, and a picture behind it. The picture was the likeliest place to conceal a safe; the *Angrezi* were not an imaginative people about such things.

"Not exactly," Sita replied. "Kali can be the demon-slayer in some legends, embodiment of the power of Shiva. Our Indian gods are like that, ambiguous. It all depends on which region and which cult you're talking about, and some are one thing in public and another privately. From that image I'd say it's one of the bad ones, where she's just a blood-drinking bitch bent on universal destruction."

"Quelle surprise," Henri muttered dryly. "Let us to work."

He'd seen prettier images in the devil huts of the shamans of European cannibal tribes. And burned them, on punitive expeditions, with the shamans inside. He walked over and felt around the edges of the painting behind the desk as Malusre checked the others and the Gurkha kept watch at the door.

This was a rather fetching landscape in a glossy realistic style, and looked ancient—pre-Fall, almost certainly; it showed a flock of sheep scattering across a bright, green landscape of pastures and wheatfields and poplar trees, while in the foreground a red-haired shepherd dallied with a milkmaid who had a lamb in her lap; rather oddly, he was offering her a moth.

A slight *click* came clearly as his fingers tripped a hidden catch. The painting swung aside to show a safe.

"Here," he said.

The other men joined him, while Sita began quickly going through the contents of the desk. Malusre looked at the safe and clucked his tongue.

"Govind and Chubb," he said, indicating a brass plate screwed to the steel. "And set directly into the stone. I could not open it without a pneumatic drill and a diamond bit or the combination. Nirad could perhaps, but—"

He motioned over his shoulder at the corpse of the little burglar. The prominent nose had been smashed completely in, and both eyes had popped out under the pressure of the massive stroke. Henri was briefly but extremely glad the man who wielded it hadn't managed to get within arm's reach. Then he noticed something odd.

"Not as much noise as I expected. Could Allenby be out?" Even traitors attended dinner parties.

"No," Malusre said. "I checked most particularly. His wife is staying with relatives—she often does—and his children are all at boarding schools at this time of year." The winter term began right after *Diwali*. "But he is here."

"Well, he's not *here*, here," Sita said from the desk. "And neither are most of his servants—a house this size should have at least twenty or thirty." A pause as she finished her quick scan of the desk. "Nothing! Nothing out of the ordinary!"

"There would not be," Henri said grimly. "This Allenby is a professional of Intelligence, even if he is a traitor. Anything incriminating would be in the safe. We must find him, and soon, or go—the police will arrive in moments. Without documents, we must have the man himself. Make him talk."

And searching this whole great house was going to take more time than they had . . .

"This way," King said.

He kicked open the door at the bottom of the stairs, ran across the room—it seemed to be fitted out as a nursery, though without any present occupants—and down another set of stairs. The door there was locked, but it was carved sandalwood, and the bolt tore out under his boot. Then he stopped for a moment, blinking in the brightness and glitter beyond. Two naked girls sat up in bed at his entry, clutching each other and screaming in high-pitched panic amid the swirling gauze curtains that hung from the bedposts. At another time he might have looked on with some interest; the girls were full-figured and very pretty, one pale cream and the other dark brown. Although they were both a bit young for his taste—around sixteen, one visibly pregnant, the other with a fading black eye.

The room was richly furnished, with a gilt fretwork ceiling set with small mirrors, and murals in the neo-Mughal style popular nowadays—all the scenes were erotic, and he realized that this must be Allenby's *bibi-khana*, his women's quarters. There were servants scattered around, most of them screaming as well—all women, all good-looking, ranging from their late teens to their early thirties.

The room would have been the base of the tower, but it was larger than the fifteen-by-twenty chambers above, with only thick arches at the corners to show where the weight bore down. Beyond those were light furniture, low couches and tables, rugs, cushions, and a sunken tub of blue-and-white marble set amid tiles and carved-stone screens.

And on the opposite side a doorway, which slammed back to admit four large men with *tulwars*, rushing in at the women's screams, and now breasting forward through a covey of bright saris and shrieks like fishermen wading through surf.

"Bloody hell," King snarled to himself. And then aloud: "Take them—but keep it quiet!"

There was plenty of noise from the courtyard below. If *his* party didn't start shooting, they might be able to get through to their objective without attracting the attention of either the occupants or whoever-the-hell it was who'd attacked the house at this *extremely* inconvenient moment. King crossed his arms downward, drawing his Khyber knife with his left hand and his saber with his right. There were no points for elegance in a melee; it wasn't like a duel.

A hysterical maidservant got in the way of his first lunge, making him twist aside at the last moment—giving her a nasty gash despite all he could do. The distraction might have been fatal if David bar-Elias hadn't moved up and caught the foeman's descending sword on his. King pivoted and stabbed his immobilized opponent under the arm with the *chora* in his left hand, in time to see Ibrahim Khan neatly trip another and hack through the back of his neck. No points for fair play, either.

Beyond him another of Allenby's retainers toppled backward with half his face gone and a mushy scream, blowing blood bubbles through what was left. The other two of David's men were hacking the last man down with economy and dispatch, the inward-curved blades of their *yataghans* throwing streams of red drops as they flashed and turned and smacked home with dull wet sounds. The brief scrimmage of clashing steel and stamping, snarling men died down; Ibrahim silenced enemy wounded with short, brutally efficient thrusts and chaffed good-humoredly at the other men as they rifled the dead. One of the merchant's retainers tore open his jacket and grunted at the sight of blood staining his shirt beneath from a deep stab.

"Back," David said. "Can you climb?"

"Yes, *sahib*. For a while, at least. I will weaken, with this."

"Back and out. Togrul will bandage you and send you on your way home."

"This way," Yasmini said, in the same dream-toned voice she had used since drinking the *bhang lassi*. "Through the door."

"Come, then," King said to Ibrahim.

"Shall I slay, and not scratch?" the Pathan said, but followed willing, leering at the women—now mostly huddled around the two on the bed, one binding another's gashed forearm.

"Down the stairs," Yasmini said. "Below."

"Through here!" Henri said, increasingly desperate.

The door was locked. He backed off to the side and pointed his pistol, covering his eyes with his sword arm.

Crack. Bits of metal flew through the air. They pushed through, shouldering the door open, and the Frenchman whistled.

"Death of my life," he said; it was a big room, and fitted out like the gaudiest whorehouse in creation.

There were a good dozen women huddled together on the bed—all of them terrified-looking, many weeping, one moaning over a bandaged and bleeding arm. And there were four dead men on the floor, *tulwars* near their hands, blood still flowing from their wounds, with an open door behind them—stairs behind it, leading upward.

Sword work, he thought; the stink of raw blood and bowel was thick, and the rich carpets near the men were sopping. *And rather well done.* All hell was lose in Allenby's house tonight, and not just the hell of his own making.

"More of the Good People, Captain Malusre," Henri said in frustration, nodding at the women. "Apart from these," he added, prodding one of the corpses with the toe of his boot.

"Pathan," Malusre said. "Not the dead men—the killer. Look, see how the throats are cut, with an outward thrust? Very distinctive."

"Which helps us not at all: *Where is Allenby?*"

Sita surprised him. She stepped past him toward the bed, and spoke in rapid Hindi:

"Where is your master?" Whimpering met her gaze, and her voice sharpened—not loud, but with a tone of cold command. "Where is your lord, you foolish women? *Now.*"

Half a dozen arms pointed to a door at the far end of the room. "There—down the stairs, in the chambers below the house," one voice said. "He—he meets with his *guru.*"

"The foreign *guru*," another amplified.

"It is forbidden to disturb him," a third said, her voice shaking.

"Get out," Sita went on. "The *polis* will be here soon. When they do, run out to them. Dress for the street, gather your valuables. Obey!"

The women were gabbling and running about as Henri led the party through the door and down a spiral staircase, down past what must be the ground floor into darkness lit only by a few gas lamps turned low.

"Why?" he said to the princess, jerking his head upward.

"Whoever's loose in the house, those poor bints don't deserve to be hurt more," Sita said. "More of the Good People, as you said."

Henri smiled for a moment. Then they were in a round space around the base of the stair with four corridors leading off to each quarter. The noises of the house above were muffled here, barely perceptible; they must be even fainter in the rooms that gave off the open corridors, for the doors he could see in each were heavy and of solid metal.

"Which way?" he said.

"Quiet," Sita replied, cocking her head to one side. Then: "*That* way. I hear chanting. If Allenby is with a 'guru'—the man Ignatieff, that Warburton's papers mentioned?—they might be holding some sort of ceremony."

"Good thinking, *ma petite*," Henri said; her ears were keener than his. Well, she was eight years younger, and hadn't spent so much time around gunshots and explosives as he.

They jogged along the corridor, between walls of rough mortared stone. The sound came louder, loud enough for him to hear as well.

"Back," he told Sita.

The Gurkha enforced that with his shoulders. Henri put his hand to the catch; the door opened inward, and the sound from behind it was loud now—voices chanting in a language he didn't understand, and the beating of a drum. He took a deep breath—small, confined, underground places were not among his favorites—and swung the door open, cutting off the chant like an ax stroke.

Within was a large room, its single half window bricked up. Perhaps it had been an ordinary cellar once; now it was walled with smooth black ebony on three sides, and dimly lit by a single oil lamp hanging from the ceiling by chains of orilachrium. The lamp was in the form of a horned head, mouth stretched in a dolorous gape to show the flame. Over the night black glossy wood of the paneling were . . . *icons*, he supposed. Religious paintings at least. Some were Indian, images of the death goddess like the statue in Allenby's office above. Others were in a stiff semi-Byzantine style. Images of Malik Nous in his aspect as the Black God—some of him fighting Christ, driving Him, slaying Him; others of his long sword cleaving the sun as he stood on a mound of ice and skulls. Yet others were of things he instantly wished he hadn't seen, to keep the memory of them out of his head.

On the fourth wall was a mosaic of a peacock, wings raised and tail spread in glorious color. The altar was before that, a block of black marble. The body of a girl was fastened to it with silver chains, and there were runnels in the dais to catch blood and transfer it to broad shallow pans. There was a great deal of the blood; he thought the sacrifice had been young, but it was difficult to tell, given what had been done to her before she died. The death was recent—the blood still flowing—and only a few of the internal organs had been removed to stand in the vessels set into depressions in the stone block. The smell was raw, but not as strong as the bitter herbal scent that came from the lamp in dizzying waves.

Rows of men kneeling with their heads to the ground filled the room before the altar; most were in saffron yellow robes that left one shoulder bare, others in ordinary street dress, a few in Imperial uniforms.

One man stood close to the altar, a tall fair-skinned man all in black, leather and silk liberally splashed with red. He turned as the door opened; a long curved knife was held in one gloved hand, a fresh human heart in the other, and an inverted cross hung on his chest. He had been squeezing the heart into his mouth like an orange for its juice, and the lower part of his face was a mask nearly as black as his clothing in the faint light.

"So," the Frenchman said into an instant of stillness. "You, I presume, are *not* one of the Good People."

The eyes above the bloody mouth were wide with surprise and shock, one brown and one blue in the pale high-cheeked countenance. Henri de Vascogne thought that he would have recognized him without that; there was only one man that this could be. A figure sprang erect beside Ignatieff; Allenby, in similar robes, but as unreachable as the Caliph in Baghdad or the Mikado at the moment.

At least as far as taking him is concerned, Henri thought grimly. *But perhaps if we alter the plan to simply making him die . . .*

Henri leveled the revolver—regulation stance, body at right angles to the target, left hand tucked into the small of his back—and emptied it at the Russian nobleman and the *Angrezi* traitor beside him. He thought one of the bullets struck, but there was no time to be sure, because the rest of the cultists were springing up and coming at them like a wave.

Whatever other taboos the followers of the Peacock Angel had, they didn't prohibit weapons at a sacrifice. More than half of them were drawing long knives or flourishing *rumals* as they came, and their eyes and teeth shone cold in the flame light.

He sprang back and slammed the door, but there was no way to bar it from the outside. Hands gripped it from the other side and began to pull. Henri's head whipped from side to side; there was nowhere to go besides the way they had come . . . and then suddenly the gaslights all went out with a series of low *pop* sounds. A minute later the hissing of the gas started again, but there was no snap of electric starter sparks.

His eyes went wide in the total darkness. "Too many of them," he gasped, as the handle twisted inexorably in his hand. "We have to get out *now*, this place is going to explode. *Allez!*"

A hand came down on the handle beside his. "Me hold," the Gurkha's voice said. "Go—save *kunwari*."

When the Frenchman hesitated the Gurkha pushed him roughly aside, feeling like a short living boulder of Himalayan granite. "My salt—my oath. Save *kunwari!*"

Henri clapped him on the shoulder as he passed. "I will," he said, holstering his empty revolver and drawing his sword.

Malusre was pushing Sita ahead of him as they groped back for the stairs. "Faster," he said. "Don't make it for nothing!"

She ran; all three did, caroming into the stone of the corridor as they went. Behind them the door was wrenched open at last. The lamp within cast a faint light out into the corridor, enough to make the five red flashes of the Gurkha's revolver less blinding. The noise was very loud in the stony confines of the corridor. Then there was a rasp of steel, a nauseatingly audible wet thud, a high shrill scream. A quick look over his shoulder showed the great broad-bladed, inward-curved knife out and sweeping in long-armed cuts. The Gurkha hacked with the *kukri* at arms that came forward with blades as the cultists crowded into the doorway, trying to push him backward by main force. At the same instant, he drove the fingers of his free hand down into the eyes of a man who had grabbed his legs and hooked him away like a gaffed fish . . .

"*Ayo Gorkhali!*" he shouted as he fought. "*Ayo Gorkhali!*"

"The Gurkha are upon you!" Malusre said in a shaken voice as they reached the staircase. "*Shabash, jawan!*" Then in a clipped tone: "I will go first."

"Follow," Henri snapped to Sita. "Cover him." He turned to bring up the rear, sword out—a touch of light in the dimness of the night-dark cellars, where faces were blurs barely arm's length away.

A flash of steel and brightness brought him around, parrying barely in time.

Name of a dog, Henri thought, as he felt the terrifying strength in the blow; his wrist jarred painfully, and then again and again as he parried. Instinct guided him; conscious thought would have been far too slow to block the tiger speed of the assault.

"Down here," Yasmini said. "At the bottom of the stairs, turn right, and seek the last door at the end of the corridor. Your man is held prisoner there."

"Move!" King said.

The spiral staircase went from marble elegance to rough mortared fieldstone as they descended. According to Warburton's information, the whole mansion and courtyard were underlain by cellars, divided into rooms by thick stone walls and the heavy arches that upbore the house. He could almost feel the massive weight above him, a quasi-physical oppression as they came to the foot of the stairs and turned right down a corridor dimly lit by two small gaslights.

"This way," Yasmini said. She paused for an instant, those eerie eyes turning behind them. "That way is a place where they worship the Black God. And where they feast. I can . . . hear . . . the chanting. It creeps through the world, like mold through bread."

"I should have spent less time at the ledgers and more outdoors," David bar-Elias puffed beside him.

But he was keeping up well enough, and he'd been strong enough to haul himself up a three-story height nearly as fast as fit young fighting men. King suspected the older man was remembering his own imprisonment in the dungeons of the House of the Fallen in Bokhara, and that was what squeezed heart and lungs. He didn't blame Elias's son for that at all. Enduring a nightmare when you had no choice was bad enough. Going back into it, of your own free will . . .

"All the better," King said. "They won't be paying so much attention to *us*, then."

"This door," Yasmini said after a silent minute. "He is within. There is a window to the outside—small, and barred with iron."

"Right—" King began.

Then there was a fusillade of shots—not close, but somewhere in the cellars with them. A chorus of yells, the clash of steel, more shots, and a shout:

"*Ayo Gorkhali! Ayo Gorkhali!*"

King's head whipped around. The Gurkha battle cry; he'd heard it more than once. Ibrahim Khan recognized it, too, wheeling, ducking, and bringing up his long Khyber knife in a single motion, eyes flickering around in automatic wariness. The mountaineers from Nepal furnished many regiments for the Raj, and they were the only men the Border tribes really feared on their own ground.

"That's only one man," King said.

Whatever in the ten thousand names of God he's doing here. Gurkhas were popular as bodyguards and armed retainers for the wealthy, as well as serving in the Imperial forces. Retired soldiers from their regiments might enlist in the police. *Could be any of a dozen reasons.*

"One man, and he's fighting many. Ibrahim—get that door open and get Narayan Singh out. Mr. bar-Elias, we'll see what's going on and hold the corridor if we must."

Just then the lights went out, leaving only a dimming red glow for a few seconds as the mantles cooled.

"Merciful Krishna," King swore, sheathing his *chora* and pulling the bull's-eye lantern from his belt. *This is getting beyond bloody enough,* he thought, feeling increasingly harassed—how was he supposed to keep all this straight?

He opened the lantern's slit only a touch—any light right now was going to make him a sitting duck—as they ran back toward the stairwell. The run turned into a silent lunge as he saw an armed man at the base of the stairs.

The man turned, smooth and very quick. The swords clashed, met, clashed again in the near-total darkness, only an occasional glint on the steel itself showing where death walked. The ugly wind of a sharp blade passed before his eyes, and then the swords locked at the hilt and the two men were wrestling . . .

"Name of a dog!" An accented half scream. "You!"

"De Vascogne!" King blurted, skipping backward. "What in the name of the Gods are *you* doing here?"

"Looking for *you*, imbecile! Or evidence of you—we found Ignatieff, and Allenby, and half a hundred others; they'll be on us in seconds."

King swore: "Shiva's dong, *you* blew the door in—no time—tell them they can contact me through Elias bar-Binyamin—there's a plot to kill the King-Emperor, and my family, and—go, man, go! I have my own way out!"

The Frenchman nodded, half-seen, and obeyed, his boots pounding up the staircase. King heard a choking sound behind him and wheeled. David bar-Elias was standing frozen, his sword half-drawn. Beyond him was Ignatieff, almost invisible in his black robes save for the pale face. From the awful stink, much of the robes' color was dried and rotting blood. There was fresh blood on his face and hands, and his blue eye glinted with a terrible merriment as he extended one finger toward the Jew's face.

"Tchernobog has his mark on you, *zhid*," he said in Russian. "The Peacock stands ready to bear your soul to the Mouth that shall eat all existence."

"Snap out of it!" King said, deliberately jostling the Jew as he came up beside him. "No need to be alarmed at a man who can't even afford to pay his laundry bill, by the smell."

The older man came to himself with a start, and they both backed a step—into the corridor that led to Narayan Singh's prison.

Ignatieff laughed, a soft grating sound. Behind him the men in saffron robes advanced, their heads nodding in inhuman unison as they hummed together. In the rear of their ranks a voice rose in song—a hymn. A hymn to Her; a song of the pestilence that was Her health, of the famine that was Her affluence; of the agony that was Her joy. Several in the first row were snapping *rumal*-handkerchiefs from hand to hand, the cloth flickering too fast to see; others brandished the short one-bladed pickaxes, or skinning knives. They edged forward, between the figure in the black robe and his enemies.

"So," the Russian said. "An *Angrezi* dog and his arse-sniffing Yid jackal. Filth, defending a world of filth. You have committed sacrilege, but you can pay immediately. Oh, *how* you shall pay!"

He half turned. "Take them! We have them trapped—take them alive for the sacrifice."

Oh, no you don't, King thought.

The corridor was a tight fit for two men, if it came to fighting; just about right for one with sword and long knife. If they could hold the enemy off—

"Fall back," King said. "Give me blade room. You can spell me if I tire."

"I have a better idea than that, my *Angrezi* hero," David bar-Elias said. "More light, please."

King brought the bull's-eye lantern up and squeezed the grips, opening the shutter more widely. David stepped up, with the odd-looking pistol King had noted in his hand. The Kali-worshipers rushed immediately, but the Jew met them with a ripple of fire that would have done credit to a Gatling gun, killing a man with each shot. That was no easy thing; in darkness and the terror of close combat most men would miss two times out of three, even at point-blank range. Most of the dead were down with head wounds; the bodies fell in the front rank, some limp, more thrashing for a few seconds like pithed frogs.

Ignatieff reacted just as swiftly, grabbing two of his followers and holding them together before him as a shield. When the sixth bullet fired and the pistol clicked on an empty chamber he grinned and threw them aside.

"Take them!" he called again.

His followers began to climb over the twitching mound of bodies. David extended the pistol and fired again. This time the sound was a softer *thudump*, rather than the sharp crack of regular fire. A circular patch of Ignatieff's robes disappeared, right over his stomach; he went down with an *uffff!* like a man punched hard in the belly. Dismayed, the Kali-worshipers wavered.

"*Shabash!*" King shouted, wishing he'd done the deed himself. *Take that for Hasamurti, you bloody maniac!* Although—had that been a gleam of chain mail beneath the robe? It wouldn't stop a normal bullet, but that had sounded like—

"Now we run!" David called cheerfully. Then, in gasps as they tore down the corridor into darkness: "French . . . bought it in Cairo . . . extra barrel, round of buckshot!"

The door to the chamber at the end was open. Within—

Narayan Singh bit his lip until the blood flowed. He was "swimming on land," hanging in midair suspended by chains that ran from each limb to brackets in the walls. A man of less than his thick-limbed, bull-necked strength would have been racked to madness long since. As it was, every joint of his limbs was a mass of fire, and the tendons that ran up into the muscles were like iron rods heated to white welding heat in a smith's forge.

Still, he managed a hoarse laugh as he heard shouts and running feet outside his prison, and then gave a bellow:

"*Shabash!*" he shouted. "*Shabash, sahib!*" And laughed again when the lights went out.

There was one guard with him, the Sikh; the man cursed, relighting the gas lamps from a taper. He looked at Narayan and raised his dagger, then shrugged and lowered it again. Instead he went to the door, listening with his ear pressed against it.

A voice spoke outside: a woman's voice, speaking in a tongue Narayan Singh didn't understand, but thought was that of the *Russki.* His heart sank, although he kept the snarl on his face and craned his neck up despite the pain. Had the Russki woman betrayed the *sahib?*

That seemed more likely when the Sikh guard unbarred and opened the door. Through it came the seeress, only her pale eyes visible through the eye slit of a hood. Behind her came Ibrahim Khan with long knife in hand, grinning and splashed with blood. The blood was as natural to him as his beard, and as for the grin—in the lands up north and west of Peshawar town, treason has always been accounted a good joke, and a better game than stick-and-ball.

The woman looked around the room. Even hanging from the

chains, Narayan felt a slight tingling chill as he met them. They saw more than human beings were meant to see . . .

She stepped aside, pointed to the Sikh guard, turned her head to Ibrahim.

"Kill," she said.

Her voice had the empty purity of water in a mountain stream. So much so that the guard was nearly caught flat-footed, his mind not taking in that the word was meant for *him*. Ibrahim Khan had no such weakness, and his Khyber knife was flicking out even as she spoke. The point of it touched the guard's belly as he sprang backwards—there was nothing wrong with his reflexes in a fight—and instead of standing to do battle, he spun and raced for Narayan Singh with a dagger held high, plainly intending to obey his instructions and see that the prisoner wasn't saved.

The young Sikh felt a surge of angry frustration—to come so close to rescue!—and then filled his lungs to meet death with a cry of defiance. He could see Ibrahim making a throwing gesture, but with his left hand, and there wasn't room under the low ceiling for a proper cast with the *chora*, anyway.

Then half a pace from him, knife raised, the guard halted. The snarl left his face, replaced by a scream of pain, and the knife fell from nerveless fingers. He clutched at his right elbow with his left hand, screamed again, turned in a blundering circle, and the Pathan was upon him. Narayan saw the point of the *chora* slam through the man's neck, and then a gout of blood struck him in the face, stinging fiercely in the cuts and bruises on his skin. He spat again and again to get the taste out of his mouth, blinking and squinting as he saw Ibrahim's face again. The Pathan was tossing a lead ball with steel spikes up and down in his left hand; it was fastened to that wrist by a long length of fine chain.

"I took it from the dead Maxdan in thy village, idolater," he said.

Narayan grunted, and looked down at the guard, whose head was at an odd angle as blood pooled beneath him. Ibrahim giggled again.

"Tee-hee! That is the way to cut a Sikh's throat. With an outward thrust; the point behind the windpipe, and the heel of the blade parts the neckbones!"

The Sikh grunted again. "So, have you come to rescue me, then?"

"Nay; I have come to squat on thy chest and talk to thee of the true faith. Or perhaps to tickle thee with *this*?"

He spun the *chora* in a bright circle. Meanwhile, Yasmini had been tugging at the dead guard's belt. After a moment she drew a knife of her own and cut the keys free, then went to Narayan's feet.

"Hold him," she said, and fitted the key to the lock on one ankle iron.

Ibrahim did as she bid, holding up the Sikh's shoulders and letting him down gently into a sitting position—Narayan wondered at it, until the weight came off his feet, and he bit his lip again to keep from shouting with an unbearable mixture of relief and fresh pain. When the cuffs came off his arms Narayan lay back, hissing.

"Now, God be thanked. And my fate be cursed, that I must give thanks to a Muslim—and a Pathan, at that. Where is the *sahib*?"

"Coming—if he lives," the Pathan said.

A third man waited in the doorway. "They come," he called.

"Not before time," Ibrahim grumbled. "Are all folk but we *Pushtun* so heavy of foot? It is a wonder known only to Allah why we don't rule the world."

"Perhaps because no two of you can agree on anything for the space it takes to cut each other's throats," Narayan wheezed.

He saw two more men—the *sahib*, thanks be to God, and the Guru!—speed through the door. One, a Jew by his dress and looks, took something from his coat, knocked the base of it against the wall, and threw it out into the corridor. Then the two of them slammed the iron door shut, barred it, grabbed several heavy instruments of torture, and tossed them against it as well.

"Greetings, *sahib*!" Narayan called. "Thy father was right—listen to the Jew indeed!"

King nodded, holding back a huge grin of relief—it would have been past bearing, if Narayan had been dead after all. Dying in battle was one thing; being done to death in a pit of human weasels like this was no fate for an honest fighting man.

"I see you have been lying in idleness while the rest of us labored, *bhai*," he said. Then gently: "Can you move?"

"Not except to crawl on my belly like a snake, *sahib*," the Sikh said. "Ai! My joints are like fire, and I as weak as a woman when there is battle to be done, curse these *banchuts*!"

King checked him over, with a quick skill born of long acquaintance with the hurts men inflict on each other. The Sikh's wrists and ankles were lacerated and bleeding, and his joints and tendons had all been stretched far beyond their natural ranges. None of the joints were dislocated, though, and he didn't think anything had torn too badly; Narayan was enormously strong, and had his life nailed tight to his backbone.

Fists were beating on the outside of the door; then something went *pop* and hissed. The pounding and shouts of rage gave way to screams of panic, retching, and pain. David bar-Elias grinned as he dashed across the basement chamber to the outer window. That was at head height, just enough for a man to worm through, if it were open.

"I dabble in chemistry," he said, breaking the glass there with the butt of his pistol, careful to leave no spikes or sharp edges. "As witness—"

He pulled another ball from his long coat, slapped it against the stone, and tossed it out through the bars. It popped in its turn, and let off a spark of bright light on the roadway outside. Almost immediately came the sound of mule hooves on pavement, and the driver of the wagon came forward with another of Elias's men. They fitted the device the blacksmith had made to the bars; it was more than a simple grapnel, more like a giant pair of iron pliers, with twin ropes on the long handles running to the rear of the wagon, and hooked claws on the business end that went around either side of the iron grille.

The driver slapped the backs of his four mules with the reins. They surged forward, and the huge leverage of the simple machine tore the iron bars inward and forward with irresistible force. They ripped free of their seating in the stone with a tooth-grating squeal of tortured metal and clanged away across the street, shedding sparks and fragments of cement mortar. The driver leapt down to untie the rope even as King grabbed Yasmini around the waist with both hands and boosted her through the gap.

Her body was warm and lithe as a mongoose between his hands as she climbed up, a little heavier than he'd thought it would be from her size and build but still no burden. He followed her, and then turned and knelt on the pavement.

"Ibrahim, then hand up Narayan."

The Pathan came through easily, and then they manhandled the limp but conscious and quietly swearing form of the Sikh out, the swearing becoming inventive when the burly shoulders stuck and had to be tugged free with no excessive gentleness. David and his retainer came last; the Jew paused to throw another of his surprises into the open window.

"*Shalom,*" he called mockingly down into the cellar, and then tumbled into the wagon with the rest of them.

The driver was already pulling the heads of the mules around, calling to them, keeping the pace down to a rapid walk—a gallop would be far too likely to attract attention, once they were safely away, and it made it easier for Togrul to sprint out, toss in his bow, and follow it by rolling across the tailboard. King looked at his watch, blinked astonishment, looked again. He was familiar with the rubber time of combat, but—

"Seventeen minutes?" he said. It was then that the full glee of it struck him, and he laughed aloud. "Seventeen minutes!"

He looked up, and saw Yasmini unwinding the cloth that had concealed her face.

"Thank you," he said.

"You are wel—" she began, then clutched at her brow. A single whimper of pain, and she fell forward boneless into his arms.

Cassandra King waited in the darkness. *This is the hardest thing I've ever done,* she thought, as acid chewed at her stomach and the cold stale smell of the small hours oppressed her. Then: *No. I think Charles has the harder part. He has to wait all unknowing, and act as if nothing was happening.*

The two *tiki-gharis* waited; she stood close to the seat where the driver of the first sat tense and let him see her revolver. Henri's man sat beside the other, a hand on his shoulder in what a casual observer might have thought was a companionable gesture. She gnawed the inside of her lip until she caught herself, forced the nervous tic to stop, then found herself doing it again.

Time stretched, more quietly after the first burst of shouts and shooting. Some of the hired *dacoits* came staggering out of the shattered front entrance of Warburton's house and around the corner toward her. Most of them were hauling bundles, some as large as they were. A few limped and clutched at wounds. Some made off on their own, probably because they'd found a bit of loot beyond their wildest dreams. Most of them came over to the *gharis* and tumbled in, chattering excitedly until she gave a crisp command for silence—and showed them the pistol. One at the other *ghari* seemed disposed to argue; Henri's man silenced him with three swift savage elliptical kicks, using his feet like fists, and chucked his moaning form into the vehicle for his friends to catch.

A time that stretched, when nobody came, and then one last bandit plunged out toward them.

Cassandra started to shout a warning, but the pursuing shadow was on the *dacoit* before she could speak. Something flashed in the night as he sprang for the man's shoulders, something white and quicker than a striking cobra. Then the *dacoit* was down on the ground, and the pursuer had a knee between his shoulder blades as he strained upward. There was a brief flurry as the victim's hands and feet thrashed at the ground, then stillness; the assassin crouched and stared about, glaring.

Sweet Mother Pravati, Cassandra thought to herself, appalled. Her hand raised the pistol without conscious decision, as she might have struck at a poisonous serpent. *A Thug!*

Thuggee was something out of legend, a tale of the Old Empire and the Second Mutiny, hardly real despite Athelstane's grim description of his encounter in Peshawar. Now she had seen one of the Deceivers at work herself, as if she'd been catapulted back in time to the Exodus, or even Colonel Sleeman and the youth of the first Victoria. She lowered the pistol to firing position, letting the muzzle fall down until the foresight filled the notch of the rear as Ranjit Singh had taught her—

There was a *vvvviwp* of cloven air. Then the Thug jerked, rising upright and pawing at his head, seeming to dance a jig as he circled. That let her see clearly what had struck; a long black-fletched arrow was through the man's head, right through the ears, and the killing handkerchief fell from nerveless fingers. He tried to scream, his mouth open in a huge dolorous gape, and then blood boiled out of it, flowing black in the faint moonlight. He collapsed with a limp finality.

What next? Cassandra thought. *I just saw a Thug kill a man. Then someone shot an arrow through his head. Who was it? Arjuna, perhaps?*

Then: *Sita . . . what if she doesn't come back? What will I tell Charles?*

The girl was an Imperial pain in the sit-upon without any dispute, but she was so alive; impossible to imagine her dead, there in that den of stranglers. *And Henri—the Frenchman is an experienced soldier,* she told herself. *He'll keep them safe.*

False reassurance. Good men died, when they met bad luck or overwhelming force; as her father had. That was the way the world worked. *What next* was a very serious question.

The next thing was a *konstabeel* in blue and yellow, walking quickly to see what had happened on his beat with such noise and activity. Cassandra stepped back into the shadow of the *ghari,* hissing imperiously for silence as the occupants shifted nervously at the sight of their natural enemy. The vehicle rocked on its springs as they crowded to the other side, anxious not to be seen through the window.

They needn't worry, Cassandra thought, fighting down a giggle she knew was hysterical as the man halted, gaping incredulously at the ruined front of the house he must have seen a thousand times whole on his rounds. Staring at shattered ruin, dead bodies, and scattered weapons.

The representative of the *polis* was a brave man. Armed only with a hardwood truncheon, a set of handcuffs, and a notebook, he took several steps forward and began to blow frantically on the whistle that hung on a lanyard around his neck.

That's torn it, Cassandra thought.

City police didn't patrol in groups, not in a neighborhood like this, but soon enough one was going to hear the whistle, use his own, and alert the whole district. Patrols would come to investigate; it was a wonder nobody's household retainers had already.

Just then the policeman stopped, the whistle falling from his lips. Out through the shattered gates of the Allenby mansion poured . . . women. Cassandra stared herself, feeling her jaw drop a little. The two in the lead were more properly *girls,* which she could see despite dimness and distance because they were wearing hastily donned saris, without either the blouse or petticoat that usually went under the wraparound garment. A dozen others followed them, their dress ranging from servant-caste respectability to trousers of filmy gauze and halters of the same. They engulfed the *konstabeel* in a wave of weeping, pleading femininity, bearing him backward by sheer weight.

For a moment he looked as if he was about to lay about him with his truncheon. Then he plainly decided that here was an excuse to depart the dangerous scene which nobody could dispute; he began shepherding the women away before him, ignoring their questions and demands and blowing on his whistle as he went. A four-mule wagon passed through the little crowd, the covered sort delivery firms used, adding a bizarre touch of normalcy to the deadly chaos.

Hardly had it gone by and the *konstabeel* disappeared that she saw Malusre appear, looking to either side. Relief and fear fought, choking her; she stepped forward and waved. Henri de Vascogne came into view next, with Sita at his side, her light sword in her hand. The Frenchman turned, running backward and firing at the same time. They came to the *gharis* in a breathless rush, tumbling in.

Cassandra joined them, and the vehicles jolted into motion, drivers lashing the ancient beasts to a lolloping approximation of a gallop. She ignored the crush, the old-sweat smell of the jubilant *dacoits*, everything but the faces beside her.

"Your brother is alive," Henri said quickly. "We saw him. Alive, free, with his own way out—he staged a housebreaking of his own, to get his man, the Sikh."

He would, Cassandra thought, torn between love and exasperation.

Not that she wasn't fond of Narayan Singh herself, in a dutiful sort of way, but for Athelstane to stick his head in the tiger's mouth once more—

He would. He dashed *well would*. Any King would, but Athelstane would be *enthusiastic* about it.

Then the world flashed white. As she flung up her hand, Cassandra saw livid flame burst from every window of Allenby's house, and a wave of hot air struck the *ghari* like an enormous heated pillow. It swayed over onto two wheels, then settled back with a crash and an ominous crinking sound from the springs. They turned a corner, but she could see stone slumping and flames licking high as they did.

"Gas explosion," Henri said grimly. "I noticed the smell before we left. With any luck, Monsieur Ignatieff and Mr. Allenby have departed this world—and will be learning how their beliefs are received in the next."

He crossed himself. Cassandra shook her head; her ears were ringing with the crash, like the end of the world from a badly tuned orchestra. Even then, the precision of her scholar's memory made her ask:

"What about that guardsman who came with Sita? The Gurkha?"

Sita had been sitting motionless, not even bothering to clean or sheathe the saber, which was unlike her—and it was dangerously sharp, with blood on the curve of the cutting edge. Suddenly she turned and gripped Cassandra fiercely, burying her head in the curve of the older woman's neck.

"He died for me!" she said, and burst into sobs. "He died for me!"

Chapter Sixteen

"And so we thought we'd better make a clean breast of it, sir," Charles Saxe-Coburg-Gotha said, standing ramrod straight.

Cassandra kept her hands still on the table before her. The audience room was one for informal conferences; plain ebony table, simple flower-and-bird-pattern tiles on the wall, and a smell of polish and, very faintly, incense. The servants had silently offered tea and juice, then withdrawn.

The King-Emperor was a man in his late fifties, also dressed informally for this occasion, in the gold-trimmed midnight blue walking-out uniform of a general in the Guards; which meant he could be addressed without the full set of honorifics, since by convention military rank always superceded civilian titles. His face was a preview of what Charles's would look like in a generation, apart from the bushiness of the old-fashioned gray-brown muttonchop whiskers that ran into an equally outdated full mustache. The skin had sunk in a little on the aquiline features, and time had worn deep grooves from nose to mouth, but he was still whipcord-lean. The monarch had only one attendant with him; his aide, a Rajput nobleman named Lord Pratap Batwa. The earldom was Pratap's Imperial title—he was a raja by rights as well, down home near Jodhpur, a position he'd handed over to his eldest son years ago. He'd been the then-heir's second-in-command in Siam and his right-hand man and voice in the House of

Lords ever since; wits were known to refer to them as the Siamese Twins.

"So."

The King-Emperor looked around the table: at his son and daughter, at Cassandra, at Detective-Captain Malusre, and at Henri de Vascogne.

"You may be seated, Charles. Now, let me see if I understand this correctly: Acting on your own authority, you allowed a foreign guest, a police officer acting in direct contradiction to orders, a lady of the court, *and your sister*, to engage in an armed raid on the home of an Imperial civil servant?"

Charles swallowed visibly, but his voice was steady. "Essentially, yes, sir. Except that I did *not* give my sister permission to do any such thing."

The King-Emperor sighed. "I'm surprised you didn't go yourself!"

"I would have, sir, except that I thought that might create too much of an embarrassment for you and the family."

"As if this wouldn't, once it came out!" He sighed again, and looked down at his knobby hands for a moment. "Do you have any conception of how lucky you are that some sort of evidence was found to back up your . . . assumptions, boy?"

"No, sir," Charles said. Cassandra darted a glance at him, as he went on: "If I hadn't been convinced that there was something to it, I wouldn't have allowed matters to go forward. It was a matter of necessity."

His father gave him a hard stare, and then a very slight smile. "And damn the consequences, eh? Well, I suppose a young man ought to think that way. A King-Emperor, however, cannot. We are not allowed to be our selves; we are the servants of our subjects. That must come before everything, including our own souls and our dearest personal friendships."

Charles bowed his head. His father transferred his gaze to Sita.

"And as for you, young lady . . ."

"I'm sorry, Father," she said in a small voice. There was little of the usual steely self-confidence in her tone today. "I . . . I shouldn't have done it. And because of me, a man is dead. Our man. I'm . . . so sorry."

"Yes, he is dead," the King-Emperor said. "Because of what we are, we have only to say a word, and men will die for us—and tonight a woman weeps for him, and her children will ask when their father is coming home. *Rajadharma.*"

Sita's eyes met her father's, then slowly filled. Tears streaked down her cheeks one by one. "Yes, Father," she whispered.

"And I don't think you will ever do that lightly again, will you?"

"No, Father. I'm . . . I'm very sorry if I've disappointed you. I'll make you proud of me, I promise I will."

Most of the time you forget how young she is, Cassandra thought, with a burst of pity. *She's barely eighteen.* The daughter of the Kings of Rexin was no stranger to the concept of responsibility, but to have *that* weight crushing down on you . . .

A little of the glacial stiffness left the King-Emperor's face.

"Your mother was much like you when we met," he said gruffly. "And she became a very great lady."

Henri put his hand on the princess's shoulder for an instant. "Yes, the weighing of lives . . . That is something any commander of men must bear. But in this instance, sir—without your soldier, either Detective Malusre or I would have had to hold the rear guard, and would undoubtedly have died—and I would have felt obliged to take the position myself, with all due respect to the detective. A commander is obliged also to know when men *must* be sent to their deaths."

"Very true, Monsieur le Vicomte. And you have definite proof of this tale of treason in the Political Service?"

"I have the evidence of my own eyes, which can be confirmed by the detective-captain and your daughter, sir," he said firmly. "I saw Allenby standing beside a Russian agent in the middle of a human sacrifice to the Black God. That *would* seem to confirm Sir Manfred's suspicions."

"It would indeed. Unfortunately . . ." He turned to his aide. "Pratap?"

"The gas explosion and fire were extremely complete—suspiciously so." The Rajput's face was like that of a middle-aged eagle carved from hard brown wood; he closed his eyes for an instant in thought, marshaling details.

"The initial forensics report states that the presence of additional explosives cannot be ruled out. Essentially, the building and every-thing in it was completely destroyed. The only survivors—presently known survivors—were a number of Mr. Allenby's women and ser-vants, and they seem to know very little. They *did* state that Allenby had been holding meetings with a 'foreign guru,' who matches Ignati-eff's description—during which they were all strictly confined to the servants' quarters or the *bibi-khana*. They knew his work involved se-crets, and thought this was part of it.

"The only other evidence to date was that of two bodies found just outside the premises. Both were scorched and damaged by the explo-sion, but one does appear to have been strangled in the classic Thug manner. The other had the remains of a tattoo on his inner eyelid—but the face was too badly burned for the police surgeon to be sure what it was."

Pratap smiled. "He also had an arrow through his head—in one ear and out the other. Remarkable. I've never seen anything quite like it."

"We've managed to keep this out of the papers, I presume?"

"Yes, sir. They've been told it's part of an ongoing investigation with political implications and that it isn't to be mentioned except as an accidental fire. That ought to work for several weeks, and we can hope that the announcement about the trip to France will bury any lingering curiosity. There's really very little for them to go on any-way."

"That's never stopped them from baseless speculation before," the King-Emperor said sourly. He paused again, then went on:

"Charles: As I understand it, before this affair at Allenby's, you were morally convinced that Sir Manfred's . . . speculations were cor-rect, but didn't have anything concrete to put before me. Nothing to substantiate such wild allegations, at least."

"Yes, sir."

"Well, for what it's worth, son, you now have *me* morally con-vinced. Unfortunately, there's not one iota more of firm evidence."

Henri spoke softly: "And that itself is suspicious, is it not, sir? That explosion and fire were altogether *too* convenient."

"Yes. I presume, then, that you don't think this Ignatieff is dead? Or Allenby either, for what he's worth."

"Very little, now that we know of his treason," Henri agreed. "But as for Ignatieff, from Sir Manfred's notes and from my own experience, I would not trust that he was dead until I had his corpse at my feet. And even then, I would cut off his head and bury his body at a crossroads with the head beneath his knee and his mouth stuffed full of garlic."

The older man gave a single dry chuckle. "Sounds drastic but effective, young fellow. And the brave Captain King is alive too, eh?"

"Was alive last night, sir. I presume he escaped with the man he came to rescue. Fortunate that he did, but a wild deed, *n'est-ce pas?*"

This time the monarch's smile was broader. "I've met a number of junior officers like that, and I'm inclined to agree. The world would be a duller place without cavalry subalterns . . . yes, Dr. King?"

Cassandra took her courage in both hands and spoke: "He's not just a type, Your Ma . . . sir. He's my brother."

"There is no contradiction between the two, Dr. King, but your point is taken." He spread his hands on the table.

"I know my children consider me something of a fussbudget and a stick in the mud," he began.

Sita had dried her eyes. She flickered a tentative smile; Charles merely raised an eyebrow.

"But there is a reason for being stuffy about the rules," the King-Emperor went on. "It's always easier to destroy a tradition than to create it, and once you break a rule for a good reason, it becomes easier to break it for one not quite so good—which is a road it's better not to start on. We *should* be able, at this point, simply to call in the relevant authorities to begin a purge of the Political Service and to hunt down these conspirators according to law."

"I wouldn't advise that, sir," Pratap said.

Astonishingly, the King-Emperor grinned. "No, you'd rather I just started whacking off heads," he agreed. "Starting with the prime minister's, if you don't like him. How many times have we had that discussion, Pratap?"

"If you include the time I recommended chaining his predecessor to an elephant's foot and goading it, and presuming you mean starting with the day we met . . . let me see . . . thirty-seven years . . . that would be an average of at least once every three days—over a hundred thousand times. However, you might discount the times I was merely expressing the frustration that you cannot—"

"Enough," he said, raising a hand. "In this case, however, you have a point. The Political Service is the instrument we'd generally *use* for such an investigation, and if we can't rely upon it, we must be more circumspect. Conceivably, we could end up so deceived that the traitors would purge the honest men."

Cassandra nerved herself to speak again: "Sir Manfred's papers indicate there may be . . . what's the term . . . *moles* in other places. The Military Intelligence services, and the Special Branch of the Imperial Indian Police, as well."

"Yes." The King-Emperor nodded. "And because of that, we must distrust our own people—which is undoubtedly a part of what the Czar's men intended by infiltrating us. Trust is the lubricant that enables men to work together, and they've thrown a handful of corundum grit into ours."

"Not to mention the political implications," Pratap said.

"Ganesha Lord of Wisdom, yes. What that damned old woman Somersby would say if he blundered into this—"

Even then, Cassandra felt a twitch of Whig resentment, before she suppressed it as absurd. The monarch went on:

"—he's competent enough at ordinary administration and massaging the MPs' vanity, but this! He'd start squawking about the Crown encroaching on Parliament's prerogatives. It's a reflex with the man."

"Sir, there's the matter of the conspiracy to kill you," Cassandra said. "Perhaps it would be wise to, ah . . ."

"Hide in the palace?" the King-Emperor said. "When this dynasty begins to allow its behavior to be dictated by threats, Dr. King, rest assured that you shall be among the first to be informed."

Cassandra felt a flash of fear, then realized he was smiling at her. "No offense, sir."

"None taken, Dr. King. I realize the source of your concern." He sighed. "In any case, making drastic changes would be sure to arouse too many questions. And I refuse to believe that the Guards have been subverted." He rapped his knuckles on the table.

"Detective-Captain Malusre."

"Sir?"

"First, my commendations. The Empire has hundreds of thousands of bureaucrats who can be relied on to follow the path of maximum security, but all too few men who'll take risks on their own initiative."

The Marathi policeman ducked his head slightly, looking embarrassed.

"And in the usual reward for good work, I'm now going to give you more work, dangerous and difficult. You will liaise with Dr. King's brother through this man Elias—not at his main place of business, though, or his home. Get any information Captain King has, and—through my son—you will also carry any instructions We send to him. Though he seems to be a young man who interprets instructions with a free hand. We must *not* let the enemy know how much we know, so contact will have to be kept to a minimum."

He rapped out a few more instructions before he left. As he did, she could catch a few words spoken to his aide:

"Like old times, eh, Pratap?"

"More leeches in Siam, as I recall—"

Cassandra let out a silent *whoosh* of relief at the King-Emperor's departure. A quiet academic life had always been her first choice; hobnobbing with the ruler of half mankind on secret matters of state . . . no, not her cup of tea, by choice.

"An alarming man, your father, in some respects," Cassandra said.

And he comes right to the point, as well. A pretty pass we've come to, when Athelstane is safer skulking like a criminal than he would be living a normal life.

Charles chuckled dryly. His eyes were on the walls, which bore portraits of his father and ancestors. Cassandra hadn't noticed them much before; Imperial portraits were something you saw so often—in schools, in railway stations, when you went to the post to drop off a letter—that they hardly registered.

Now she followed his eyes and looked: There was Victoria I, dour and dumpy and indomitable in archaic black widow's weeds. Her son Edward with his plumply good-natured face and the haunted survivor's eyes of a man who had lived through the worst of the Fall and Second Mutiny, witness to the death of a world. Edward's son George, in a plain turban of naval blue, the bluff tongue-tied Sailor Emperor. George's daughter, Victoria II, draped across the Lion Throne in a daringly tight and gauzy sari covered with a tiger-skin sash, portrayed as she'd always insisted she be portrayed in life: a pen in one hand and a wine cup of carved white nephrite in the other. Gorgeous and mad and brilliant—Charles would have been totally out of place at *her* court, which the more respectable history books still skipped over rather lightly. Although even the censorious admitted her love poetry had been first-class in three languages, despite the embarrassingly wide spectrum of objects of adoration.

She'd had no children: Albert I was her cousin, a professor of Indo-European Linguistics most of his life, and Cassandra's imagination put a *you want* me *to be* what? behind his wide blue eyes. His daughter Elizabeth, only twenty years dead in this year of grace 2025, the Whig Empress as they'd called her, the one who'd pressured and intimidated Oxford and Cambridge and the Imperial University into opening their doors to women.

And John II, Elizabeth's second son, whom she'd now actually met and chatted with . . .

"You're lucky to have him," Cassandra said. "Not the King-Emperor, but a father. I can scarcely remember mine; the first thing I *really* recall is his ashes and sword coming home, when I was about five."

"Yes," Charles said. "My mother died when I was about that age; Sita can't recall her at all, although she's supposed to be the image of her. Looking up there, though—I was wondering how long before I'd be a set of names and dates schoolchildren had to learn. At least I'm the oldest son; Father had it dropped on him unexpectedly, after Uncle Edward broke his neck playing polo. *He* wanted nothing more than to stay in the Army."

"Would you, Charles, if you weren't heir?" Cassandra asked.

"Lord, no, although it's better than what Father has to go through. Most of military life is routine . . . well, you know that."

She nodded; you couldn't be the daughter and sister of soldiers without getting some idea of what life in the officers' quarters of a base was like, or the boredom of endless drill and field days. There was always some skirmish or other going on—it was a *big* Empire—but the Imperial Army was also big, large enough that most of its units didn't see action in any given year, for which she thanked the Gods. The heir to the Lion Throne went on:

"What I'd like—" He paused, and blushed slightly. "Well, it sounds a trifle silly, coming right out and saying it . . . what I'd *really* like is to do something like what Henri did the other night. Or what the first Raja Brooke did, or . . . well, I'd like to have adventures. Not just amusing myself, hunting and so forth, but doing something *important* with my own hands and wits, and a few friends."

He looked at her, raising a brow. "Instead I'll probably turn into my father. D'you think the less of me, then?"

Cassandra took his arm and squeezed slightly. "Charles, I long ago reconciled myself to the fact that men are men—which is to say, that they have a lot of boy in them, even when they're grown-up. The ones who don't aren't worth much."

Yasmini moaned in her sleep. Athelstane King felt her forehead again and frowned; then he used the thermometer, holding her mouth gently shut. His hand could cup right around her jaw, but he was careful of that—she seemed to grow distressed when she felt herself held against her will. Considering some of the things she'd babbled in her sleep, that wasn't surprising at all.

Ninety-nine, he thought, reading the instrument, flicking it sharply to drive the mercury down, and then returning it to the glass by the bedside. He gently folded a damp cloth and laid it on her brow; she muttered something under her breath. This time the fever spike was lower and it broke in sweat sooner. She muttered again, louder.

I wonder what that was she said, he thought. *Sounded like . . .*

"*Mati*," Elias bar-Binyamin said softly. "Mother. That much we all have in common."

King nodded, and so did the old Jew's son, where he sat quietly beside his father.

The Lancer officer suspected they'd both seen enough men die ugly deaths to know that *mother* was the last thing most of them said—screamed, if the pain was bad enough. Although *water* ran a close second. That was certainly the way it was on battlefields. Probably the same for dying women, too.

His lips quirked; he remembered lying sobbing in bed, a small boy who'd lost the father he'd adored, and *his* mother coming to him. There were probably earlier layers of memory he couldn't reach, lying under that, back to . . . well, perhaps back to the womb—memories of comfort, of safety, of everything being made *right*. He'd read a few things like that; his taste ran to the classics, but he'd dabbled in avant-garde fiction now and then, or even a few books by academic alienists Cassandra had recommended, with their theories about childhood and the unconscious.

It's no wonder we're never great heroes to our mothers, he thought ruefully. *They remember, too.*

"I'm worried that she's not waking," he said. "It doesn't seem like a coma or an infection"—the doctor hadn't thought so, at least—"but it's not natural."

"What she is, that is not natural," Elias said.

Seen close to in the clear warm winter sunlight of Delhi, the older Jew's skin was like parchment that had been rubbed smooth and reused several times, a network of infinitely fine wrinkles; King had begun to suspect that the dashing but middle-aged David was the son of his host's old age. They were sitting in a pool of the light that came through an arched window from the courtyard, stopping just short of the low bed where Yasmini lay. Elias's daughter-in-law had just bustled out, leaving a pile of fresh-baked flatbread and homemade yogurt with chunks of fruit in it, orange juice, and coffee. The coffee was good enough to convince him there was something to the beverage, even without cardamom. An elderly, stiff-jointed cat wandered in, sniffed, climbed painfully into David bar-Elias's lap, and went to sleep; the man stroked it absently, and it began to purr in its slumber, kneading its paws and drooling a little.

"It may not be natural, and it certainly seems to take it out of her—but she used it for us," King said.

There was a chess set beside the bed as well, the black jade one Elias had been using the night King came knocking on the door of his warehouse. They'd had several games, with Elias spotting the younger man a queen and two knights; King had even won, once. He suspected that was because his own headlong style had simply surprised the other man with its recklessness—it certainly hadn't happened since. The enforced concentration still did him good; waiting had never been his strongest point, and a soldier needed patience.

He slid a bishop forward. At least, he *thought* it was a bishop; the set was East Asian of some sort, perhaps Chinese. Elias said one of his ancestors had bought it from one of King's in Old Empire times, though that meant little—men of the *Angrezi* breed had been picking

up spare valuables all over the world for a very long time. Walking off
with whole continents, come to that.

"Ah, you are improving," Elias said, smiling to himself.

There was a final flurry of thrust and parry, and then a long pause.
King nodded, and tipped over his king.

"Tcha-hey!" Elias said, setting up the pieces again. "You have no
patience—a young man's fault. You could have held me off for another
six moves, perhaps eight."

"Would there be a point?" King said ruefully.

"There is *always* a point!"

He reached across the board and prodded King between the eyes
with a finger:

"Would you fight so with a sword? No? I thought not! You would
try to cut your enemy even as his blade split your heart. That is the
Angrezi vice; you would rather die than go to the effort of thinking.
You are not stupid, but you are lazy—" He touched the side of his head
to show what he meant. "You will toil like bullocks with your bodies
rather than make your brains sweat."

King grinned. "Well, at least you're not claiming the national vice
is a taste for getting our bums switched. But I thought fear of embarrassment was the great *Angrezi* weakness?"

David bar-Elias stifled a snort of laughter. His father grumbled on:
"Another aspect of the same thing. Look at this message from your sister—"

"And the King-Emperor," King pointed out. *Krishna, but it's odd to
think of Cass mixing it in at court!*

"And the King-Emperor, may the Lord save and keep the right-
eous ruler who has been good to the Lord's people. He and the ones
who know the threat—they will do nothing—nothing!—because
they are afraid they can't *explain* why what should be done should be
done. And the politicians, the bureaucrats, the ones they are afraid
of will not listen because the facts do not fit their preconceptions!
They cannot bear the pain of having to reason from first principles.
Tcha!"

"Maybe we should pick men of your people for our governors,"
King said, stroking his clean-shaven jaw. "Then they could do all that
unpleasant thinking, and suffer the embarrassment—"

"You did," Elias pointed out. "Your St. Disraeli. And *he* saved you all, because he was not afraid to think—to imagine—to use his mind instead of his instincts and prejudices and his belly. How do you think of him? Your Moses? But *he* thought of an Exodus from a land under the curse of God. An apostate, but he thought like one of us."

"A hit," King said, smiling still.

It was easy to smile, on a sunlit day, when you'd dealt your enemy a stinging defeat.

Perhaps Ignatieff is dead, he thought. And even if he isn't, we've exposed Allenby, and we've broken the secret of the True Dreamers, and Cass is in, well, not safety, but as close as she can get until we win the final battle. And I did save Narayan. With Ibrahim's help, and David bar-Elias's, and Yasmini's, of course, and Togrul and his handy bow. And Elias here really does have a good point about St. Disraeli. Would anyone else have thought of the Exodus, and been able to organize it, to talk and bully and inspire enough men to bring it off?

"A *very* palpable hit," he repeated.

"Yes," Yasmini's voice said, soft and breathy.

King rose quickly and went to the side of her bed. She looked pale but conscious; he slid a hand under her head, beneath the sweat-dampened curls, and raised it for her to drink.

"More?" he said. "Water is good for a fever."

"*Spacebo*," she said, her voice a little stronger. "*Gospodin* Elias is right. I have seen Disraeli in the dreams, many times. A wise man—very wise, very kind, and so wise he knew when he must be hard. And *Gospodin* Elias is also right about thinking."

King sat easily with his back near the railing of the balcony and his legs crossed, slippered feet resting on the opposite thigh.

"*Spacebo* for our lives," he said. "And don't tire yourself."

"No, it is no matter, I will recover," she said. A shrug. "If I do not die in the trance that follows the waking dreams, then I have nothing to fear. I will be weak for a time, yes. Longer this time than before. Each time a little longer, until I do *not* wake, or stop using the drugs, or the madness takes me."

King winced inwardly. *This girl has guts,* he thought. *Smart as a tack, too—apart from her . . . abilities.*

Elias spoke, his voice wary but friendly enough. "I thank you for your kind words, young miss. Although *Gospodin* is not a title I crave."

Yasmini stared at him with a flash of temper. "I use it as it was used

when the *Russki* were clean. Should I forget that there was a time before my folk learned to worship devils or to eat man's flesh?"

"My apologies," Elias said, bowing slightly from where he sat.

Yasmini had been very slightly tense as she spoke; almost as if she
expected a blow for her words. At the soft reply she relaxed; King
touched her forehead again and found the fever gone. It might return,
but for now she was calm.

"That is a good answer," Elias went on. "You call yourself a
Russian, then?"

"By blood I am, mostly, with a little Tadjik," Yasmini said. "The
first of the Sisters was *Russki*—a holy sister, a nun. What the priests say
about the dreams being a gift of the Peacock Angel is a lie."

"What is the truth, then?" Elias asked, his eyes bird-bright with
curiosity. "The lies of the priests of Tchernobog, those I know."

"The truth? Czar Nikolai—the Grand Duke, he was then—heard
of her among the refugees as they fled south from Kazan through the
Kazakh marches in the second year of the great dying—heard that she
had prophetic dreams. She was near death because she would not
eat . . . that . . . but none dared to slay her to devour. A Dreamer must
fast near to death for the first dreams to come, in any case.

"When the dreams proved so useful for him, the Grand Duke ordered that she be given to eat of whatever clean food they had, and so
she lived. He sought out others, men and women of many peoples,
those with some trace of her gift, and declared them his personal
slaves. In the charge of his priest—the man who turned from Christ
to the Peacock Angel and persuaded others, the first of the High
Priests of Tchernobog. From them was bred the Sisterhood. Boys
with the talent . . . their minds cannot bear the knowing of things that
are and are not at the same time, and they go mad when they come
to manhood and the dreams come upon them. That is one reason we
are so few."

Elias nodded. "Some of this I learned in Bokhara," he said, and
was silent for a pause that stretched. "And the thinking? What did you
mean by that?"

"That the Master, Count Ignatieff—he has won many fights by
cunning rather than heavy blows. I was never far enough from the
count to think of him as anything but the Master. Now I am—oh,
ochen khorrosho, most excellent!

"And . . ." She turned to King. "How do *you* think of him?"

"As the Czar's arm," King said. "An agent of Russia."

"And are all agents of the Empire as one, then?" Yasmini said shrewdly. "Shall I tell you what Ignatieff most feared, at . . . back within the Czar's domains? He feared to have his schemes discovered."

Elias made an interested sound. King nodded slowly. "You mean, not all his superiors would like what he's doing?"

"No. Not even all the priests of the House of the Fallen. The Czar follows Tchernobog's cult, but he is not eager to meet the Peacock Angel. To weaken your Empire, *da*. He thinks—"

She nodded to the chessboard.

"Russians are chess players, yes," Elias said musingly. "Not polo or cricket: chess."

"*Da*," the girl said. "But against each other, no? The Czar thinks to hand down power to his sons and grandsons. He would not seek the death of all that lives—not in deeds, though he might pray loudly in public to Malik Nous to bring the ending of all things."

"You think we could get Ignatieff . . . recalled?" King said.

Yasmini shook her head, then winced slightly at the pain the motion brought. He gave her more of the water, and she continued:

"No. He is of too much power at court, and would not the Czar believe that it was a plot to divide his forces? Especially while to say so would anger Ignatieff's faction and kindred."

"Tcha-hey," Elias agreed. "Captain King, you cannot conceive of what it is to live in that land—such suspicions, such a viper's nest of murder and betrayal—treachery and black intrigue—not unless you have breathed its air. Samarkand is bad. Bokhara is worse."

Yasmini nodded. "But if the Czar were to learn of Ignatieff's mission—his *full* mission—after it failed . . . then he would have a lever to move against the Patriarch. Many *boyars* chafe at the power of the priesthood, or envy its lands and wealth. And factions within the House of the Fallen, more interested in riches than the coming of the Black God, they would join him to throw down Ignatieff's patrons. The Czar is Supreme Autocrat—Tchernobog's Claw upon Earth, much though the Patriarch envies him the title. He could demand that the Serpent Throne be given access to the Dreamers, to prove or disprove."

"Never thought I'd be considering giving the Czar a helping hand," King mused.

Elias shuddered. "The Czar is bad. The House of the Fallen . . . worse. Much worse. Tyrants can be outlived—bribed—outwitted—fought. It was not for power or wealth that the Crusaders slaughtered us until the streets ran with blood, or the Inquisition hunted us like rats for flaying and burning—although they robbed us, too, yes. It was for ideas, for religion, for belief in things they thought holy. The worst in men is the best corrupted. Ideas kill more than kings; brains are more dangerous than fists. That is the *Angrezi* strength, though: you will not follow ideas if that means doing things that are . . ."

He dropped into upper-crust Imperial English for a second: *"Just not done, old chap."*

"Well, that leaves us with Ignatieff to deal with first," King said practically.

A quiet streak of Punjabi blasphemies came from the corridor outside, along with a squeak of rubber and a raw Pathan whoop of glee—King was immediately reminded of an old Afghan saying, that the sound of the Pushtu language was like listening to rocks falling down a mountainside. Ibrahim pushed Narayan Singh through the door, in a wheelchair. The Pathan thought that a marvelous invention, though more as an instrument of torture than of healing. Sir Manfred Warburton followed, not using a cane anymore or looking quite so much like an old man; David bar-Elias rose to give him his arm. Warburton lowered himself inch by inch into his cushions; David sat beside his father; the Pathan squatted on his hams beside the Sikh's wheelchair.

"So, you mend, *bhai*?" King said.

"With every day, *sahib*," Narayan Singh said. "Already I can walk a little. In a week's time, I will run—two, and I will be fit for duty."

He looked drawn and a little gaunt, but good feeding and an expert masseuse—brought in blindfolded, and led out the same way—were mending the damage, aided by youth and native strength.

King nodded, feeling a vast relief. Being without Narayan Singh was like lacking his own right arm.

"Well, we'd best take counsel," he said.

David bar-Elias nodded. "Men *have* been watching our house on the Chandi Chowk," he said. "I have confirmed it."

King hissed. "Ignatieff's alive, then," he said. "More lives than a cat, that one."

"The devil protects his own, they say," Warburton said.

Elias stroked his beard. "Ignatieff saw my son—knew him from his time in Bokhara—at Allenby's house," he said. "That he would have our known properties watched—that is only reasonable, from his point of view."

King winced slightly. "Poor return for your hospitality," he said.

Elias cackled, stroking his beard, and David bar-Elias laughed, glanced at his father, spoke when the older man nodded permission:

"We owe your family a debt, Captain King. And there is also a debt between us and Count Ignatieff, and the House of the Fallen."

His hand closed on his knee where he sat cross-legged. "My family are business folk, not nobles who think honor means to keep no count of costs. Our debts must be paid, in full. And those owed to us, collected. As Count Ignatieff will find, we collect fairly—*to the last jot and tittle*. He could not pay us in cash, not with all his lands; so we will take our"—a sly grin—"to coin a phrase, our *pound of flesh* from him."

Remind yourself never to get on that family's wrong side, King told himself, searching for a half-remembered memory of the words. Sir Manfred was more current with the classical literature of the Old Empire, and snorted laughter first.

"Now, this royal trip to France," he said. "I suppose there's no prospect of getting it canceled?"

Elias shook his head. "The detective—the Marathi—said he heard from the Padishah's own lips that he would not be turned from his path by fear." He shook his head dolefully. "A stubborn man."

"*Dieu et mon droit,*" King quoted. "Fancier than my family's motto, but it does mean about the same thing. *Kuch dar nahin hai!*"

Elias made a guttural noise of derision at the back of his throat. "God gave men fear to warn them from folly," he said. "A man cannot be ruled by fear, no; but he who pays it no heed is a fool, not a hero."

Warburton sighed. "There's a good deal more involved than stubbornness. The alliance with France-outre-mer and the Egyptian question are matters of the first importance," he said. "The King-Emperor and the Foreign Office have been working on this for a decade."

Elias stroked his beard, shifting from Hindi to Imperial English with an almost imperceptible glance at Ibrahim, who was as innocent of that tongue as he was of higher mathematics.

"I have also heard something of that." At King's surprise: "Many of my people dwell in the lands of the Caliphate, in Egypt, and in France-outre-mer; many have since the Babylonian Captivity, and before. We also have an interest in these matters, and not only those of us who are Imperial citizens."

"The Caliph's government aren't such brutes as the Russians," King said, curious. "Fairly civilized, in their . . ." he did not say *woggish* ". . . fashion."

"No. And there are those here—more in France-outre-mer—who do not love us."

His voice held a strain of dry, pawky understatement. "But in the *Dar ul'Islam* we are not citizens. Tolerated, yes, somewhat. *Dhimmi* they call us, People of the Book. We are allowed our faith, but on sufferance; we must pay heavier taxes; wear special clothing; build no house higher than a Muslim's; build no new synagogue without permission; and there are many other pinpricks. And at any time the greed of a ruler, the spite of the *mullahs*, the anger of the mob, may fall on us. Here in the Empire we are equals before the law, one folk and faith among a hundred hundred others, and treated no differently by the *sahib-log*. There are even a few of us in Parliament and the House of Lords."

"There would be one more in the Lords, if you'd pushed for it anytime these past twenty years, sir," Warburton said.

"Tcheh!" Elias indicated himself. "I should sit with generals and rajas and *bishops*? At my age, better to read Torah and pray than play such games."

He smacked his son lightly on the back of the head when the younger man made a skeptical sound.

"Show respect!" Then: "But we would not be sorry if Egypt came under the Raj, or France-outre-mer, or both," he concluded. "And close to Egypt is Jerusalem."

"That's if all goes smoothly," King said. "I suppose the thinking is that if we and France-outre-mer are strongly linked, the Caliphate will back down when we take Egypt and rebuild the Canal? After which they won't be able to *do* damn-all."

"Yes," Warburton said. "But if the alliance were to fall through, or even be seen as weak, they'd fight and fight hard. The Caliph *is* technically the religious overlord of a substantial percentage of our population, too; and he has influence in Afghanistan. He could declare a *jihad* against us. And then very likely Dai-Nippon would come in, attacking us in Southeast Asia when we were tied down in the Middle East—the Caliphate is a bloody enormous place, a lot of it as bad to campaign in as the Pathan country. Egypt is one thing—anyone who controls the Nile owns the place. Trying to take on an empire that runs from the Danube to Khorasan is another entirely. Oh, we could beat them easily enough in pitched battle, but that's not the same as winning a war. What's more, Dai-Nippon is nearly as strong as we are at sea and in the air, too. With them involved, it could be a very nasty business."

"Yes," Yasmini said again. They all looked at her. "I have . . . dreamed it. War over all the world, cities burning and bombed from above, both sides building new and terrible weapons, and uprising within the Raj stamped out in rivers of blood. Everywhere hatred and death, the Great Powers fighting until they are exhausted, and then the Czar holding the balance."

She shivered. "Vast would be the domains of Samarkand, and the cold glee in the House of the Fallen. Much feasting before the altars of Tchernobog. And then, a hundred years from now, death from the sky—"

"Well, that's not going to happen," King said stoutly, as she raised her eyes to the heavens and shivered.

Not if I can help it, he thought. *We soldiers hold the Border and keep the peace, and that lets people like Cass make the world better while ordinary folk get on with their lives.*

War was necessary now and then; war waged by professionals like him, men of the martial castes, born to the sword. War to put down barbarians and pirates, to keep the peace between the Empire's sometimes-fractious peoples, to add a province or adjust a border. Ugly enough, but not the sort of struggle Warburton and Yasmini hinted at, whole nations wrecked and beaten into dust. The Gods knew the Empire had its faults, but what was it *for*, if not the Imperial peace that held half mankind in order under the rule of law?

Which, stuffy though it may sound, it's my duty to uphold, in whatever small way I can, he told himself.

"Well, then, to work," King said. "They obviously plan to strike at the King-Emperor, the royal family, Cass, and the special emissary from France-outre-mer. Probably they and their tame traitors—their moles—have got some cock-and-bull story ready to put in place once the dirty deed is done, to set us all at each other's throats and bring on this general war, this . . ."

"World War," David bar-Elias said.

"Yes, World War. Merciful Krishna, what a ghastly concept!"

"It is," Warburton said. "If there hadn't been a Fall to throw back progress, we'd be beyond the possibility of such things already. Probably the Empire would have united the world by now."

King saw Yasmini stir out of the corner of his eye, then subside. *Ask later,* he thought. Aloud:

"Well, what is His Royal and Imperial Majesty doing about it?"

"Not all that much, I'm afraid," Warburton said.

"Oh, bugger," King said with quiet conviction.

"That's the hell of it. He *can't.* Not if the rot's spread as far as we think." He looked at Yasmini. "If this were an ordinary conspiracy, I'd say to hell with it, and advise emergency measures. But if we did that, Ignatieff would simply withdraw and—with the aid of talents like this young lady's—try again."

Narayan Singh spoke for the first time: "But if we follow, we can catch this *E-rus* at his work, and then—" His hand made a gesture, like the drawing of a sword.

"Hey-vey, do you think you can solve all problems with a *tulwar,* Sikh?" Elias asked.

"Most of them, Jew," Narayan said, showing white teeth in his dense black beard. "What we need is a plan to put us within striking distance when the time comes."

King nodded. "My *daffadar* is right."

Warburton made a frustrated gesture of agreement. "The problem is that the very structures set up to protect the King-Emperor are the ones most likely to be penetrated," he said. "That means that not only can they not be trusted to do their job, they can't be told about *us*—even to the extent of being told not to notice us!"

"Which means we have to *genuinely* penetrate Imperial security," King said. "A nice dilemma."

Ibrahim Khan spoke: "Why do you not share your thoughts?"

"Oh. Sorry," King said absently, dropping back into Hindi. "Our problem is this, man of the Hills. We think the *E-rus* plan to strike at the Padishah as he flies in one of our ships of the air—"

"Dirigibles, yes," Ibrahim said. "Some of the tribes in the west of our country, in Uruzgan and Ghowr, use them—smaller than yours, but they learn—as my tribe has been learning to make better weapons, like your mor-tars. The western tribes buy the engines and hire learned *hakims* from Isfahan and Baghdad—even Damascus itself—to teach them how to use and care for them."

King's brows went up; he looked at Warburton, who shrugged in an embarrassed fashion. "You can't keep a law of nature secret forever," he said. "And the Russians have passed on data and copied machinery from Dai-Nippon to the Caliphate, to hinder us. Nothing Damascus makes is anywhere near as good as *ours*, and I doubt the Afghans will even equal *them*."

Ibrahim gave him a hard look, then went on: "They're dangerous and tricky and sometimes they burn, but you can take an enemy by surprise—land warriors where your enemies least expect—carry away plunder. You *Angrezi* taught us that trick, these last twenty years."

If you play chess with good players long enough, you learn to play good chess. King winced behind an impassive face, stroking his mustache. He remembered something from his course in the Ancients at school, a poem of the ancient Spartans, saying that it was unwise to fight the same enemy too long, for just that reason. The Pathan went on:

"Well, if your Padishah is going to fly, either the *E-rus fakir*-who-isn't will attack them with other ships of the air, or he will try to put his own men on them."

A predatory grin. "What a ransom, to take captive the Padishah of the *Angrezi*! A *crore* of gold *mohurs* . . ."

"Yes," said King grimly. "And then a *crore* of blades come riding to take the money back, and burn your villages about your ears."

"Well, there is that. You lowland infidels have no appreciation of artistry." The Pathan scratched in his beard. "So. You must track the trackers—do as they do, and enter the dirigible in disguise. When they strike—you strike at their backs. And when we take the false *fakir*'s head, forget not the two hundred gold *mohurs* you owe me. Half of which should have been given in advance anyway," he added.

"And you have me to help you with that tracking," Yasmini said.

It does certainly seem to take it out of her, though, King thought. *I thought we were going to lose her for a while there.*

"I will not chance the drugs again, unless it is very necessary," she said, seeming to sense his doubt. "But if it is necessary, we will." She looked at King, and smiled—the first time he'd seen her do that wholeheartedly. "I would not wish to live in the world that will be, if we lose."

The sunny feeling he'd had at the beginning of the day left King abruptly. *It's one thing to have a small part of the Empire as your responsibility*, he thought. *The whole thing is too* bloody *much*.

Chapter Seventeen

Count Ignatieff had switched to a fresh set of his robes and put the other in its sealed box. The rotting blood of the old was holy, but—he confessed to the weakness in the privacy of his mind—too uncomfortable to bear for more than an hour or two, and it could literally betray him with its stink at half a mile in the open air. The ruined temple a day's ride from the southwestern outskirts of Delhi would do for now as a hiding place; he had several servants from the followers of Kali with him. It was actually easier to move without the Dreamer . . .

One of the Deceivers sent to serve him flinched away from his face, and he mastered himself. He would recover the Dreamer or kill her; he *must*. Ignatieff did not deal in self-delusion. He knew exactly what was in store for him from the Okhrana if he betrayed the unprecedented trust that had been given him—and the worse things that the Hierarchs of the Fallen could deal out. Nor did the Peacock Angel pardon failure, in this life or the next. The thought brought anger, not fear; but he strove to master that as hard as he would have with terror, pacing steadily across the uneven surface, steady as if it had been the floor of his hereditary castle where the Tien Shan peaks rose above Fergannah.

The temple had been very old when the Afghan warlord Mahmud of Ghanza sacked it more than a thousand years before. Little was left now but a pyramidal mound of stone, here and there a carved lotus or a hand held in a curious gesture. The outside was overgrown with scrub, for this was the center of a *doab*, the—slightly—higher ground found here and there on the Ganges plain. If you climbed to the top of the fallen tower, you could see the geometric glint of moonlight on irrigation canals in the distance, the dark shadows of a village surrounded by mango trees. Distance hid the manor that held this land, through air dry and chill with the nighttime coolness of the North Indian winter.

The wild part of this holding was seldom visited; the natural scrubland was the *zamindar*'s hunting preserve, and the estate was currently managed by a widow with no grown children. Even when it was used for the chase, few would bother to ride into the dense thorn-thickets around the temple—ruins were many in this land, where history lay layer on layer. The central part was clear enough to hold a fire that the walls hid, and over the generations the local lodge of the Deceivers had made discreet improvements—natural-seeming pathways and tunnels into the stone bulk. It was a place to plan, to store booty, to hide travelers favored by the Dreadful Bride, to leave secret signs telling of Her votaries' plans. So it had been for six hundred years.

A shank of mutton roasted over the fire, and a pot seethed with rice and dates. After a while he crouched by the spit, cutting off slices of meat with a folding knife from his belt and scooping from the pot with a horn spoon. The meat was dry—nothing like the melting tenderness of a roast suckling Uzbeck from his own lands—but it and the rice were fuel. As he ate he considered, shifting elements of plans in his head, conscious of the men slowly arriving and gathering, one by one, behind him. The servants withdrew themselves, lest they see that which was forbidden.

All things are thrown into confusion, he thought at last. *Good. A plan too stiff to change with circumstance will shatter.*

At last he turned and rose, a black outline against the dying red coals. Six men waited for him to speak. One was in the dress of a *babu* in the labyrinthine lower levels of the Imperial bureaucracy—not the Imperial Civil Service, of course, which was another thing altogether. Another wore the blue uniform of the Raj's Navy, with a branch-of-service flash from one of the technical branches on his arm. Next to him stood a stringy near-naked ascetic with the three yellow ash-marks of Shiva on his brow. The others were likewise disguised—

disguised in the lives they drew about themselves from infancy on. Those who could not live the double life did not live at all past child-hood; not for nothing were they called the Deceivers.

The votaries of Her rarely wore their own garb. And the century-old link between them and the cult of the Peacock Angel was the deep-est of their secrets. The men were motionless, save when a bat flew through the fading fire glow; that brought an infinitesimal relaxation. Ignatieff sneered inwardly; bats were merely a symbol, in themselves nothing more than an animal of the vile material world, for all that the ignorant Cossacks called them Tchernobog's Chickens. Still, it was a useful touch. His hold over them was shaken by the loss of the Dreamer, badly shaken.

Richard Allenby also stood before him. *His* garb was plain street dress, and there was despair in his eyes. Ignatieff smiled at him, then smashed a gloved fist across his face. As the man folded to the ground he kicked him once with savage precision. The other watchers leaned closer at the scream, their eyes intent.

"Shall I give you more gold, Allenby?" Ignatieff said softly, in the Hindi that was the common tongue of those watching. "Shall I hide for you once more the evidence of the girl-child you slew, being over-hasty in taking your pleasure?"

"But—" Allenby had managed to lever himself up to his knees. "We had a bargain—I did everything you asked, everything—"

Ignatieff laughed. "Did you think you could make a bargain with Malik Nous, Allenby? That is superstition. The Black God never buys human souls. There is no need. They *give* themselves to Him."

He struck again, with a precision that could inflict a great deal of pain without much damage. "You are not my partner. You are not even my accomplice. You are my serf, my slave, the slave of my slaves, less than the least of the Deceivers here. Or will you run to the Sirkar, with the taste of *His* meat upon your lips?"

Allenby broke completely at that, groveling on the shattered stone of the temple and weeping. Ignatieff smiled benignly, and the six watchers nodded. That was an ancient truth—once a man had passed initiation, he was lost to his former life, for he had committed the sin for which there was no forgiveness. There was no company for him then but his brothers in the cult. So the Deceivers had known for cen-turies, and so the Grand Duke and the first of the High Priests had found in the days when the heavens themselves revealed who ruled this universe.

For Your gift of wisdom I thank You, Black God, Ignatieff thought. *Angel of the bottomless abyss, spread Your wings over Your servant's head.*

"Get up," he said aloud. Allenby obeyed. "Command yourself, or I will know that your only usefulness is as blood and meat. There is still work for you to do."

"Master, they know me now! If I am seen, I will be taken."

"And will talk," Ignatieff said contemptuously. "No, you will not be seen. You have some skill at disguise; and you know names; and our enemies will not announce your treason, lest it alert others. You will keep watch for us—and others will watch you. Do not fear. You will not be taken alive. If you manage to kill King, or recover the Dreamer, you will even be forgiven—richly rewarded, and given a new identity."

He gave further instruction, and at last the *Angrezi* stumbled away. The others watched Ignatieff with new respect; the humiliation of one of the *sahib-log* pleased them greatly.

"We also will watch," he said to them. "We may yet find the ones we seek; and if we find and slay, all will yet be well."

The *babu* spoke: "Will they not inform the higher authorities, who will change all things, if a hint of our plans has reached them?"

"No," Ignatieff said. "Their laws and customs will bind them. The fire carried away all evidence at that one's house. And they do not know which of *their* men are *ours*. We would put a thousand to the torture and find the tracks of our enemies; they will march to the slaughter like sheep—*if* we are careful."

The sun was paling on the eastern horizon, red and swollen with the city smoke of Delhi, before they were finished.

"You're about recovered, *bhai*," King said, stepping back and letting the point of the practice saber fall a little.

The small courtyard of the house Elias had found them made a splendid practice ground; the fountain and planters and the archways about it kept it from being too unrealistically smooth and open. Duels and fencing matches were all very well, but a real fighting man had to be aware of his surroundings every moment—unless you were, then a trip, a bump, a flash of light off a bit of glass, an enemy's friend coming up behind you, could all mean death. And he'd never heard of a battle or skirmish where the opposing sides stopped to rake and roll the field beforehand.

"Of course, you always were rather slow," he went on, with a taunting grin.

Narayan Singh gave a roar and lunged again. King beat it aside from the wrist and backed a little, laughing to himself despite the sweat that ran down his body in rivers beneath the training armor—a leather coat with metal bosses riveted to the outside, padding beneath, a helmet with a gridwork of bars over the face. The *tulwars* had no edge or point, but they were regulation weight, and a blow with his or the Sikh's arm behind it was no joke. His breath came deep and quick but controlled, and it was a familiar pleasure to push himself to the limits of capacity.

The swords rang off each other again and again as their booted feet rasped and scuffed over the tile, thrust and cut and parry blurring them into silver arcs, breath coming deep and hard. Then the steel met again with a slithering rasp, and the long blades locked at the guard. King caught the Sikh's left arm at the wrist and they strained against each other for a moment; then he tried a risky hip throw, switching stance and twisting. Narayan went down on his back and cut at King's legs; the Lancer officer skipped nimbly over the blade and leapt in to thrust at his body. A hamlike hand grabbed his ankle and pulled; King went down on his backside in turn.

"You wouldn't have tried that with real blades," King complained, as they rose and stripped off the practice gear. "I'd have had your hand off at the wrist."

"Not before I turned thee into a kebab," Narayan Singh said cheerfully.

When the Sikh had stripped to the waist he thrust his head and shoulders into the basin of the fountain and laved water over himself with both hands. He was blowing like a grampus, his hairy torso covered with sweat—and the multicolored, fading mark of bruises. King followed suit, grunting relief at the feel of the cool clean water, and they sluiced down their torsos—for the rest they were wearing soft boots and loose pjamy-trousers of undyed cotton. The Sikh wrung water out of the blue-black mane of beard and hair his faith required, tying a rough topknot, and then spread his arms in the challenge-gesture of a Punjabi wrestler.

"Two falls of three, *sahib?*"

King shook his head, picking up a towel from across the back of a bench and tossing another to his follower.

"Not today. I beat you two matches in three with the sword—you will beat me two in three when we wrestle. We've had exercise enough. Why waste the effort to prove it again?"

Narayan nodded, suddenly serious. "It's hard to learn when we spar; we grow too used to each other's tricks."

King smiled. "I think our enemies will give us enough variety, and soon," he said. He slapped the Sikh on the shoulder. "We leave tomorrow—best give the gear another check. I must talk with Elias and Sir Manfred again."

"*Han, huzoor.* It will be good when this matter is settled and we can return to real soldiering. The Second Squadron will grow slack, without us to drive them. *Rissaldar* Mukdun Das is too soft on them."

I wish I had his self-confidence, King thought as the Sikh picked up the practice gear and trotted off. *Or, on the other hand, maybe it's just that he's as good an actor as I am.*

Yasmini watched from the shadow of a pillar as the *Angrezi* officer stood in the mild winter sun, water making rivulets down his body as he toweled himself. He was big without being bulky—the Sikh had looked like a great hairy bear beside him—with broad shoulders tapering to a narrow waist, deep chest, long legs, long arms, and the enlarged wrists of a swordsman. His skin was smooth save for a few scars and a light thatch of hair across the arch of his chest; muscles swelled and slid under wet skin the color of oiled beechwood as he moved, each clearly defined, like living shapes of metal.

She was close enough that she could even smell him a little, a clean masculine scent unlike the all-too-familiar wolf musk with a hint of blood taint of the Master. His face had an intriguing narrow cast, and it was strong without cruelty; the face of a man who could kill without passion or regret when it was necessary, but who would be safer than a mother to all save his enemies.

Altogether it was a fine sight.

The more so as I can look at a man without fear of punishment, now, she thought, with a feeling of guilty pleasure.

She cleared her throat, hoping to make him jump—she had

learned early in her life to creep and steal about the House of the Fallen like a mouse through the wainscoting, with a whipping and a day and night locked in the Black Box for punishment if caught. She knew she was stealthy even by the high standards of the Okhrana schools, where the punishments were far worse, but he was not startled. Instead he lifted his face from the towel and smiled at her.

"That's all right, miss," he said, giving her the title of respect he would have a woman of his own people and class.

Such a pleasant change from slave *and* bitch, she thought.

He went on: "I knew you were there, but thought you might not want to be seen, as it were."

"Thank you," she said. "I have seen you so often in dreams, you see. In person, it is a little different."

That startled him, though he hid it well for an *Angrezi*. It did not frighten him, she thought: But it puzzled, and left him a little off-balance. He nodded—good that he knew when it was better to keep silence—and dressed, pulling on the loose round-collared shirt, then the high-necked jacket that lapped over from left to right and was secured by a tie-off near the shoulder and a sash about the waist. His sword belt went over that, cinched tight, and he settled it comfortably with a slight movement of the hips and hands wholly automatic.

A fine figure of a man, and the more so because he knows it—but dwells on it only a little, she thought, before saying:

"The others wish to discuss the departure with you. They do not like my idea, although *Gospodin* Elias acknowledges it has merit."

"Idea?" King said.

"About the *burqua*," she said, and grinned at him—not an expression he had seen on her before, but then, there had been few occasions for it.

"It's a good disguise," he said, nodding. "Never approved of the damned things, myself, but they're convenient."

"No, not for me—that is, yes, I will wear one. But that is not enough. The watchers will look for one woman, you see, however she is dressed; and I cannot pass for a man in disguise, because I am too small, and my face too different. So there should be two women in the *burqua*; myself as a young noblewoman, and Sir Manfred as my *cheti*— my handmaiden—he being the only other one of us of suitable height and build. Or my *ayah*, if I were to pose as a child."

King stared at her for a moment, then delighted her with a roar of laughter. "Oh, ripping!" he said at last, wheezing a little. "*Shabash*, Yasmini! And Sir Manfred didn't like the idea?"

"No," Yasmini said demurely, dropping her eyes a little. "And when I said that if that was not to his taste, he could be my mother instead . . . somehow that did not please him either."

"By the ten thousand faces of God, I'll give you odds it didn't!" King said, still chuckling. "Am I mistaken, or do you dislike Sir Manfred the least little bit?"

Yasmini hesitated, then decided on the truth. "I should not, perhaps. It is unjust; he is not like the Master, and has never treated me badly. But he *does* look at me like a tool, a thing to be used for a purpose, and that *is* like the Master. That is why I *left* the Master, because I wished to be my own, and use myself for *my* purposes."

He paused, nodded slowly, and held out his left arm, bent in a crook. "I must confess an occasional irritation with Sir Manfred myself. Shall we, then?"

She looked at him in puzzlement, then remembered the *Angrezi* custom and slid her small hand through his elbow.

"Perhaps if he could be my elder sister?" she murmured, as they moved off—he shortening his stride to make it easier for her, and joining his deep laugh to her silvery one.

"Perhaps we should revive the waltz more often," Prince Charles said, leading her off the floor.

"Perhaps we should," Cassandra King replied, snapping open her fan and fluttering it.

His mouth gave a small quirk at that; he knew full well that she had received all a gentlewoman's training in the social graces at home and school, mastered them well, and gratefully dropped them down an oubliette when she became an Oxford scientist and—since she was also a woman, and young—by definition a hopeless eccentric and prospective spinster.

Or unnatural bitch to a good many faculty wives, she thought. *But not having to spend half my time remembering social sign language and ritual is a compensation.*

The ball was theoretically in honor of Henri de Vascogne; the nature of his mission was quasi-public knowledge now; the antique waltzes were in his honor as well, since that style of public entertainment had never fallen out of favor in France-outre-mer. The ballroom was designed for it, in any case; usually for the annual revival on Victoria Day—honoring the first sovereign of that name, not the second, whose idea of a jolly evening had been much less proper. Accordingly, the room was in the classic Old Empire style, strange to modern eyes—nothing but a little carved plaster on the ceiling, the stretches of wall between the gilt-framed mirrors in a plain red wallpaper, and chandeliers of clear translucent crystal drops above. The orchestra was tuning up for the next dance on a dais in one corner, and there were chairs all around the walls elsewhere except for the outer wall, where tall glass doors gave on a broad terrace. Even the scents were old-fashioned, less complex than the patchouli-musk-sandalwood-jasmine-rosewater of contemporary perfumes.

"I think I'd rather watch this one," Cassandra said. *Of course, there are limits. None of the women are wearing corsets or bustles.* In fact, most were in the same sort of *shalwar qamiz* outfit that she was herself, long tunic and trousers; it was more practical, for dancing.

Charles nodded, snagging two glasses off the tray of a passing servant and handing one to her. It was wine punch with sparkling water, and she sipped at it gratefully; despite careful design and those twenty-foot glass doors, the room was a little warm. She watched Sita and Henri talking while the music began, the girl laughing up into his face.

Then he bowed, in a smooth but foreign fashion—right arm folded across his body, left out. Sita curtsied in turn; unlike most women here tonight, she was wearing a sari, one shimmering in rose silk and picked out at the edges in diamonds. Despite the confining skirts of the wraparound garment, she followed him easily out onto the floor, with one hand on the back of his, then launched into the waltz with a swirling, swooping grace. Henri was in French costume tonight, narrow trousers and black tailcoat jacket with golden epaulets. He moved with a swordsman's grace . . .

And more practice in this dance than any of us, Cassandra thought, as a murmur of applause spread through the watchers, and then more and more couples moved out onto the pale marble of the floor. Soon it was a fantasy of color, swirling silken fabric and plumes, flashing feet in jewel-crusted sandals, bright uniforms . . .

"Ah . . . Charles, I know it's none of my business . . ."

"Well, don't let that stop you," the prince said. "It hasn't so far, hey?"

Cassandra gave a small incredulous snort of laughter, glancing aside at him; there was a definite twinkle in his eye, not something you saw every day—the *kunwar* of the Raj was something of a sobersides.

"Perhaps outside—" she said.

They turned their backs on the dance and slipped out on the terrace. It was broad and quiet, lit by crescents flickering on tall pillars. The surface was Rajasthani marble, a pure creamy white divided into squares by narrow strips of lapis lazuli and inlaid with interlinking patterns of tulip, lily, iris, poppy, and narcissus; *pietra dura* work of red carnelian, turquoise, and malachite. The expanse was spotted with high-backed, carved-stone benches curved for easier conversation and padded with snowy linen from the South Island of New Zealand. A few folk were about; couples taking a break from the dancing for flirtation or a snatched kiss, the odd individual taking a smoke. Cassandra and her escort walked over to lean on the balustrade that circled the terrace, looking down on the ornamental pool that surrounded it a dozen feet below.

Beyond was an avenue of fountains flanked by sculpted elephants, jets of water surging and crossing in an intricate repeating pattern; beyond that were the domes and towers and gardens of the Palace of the Lion Throne, dim-lit and mysterious under the frosted stars.

"Hmmm . . ." Cassandra said. "How shall I put it—wasn't Henri's job supposed to be getting Sita to like the thought of marrying his *prince*? Rather than himself, that is."

"Eh?" Charles seemed to start a bit. "Sorry . . . yes, of course. Although the marriage can wait a few years, if needs be, no harm in an engagement of some length. Henri is just getting her to like the idea of living in France-outre-mer. Quite a charming chap when he sets his mind to it, isn't he?"

"He could charm a snake out of its skin," Cassandra said forthrightly. "And he knows *just* the way to go about it with your sister, too. Not throwing her out of the carriage the other night when we went to call on Allenby, for example. *That* made him a hero to her for good and all. Is his Emperor—and this prince of theirs—*insane*?"

"I understand he and the prince are extremely close—playmates since childhood—virtually brothers."

"Still . . . Charles, I've become very fond of Sita. I'd hate to see her with a broken heart; and as I believe I told you, that girl is going to fall seriously in love with *somebody*, and soon. I don't doubt Arthur was close to Lancelot, too—and at least he didn't send du Lac to court Guinevere for him."

Charles produced a cigarette case and offered her one. She shook her head, although she'd once been fond of a quiet evening hookah herself. Some of the Medical Department statistical programs run on the Analytical Engine at Oxford had been coming up with disturbing correlates between tobacco and a galaxy of very nasty diseases, and she'd thrown out her hubble-bubble and sworn off tobacco after reading them.

Instead she watched his face in the dim light as the smoke curled up around his narrow features. She had to admit that cigarettes *did* make an extremely effective aid to conversation.

"I'm glad that you care, Cass," Charles said. "Sita needed a friend—a levelheaded friend—someone a little older and steadier to look up to. Most of the girls her age around court make her look like a rock of stolidity."

"So, I'm to supply stolidity as well as the sciences?" she said.

"*I* don't, ah, find you stolid," he said, turning away slightly as if to watch the view.

Not even the kunwar is immune to our national disease, she thought. Although he couldn't be used to suspense, when it came to women.

"Charles." She laid a hand on his arm, wincing slightly at the look in his eyes. "I like you very much, Charles. And I'm fully aware of how the court biddies have been clucking over how many times you asked your sister's tutor to dance."

"Not every dance," he said defensively.

"No; just as many as you could get away with, after dutifully dancing with your sister and your aunt—Charles, I *do* like you. I enjoy your company and your conversation; I even like simply being with you. I think you're a very attractive man. But I am *not* going to let my emotions run away with me. I have absolutely no interest in the position of an Imperial mistress. My career has far too much of my heart, and I worked too hard and long on it."

The prince flushed enough to be visible even in the darkness. "I— ah—"

"And please, you *know* that your father would absolutely never under any circumstances permit an offer of marriage to an untitled nobody from the provinces—and a Queen-Empress astronomer living in rooms at Oxford? One of the things I like about you is your realism. *Please.*"

He gave a long sigh and flicked the end of the cigarette into the night, like a miniature comet with a trail of sparks. "You *do* have to stay at court until this business is wrapped up, don't you?" he said hopefully.

"Yes. And I'll enjoy being your friend while I do. Fair?"

"Fair. Although I doubt women ever appreciate the doomlike knell of the word *friend* in these circumstances." He surprised her with another laugh. "And accordingly, why don't we go have a friendly waltz?"

Chapter Eighteen

"**R**ailways are out of the question," Warburton fretted. "So is anything where the opposition could be watching. And we must get to Bombay within three weeks—they can't delay the departure any more than that without Parliament starting to take notice and ask questions. They can scarcely tell the prime minister that we needed the time to recover from our wounds."

"Trust me," Elias said. "There are many ways to Bombay." He smiled, the wrinkled face suddenly looking like a map of some mysterious, mountainous country in the bright morning sunlight.

"This was a very old land before the first *Angrezi* dropped anchor off Malabar," he said. "And in every age there have been those who had absolute need to travel, or send goods or letters, without the knowledge of those who dwelt in the seats of power. Smugglers' routes, pilgrim pathways, roads that run alongside and through the roads of day, from one house to another—established for religion, or for politics—you would know more of those, Sir Manfred—or to avoid the cadasters of the tax collectors."

"And you know them?" King said curiously.

"Some. Some, a little. Tche-veh! I am ancient in this land myself!" He grinned. "And not all our family's business over the generations has been so respectable as selling your apples and cheeses and dried apricots and remitting net-minus-four-percent-plus-shipping, young lordling."

Well, I can take a hint, King thought, quelling any further questions. *And life is full of new experiences.*

Up to now, he'd never run across someone who found the landed gentry *amusing*. His mouth quirked; he'd met plenty of resentment, buried or overt—you had to have much, much more money than a *zamindar* to equal his social weight, if the money came from trade. No amount of business money would get you an Army commission, for instance—a regiment's officers had to vote unanimously on admitting new subalterns, and they'd blackball anyone with the wrong background.

But never before had he met a subtle sense that those to the manor born were faintly *ridiculous*.

The other members of the party were bustling about with bundles and parcels. Yasmini came dressed in the *burqua*, carrying another—hers was of the type where even the slit between nose and brow was covered by a mesh, lest the color of her eyes attract attention, and with sleeves long enough to reach the fingertips. Warburton put his on, and—being a professional, after all—immediately altered walk, stance, and movement. Yasmini looked at him critically, and after a moment said:

"It will do . . . Mother."

"A child should obey!" Warburton replied. His voice had become a querulous old lady's, his walk a limping waddle. "Children today have no respect—none—none for Gods or parents."

King raised his eyebrows at the motortrucks waiting in the courtyard. "First-class service," he said.

"As far as the outskirts," Elias said. "Hired—through intermediaries. The delivery company has no link to me. With luck, that will delay any seekers for a while yet. Better yet if you could have left this house earlier, but—" He shrugged; their wounded had needed the time. "Go with His blessing, and mine—for what that is worth. And come tell me of what passed, when it is over."

"I will, sir," King said, taking his hand. "My father never did a wiser thing than telling me to take your counsel."

"Keep your own counsel—and use your head for something besides a battering ram, that is my advice to you. Keep up your chess; it stretches the mind and makes it supple. Go then!"

King helped pass the bundles into the forward truck. He saw David bar-Elias climbing into the second, in his traveling garb once more, with his retainers. That was reassuring; the middle-aged Jew was a good friend to have at your back, and had proved it abundantly in the most concrete way possible. He gave the man a thumbs-up gesture and settled into the motortruck's compartment; it was a little warm and stuffy with the doors closed, despite the mild winter's day.

The vehicle had an advertisement above the rear doors proclaiming that none but Brahmins were allowed to touch the interior or handle the goods, which meant its regular business was probably delivering high-priced fresh produce; there was a faint smell of butter and ghee to confirm it, and shreds of some leafy vegetable caught in cracks in the planks which made up the cab. There was also a narrow slit in the front which showed the open seat where the driver sat at his big horizontal wheel; he set his back to the thin wooden boards and squatted easily as the motor started with a soft *thudump* of kerosene burners.

The sides of the the motortruck creaked as it turned and made its way out into the street. None within saw the eyes that watched over a compound wall whose top was set with shards of broken glass.

Narayan Singh grinned at him from the other end of the cab. "So, *sahib*—we are away, the game is afoot, and our enemies none the wiser!"

"If they were the wiser, would they send a message so that we, too, might know?" Ibrahim Khan said. "Would they beat a *dhol*-drum, lest we be in doubt? Light a fire and dance about it, snapping their fingers and singing—"

"Peace," King said, and both the younger men settled down with a slightly sulky air.

The chaffing between the Sikh and the hillman was only half-serious. On the other hand, half of it *was* serious, and neither was a man to be trifled with or take lightly in a quarrel. Narayan Singh had his strength back, and an agreeable prospect of further revenge on the men who had dared to abduct him and torture him and—even worse—think that they could wring betrayal out of him; and at the best of times he had a rather stuffy sense of his own dignity as a non-commissioned officer. The Pathan was in good spirits because he'd helped carry off a daring raid, and because he'd found an agreeable servant-girl, which gave him a high opinion of himself—coming as he did from a land of reavers where all women were under guard, and for very good reason.

They were both on edge and ready to strike; it was a leader's duty to see that the blows went in the right direction.

The black *burqua* that covered Yasmini somehow conveyed an attitude of acute interest; King gave her an imperceptible nod. Warburton moved a little, too. King looked at him with a raised eyebrow. You could see out of the mesh in a *burqua's* eye slit much better than anyone at a distance could look in.

"Wish Mr. Bar-Binyamin was in the Political Service," the agent said—and the man's voice was astonishing, because the whole posture beneath the all-concealing garment was female, and elderly. "We've got two tasks—one, get to Bombay. Two, get aboard the *Garuda* and stop the deviltry planned. How"—the shrug was verbal, rather than a gesture—"we'll see."

The motortrucks were fast, once out of Old Delhi and on the broad highways leading west: a good thirty-five miles an hour, faster than anything else on land except a train. The problem was that motor vehicles were impossibly conspicuous anywhere beyond city limits. Driving one through a village would set tongues to wagging for a year and a day, and the enemy seemed to have a disconcerting number of ears.

We might as well put up a sign, HURRAH, WE'RE HERE, King thought. He'd never seen a motor vehicle in his life until he went away to school and passed through Oxford. Even in most of Delhi they weren't so common that you saw one at every glance on the streets, and there was more motor transport within the city limits of Delhi than in all the rest of the world together—over twenty thousand of them all told.

When he voiced the thought aloud, Warburton chuckled through the *burqua*.

"Trust Elias," he said, speaking softly—Yasmini had laid her head on a rope-wrapped bundle beside him and was sleeping, one small hand beneath her head. "He knows West Delhi better than you. Has property there, he told me."

King looked out the slit again. The packed urban mass of Delhi was fraying, opening out into greenery—but not green fields. The houses looked like miniature manors, and were set in large gardens that looked pretty even in winter; above one brick boundary wall he could see the whirling plumes of a sprinkler keeping lawns green, never easy in the lowland climate. Children played amid the trees and flower banks, gardeners clipped and mowed and watered, ladies in bright saris or tunic-and-trousers took postbreakfast strolls with parasols. Yet there were no fields beyond the gardens, no villages or plowland, and after half an hour he'd seen enough mansions behind wrought-iron gates to furnish manors for a province. A light dawned:

"Oh, I'd heard of this—read about it in a newspaper. The New Garden City, isn't it?"

A good third of the houses seemed to have small buildings for motors attached, many converted from stables.

"Yes," Warburton replied, the *burqua* giving an eerie disembodied note to the speech. "When I was your age, this was all farms. Myself, I wouldn't want to live here—it's neither country nor city, fish nor fowl nor good red meat, and I was born inside the Old Delhi walls."

"Hmmm," King said; it seemed unnatural, but . . . "I suppose in a city of four million, you get a lot of everything—even men willing and able to buy motors just to drive to their work, or manor houses without estates."

He racked his memory and came up with the Latin tag the newspaper had used for areas of this sort: *rus-in-urbe*, or *rusurbs* for short.

The *rusurb . . . ghastly name . . .* ended in an ocean of building sites, half-dug cellars and half-built walls, streets in every stage from sealed tarmacadam to trenches for water and sewer pipes, piles of sand and stone and brick, timber and iron and doorframes. The quiet half-life of the Garden City gave way to a semblance of noisy urban bustle, with hundreds of horse carts and oxcarts, thousands of bare-legged laborers in *dhotis* chattering or chanting as they worked, dirt flying from shovels, women carrying traylike baskets of it on their heads, foremen with *lathis* of split bamboo yelling, contractors arguing and waving papers, craftsmen working with plane and chisel and saw. The *tink-tink-tink* of hundreds of masons sounded, as they squatted amid piles of chips to shape stone with flying hammers.

I'd hand out punishment detail to men who made that much fuss on a work detachment, he thought. *Civilians!*

The motortrucks pulled up behind several huge piles of building materials, and a line of young trees with their root balls wrapped in burlap. Four big oxcarts were waiting, each with two painted wheels as high as a tall man and a pair of huge white Gujarati oxen, plus gaudy designs on the sides and an overhanging curved roof—what conservative but modestly affluent country folk would use for a trip to town. Horses were tethered nearby, including the ones on which King and his two followers had ridden into Delhi. Those looked sleek with good feeding; Ibrahim gave a grunt of satisfaction at the sight of his Kashmiri gelding, doubly his since King had bestowed it and he'd killed the previous owner of the—stolen—beast.

King jumped down immediately, shaking Yasmini gently by the shoulder. She started up, shivering and looking around her as if bewildered, then began to speak. He gave her his hand, making a slight *shush* gesture, and then both of them were clucking solicitously over their "mother."

In a nondescript turban and countryman's traveling clothes, King could pass at a distance for a wealthy North Indian Muslim; Ibrahim Khan added to the picture, for he was just the sort of swaggering fortune-seeking Afghan blade such a man might hire as armed retainer—if he had high confidence in his womenfolk, or none of nubile age. An unmistakable Sikh spoiled the ensemble—the Protestants of the Hindu world had never forgotten how many of their early Gurus were killed by Muslim rulers—but Narayan was undercover again soon. David bar-Elias vaulted into the rear of the cart; he had his side curls up under his turban, and could have been of any dozen faiths or peoples himself.

"The drivers are our men," he said, and pulled out a map. "Now's the time to decide on our course."

He laid the paper down on the floorboards of the cart, swaying easily as it lurched into motion. "Here we are—just southwest of Delhi. There are three paths we could take to get to Bombay, avoiding the trunk roads and the railways. I suggest going through Alwar and then—"

"No," Yasmini said.

They all looked at her; she unfastened the buttons beneath her hood and pushed it back. Her eyes didn't have quite the blank look they had when she'd led them through Allenby's house, but they were intense enough.

"Death, here," she said, sketching a finger along the most direct of the routes between the capital and Bombay. "Many forms of death—

many men waiting for us. Nearly as bad here. And further west—least bad." She frowned. "I am . . . crossing the path of my own earlier dreams here. It makes things . . . hazy. Makes more the possibilities. But that is as much as I can give you."

David looked doubtful. King, with more experience of Yasmini's talent, held up a hand for silence, finger on the map. "They must have spotted us leaving Delhi," he said, looking at Yasmini.

She shrugged, wiping one palm across her forehead, looking shaken and wrung-out from her sleep instead of rested. "I cannot be sure. Only that they are waiting, as I said."

"Not sooner, Yasmini?" King asked.

"No. Not before then—I did not dream more than a flicker of an attack in the next three days. That was . . . far away, where none of us were as we are." Seeing their confusion, she added wearily: "Call it a chance so slight we need not be concerned."

King paused for thought. "All right," he said at last. "They know we're going overland, not by rail, and they know we're heading for Bombay. We should use the knowledge against them—it isn't what you don't know that'll kill you; it's what you think you know that isn't so. Here's what we'll do instead . . ."

When he finished speaking, David stroked his beard. "I know that country—we have friends and clients there. Can you all ride a camel?" he said.

"I wouldn't call myself or Narayan experts, we're horse-soldiers, but yes," King said.

Krishna, but I loathe those smelly brutes, he added to himself. *Still, the best bet for what I want.*

Warburton nodded silently.

"*Da,*" Yasmini said.

Ibrahim snorted indignation at the question: "Am I weaned, Jew? Can I walk?"

"Good. Then we can *perhaps* do what you suggest, Captain King. Your father thought well in a tight spot, too."

He stuck his head out of the cart and called one of his men, giving quick orders. The man nodded, untied and readied two of the horses; master and man swung into the saddle and pounded off, each with another behind him on a leading rein. White dust spurted up behind the hooves and drifted downwind; they were out on an ordinary graveled secondary road now, through ordinary low-country villages.

Even in November, at noontime it was comfortably warm for lying in the shade, sweating-hot if you had to work in the sun. The winter wheat had just been planted, and a few shoots were showing green in fields damp from irrigation. *Ryots* were at work with shovel and mattock, clearing channels, building up and breaking down the banks.

A few looked up to wave as the carts went by. King saw more stopping work and salaaming, and heard the explanation a moment later when a bugle's harsh cry rang out from the middle distance southward.

It sounded again, closer, an insistent four notes that said: *Make way! Make way for the King-Emperor's men! Make way, for the lords of humankind!*

The bullock-men of King's party pulled aside, like the other farm vehicles and the more numerous travelers on foot. An infantry regiment came swinging down the road after the martial music, with a long plume of khaki-colored dust smoking behind them. They were headed northeast toward Delhi; the colonel in front on his charger with the tall poles of the colors following—regimental and national flags, furled inside the leather cover casings now, carried by picked men; the company officers riding by the side of the road; the other ranks in columns of four sweating in the dust behind the band, which was silent except for the *thrip-rip-rip* of the drum. The mule carts hauling baggage, kit, ammunition, machine guns and a few men unable to keep their feet brought up the rear.

Imperial Service outfit, King thought—the faces in the ranks were all *sahib-log*, and mostly in their late teens or early twenties. They marched well, booted feet swinging in unison, rifles over their shoulders. *Well enough, for short-service men, that is.*

He was prejudiced in favor of professional units like the Peshawar Lancers himself, of course. All members of the martial castes had to do a few years with the colors and train periodically for the reserve until they were middle-aged, but even within those groups only a minority made the Army their life's work. From their brown tans and the look of their uniforms, this lot had been at field exercises somewhere down in Rajputana, somewhere hot and dry.

Right where we're going, King thought grimly, looking at the map again, examining the routes that crossed the Thar Desert. *Or even drier.*

Then he folded it and settled down next to Yasmini as the cart lurched back into slow but steady motion. She was lying on pillows— the carts were fitted out for carrying womenfolk, with rugs and cushions, and water bags of canvas hanging from the roof kept cool by their sweating skins. Her eyes were open, but her face was still drawn.

"Are you all right, miss?" he said. "I'm a little worried for you."

She turned her head and smiled wanly at him, murmuring in Russian. He repeated his question in that language, a little alarmed when her eyes glistened.

"You used the old words," she said. He nodded; his Russian was book-learned, much of it from texts dating before the Fall. "My mother used them—some of the other Sisters, too. Never where the priests of Tchernobog could hear."

"Old words?" he asked.

"Words of kindness," she said.

A small hand crept into his; it was work-hardened, but tiny and fragile inside his sword-callused one. He closed his fingers gently on hers.

I've never had a girl keep comparing me to her mother *before,* he thought. *And I wouldn't have thought it was so flattering.*

"You didn't answer my question, though, miss," he went on aloud.

"Yasmini—you called me that before," she said.

"Ah—" He flushed slightly with embarrassment. "Sorry . . . hadn't asked . . . irregular situation . . ."

"You have my permission, Captain King," she said solemnly.

"Ah . . . thank you. Athelstane, then. And you *still* haven't answered it."

She looked at him for a long moment. "I am growing too old to be a Dreamer," she said.

"You're barely a child!" he blurted. Then: "Well, you look like one. Sorry."

"We often do. I am four years and twenty—ten years now since I became a woman, and began to dream. That is more than most can bear. Every time I dream, control is less—I have passed the point where more skill and practice can match the growing power. If I dream much longer, I will be lost in the dreams . . . mad, not knowing if I am *this* Yasmini"—she touched herself between the brows—"or a thousand thousand thousand others from one instant to the next. And they may think themselves me. A chain of madwomen across time."

"Oh," he said. "I see."

He was also a bit shocked; he'd have sworn she was hardly sixteen, eighteen at the most, rather than nearly his own age.

"*Nyet,*" she said. "You do not. I fear that, yet I fear the loss of my dreams as much as you would the sight of your eyes, or the use of your legs, or the strength of your arm."

"How do you stop?" he asked. "Is it a drug you take, or . . . ?"

She told him, bluntly; modern Russian, even the High Formal mode, had little reticence about such matters. He winced—in fact you had a choice between the brutally animalistic and the subtly cruel, in the language of Samarkand. The tongues men spoke shaped how they lived and thought, but the process worked the other way 'round as well.

She shivered and rolled tighter into a ball. "Yet what is Yasmini if she cannot dream? Nothing but another broodmare in the pens."

And as a cripple to boot, he thought, trying to imagine living as a blind man begging on street corners.

"We can find something better than that," he said stoutly. "My word of honor on it as a King. *Kuch dar nahin hai,* remember?"

"With you, I can believe that . . . sometimes," she said, and dropped off to sleep again, curled up against his flank like a puppy.

King glared down Narayan's brief inquiring look; Ibrahim was giving him a glance of mingled respect and fear, since he would rather have cuddled a hooded cobra himself. The Lancer officer dug into one of the bundles, pulling out a copy of *Bradshaw's Indian Imperial Railways,* by Newmans of Calcutta, and lost himself in thought.

Yasmini's hand remained firmly clamped on his.

They came to a manor just inside the borders of Rajputana, as the moon rose enormous and smoky red with dust, and the white road wound before them like a ribbon of silver. The land had grown drier throughout the three days of oxcart travel, as rocky hills grew common and the deep rich clay of the northern river plains gave way to country where the bones of the earth showed. The *zamindar*—or *thakundar,* in the local dialect—was a Rajput himself; the gentry of this hotbed of feudalism had remained stoutly loyal during the Second Mutiny, and none of it had been gazetted—confiscated—in the great wave of *sahib-log* rural settlement that followed the Exodus.

It was a great deal less tidy than estates in more modern parts of India. A big tile-roofed house-fort stood on a hillock at its center, surrounded by huge green pipil trees with hordes of sleepy monkeys in their branches, both protected for their sanctity. Below the hill was a small river with an arched stone bridge; about that were blocky stone houses thrown together, with smaller and humbler dwellings of mud-brick and thatch some distance away. The only modern touches were the abundance of window glass, the whirling wind pump and water tank near the mansion, and the odd piece of factory-made farm equipment lying against the wall of a house or shed.

The fields round about—wheat, sorghum, cotton, sunflower— were harvested stubble, but today they bore other crops. The lord of the estate was holding a polo tournament, and the national game of the Imperial gentry had a fanatical following in Rajputana among all classes—all Rajputs thought of themselves as the sons of kings, after all. Tents and shelters sprouted far and wide, from mere bothies of sorghum stalks to vast colorful pavilions; canvas enclosures held rows of ponies and pampering, lavish grooms; there was even a brace of elephants, leg-tethered by chains to deep-pounded posts.

The manor house was bright with lanterns and noisy with festivity—a feast for the teams and the noble visitors, another for their ladies. Their retainers and servants made a swarm in the little town below, and following them had come acrobats, men who swallowed fire and juggled flaming torches in bright arcs through the cool night air, trained horses prancing on their hind feet, performing bears holding wooden swords in their paws, troops of nautches—dancing girls— with fantastic jeweled hoops through one nostril and gaudy saris and gliding steps, storytellers, singers of the interminable Rajput ballads of mad gallantry and courtly love . . .

Perfect disguise, King thought, as he handed Yasmini down. *Four more oxcarts? Nobody'll notice 'em, though we'd be a four-week wonder here if we arrived in normal times.*

The carts had stopped beside a small, half-ruined temple a quarter mile from the village; from the flowers and bowls of *puja* offerings on the steps, it was still in use but left tonight to the birds and bats and scampering monkeys. The scents were mostly sweet, underlain by dust and packed humanity, horses, and the hard dry smell of the working oxen that pulled the carts. The party made camp in its usual fashion; King helped with the horses, Narayan and the bar-Elias retainers set up the tents, and Ibrahim Khan sauntered off to "scout," by which he meant that he was a Pathan and would never dirty his hands with manual labor of any kind, as long as someone else would do it for him. Trying to force him to it would simply turn him sullen and dangerous.

That's more *dangerous*, King thought.

Yasmini looked wistfully at the crowds and lanterns a little distance away, the murmur of voices and laughter and song carrying over the shrill chirping of insects.

"All those people together, and nobody fighting or killing or beating anyone," she said. "So many laughing, and the shows and . . . that looked like . . . what's the *Angrezi* word . . . fun?" she said. "I would like to, to *have fun* someday."

King stopped himself from a casual joke along the lines of: *Haven't had any before, then?* He'd spoken with her a fair bit as they traveled, trading stories, and from what she said that was literally true. Or at least not except as something rare, snatched, furtive. Living in the Czar's dominions was miserable enough anywhere, but to be brought up in the Peacock Angel's city, in the very House of the Fallen . . .

He shuddered inwardly. *Yet she seems to be sane enough*, he thought. *Got a wicked sense of humor, too, and plenty of guts. Good company. Reminds me a bit of Cass, actually. When I think of some of the social excruciations I've been through with giggling debutantes . . . Three days in an oxcart with them would drive me bloody mad!*

"You should see the *Holi* festival at Rexin," he said. "Now, *that's* fun."

"Thank you," she said.

"What for?"

"For telling me about your family," she said.

King found himself flushing again and turned with gratitude as three riders made their way out to the camp. David bar-Elias and his oddly named Mongol retainer were two; the other was a tall thin Rajput noble, with grizzled whiskers trained to flare out a foot on either side of his face, an enormous turban of red silk, and enough jewelry to start a shop, with still more on the hilt and scabbard of his *tulwar.* His horse was splendid, lifting long slender legs in a high trot, and he kept the saddle as if he'd been grown there, but the beast had been *painted*—spots and stars and stripes in gaudy hot crimsons and yellows and greens. The lord of Rexin winced inwardly, ever so slightly.

Hell of a thing to do to a good horse, he thought, as the Rajput drew rein. *Customary at festivals, but still . . .*

One *sowar* of the Peshawar Lancers had taken a horse home for a wedding and decked it out like that, and been unable to get the paint off in time when he came back from leave. Colonel Claiborne's remarks when the luckless trooper showed up on parade had been memorable.

The Rajput's hard dark eyes met his for a second, then flicked away in the elaborate, deliberate disinterest of a man determined not to notice something.

Soldier's eyes, King thought. *Probably high-ranking in his day, too.*

The Rajput rider turned to David bar-Elias:

"Yes, I can provide the beasts," he said, in good Army-style Hindi, based on the Delhi dialect but shot through with loan words from English and a dozen other languages.

Well, I was right about that, King thought, stepping back into the shadows.

The Rajput gave a wave of the riding crop. "With this bally crowd here eating me out of house and home for the polo match, half the neighborhood is trading and bartering animals on the side—oxen—horses—camels—nobody will notice the extras."

His gaze rested on King for a space, and on Warburton in his hastily donned *burqua,* and on Narayan Singh—who always wore civilian clothes as if they were the silver-gray dress tunic and knee boots of the Peshawar Lancers, and had even before he enlisted. They flicked over Yasmini with an arched brow; she was not in the tentlike garment herself—it was a little out of place in this part of Rajputana, where Muslims were few—but she was holding the tail of her head scarf over her face. That was perfectly acceptable behavior for a woman in the presence of a strange man; a trifle old-fashioned in Delhi, but nothing out of the ordinary here in the backwoods. The curl of blond hair peeping out at one side was not, however.

"And as you said, old chap, it's better that I not know too much. My regards to your pater, eh, what?"

With that he turned his horse with an imperceptible movement of his thighs. It floated off, the trot breaking into an equally fluid gallop.

I'd pay five mohurs *for that horse,* King thought for an instant, as he absently reached over and tucked away the betraying curl.

From the way Ibrahim Khan was fingering his knife hilt as he came back into the firelight, *he'd* been thinking of stealing it. King frowned at him, meeting an innocent grin in return.

He knows that I know that he knows, and so forth, King thought. *Not a bad johnny, in his way, but wearing.*

"That man can ride, *sahib,*" Narayan Singh said. "And that horse is worth the riding, by the Guru!"

"True, true," Ibrahim said. "A dancer with the wind—although I'd like to see how those dancer's legs stood up to the trails in the hill country before I bred from it."

David bar-Elias swung down from his saddle, looking a little worn—he'd traveled considerably faster than they. "Horses, trains, camels—they take you where you wish to go. Motorcars would be better, if they were cheaper and more reliable. Airships better still."

Sahib-log, Sikh, and Pathan looked at him in horrified incomprehension. He shrugged.

"Well, we have what we need," he said. "And no stinting. Our host will say nothing. Neither will the servants he sets to this matter."

King nodded, and spread his map again on the tail of a cart. "All right," he said. "We're here—northwest of Sikar. What we're going to do is head straight west."

"Allah aid me, how will that get us to Bombay?" Ibrahim asked.

"If you were less fond of the sound of your own voice, you would find out more quickly, child of misbelief," Narayan Singh said with heavy patience.

"Peace," King said. *That's quite true, Narayan, but he's not a trooper in the Lancers.*

"We have to cross this country here—the Thar," he went on. At inquiring looks from Ibrahim and Yasmini, he explained: "Desert. Bad country at any time of year, although not as bad in the cold season, thank Krishna; no sandstorms, at least. No water to speak of, and it's lawless—by our standards," he added a slight ironic tone directed at the Pathan. "On camelback, and pushing it, we can reach the rail line *here.*" His finger stabbed at a point on the map. "Between Pokharan and Jasalmer, in about a week. Even a slow train will get us into Bombay in good time after that."

"But you said the trains were too dangerous," Ibrahim pointed out. A moment later: *"Huzoor."*

"The passenger trains, and the stations," King replied, with a grin. His free hand tapped the *Bradshaw*. "And here I have the schedules. We'll stow away aboard a freight train as it crosses open country—there's heavy traffic on the Multan-Bombay line; it taps the lands watered by the Smith Canal. I should have thought of that earlier. We can bribe the engineer or brakeman if we're discovered."

Yasmini shrugged when he looked at her, and spread her hands. "Nothing. That might mean there is nothing, or that there is. I feel no great fear of that route—but everything along our path is dangerous."

"But what of my horse, if we must travel by camel?" Ibrahim cut in. As everyone else looked at him: "It is a good horse! And part of my miserable pay—the greater part. It is not fitting that the son of a great chief return to the hills without at least a good horse."

"Our host will care for the horses and return them to my father's house in Delhi," David bar-Elias answered.

"And I will replace the horse if it is lost," King said, slightly impatient.

It was natural enough for the Pathan to think the horse lost as soon as it was out of his sight. In Ibrahim's home range, you tethered a horse by tying left rear to right forefoot, and then anchored that to the ground by driving down a hooked iron stake, and then you guarded it all night anyway. In a country where kidnapping women was considered a good practical joke by everyone except their husbands, fathers, and brothers, mere horse-stealing was an art form.

Grumbling, the Pathan subsided. A pony-trap came out from the mansion, with a man driving who had *cavalry trooper* written all over his weathered brown face. In the back was food in covered brass bowls. Festival food at that; tandoor-baked chicken, fragrant basmati rice, *nargisi koftas*—lamb meatballs shaped around hard-boiled eggs—and fiery sauces.

Another benefit of coming during a social gathering, King thought, nose twitching and appetite stirring. A Rajput noble would live on sorghum porridge for a month if he had to, rather than appear a miser before his assembled peers.

Ibrahim carefully sniffed to make sure none of the meat was pork, which Rajputs did eat, particularly in the form of wild boar, and then took his portion aside. So did several of David bar-Elias's retainers; he himself avoided the meat save for lamb without the cream-based sauce, but ate with King's party. Except for beef, Narayan Singh would cheerfully eat anything with anyone; Nanak Guru, the founder of the Sikh faith, had disliked caste and the ritual-purity rules about who could eat with whom. He and the others sat down around the food, rolling up their right sleeves and using balls of rice or chapatis to dip up the sauces and meats.

King watched Yasmini a little, out of the corner of his eye. There was something fascinating about the catlike way she moved, the precision of the small hands and the delicate flicker of her rather pointed tongue as she licked her lips . . .

Business, Athelstane, he thought to himself, rather flustered. Aloud: "Eat hearty. We're on cold dry rations for the next week."

The Rajput squire's men came back, this time with the first of the camels. King went to inspect them as they came in; the drier parts of Rajputana bred the finest and fastest camels in India, and some said in the world. These raised his brows—long-legged beauties (as camels went), a foot taller than his head at the shoulder, and all young and fit. Considering that there was one and a remount for each of them, plus baggage beasts, a fairly considerable sum was involved. Whatever sort of connection Elias's family had with the Rajput, it was solid. Any of the animals here could carry six hundred pounds, and do thirty miles a day or better for a week on no water and no better fodder than the thorn scrub of the *jangladesh*, the dry country.

David bar-Elias went also, and he was a true expert, as King was with horses. Harnessing went quickly under his eye, and that of his caravaneers. The beasts bit, and kicked, and spat gobs of green mucus, and complained with guttural abandon as the unfamiliar handlers saddled and loaded; there was a fair bit of cursing and whacking of sensitive noses. Camels were never amiable, and saw no reason they should walk long distances under heavy burdens just because men wanted them to. When the process was well under way, the Jew went back to one of the ox wagons and pulled up the carpets that covered its bed. Then he pushed and pulled until sections of the planking came up in turn, revealing short burlap-wrapped shapes beneath in a shallow hidden compartment between the real and false floors of the cart.

"I'm not here in an official capacity," King said hastily—the rifles were hideously illegal, unless the owners had permits.

"Properly licensed—just not licensed for use inside the Empire's borders," David said, smiling as he handed the weapons out.

They were Martini-Metford carbines, somewhat out-of-date but still very usable; King had trained on them as a cadet, before the Metford magazine carbine became general issue. He stripped the jute sacking off his and let the familiar weight of wood and steel settle into his hands, smelling of iron and the faintly nutty scent of gun oil. He shook it gently, to make sure there was no rattle of loose parts, then worked the action—thumb through the lever below the stock; push down, and the block sank to lay the chamber bare, pull it back up and the action closed and cocked.

A metallic *chick-chack* sounded, and then a *snap* as he pointed the muzzle skyward and pulled the trigger. The whole sequence was glass smooth; when he looked down the barrel with the action open the seven shallow grooves were well marked in the glitter of the firelight he was aiming at, so the lands hadn't been shot out—always a risk, with old weapons in the Reserve armories or civilian hands. The round was the same .40 cake-powder semirimmed as the modern gun, and the ballistics identical, so he wouldn't be thrown off his aim.

David noticed him checking. "We carried those to Bokhara in your father's time," he said. "And they've guarded a good few caravans outside the Empire for Elias and Son before and since. I'm not a soldier, Captain King, but I treat my tools properly."

King dipped his head slightly. "I'm sure you do," he said sincerely. "But I *am* a soldier, and I also always check my tools and my men's. Good habits keep you alive—and it's worth the trouble to keep them up when you don't have to, for the times you do."

"Something to that," the Jew admitted, pulling out bandoleers of cartridges, slinging one over his shoulder, and handing the others to the men who'd taken rifles.

The brass cases had been enameled a dark, nonreflective matt green, which was a touch King appreciated—many a patrol had been betrayed by the military mania for polishing things brightly, and dulling all metal was something he always saw to before his men went out the cantonment gate.

Narayan Singh had checked his own rifle, just as expected; he wasn't surprised to see Warburton do the same, or Ibrahim Khan take his weapon with a delighted whoop, examine it with familiar confidence, or drape two bandoleers crisscross over his sheepskin jacket with piratical élan.

It did raise his brows a little when he saw Yasmini take a carbine of her own and dry-fire it with practiced ease. With the butt on the ground it came up past her breastbone, the way a full-sized infantry rifle would on a soldier. She handled the seven-pound weight easily, though; he remembered from her touch that she was surprisingly strong for her size.

"The Master . . . I mean, Ignatieff, had some of his Cossacks train me with saddle guns," Yasmini said. "For emergencies, because I was so valuable to him. The priests agreed."

A smile, this time a little harder than he was accustomed to from her. "And now I will guard myself because I am valuable to me, and you. This bandoleer is too long, though."

It was, drooping past her hip almost to her knee; he smiled at the sight. *Makes her look like Cass did, that time she dressed up in Mother's things when she was seven—the pearl necklace that reached right to her feet, for instance.* Except, of course, that Yasmini most definitely *wasn't* his sister.

Her slim figure looked almost like a boy's, too, in the rough dark *kurta*-tunic and pjamy-trousers and riding boots. Except that boys didn't affect him this way, which was something he knew with absolute certainty, after spending over half of every year from six to sixteen at United Services boarding school.

"You looked a little like my sister then," he explained as he took the length of leather from her and trimmed it deftly with his belt knife, cut a new tongue for the buckle, and handed it back. The cut leather all came off the part that went across her back, which didn't have cartridge loops.

"Yes, that is much better," she said, adjusting it. "And I would like to meet your sister. From what you say, she seems to be a woman of much spirit."

"That she is," King said. *Good Ganesha tell me, what* would *Cass make of her? Or Mother . . .*

"*Chalo!*" he said aloud. The thought was irrelevant with diabolists, Thugs, and spies on their trail. "We've got a lot of ground to cover."

A touch of his foot, and the camel he'd picked knelt. He swung up into the high-cantled rest that spanned the animal's hump—it was more like straddling a divan than sitting in a horse's saddle—and looked up at the stars.

"Follow me!" he said, and grinned, tapping the camel again so that it rose, grumbling, rump first. "Tally-ho!"

Chapter Nineteen

"I like Bombay," Charles Saxe-Coburg-Gotha said, speaking loudly to be heard over the roar of the crowd as he waved.

He took an instant from official duty and brushed rice and flowers off his uniform. Cassandra King leaned over from beside Sita in the front of the open howdah and brushed off a few more, feeling a rush of tenderness she knew was absurd.

"Your *dupatta* is covered with the stuff," he said.

"Oh!" Cassandra said, and shook her head shawl back off her piled chestnut hair before replacing it—this was a little public for even a daring Whig professor to leave her hair uncovered for more than an instant.

The *kunwari* of the Raj squeaked a little. "Now you're getting it on me!"

"*So* sorry," Cassandra said, flustered. "Not used to having people throw things at me. Except brickbats, metaphorically."

"Better flowers and rice than bombs," the heir to the Lion Throne said grimly, his smile fading.

"Or bullets," Henri de Vascogne agreed.

The howdah swayed slightly as the elephant strode on; it was a thing of glass and silver filigree to all appearances, but far from fragile. Howdah and elephant put them a good dozen feet above the surface of the street; most of the flowers flung up at the riders ended up beneath the feet of the great gray beasts. The elevation of the howdah didn't hinder the manifold thousands of well-wishers showering blossoms on them from the taller buildings along the way, of course.

This elephant was second of twelve. The first held the King-Emperor and his aide and sister, Dowager Princess Jane; behind came that of Sir Benjamin Sukhia, KCBE, the Parsi mayor of the city, and his lady; from there the procession shaded off into lesser dignitaries in mere carriages. Many of them owned the office buildings that towered four, five, and even six stories on either side in a rococo splendor of carved-stone balconies, columns, polychrome statues, glass, gilding, and mosaic, and stretched ahead down the Avenue of the Adventurers—the headquarters of the great textile and shipping firms and the world's most powerful banks.

The flowers thrown by the crowd from windows and balcony-terraces and rooftops filled the air in a brilliant rain as heavy as the monsoons of summer, turning the avenue ahead into a tunnel of brightness and scent, a thundering blaze of color and cheers in air heavy with smoke, incense and sea salt. The elephant's flanks from the howdah nearly to the ground were covered by a gold-mesh fabric with the Imperial arms and the patron goddess of Bombay, Mumba Devi, blazing and glittering as it rippled in the bright winter sunshine—although wits claimed that the real city divinity was Mahalakshmi, goddess of wealth and business. Charles was in the dress uniform of the Poona Lancers, of which he was honorary colonel-in-chief; indigo blue tunic frogged with silver lace, gray trousers, and polished high boots, his turban cloth-of-gold and lavishly plumed, a jeweled *tulwar* held between his knees. The ceremonial escort trotting along on either side were from the same regiment, a mass of bristling points, pennants and glossy hides showing endless work with currycomb and polish. The faces under the turbans were dark brown and mainly clean-shaven, reminding her of Detective-Captain Malusre; the Poona Lancers were a Marathi unit.

Infantrymen stood to attention and presented arms along the sides of the street—and behind them another file stood facing the other way, rifles held horizontally to make a living fence and keep the madly cheering crowds at bay. Some of the *jawans* doing parade duty were from the Gurkha regiment of Foot Guards, sent ahead from Delhi by train. More were Imperial Marines in scarlet coats and archaic-looking pith helmets, and more still were Navy men in blue sailor-suits and turbans. Bombay was the main headquarters of the Royal and Imperial Navy, as well as the country's largest trading port.

"Why do you like Bombay specifically, Charles?" Cassandra asked.

"Because Father doesn't? No, really—because my namesake founded it. Charles II."

Let's see, 1662 . . . Cassandra thought—with a quick memory of chalk dust and a well-chewed pencil. *Three hundred and sixty-three years ago. Charles II got it as the dowry of Catherine of Portugal . . . Right back at the beginning of the Old Empire.*

That made it a young city, by Indian standards. "I see your point," she said. "There was nothing here but a swamp, some islands, and a run-down Portuguese fort. We built it, we *Angrezi*—or at least it was built under us, and the Empire's peace."

Henri de Vascogne gave a smile. "We in France tend to remember those years as a time when our ancestors fought yours for the dominion of India," he said. "If that had gone otherwise, we might still be having this conversation—but in reverse."

Prince Charles laughed aloud. "Vishnu preserve us! A Franco-Indian Empire . . ." He shook his head. "Well, the moving finger writes, and all that. No offense, but I'm glad it came out the way it did."

"None taken. All men tend to think the present is the best of all possible worlds, for it leads to us, our ineffable selves," Henri said. "Permit me to say that the *Angrezi* triumph was not *all* to the good. I remember that railway station with disbelief, twice. On my arrival, and just now finding that my memories had muted the horror."

Cassandra looked behind her: The great prickly pile of Victoria Terminus—named for Victoria the Good, not her great-granddaughter Victoria the Wicked—was barely visible. It had been built during the last years of the Old Empire in a leaden High Gothic Revival style that the twenty-first-century *Angrezi* eye could hardly grasp, all gargoyles and bell towers and fussy arches. Even after seeing it with your own eyes you could hardly believe that it could have been commissioned by men who ruled the country of the Taj Mahal and lived with the Palace of the Winds.

"Well, there is *that*," Charles said. "But as a city, Bombay's less stuffy than Delhi."

That made her blink again, until she realized he was talking about the very top echelons of society. In Delhi that meant people with seats in the Commons or Lords, generals, courtiers, and ICS upper-roger bureaucrats. Despite its size, wealth, and the growth of industry in the last few generations, Delhi was a political city, with the military and landed aristocracies and their retainers and hangers-on at its heart. That had been true since Mughal times and before.

Bombay meant new men and new wealth, looking out onto the Arabian Sea and the wide world; here financiers and factory owners and shipping magnates set the tone. Even the military component was largely naval, and that was the middle-class service; the Army was too firmly rooted in the land and its time-encrusted hierarchies to have much place for box-wallahs or banians.

"Let's see," Charles said. "I've made *puja* at the city goddess's temple—I'd swear that Brahmin burned my hand deliberately when I took *darshana;* they'll always take a chance to do a *kyashtria* down— Father heard mass at St. Thomas, Aunt Jane cut the ribbons on the orphanage and slum-clearance project, Sita opened that library Aunt Jane endowed . . ."

"That was a really splendid book they gave me, though," Sita said. "I've always admired Vasami's engravings. The hand-coloring was exquisite."

She tapped a foot against it where it rested in a rosewood-and-ivory box on the floor of the howdah. Cassandra felt herself flushing a little; the choice had been a lavishly illustrated edition of the *Kama Sutra,* probably in honor of her rumored-to-be-impending nuptials. Luckily, a nudge from a lady-in-waiting had reminded the *kunwari* to confine herself to a gracious word of thanks and a quick flip, rather than diving into the volume right then and there.

"What we *really* ought to be doing," Sita went on, with a wink at Cassandra, "is to be making *puja* to Santoshi Mata."

The three *Angrezi* chuckled—the two members of the royal family, she noted, without showing an unseemly expression to the crowds or halting the graceful, economical turn-the-wrist waves she'd been trying to imitate.

It must be practice. Or maybe it's genetic. The motion made her forearm ache.

Henri looked from one face to the other. "What, or who, is Santoshi Mata?"

"A recent goddess," Cassandra said, taking pity on him—Sita looked set for one of her Epic Teases, which could go on longer than a full performance of the Ramayana and reduce the victim to a gibbering madness of frustration. "She's the goddess of . . . ah . . . modern aspirations and career success for women."

"She's a kinematograph goddess," Sita went on. "No, Henri, I'm *not* pulling your leg. This time. Bombay is the kinematograph capital of the Empire, you know; all the best studios work out of the Bombay Sacred Wood district. There was a goddess in a kinematograph play made here, and none of the pantheon quite fit—so they made one up."

"Ah," Henri said. "A joke, then." With a wry smile: "The small jokes, they are among the most difficult things to learn in a foreign land; of a sudden you trip over one, and realize you are far from home."

"No," Sita protested. "No, really! She's a real goddess—with a temple, and everything. Career girls pray to her—make offerings so she'll bless them and they can afford to buy a sewing machine or learn to use a typewriter, or have a telephone in their office. I've made *puja* to her myself, but she's not . . . mmmm . . . weighty enough for an official occasion like this."

Henri blinked, goggling. "And people of a veracity *believe* in this goddess?" he asked, his accent suddenly a little thicker.

Cassandra had the impression that France-outre-mer's Christianity had absorbed some of Islam's sternness, or perhaps merely kept such a quality from before the Fall. Whereas the Established Church of the Raj . . .

"Henri," she said, "if you're going to understand our religion, you're really going to have to understand how . . . flexible . . . it can be. I'm quite content with the Established Church, myself—and an occasional offering to Saraswati, which is where my *bhatki* would go if I were inclined to devotion."

Especially considering the current theological controversy over whether Christ is an incarnation of Vishnu, or possibly His son.

The Bible's God was far too active post-Creation to be readily assimilated to Brahma, but He fit Vishnu and/or Shiva rather neatly, and since those three were the Hindu *trimurti*—Trinity—the missing pieces of the jigsaw were being earnestly sought.

Charles added: "Saraswati—wife of Brahma—goddess of learning. And beauty," he added, glancing at her.

Cassandra flushed again. *He's been a perfect gentleman*, she thought, scolding herself. *It's not fair to him to hint that you wish he wouldn't be.* Of course, it also seemed vilely unfair that Charles could work out his frustrations with some nautch-girl and nobody would think the less of him for it, while she . . .

While I wouldn't want to even if there were *dancing-boy equivalents*, Cassandra thought dismally. *I wished I could have flirtations, like other women. I should have been more careful about that—how much work would I get done in this state? The sooner I get back to Oxford, the better. There's always daydreaming and solitary vice.*

Admiralty House loomed ahead. *Another banquet*, she thought— and with so few opportunities for rock-climbing or even long walks, she'd gained five pounds since she came to court.

Charles echoed her thought. "More stuffing. I do hope I'm next to the mayor, though—quite an interesting chap. Worked for several years in Zanzibar, helping set up a bank there, after we conquered it and ran the Omani slavers out."

He looked southward. "You know what I'd really like to do? I'd like us all to put on disguises and go to Chowpatty Beach."

Sita clapped her hands, forgetting to wave for an instant: "Oh, let's! Like Haroun al-Raschid in the Thousand and One Nights!" She had a well-thumbed copy of Burton's translation. "We could ride on the Ferris wheels, and dunk someone at the coconut shy, and eat *bhelpuri* from the stands—"

Cassandra caught Henri's smile, and joined it: Sita *was* just eighteen. Her brother's expression was wry:

"And Father would have us both thrown into an active volcano, and rightly so—Sita, *do* remember what's been happening. Although," he added, "I'd at least find out what people *really* thought of us."

"I think this is reasonably genuine," Henri said, indicating the crowd.

They were approaching the City Hall, just off the round park of Horniman Circle, where a famous banyan tree that had sheltered the city's first stock exchange still stood. Policemen in yellow derby-shaped hats began to replace the soldiers as the imposing neo-Classical bulk of the building came into view. The crowd there was even gaudier than that which had lined the Avenue and, if possible, even more enthusiastic. Some of them managed to break through the line of *konstabeels* and perform a full prostration, tossing handfuls of vermilion powder on the feet of the King-Emperor's elephant. That elderly beast was well trained in public ceremonies, and managed to kneel without excessive rocking or squashing some unfortunate loyalist.

"Father says that it's because business is so good," Charles observed, as their own mount began the slow folding process and attendants came up with a wheeled staircase.

Cassandra clutched a handhold unobtrusively—there weren't many elephants in Kashmir, and this was her first long ride on one—and spoke:

"That's not a bad reason for people to like their rulers, Charles," she said. "I wouldn't like to live here in Bombay, myself—but business is what puts roofs over these people's heads and feeds their children, lets them get on with their lives and better themselves."

"Well, *we're* not responsible for that—or not much," Charles objected.

Henri shook his head. "A regiment's colors are merely wood and cloth," he pointed out. "Yet men see them, and for them will do things that you would swear men could not do."

"That's the politest way I've ever heard you called a totem with a flagpole up your bum, brother dear," Sita said sweetly, waiting with cruel exactitude for the moment his foot sought the first riser.

The vice admiral waiting to greet the party of the *kunwar* and *kunwari* at the bottom of the stairs went rigid with alarm, as the heir to the Lion Throne seemed to stumble and almost fall. Then he smiled in relief himself, and again more broadly when he saw their faces; the heir and his sister and their companions all seemed to be in high good humor.

Wakeful, Athelstane King lay on his back and looked up at the desert stars as he waited for his turn to go on watch. He was humming very quietly under his breath, a tune whose words went:

> *"On a battlefield*
> *Six thousand years ago—*
> *In the midst of danger*
> *Arjuna dropped his bow . . ."*

The moon was very large as it hung near the horizon, and bright enough to pale the stars near it. Elsewhere they hung like frosted silver dust in a sky blacker than velvet; the small campfire had long since been banked, and the others were mere black shapes on the pale silver sand. The air was cold, cold enough to make the yak-hair blankets Elias had thoughtfully provided more than welcome. King sat up and gathered his around his shoulders, trying to spot the sentries, and failing—David's men knew their business.

He listened to the sounds of the desert night. There was an occasional crinking of insects—which reminded him to check his boots carefully before he put them on again; this place swarmed with scorpions. The big black kind, often fatal. Last night he'd heard a lion roar, and in the morning ridden past the three-quarters-devoured *chinkara* gazelle the pride had brought down. Tonight there was only the far-off yapping and moaning howls of a pack of *dhole*—red-coated wild dog. The desert air was painfully dry, but it had an exhilarating cleanness.

The camels were some distance off, kneeling in sleep, with their long heads outstretched. They knew their business, too, and had kept up splendidly. Everyone was worn down and tired, but the party ought to make the railroad early tomorrow, well before the noon break—

Yasmini gave a muffled scream and sat bolt upright. King leapt to his feet reflexively, pistol in hand. The other men did likewise; Ibrahim Khan shot over the crest of the dune behind them and cast himself down, carbine to his shoulder and eyes glaring for danger.

Athelstane knelt gently by Yasmini's bedroll. "What is it?" he asked.

It need not be a vision. The poor girl had "natural" nightmares enough; sometimes he was surprised that she ever got a good night's sleep at all.

"Men come," Yasmini said thickly.

Then she threw herself on him, clutching him around the neck and burying her head in the hollow of his shoulder. He could feel the quick thudding of her heart against his, and the tense, lithe body within the curve of his arm. Nightmares were bad enough. When you knew, from cold fact, that the nightmares could come true—

"Many," she whispered. "Horsemen from the west. They come to kill. I saw them kill, kill us all, I *felt* it."

My dear, I don't envy you your gift at all. However useful it might be. He repeated her words aloud as she shuddered back to self-control; he saw puzzlement on the others' faces that matched his own. Westward was only the worst of the Thar, and then the Ran of Kuch—salt-marsh even more hostile to man than these empty sands. Then his face changed.

"*Sahib?*" Narayan Singh said.

"The *railway*. We're heading for it, but if you suddenly got a report that we'd headed out into the desert, learned too late to pursue us from behind—how would you get horsemen into place to intercept us? By *train*."

"Or perhaps less a report than a rumor," David bar-Elias said, scrubbing at his face with both hands to rub the sleep out of his head. "If you were one of the enemy leaders, and had most of your men watching more likely roads, then heard a *rumor* that a party had left to cross the Thar—"

Yasmini cut in. "We must kill them all. Not one can escape. If any does—we die."

King nodded grimly. "Can you describe them?" he said.

She did; thin men, with long, embroidered coats and cloaks over them, large bulbous turbans; all ragged-looking and none too prosperous, some riding barefoot with their big toes thrust through ring stirrups. One or two dressed otherwise, but mostly so.

He could identify them: Rabari shepherds, quasi-Gypsies who were the nomadic tinkers and herders of the Thar. Even as many Rajputs lived outside the "land of princes," so likewise not everyone who dwelt within it and spoke the tongue were considered Rajputs. The Rabari were a good example. Not quite an officially listed criminal tribe, but they had a bad reputation for horse-theft and occasional high-binding; they'd been much worse in the old days.

That means David's right, too. This is something someone on the other side is doing on a guess, hiring what muscle he can get. Wave a little money around some Rabari camps out on the edge of cultivation, and you could get hired blades enough. Our camels alone would be a big lure, if whoever-it-is can persuade them the police won't find out. They won't be martial caste, but your average Thar Desert goatherd is plenty tough. Bring them in by the rail line we're *trying to reach—no reason the railways would stop a bunch of*

Rabari goatherders from shipping horses and water out to Stop Number X on
a local, if they had the money.

"How many?" he asked.

"Twenty, thirty," she said.

That meant odds of two or three to one. King scanned the group;
he doubted that any bunch of scratch hirelings could match their quality, but they weren't a trained military unit. Of course, neither was the
opposition. With a ten-man file from his own squadron of the Peshawar Lancers, he'd be completely confident of the outcome and trying to figure out a way to do it without loss on his side. As it was . . .

"If they disappear, how long before their side notices?" King wondered aloud.

"Not soon," David bar-Elias said. "If these are local hirelings, the
man who bought them will wait until success to report to his superiors. Less chance of punishment if he fails—more credit if he succeeds
and presents them with our deaths."

King raised an eyebrow. He'd met a few officers who operated that
way, always trying to keep their own arses in a protected corner, but it
wasn't wise to underestimate the enemy.

Yasmini nodded. "Yes. That is how things are, under the Peacock
Angel. How not, when no man trusts another not to take advantage?
I would not have known men could live otherwise, save for my dreams
and my mother's tales."

"Good," King said grimly. *They have the firsthand knowledge of how*
the enemy operates. Which means . . .

"Yasmini's perfectly right. We have to kill all of them. If we do, we
have a chance of making a clean break to Bombay; they won't have an
earthly idea where we are because whoever's running them wouldn't
have told *his* superiors."

Ibrahim and Narayan Singh had thrown themselves prone and
pressed their ears to the ground not far off—on a patch of hard sand,
where the looser surface accumulation had been blown aside. After a
moment they both rose, dusting the powdery stuff off their clothes.

"It is true, *sahib*. Many horsemen, and coming in directly from the
west."

"In alignment with the last well, to cover the paths anyone coming from the closest water would take to reach the te-rain," Ibrahim
added. "They must know this countryside."

"We have fifteen minutes, twenty at most. Perhaps Allenby *sahib* leads them," Narayan said, a savage eagerness in his voice.

Then he worked the action of his carbine, snapped the shell out of the air with his hand, and licked the bullet before reloading with a *click-clack*. That was a Sikh gesture of a particular, exact significance.

And Allenby would be very, very unhappy to see it, King thought, catching his orderly's eye and nodding with a grim smile.

Then he looked around, drawing the lay of the big soft-sided dunes and occasional wind-scoured rock into a mental map. "Do you remember how Colonel Claiborne caught the Baloch in his trap, that time they were raiding Scinde?"

"Indeed, *sahib*," Narayan said. "But here are no large rocks suitable for hiding men."

"No, but we can substitute," King said. "On a smaller scale. Here's what we're going to do. We'll need a couple of mirrors and some stiff paper or leather—"

David bar-Elias nodded, went to rummage in one of the capacious camel saddles, and tossed a rectangular object to King. The Lancer caught it, turning it over in his hands, then snapped the device of leather-covered tinware open. It was a black periscope, with an eyepiece below and a rectangular slit on the other end.

"Capital," King said. David listened gravely to the rest of the plan and offered a few refinements. When the scheme was complete, Narayan Singh chuckled again and tapped the breech of his weapon.

Ibrahim Khan drew his *chora*, laughing aloud as he spat on his pocket hone and touched up the edge, new respect in his eyes when he looked at King.

"I will show you how to cut throats!" he said. "The point goes in behind the windpipe, and the heel of the blade separates the neck-bone! That is the way to slay a Rajput!"

Athelstane King lay in hot, stifling darkness and waited, eye pressed to the eyepiece of the periscope, tasting the sweat that ran onto his chapped lips and stung, smelling on himself the results of a week's desert travel without clean clothes or washing water.

In his trench in the sand he could hear the approaching hooves clearly. They had stopped a while ago—that would be while the enemy sent scouts forward to confirm their position. The camp lay in the hollow between two big dunes that met on either side, leaving an almond-shaped hollow by some chance of the winds; they would have a man crawling up to the crest, to check on their target. Perhaps to left or right of the dune's midpoint, for the wall of sculpted sand was steep in the center, like a frozen wave about to topple. It was near-vertical on the side facing the campfires.

The Lancer officer smiled wolfishly. That man would see a picket line of tethered camels at some distance, gear and saddles, two low fires of dung and thornbush separated by a pile of stones, and a man sitting with his head on his knees, asleep—near him the blanket-covered shapes of nine more sleepers. His mind provided him with the image of a snaggle-toothed snarl of contempt for travelers too stupid to set a better guard, and then—

The hooves grew to a drumbeat next to his ear, but he waited until he saw the moonlight shimmer on the dust that galloping horses raised. Then he used his shoulder to push at the sand-shrouded blanket above him; the draught of cool desert-winter air was inexpressible relief, but he didn't want to draw attention to himself. His head and shoulders came out of the gravelike pit he'd dug, and he saw the night with almost painful brightness, after half an hour in utter dark save for the trickle through the instrument.

A long line of horsemen crested the top of the dune opposite and rode whooping down the steep slope below it, breaking like a curling wave around the steepest central part and flowing down toward the camp.

Thirty men, he snap-counted, robes flapping in the rushing night air, swords swinging, some with couched lances glinting in their hands. Some of them reined their horses back onto their haunches to descend the slope; all of them whooped and screeched out war cries. Good horsemen—only one lost his saddle coming down, and managed to dodge his mount as it stumbled and rolled.

The others raced into the camp, some stabbing with lances at the sleeping forms, another swinging his *tulwar* in a great sweep at the head of the drowsy guard, steel glinting in starlight. Their harsh cries split the night as they struck to kill. King smiled at the sight, as he brushed sand off the breech of his carbine and took a turn of the sling around his forearm. With his left elbow on his knee, that gave another point to steady the aim. Ten yards to either side, Narayan Singh and

Ibrahim Khan were doing likewise. The aiming point was a scrap of white cloth, on the mound of dense granite rock between the two fires.

King let out a slow breath, let the foresight steady down on the mark. He waited an instant, while a bewildered horseman reined his mount out of the way and prodded at the sand-stuffed clothes that "sat" by the fire. A few of the riders had even jumped down to rummage among baggage and blanket rolls, as if the victims they'd expected to find, kill, and rob were somewhere there.

Now. The trigger release on this carbine was extremely smooth. *Crack.* And *crackcrack* from the other two men. A second of suspense, while he worked the action and slid another cartridge into the chamber, pausing to blow on it first. You had to be very careful about getting sand in the action of this model of carbine; otherwise, it was liable to jam when hot from rapid fire.

And . . . *KE-RRRACK!*

A spot of white radiance hit his eyes; he blinked against the floating purple afterimage, cursing himself for not looking away. David bar-Elias had put ten pounds of guncotton under those rocks, and the explosion had turned them into a hail of lethal missiles whipping and pinwheeling through the night. King hated guncotton, despite its usefulness; it was unstable, liable to sweat beads of nitro when stored in hot weather and then to go off unpredictably. He'd always preferred to use the tried-and-true black powder for blasting, even if it wasn't as powerful. David had sworn that *his* variety was reliable, and evidently he was right.

Screams of pain split the sudden darkness, human and the louder, more heartrending cries of the horses—he sympathized with *them.* Nobody had asked the horses if they wanted to play bandit. Dimly seen forms crawled or staggered or thrashed about.

King took careful aim at a flash of bright clothing atop a bucking horse, stroked the trigger again. *Crack,* and a harsh red spear of light in the darkness. He let it fade, picked another target, worked the action, fired. The recoil against his shoulder was a surprise, as it always was when you were shooting well.

"Concentrate on the ones still mounted!" King shouted as he fired again. *They're the ones most likely to escape.*

Some of the bandits retained sufficient presence of mind to fire at the muzzle flashes from the crest of the dune. King heard a slug go by in the night with an ugly *whit-whit-whit*, and saw the flash of muzzle and frizzen at the same time, just before several more volleyed at him. Flintlock *jezails*, then, the only sort of firearm a bunch of Thar Desert goatherders were likely to own, allowed them to protect their herds from predators.

His chance of getting hit by one of the smoothbore abortions under the present circumstances—dark of night, fifty yards away, and ten yards above their heads—was about on a par with slipping in the bath and breaking his neck. *Their* chances of reloading successfully were rather less.

As he fired his third round—less than twenty seconds from his first—some of the surviving riders reached the same conclusion. They turned their horses around and spurred frantically along the path they'd arrived on.

If the bandits had had enough time, they would have led their horses up the slope; it was much steeper than the reverse, as is the way of wind-moved sand—the central part of the dune was near-vertical. With even a little time, they would have taken the slope at an angle, to put less strain on their horses—they were experienced desert dwellers, after all. Right now they were in a panic. The horses labored, throwing up plumes of fine sand that glittered in the moonlight, legs churning but making slow progress. One reared and toppled over backward on its rider, crushing him like a beetle under a boot, save for the brief scream of terror.

And the other seven members of King's party erupted out of their hiding holes just below the steepest part of the dune's crest to slam a volley into the horsemen's faces. David bar-Elias didn't fire right away. He kept his carbine in the crook of his right arm and pulled small cloth-wrapped bundles out of his robes, tapping them on the stock to start their fuses before tossing them down into the mass of men on horse or foot. Three exploded with a wicked *snap—snap—snap*, sending fragments of the nails bound around their core of gunpowder to savage flesh. The fourth and fifth hopped and sputtered, shedding a bright weird light on the scene, revealing torn bodies and turning shed blood black, a magnesium flare in Hell.

The Rabaris' war yells had turned to cries of panic now. The light blinded them, leaving them in a bubble of brightness surrounded by an impenetrable darkness out of which bullets came—and arrows driven by a powerful Mongol bow, perhaps less dangerous but more demoralizing. King watched coldly as the wailing men were shot down, using his carbine with implacable skill.

Then a small figure came running and sliding down the face of the dune. *Yasmini!* he thought. *What the hell is she—*

Even as he ran toward her, the hair prickled up along his spine. Half a dozen of the enemy had broken away from the others, and they were spurring their horses toward the southern edge of the hollow that held the camp, where the two main dunes met in a V.

But she started to move before *they did,* he realized, shivering.

Running through deep soft sand was like running in a nightmare, the very earth dragging at your feet; he was vaguely conscious of Narayan and Ibrahim behind him, less so of calculation. He was in a very bad position for a shot, with dark shadow hiding the targets, making them indistinct save for glints off metal. Yasmini's—literal—foresight had put her in a position to catch them between her and the flares that lit the "campsite."

Much better shooting ground; from here I wouldn't have time to fire more than twice, and I'd probably miss at least once. Just *time to get there, though, if I hurry. Move your boots, Athelstane.*

She took stance, aimed with cool care, and fired. A Rabari threw up his hands and tumbled backward over his horse's rump.

Then she worked the lever . . . and it refused to function. He could see her struggling with it for an instant, then reversing it to grip by the barrel. *Can't have that,* he thought. She was a good rifle shot, and brave enough for two—but using a wood-and-iron club to effect took heft that a woman barely five feet and perhaps ninety-five pounds soaking wet just didn't have.

He arrived just in time to take stance before her. A Rabari drove toward him with lance couched, outlined stark against the magnesium fire that turned his spearhead to glimmering blue-white. King's teeth showed in a mirthless grin; he hadn't spent the last six years in a Lancer regiment for nothing. His left hand went out for balance as he crouched, and he brought his saber up in a guard position with the hilt above his head and the blade slanting down to the front. The lance head came at his face with a galloping horse behind it, and he pivoted aside at the last instant, too late for the Rabari to correct his aim, bending his body aside like a toreador. The sword lashed down in a blurring stroke as he did, slicing through the tough bamboo in a cleat cut, then up, around, backhand in a whistling horizontal slash at his own eye height.

The Rabari had just time enough to scream as the sharp curved edge took him under the short ribs; a soft heavy jarring thump struck King's wrist. His foeman flew backward in a fan spray of blood that shone like black rain for an instant in the unnatural light. The horse reared in panic, flailing its forehooves. King ran in, dodging, grasped a handful of mane, and jumped. The stirrups were rawhide, and much too short for him, but he got his feet into them and the reins into his free hand. The horse turned in a single tight circle and submitted.

That let him see what happened behind. Narayan Singh ran after a horseman, with no hope of catching him, but then something silver flashed through the air, turning, close enough to make the Sikh curse and dodge. The haunch of the horse suddenly sprouted half a *chora*, and the animal shied and went into a frenzy of heaving leaps, screaming, shedding its rider. The Rabari was agile, rolling and coming back on his feet like a cat, wheeling with curved sword in hand. The Sikh met his defense with a smashing overarm cut that rocked him backward; the next stroke snapped his sword in half, and the third sheered off half the nomad's face.

Ibrahim Khan went past him at a dead run and snatched the *chora* out of the ham of the bucking, kicking horse in an astonishing display of agility. That put him alongside a horseman as the mount began to labor in the softer sand of the rising dune; the Afghan dodged under a backhand slash, leapt up behind the man, and slit his throat to the neckbone with a long drawing cut.

"After them! After them!" Yasmini called, pointing.

The last two of the six Rabari were spurring their horses up the short but steep face of sand where the dunes met. King shouted, "Guard the woman!" to Narayan Singh, and kicked his borrowed horse into a gallop, cursing. Ibrahim Khan drew up beside him, and the Lancer rapped out:

"Yours the left! Mine the right!"

King's target was a tall man in black robes on a better horse than the rest of the nomads, riding it with reckless skill. The fleeing man reached the dune before King and put his horse at it, crouching in the saddle and firing behind him with a revolver. The dimly seen muzzle spat little jabs of red fire at him, and something struck the horse the Lancer had seized. He kicked his feet loose as it bucked and plunged, felt himself fly free for an instant. Then he hit the soft sand with a winding thump, forced himself to his feet while he was still struggling to draw breath.

The black-robed rider's mount was just ahead of him, haunches bunching as it churned at the sand. *Hate to do this*, King thought, as he raised his saber and flung himself forward.

The keen steel bit just above the horse's right hock, and King whipped the blade across in a drawing cut. There was a heavy impact that rattled up his wrist to his shoulder, and something parted like a wire under tension before the saber grated on bone. The horse screamed, a raw enormous sound, unbearably piteous, and toppled backward; he could smell the sudden salt-and-copper stink of blood. The rider managed to get off it before he was crushed and scrambled to climb the dune his horse had tried in vain. King dodged as well, barely avoiding a flying hoof that clipped his turban and would have spattered his brains if it had been a little to the right.

The shots behind continued, but they slackened a bit and there was a clash of steel as well. King wasn't worried; the Rabari were shattered. In an affair like this numbers meant little, surprise and position everything. What was important was to see that there were no fugitives to carry the tale. He lunged forward and grabbed the ankle of the fleeing man, dragging him back and flipping him over in a single surge of strength. He raised his blade, dripping with the horse's blood, then paused:

"You!" he snarled, as the man lying beneath on his back screamed and held up his arms against the steel.

It wasn't Ignatieff; that was too much to hope for—and the Russian would never have let himself be taken like this. Richard Allenby slowly let his arms fall.

"Finish it, then," he gasped. He was panting, and his face was slick with sweat. "Finish it." His face slowly relaxed and went calm. "I've earned death, but let me die like an Allenby."

"No," King said grimly.

"What you've *earned* is a pi-dog's death and a slow one." King laughed harshly as Allenby blanched. "But you're luckier than you deserve—*we* aren't Kali-worshipers."

Instead of striking, he reached down and took the man by the neck, hauling him erect and pushing him before him into the space where the campfires had been, and where David bar-Elias's lights still sputtered. Nothing moved except wounded horses and his own party; Yasmini and the Jew were bandaging hurts. Ibrahim Khan came back out of the night leading his horse, plunging his *chora* into the sand to clean it as he came down a dune in something between a fall and a stroll.

"No escape from *me, huzoor*," he called cheerfully. "He got a hundred yards. I took him from behind, *thus*—"

King held up a hand for silence, looking for Narayan Singh. "*Daffadar!*" he called.

The Sikh had been helping with the first aid; he gently held down the eyelids of one of the Jew's retainers before he rose and turned. His face changed as he saw who stood before King with the point of the Lancer captain's sword resting between his shoulder blades.

"*You!*" he said, and his hand darted to the hilt of his *tulwar*. Then he stopped, and looked at his officer.

"He's yours, *bhai*," King grated.

Allenby started. "No—you can't do that, King! For God's sake man, I'm *sahib-log*, too; you can't let a native—"

"You've got a saber, Allenby. I suggest you use it, unless you want to die begging on your knees. Death by an honest soldier's sword—it's more than you deserve."

He turned away, cleaning and sheathing his blade, then unslinging his carbine. Not far away a horse lay on its side, thrashing and trying to rise despite a broken leg. They'd have to kill all the horses they could catch, too; someone might recognize them. He looked to both sides. With a little labor, they could pull dune sand down and bury all the bandits and their animals ten feet deep. Eventually the wind would uncover the bodies and the jackals would feast, but by then it wouldn't matter.

Steel clashed behind him, briefly, as he put the muzzle of the carbine to the horse's head. It rolled its eyes at him, begging mutely for help: The *crack* of the shot and Allenby's cut-off scream came together.

Yasmini came up beside him, gasping. King took the carbine from her hands and examined it; the extractor had torn off the base of a cartridge. A flick of his knife freed it, but the woman almost dropped the weapon.

"What's the matter?" he said, sharp concern in his voice. "Are you wounded?"

"No." She turned her eyes on him, enormous with fear. "I saw where they would go. I Saw it."

"Damned good thing, too; they might have gotten away."

"No, you do not understand. I *Saw* them with my waking mind, for an instant, without the drugs. It should not be so. It should not!"

The Thar sun had risen, warm even in December but welcome after the bitter night, and the northwest wind flicked grit into their eyes. King and his companions stood with their heads bowed, as David bar-Elias prayed beside two graves marked only by oblong mounds of stones. When they mounted, he rode beside the older man, the sun hot on the back of his neck, swaying with the motion of the camel.

"Sorry about your men," he said. "I know how that feels."

David bar-Elias nodded, looking over his shoulder for an instant. His voice was musing as he replied:

"I bought Hassan in Basra."

King nodded; slavery was illegal in the Empire, of course, but widespread in the Caliphate. "The black with no tongue?"

Bar-Elias nodded. "Long story. Bought him and freed him—it's a *mitzvah*, a good deed."

"And the bowman, Togrul?" King asked.

There are times when you have to talk, he thought. *Otherwise, the pain gets too much to bear, and the only alternative is drinking alone. Talking hurts a lot less next day.*

Both the caravan guards had been unlucky; the black trampled by a wounded horse he was trying to catch, the archer shot in the belly at point-blank range by a Rabari who was probably too frightened to fire until he saw the troll shape looming up out of the darkness. Skill took you only so far in a fight. Sooner or later bad luck put you in precisely the wrong place at the wrong moment, and then nothing helped.

"Moishe Togrul was probably the only Jewish Mongol in history, did you know?" David shook his head. "I picked him up outside a caravanserai in Gansu—dried him out, too. I liked the way he kept crawling back where they'd just finished beating him up and throwing him out. Crawling back and trying to fight again; a crooked dice game with some Nipponese soldiers and too much *kumis*."

A smile. "I told him I had a job for a good man, but not for a drunk, then a month later sent him into a town we passed, sent him with money to buy supplies. He didn't come back."

"Went on a spree?" King said, doubt in his voice. David bar-Elias struck him as a kindly man, but shrewd as any he'd ever met, and not an easy mark.

"No, he got knocked on the head from behind and robbed. Then he tracked down the men who did it, killed them, got the money back, bought the supplies, and caught up with the caravan on his own, half-dead and raving. When we got back to Delhi six months later, he started pestering our rabbi. It isn't easy to become a Jew—not impossible, but you have to prove you really mean it. It took him three years, and he ended up knowing more of the Law than I do. That was twenty years ago, and he traveled with me from China to the Danube and back . . . and to Bokhara."

He shook his head. "I thought we'd both retired from that sort of thing. He had a wife in Delhi; distant relative of mine. The Lord gives—the Lord takes—blessed be the Name of the Lord."

King set a hand on his shoulder for a moment; the rest of the morning's ride was in silence. They were all too weary with the aftermath of victory for anything else, and with lack of sleep and the strain of a week's hard travel through the wasteland.

The sun was well past noon when he stood in the stirrups with a cut-off oath. The railway was not far off, half a mile perhaps and downslope, stretching in a line of shining steel from north to south through a desolate landscape of thorn and scrub, dune and low rocky hills. He unshipped binoculars and focused them; there was a cutting directly ahead, and far to the right—northward toward the distant Punjab—a tiny plume of smoke. Nothing else moved in the whole vast landscape save dust devils and a circling of vultures far above. A few others perched motionless on the telegraph wires that swooped from pole to pole along the train tracks.

"Be a bit of a stretch to make that one," he said. "The next will have to do."

"No!" Yasmini said, coming up beside him. "I recognize now— *that* is the train we must take."

King suppressed an impulse to snarl; Yasmini couldn't help the fact that her dreams came to her in fragments, or that she often only realized what they meant when she met the reality head-on. As far as he knew, she'd never told him anything but the truth as she knew it.

He turned to David bar-Elias, and fished in his tunic. The Jew's eyes widened slightly when he recognized what King was holding out—Elias's half of the *tessera*, returned to King in Delhi. His hand snapped it out of the air reflexively as the Lancer officer tossed it underhand.

"Whenever you need me or mine," King said. "For now, stay here—you've got men hurt, and they need rest. We'll abandon the camels, and you can pick them up by the line."

They leaned far over to clasp wrists, and then the Jew started pulling things out of his robe. "Take these," he said, as they jounced along side by side. "A few extra of my lights—they may come in useful."

"Thanks!" King called. The Jew nodded, and pulled up as King flicked his own camel with the riding crop thonged to his wrist.

"God go with you!" bar-Elias called.

"Hup! Hup!" King called as he waved an answer, and the racing camel seemed to find a new reserve of strength. It pounded down the slope and over the flat toward the distant cutting, speed building as it sensed its rider's determination.

Yasmini's beast had less trouble; it was carrying barely half the weight. She herself worried him. The brutal week of travel and the tension of the fight had worn even the Lancer officer down—he felt every jolt of the camel's feet right up into his spine—and she had fewer physical reserves . . . and hadn't slept well at all. There were huge dark circles under her eyes, and the elfin face was thinner, her lips peeling and chapped from the endless dry wind. She seemed to be holding on by sheer willpower; plenty of *that*, but it could take you only so far before the flesh rebelled.

Narayan Singh's face was set in grim determination, but he hunched over the pommel of his saddle and gripped it with both hands.

Not surprising, King thought, worried a second time. *He really should have been on bed rest for twice as long, after what that swine Allenby and his goondahs put him through.*

Only Ibrahim seemed untouched; the hardships that ground down the others had merely made him irritable, as if the desiccating Thar wind could only dry the rawhide of him harder.

King calculated angles. The freight wasn't a fast train; still toy-tiny at this distance, but it looked like a Danavas-class 482, a standard heavy hauler. That meant forty miles an hour or so, on a straightaway and flat ground.

"Look!" he shouted, and repeated it until he was sure all had understood. "We'll hide behind that hill." It had been split in half by the track-cutting, and there was an upgrade on the slope leading to it.

"When the engine is past, watch me—we race out and jump onto the train. Me first, then Ibrahim, then Narayan, then Yasmini. Understood?"

They all nodded. The swift rolling of the camels brought them closer and closer to the cleft hill, a pile of rock with a single dead acacia in a crack in its side. King kept his head moving, watching the train until the rising ground ahead cut off his view. It was a freight all right, mostly flatcars loaded with huge Himalayan cypress logs a yard through and thirty feet long. They were in pyramidal stacks, a bottom course of three logs, then two, then one, all held secure by thick chains. Other flatcars carried cotton in five-hundred-pound bales, stacked square and too high to climb, and a few boxcars toward the rear might have anything; most probably grain in sacks.

Then they were behind the hill, with their heads turned south and the rail to their right. The camels seemed to think they had permission to lie down once they'd stopped, and had to be dissuaded. There was a moment of brutal work with boot, whip and reins—those ran to brass rings in the camels' noses—amid a chorus of guttural groans and angry squeals and shouted curses in Hindi, Pushtu, and Russian. Yasmini shook her head violently and forced herself up from a droop after her mount nearly threw her.

"Everyone, drink some water," King snapped.

He pulled the goatskin *chuggle* up from his own saddlebow, rinsed out his mouth, spat, drank, rubbed a handful over his face, and felt strength flowing back into him. The others followed suit, Ibrahim smirking a little, Narayan Singh sitting more upright, Yasmini letting the water dribble across her chin and going into a coughing fit. They set their beasts moving as the noise grew behind them, the shriek of the steam whistle, the chuff of the cylinders and rhythmic whuffling giant's breath of the stack, an iron squeal and rattle of wheels.

"*Now! Chalo, chalo, chalo!*" King shouted.

His own camel spurted into the lead as the engine swept by, a great length of dark gray steel, the driving wheels pounding at the rails and connecting rods pistoning back and forth. Bitter sulfurous coal smoke mixed with wet hot steam flared back into his face, and the camel's— the animal snorted and tried to whip its long snaky neck around, but he mastered it and drove it on. The train was laboring, slowing to less than a horse's best pace. He came up alongside one of the flatcars of timber, and tossed over his bundled goods. They bounced, but did not quite fall, settling instead in the curve of one of the pine trunks. King forced everything but the distance out of his mind, took a deep breath, brought his long legs beneath him, and leapt.

An instant of flight, and then he landed with a grunt against the hard wood and rough bark. His fingers dug in, and he turned to the others. Ibrahim tossed him his bundle, gauged his time, and leapt with the surefooted grace of one brought up on knife-edge heights, touching down with two feet and a hand. Narayan Singh made a strong jump, but his camel chose that moment to swerve away, and the other two men grabbed desperately for his arms. They touched, enough to swing him down so that his thighs made bruising contact with the edge of the flatcar; he howled and dragged on their arms with gorilla strength, and they hauled back to put him on his feet.

That left Yasmini. King would not have been worried, if she had had more rest; he remembered her jumping the alleyway as they fled over the roofs of Delhi.

"Yasmini! You can do it!" he called, trying to pour strength through his voice as her camel raced by the train's side; the engine was beginning to pull them faster as the track leveled.

"You'll make it!" he called, as she hesitated. "Just *jump*."

She almost did make it, but one boot slipped on the camel's saddle; Thar sand, perhaps, turning the rough leather into something slippery as mountain ice. King acted without thought, throwing himself out—and felt Narayan Singh's hand close on his sword belt right over the small of his back. Without that grip he would have fallen, too; with it, he had just enough reach to grab one wrist, and wrench back with huge and desperate strength. The Sikh pulled from behind. Yasmini catapulted forward into him, knocking him back against the logs, her arms around his neck.

"I felt myself die!" she whispered, her face against his, cheek to cheek. "As I jumped—I felt myself die, in a thousand lines of time near this one—I *felt* the wheels grind through me!"

Merciful Krishna, King thought, hugging her to him. *She gets to die the thousand deaths* without *even being a coward and deserving it.*

"It didn't happen," he soothed. "You're here. You're alive. I caught you."

She pulled her head back, and her blue-green eyes were wide with horror. "You don't understand: I *felt* it. With my waking mind, without the drugs. Again. The madness—it has begun."

Chapter Twenty

Cassandra King found herself on an elephant again, but enjoying the experience more; for a start, the walls of the howdah were solid, made for hunting and travel rather than parades.

Bombay was built on islands, and most of the largest, directly north of the city, was within the boundaries of Borivali Imperial Forest. The main railroad ran through it, and there were villages along the west coast, but otherwise the hills between Powai Lake and Bassein Creek were wilderness—three hundred square miles of it, and once past the perimeter fence you could hardly believe that a city of nearly two million was an hour's travel away. Admission was priced at ten rupees, about a week's average wage for a laborer, and apart from the most traveled areas, you might almost have been in a world before man, or after.

Despite anticipation and nagging worry, she lost herself for a moment as the great beast swayed through meadows of tall grass, sere with winter but yielding explosions of butterflies at each stately pace. Jungle climbed the low rolling hills ahead; big-buttressed trees with pale trunks arched cathedral high above her as they plunged into the cool shadowed depths, lianas dangled, and monkeys swarmed through, chattering. They paced by a lake edged with swamp where shaggy brown sambhur raised dripping muzzles and long horns from water laced with jade green reeds, bounding away not in fear of the humans but of a tiger that darted through in a flash of yellow-and-black grace. The smell was wild, damp, with a taste of musk and spice; the air was full of brilliantly colored wings and their raucous cries.

"Like it?" Sita asked.

"Very much," Cassandra answered. "This isn't a part of the country I've seen much of—I've been *in* Bombay for astronomical conferences, twice, but never outside it." She paused in thought. "You know, apart from the cities, I really haven't seen much of the *country* except Kashmir. And that's extremely different. Perhaps I should travel more."

The two of them were alone in the howdah, but Guardsmen and servants followed on the little train of elephants behind them; that was as little in the way of escort as the *kunwari* could arrange, and it had brought Cassandra looks of scorching jealousy from some of the ladies-in-waiting who resented the princess's new friend.

Guards and hangers-on are something I could do without, if mad devil-worshiping assassins weren't after me, she thought. *Sita and Charles have to put up with this nonsense all their lives, and it's a severe drawback of the family business.*

Plus Sita had gone into a fit of giggles when Cassandra told her of the resentment about her new friend, deliberately misinterpreted it, and started giving her tutor melting looks occasionally in public; which was *thoroughly* embarrassing and started the Palace rumor mill working overtime and added outrage to the jealousy shown the newcomer. Bad enough to have rumors about her and Charles flying about, but being suspected of involvement with *both* siblings was like something in a bad historical novel about the court of Victoria II.

Which, of course, had been exactly what Sita intended; she was quite merciless when it came to her jokes.

The girl takes mischief to the level of an art form, Cassandra thought. *Although to be fair, she's a good sport about it when the tables are turned.*

She went on aloud: "Do you hunt here?"

The howdah had come equipped with two beautiful Purdy side-by-side double rifles, in scabbards on either side; they probably would have entranced her brother. She could appreciate their craftsmanship herself, not to mention the delicate wildlife scenes engraved in hammered gold and silver thread on the locks.

"Mmm?" Sita started out of a brown study. "Oh—no, we couldn't. Well, theoretically we could, but the Imperial Forest Service says this reserve isn't big enough for issuing hunting licenses, so we don't either. It would be unfair, when we couldn't let anyone else do it, and so close to Bombay."

Her eyes sparkled. "Now, the Terai Forest, *that's* a different matter. Tiger hunts there are *such* fun. Someday we should . . ."

She stopped, subdued. "If there is a someday."

"There will be," Cassandra said stoutly; then with forced brightness, for the onlookers' sakes: "Here we are!"

The long cliff that cut the hillside ahead of them didn't exactly contain a ruined temple. Generations of Buddhist monks had make their *vihara*-monasteries and *chatiya*-temples here in the Kanheri Caves, a millennium and a bit before, digging and shaping for century after century before the faith of Siddhartha Gautama faded from his native India and the wilderness returned. The Forest Service rangers kept the jungle at bay, and there was usually an attendant to see that visitors behaved themselves. Sita's Imperial whim had ensured that they had the place to themselves today. The elephants came to a halt on a stretch of open ground before the largest of the *chatiyas*.

For a moment they fell silent, looking up into the faces of the two great Buddhas that flanked the entrance, at the long row of columns to either side. Then Cassandra shook herself and let down the ladder. Two of the Gurkhas sprang to hold it as the ladies descended; the others fanned out to cover the approaches, kneeling with their rifles ready. Their *jemadar*—lieutenant—was a Sikh noble from the client kingdom of Basholi, a humorless young man who'd still managed to give Cassandra a smile when she talked to him in his own language. He approached, saluted, bowed, and spoke briskly:

"*Kunwari*, since you and this lady are alone, I will detail two men to accompany you into the temple and carry your—"

"*Jemadar* Singh, I *said* that I didn't want an escort! This *is* a closed cave, you know. No way in or out except through the front door. My friend and I will examine it alone."

"*Kunwari* . . ."

"*Jemadar* . . ." Sita fluttered her eyelashes at him. "You *do* realize that there are times a princess needs . . . privacy . . ."

"Oh."

The officer was too swarthy to blush, but did his best, as the attendants came up with picnic baskets and blankets and cushions, and the Imperial princess took some of them with her own heaven-born hands. He cleared his throat and looked above her head in a military fashion as he replied:

"Oh. Of course. I kiss feet, *Kunwari*. We will guard your privacy most carefully."

As they walked into the cool dimness of the caves, Sita giggled. "I could *hear* your teeth grinding, Cass!"

"You need your Royal and Imperial backside paddled, my girl!"

"Oh, *would* you?" Then she cowered back in mock-terror. "No, no, I promise I'll be serious now. Sorry."

They went farther back into the darkness; Cassandra paused to light a lantern. At last a man stepped around a pillar; it took a moment for her to realize that the dirty, ragged, bearded form was her brother. Then she carefully set the lamp on the floor and threw herself at him with a muffled shout. He gave a slight wuff—she was not a small woman—then picked her up and squeezed her, something he hadn't done since she was eleven.

"Oh, thank Pravati," she whispered.

He smelled, of sweat and camels and smoke; the jowl that touched hers had gone past bristly. There was a little dried blood on the right cuff of his jacket. It still felt wonderful to hold him.

"I was so worried about you," she said. "And I couldn't tell anyone—not even Mother—telegrams not safe—"

"I know," he said.

Then he turned to Sita, realized who she was, and went to one knee.

"*Kunwari*," he said, with a courtliness that clashed horribly with his present state of dishevelment. "I would kiss feet, but I'm afraid I might give you lice, in my present state."

Sita offered her hand, smiling warmly as he kissed it and rose. "Henri has told me about you, Captain King—and so has Cass, a great deal. I feel I know you already."

Cassandra blinked to herself; a schoolgirl one minute, and then you realized she *was* an Imperial princess. Narayan Singh and a drawn, slight blond girl made their salaams to Sita, and the Sikh gave Cassandra a warm *memsahib*, which made her feel a little guilty; the man had endured unimaginable torment for his salt. Cassandra shook hands with him, then realized with a cold shock that the young woman half-hidden behind him must be the True Dreamer—Yasmini, the underminer of her rational certainties.

Why, she's afraid of me! Cassandra thought, and smiled reassuringly. Then she was all business.

"Here are the documents," she said. "Plans, schedules, passwords. Uniforms, and the toilet things you wanted. Charles—the *kunwar*—"

She saw her brother raise a brow at the use of the heir's first name, then shake his head and put it aside.

"—got them from a Sandhurst friend of his, one who was willing to do it without an explanation and say nothing to anyone, whatever happened."

Athelstane shaped a silent whistle. "Now there's a man willing to put his career on the chopping block for friendship," he said. "Not to mention other sensitive things."

Sita nodded. "The women's things are an old set of mine—they ought to do." She looked curiously at Yasmini, then blossomed into a smile; probably because she was sensitive about not being taller, Cassandra thought, and found the doll-like Russian a welcome change from being loomed at. "I think the size will be about right."

Yasmini nodded, but she seemed to be distracted. *Well, I suppose a seeress should be strange.*

"And the documents—the laissez-passer, and the blank, and the pens and ink, and the photo of you," Cassandra went on. "And the letter from . . . Sita's father. The pass doesn't have your description, though, and—"

Sir Manfred pounced on them; for an instant she didn't recognize him, with his skin and hair dyed, in ragged nondescript off-white clothes.

"Leave that to me, Dr. King," he said eagerly, flipping open the folder. "Yes, yes . . . this is a copy of the boarding list?" He looked up at her and smiled. "Duplicating a laissez-passer I can handle." He flexed his fingers and moved over to where a crack in the ceiling let in a puddle of good light. "Forging documents is one of the staples of my trade, and I'm still quite good at it."

"And you've brought some food, I hope," King said. "We've been hiding in here for forty-eight hours, while Warburton found Malusre. There's water, but nothing to eat unless you like insects."

"Yes, in the other basket—chapatis, cakes, some cold chicken, fruit," Cassandra said. "And . . . you *did* want some *bhang lassi*?"

The pleasure of seeing her faded from Athelstane's face; he glanced over at Yasmini. "It probably won't be necessary, I'm afraid," he said, and cut off her questions. "No time. Thank the merciful Krishna that the airship port is so close to the Imperial Forest."

"Captain King," Sita said.

He looked up sharply; his eyes narrowed a little, appraising. With a sister's experience, Cassandra could hear *Young, but no fool, this one,* running through his head.

"I, my brother, and my father know something of what you've been going through for us, and for the Empire," she said. "They both send their thanks. To you, and to your companions."

"*Kunwari,* we haven't had much choice about what we've been going through," Athelstane said, and grinned.

Always his best expression, Cassandra thought. Sita seemed to like it, too, and returned it.

"But it's very pleasant to be appreciated," he went on. "After all, if a story has vile villains, daring exploits, and supernatural mysteries, tradition demands a beautiful princess, too."

Her laugh was clear and delighted, echoing off the ancient stone. Cassandra wondered if the cave had ever heard such before.

"It also demands a gallant knight," Sita said. Soberly: "God guide your swords, Agent Warburton, Captain King. You draw them in a good cause, and against a worse enemy than the demon king Ravana himself."

Sita was in a somber mood as they returned to the cave mouth. "That girl, Yasmini. She was trying hard while we gave her pointers, and she's a natural actress, but . . . is there something *wrong* with her?"

Cassandra shook her head. "I hope not. Everything depends on her."

The princess's mood lasted almost all the way to the entrance. Then she beckoned Cassandra close as if to whisper in her ear, and planted a smacking kiss on the side of her neck.

Cassandra hadn't quite scrubbed the lip rouge off her skin by the time they reached the outside.

"I can hear your teeth grinding again," Sita murmured, as they climbed the ladder to the howdah.

Even a cold-water bath and shave made Athelstane King feel halfway himself again. Beneath that was a taut eagerness; the next day or so would see this ended—victory, of course. Or he would be dead, in which case the question was moot; but he didn't intend to die. He examined his face in the hand mirror; the sideburns had been trimmed back to his ears and the mustache removed. That was a bit of a wrench, but the disguise kit Warburton had received made the skin tone match the weathered olive tan of the rest of his face. He used the little mirror to adjust his military turban and the hang of the tail that fell halfway down his back.

The uniform did even more for his morale, although it wasn't that of his own regiment; it was khaki field dress, working clothes, only the shoulder flashes to show that the wearer was supposed to be a captain in the Guards cavalry.

Have to watch how I talk, he thought, a little snidely; the cavalry regiments of the line had no particular love of their Delhi counterparts, not least because Guards officers tended to more in the way of titles and wealth.

Have to haw-haw a good deal and avoid any conversational subject that requires literacy. Cultivate the appearance of an overbred collie dog.

Warburton was dressed in the colorful but not-too-expensive clothes of a Eurasian valet-cum-secretary; the sort a young Guards officer might have inherited from his father, and who did all his military paperwork behind the scenes. He'd already stained skin and hair, and the eyes weren't a particular problem. Narayan Singh, to his own delight, was uniformed as a Sikh *daffadar*, which was a part he could play to perfection. He'd taken even more delight in Ibrahim's role, which was as a lowly servant carrying their baggage. The Pathan hadn't complained, probably because he had endless patience when practical matters required it. He could crouch for a day and night in ambush without moving more than he needed to breathe; a few hours as a bare-legged Bombay peon would be child's play.

King looked through his papers. "I see I'm supposed to be fabulously wealthy," he said. "Indigo plantations in Oudh, Tata Steelworks stockholder, and shares in mines in Australia and the Cape."

"Yes, my lord," Warburton said, with a slight singsong Bombay accent. "You're just back from a hunting trip to the North American colonies, as a matter of fact. You have been a trifle out of touch with events."

"And I'm taking my little sister to see the *Garuda* off," King answered. "Yasmini . . . Yasmini?"

The Russian woman started. "*Da*, I mean—yes. Yes . . ." Her eyes went out of focus again.

King shuddered. She was seeing more and more of the possible *nows*, pulled apart into fragments of possibility. *And I can't do a damned thing for her*, ran through him with bitter frustration. *I couldn't stop this even if it were in my power, because we need her talent too much.*

"Now. We should leave *now*," she said tonelessly.

Bombay's civil airship port was near the cityside border of the reserve that held the Kanheri caves, where the land flattened toward the outskirts of town, south of Powai Lake. Most of it was open fields of cropped grass, carefully leveled. The mooring towers for the airships were tall narrow pyramids of iron, perfectly functional despite the fanciful embellishments of bronze foliage curling around them; the airship port was an important symbol of the great city's touchy civic pride.

To the east was the technical side of the operation; twelve huge arched sheds of bamboo-resin laminate with clamshell doors, and the clanking steam traction engines that hauled airships in and out of them. Also there were the huge underground storage tanks for hydrogen, kerosene fuel, and water ballast, machine shops for repairing air engines, offices, workmen's quarters, all the latter hidden by earth berms planted in trees and flowering shrubs. Today half the field had been cleared of civil traffic; only a few smaller airships were tethered to the masts. At the base of the one nearest the terminal buildings was the *Garuda*, winched down to ground level.

The passenger entrance was to the west of the fields, close to the rail and road lines that passed down the coast to Bombay itself. King made himself languid as they disembarked from the Kanheri local, with an air of bored indifference. He strolled toward the pillared triumphal arch that soared over the broad pathway of many-colored stone leading from the rail stop. Facing him in three-quarter relief above it was a huge statue of Ganesha, the elephant-headed god of good luck, lord of new beginnings, and patron of scribes—the broken tusk he held in one of his four hands was said to have been the first pen; after Mumba Devi, he was the favorite divinity of Bombay.

Beyond was a long rectangle of garden and parkland, with many brick pathways benches sheltered by arched iron-and-glass parasols, and statues of various worthies; St. Disraeli, another of Bombay's spiritual patrons—the city liked to claim he would have take up residence there, if he'd survived—and others from Sivaji on down through Tennyson and Sassoon. Travelers were strolling about, sitting, admiring the grounds, eating ices from little glass cups, and thronging the pathways in numbers sufficient to conceal a hundred parties such as King's. He began to feel less conspicuous by the moment; you could be more anonymous in a crowd than in any wilderness.

The terminal proper stood on the other side, fronted by a colonnade of three-story pillars of pink granite topped with gilded lotus flowers. That supported the huge barrel-vaulted hall, its ceiling coffered and gilded; mosaic murals of the history of Bombay ran around the wall below. A great four-sided clock hung from the top of the arched ceiling, showing Bombay, Adelaide, Cape Town, and Delhi Mean Time . . . but not, he noted with amusement, that of Calcutta, this city's great rival.

This isn't civil pride, this is civic megalomania, King thought; you got a strong ant-on-a-table feeling in buildings like this. And what was that saying—"Bombay is a religion which doesn't believe in Calcutta"?

One stretch of mural showed a map of the world, with airship routes webbing it in little lines of rock crystal—including routes to places that were still howling wilderness inhabited by cannibals with bones through their noses, if at all.

Still, no denying the city magnates dream grandly.

A substantial crowd milled around within; a fair number of them had big cameras with flashbulb attachments, going *pop* and lighting the gilt ceiling and the windows of the expensive shops that lined the interior walls. The object of their attention was a corridor marked off by crimson velvet ropes on stands, and more emphatically by Gurkhas with fixed bayonets. The royal party had gone by; King checked his watch and found they were exactly on time. Various dignitaries, hangers-on, and courtiers were following for the send-off, though, and the social pages of the papers would be full of who was with whom, and at what point in the proceedings.

"Right," he muttered to himself, and walked up to the gap in the rope.

"Captain Lord James Conrad, Baron Rhotak," he drawled to the officer of the detachment. "Agra Dragoon Guards, on extended leave at present."

The officer there saluted, and King returned the gesture. The man in charge was in subaltern's uniform, looking absurdly young but keen enough, with searching blue eyes. He wore a pith helmet instead of a turban, and when he spoke his Imperial English had a strong clotted accent, swallowing the beginnings of his words and stretching the vowels—Australian, doubtless the offspring of some squatter or station-holder family; Australian titles of nobility were as eccentric as the rest of the place.

"Lieutenant Harold Ickles, sir: holder-scion of Bungaree Station. I must ask for your papers, my lord," he went on, with a polite nod. "The royal party is still in the port buildings and unauthorized persons may not approach."

The Gurkhas he commanded were in tight dress uniforms of green and black, pillbox hats at a jaunty angle on their close-cropped, black-haired heads. The rifles they ported across their chests were loaded, and had a round in the chamber—and if the officer told them the man in Guards uniform was a danger to the King-Emperor's safety they would shoot him down like a pi-dog. Would do the same to the Archbishop of Delhi, for that matter, and probably their own mothers.

"Samuel, show the man—there's a good fellow," King said, taking out his cigarette case, flicking it open one-handed, and offering it to the young Australian. He shook his head, and Narayan Singh wordlessly came forward with a match for King.

Warburton bustled up officiously and handed over the documents. The subaltern read through each completely, holding up the pictures of the "captain" and his "*daffadar*" to compare them with the living men before him. King lounged with his gauntlets in his left hand and the hand resting casually on his sword hilt, smoking the cigarette in an ivory holder. Yasmini was quivering beside him, a fold of her crimson-and-silver sari over her head and her face downcast.

"My lord, these are for yourself and the *daffadar*," the subaltern said. "They authorize you as a member of the Household, but no others."

"Oh, really, my dear young fellow: *Khoi bat naheen*, surely? My valet, the chappie with our gear . . . and my lady sister, of course. I promised you you could see the King-Emperor leave close-up, didn't I, Indira?"

Yasmini nodded wordlessly, clinging to his arm; only he could feel the tension in her hands. Her face was childlike enough anyway, and a little artful makeup and the *kunwari*'s very slightly oversize clothes made her look like a mature twelve-year-old. She turned her huge blue-rimmed green eyes on the young officer.

"Please," she whispered.

"Ah—oh, very well, my lord." With a bow to Yasmini: "Far be it from me to disappoint the little lady."

The subaltern snapped the little booklets back together and handed them to Warburton without looking at him—merely a valet, after all.

"No need for me to get *stroppy*, as we say at Bungaree Station. Just back from the American colonies, I see? Any trophies, sir?"

"Haw, yes. Bloody awful wilderness, and bloody awful colonials, but the *shikari* was top-hole. Haw. Got a bison that may be a record, two good plains lions"—descended from zoo stock gone feral maneater during the Fall—"and a panther. Recommend it; but be sure to get a first-rate native guide and bearers. Galveston's the best start; town's a dreadful little hole, though. Bring your own brandy."

"I may take a trip there someday, my lord. Ah, no firearms beyond this point for anyone not on active duty with the Guard, as I'm sure you know."

Well, not mentioning it was worth a try. Narayan Singh handed over his pistol. King drew his and automatically flipped it around in his hand with a twirl and a finger in the trigger guard, a motion that left it butt first. *Oh, bugger, shouldn't have done that. Out of character.*

The subaltern did raise an eyebrow, but there was a little more respect beneath the formal politeness as he stepped aside:

"Enjoy the launch, my lord, my lady."

Thank you, Lord Krishna, King thought, taking another casual drag on the cigarette and feeling sweat trickle down his flanks under the uniform jacket. *Now what?*

They followed the crowd out toward the final exits, where marble steps gave onto a roped-off enclosure not far from where the *Garuda* waited, its gondola rails resting on the turf and the ground crew squatting beside them. *That* wouldn't do them any good at all—they'd be able to wave good-bye, and no more.

"Yasmini," he said quietly. "*Yasmini. Now. You must.*"

The seeress leaned against him, panting. Then she straightened, looked about.

"Left," she said.

He swerved casually, crossing the marble-floored, glass-walled corridor. A door stood closed, teak and brass with an *Airship Port Personnel and Imperial Indian Airways Personnel Only* sign on a stand next to it.

"Wait," she said.

They did, elaborately nonchalant; King flicked the cigarette into a brass cuspidor, where it sizzled in the expectorations of betel-nut chewers.

"Now. The lock will break. Will break. Would break. Did break—"

He reached out and turned the knob. It was locked, but the lock was a simple turn-handle type in the knob itself, not a dead bolt. King took a deep breath, and as he let it out twisted and pushed with all the power of his arm and shoulder. His right wrist had swung a saber for several hours a day most days since he turned twelve; the tendons stood out like iron cables, and a seam on his uniform jacket began to yield, giving with a rip of parting thread. Then there was a *snap* and tinkle from the door. He swung it open, onto a covered walkway that led onto the turf. A dozen large, wheeled dollies of baggage stood there, and their crews were gathered at a little distance—smoking themselves, he noted, crouched in a circle, and well back of the red line that prohibited open flame closer to the airships. Their eyes were fixed on the bouncing dice one tossed.

"Here," Yasmini said in the same sleepwalker's voice. "Between the trunks."

Those were substantial wicker-and-brass affairs, piled up over six feet high on either side of the carts.

"Won't they—" he began, then silently motioned the others. *No, they won't. She would have* Seen *it if they did.*

He took the first cart himself; there was an aisle most of the way down the center between the piled crates, accessible only from the top and large enough for him and Yasmini—just barely. He eased his way in, then crouched. The Russian woman followed, collapsing against him, dangerously limp. He worked his way around until she could rest with her back against his chest. She was still quivering, but seemed only semiconscious in the gloom, and he could see her eyeballs rolling up until only a trace of iris showed at the top.

"Losing me," she whispered in her own language. "I am losing me. Losing me. Losing me—"

It trailed off into a breathy whimper as he pulled her face into his shoulder. King felt a lurch as men tailed on to the cart; pressing his eye to a crack between two trunks, he could see six at the pushbar and as many at the puller, wiry near-naked brown men in loincloths and turbans. They set up a wailing chant as the baggage carts moved, trundling across grass and the hard clay beneath. Shadow fell across them, the shadow of the *Garuda's* eight hundred fifty feet of hull, looming over them like a mountain, like a whale flying. He craned and saw the great cruciform tailfins go by, the Union Jack proud on their covering of doped cotton cloth, and an engine pod.

Then the baggage cart lurched again—tilted, as the men shoved it onto the beginning of the ramp that led into the belly of the gondola. Darkness fell, full of rumbling and clicks—and then the trunks around him squeezed slightly as the cart was shoved into a slot between two others. For a moment he thought he would be crushed to death in the darkness, and then he realized something that his eye had slid across when they came through the door: the Imperial family crest *on the baggage wagons*. The knowledge flowed through him as silence fell, save for the creaking of the airship's laminate frame and faint sounds from outside the hull.

"Merciful Krishna," he whispered to himself, in rising glee. "You did it again—they must carry these carts as part of the yacht's equipment!"

And load and unload them as units; filled with gear for a royal visit that was needed only on the ground. They were probably coded somehow, and stored in fixed order so that everything would be there whenever the *Garuda* landed . . .

Outside a great hoarse cheer went up. Somewhere a signal gun was firing a salute—twenty-one and then twenty-one again, in quick succession: the King-Emperor's greeting, alone of all the many rulers within the borders of the *Angrezi* Raj. Then a band struck up the national anthem, and a thousand voices sang—with one half-stifled, mouthed accompaniment from the baggage hold:

"Gods save our Padishah—
Dillishvaro wa Jagadishavaro wa
From Delhi rule Universal Lord
Mulk-i-Padishah, hukum-i-King-Emperor—"

It was Yasmini who brought him back to himself. She suddenly writhed in his arms, back arching, gasping for air. His belly lurched with terror, and he did his best to pin her arms and legs as she flailed bruisingly against the shapes that contained them, a thin helpless wail breaking out of her mouth. For one moment of horror he thought she would tear her flesh loose from her bones or break her own spine in the violence of the fit. Then she collapsed for an instant into a boneless limp mass, panting like an animal in a trap; a moment later she had writhed around to face him—something he wouldn't have thought possible in the strait space available.

"Please!" she said, her mouth almost touching his, the cardamom-and-cloves scent of her breath strong, and the feminine musk of her sweat. "Please—help me . . . you must . . . *Pajalsta—pajalsta!* I must have!"

The raw agony in her voice shocked him. "How?" he said. "Tell me how, Yasmini."

"Free me—free me. I am losing me—I will be lost forever. Free me!"

He remembered what she had told him, and almost burst out with an: *Impossible.* And almost laughed: *What, here and now?*

There was another whimper of terror; and no terror would be worse than your very mind drowning in the dark.

"All right," he said with infinite gentleness, kissing the trembling mouth. "Don't worry. Whatever you need."

Chapter Twenty-one

Henri de Vascogne looked around the bridge of the *Garuda* with alert curiosity and more than a little envy. France-outre-mer had airships, blimps much like those the Caliphate made, and even so his people had to buy many of the engine parts from Imperial or Nipponese traders under severe restrictions. Those rope-slung, disaster-prone expedients were useful enough, but nothing like *this*.

"... million cubic feet of hydrogen, giving a useful lift of over sixty tons," Captain Albert Pienaar finished.

He spoke the Delhi-style English service language of the Royal and Imperial Navy, but with a harsh accent, clipped and guttural at once, that marked his birth near Simonstown in the Cape Viceroyalty; a big stocky muscular man in his thirties, in a blue uniform with four gold bands on the cuffs and short-cropped blond hair under a peaked cap.

"Is that inclusive of fuel?" Henri asked.

"Inclusive of our standard load, for a range of five thousand miles at a cruising speed of fifty-eight miles an hour," Pienaar said with pride. "That's more than twice the distance from here to the Imperial base at Aden, our first stop. This is the latest design—better engines, better materials for the gas cells, stronger and lighter hull structure—radical improvements in capacity. That's why I transferred from surface ships; man, the changes I've seen in ten years with the Air Service!"

They stood together near the rear of the bridge. That was built into the nose of the long boat-shaped gondola fared into the bottom of the orca-shaped hull. Most of the forward three-quarters of it was glass, curving in below so that the helmsman at the ship-style wheel in the very front could look down to either side as he controlled the rudders. Behind him were the two vertical helmsmen, their spoked wheels set at ninety degrees to his, governing the ailerons on the fins at the rear. To the rear of them was the map table, the engine-telegraphs that set the speed of the eight Stirling-cycle motors, and banks of brass gauges set in consoles of thin, beautifully varnished wood, levers decorated with filigreework, and turned-rosewood pulls at the ends of tubes that hid control wires running up into the structure of the craft.

Through it all ran the laminated structure of the hull itself, curving in from above in organic shapes like the ribs of some great sea beast, triangles of slender strands held together with stiffening O-rings.

"*Magnifique,*" Henri said sincerely.

The trip to Aden was a warning, too. Ships like this, based there, could reach Damascus itself and return, as well as reaching Tunis without stopping in Egypt.

"And the fire hazard?"

Pienaar snorted impolitely. "What hazard? *Ya,* hydrogen burns, and it leaks through everything, but it leaks *up.* Only mixtures of air and hydrogen are dangerous. Provided you flush the gas cells regularly and—but you must excuse me, my lord."

Henri nodded, stepping back, as a barrage of technicalities flew between the captain and his bridge crew. Finally:

"She's eight hundred pounds heavy, but the ballast looks normal, Captain."

Pienaar frowned. Sita spoke, breaking her unaccustomed silence:

"There won't be any delay, will there, Captain? That would look *very* bad."

"Nie . . . no, *Kunwari.*" The captain of the *Garuda* shook his head, looking a little like a bull testing the air. "Probably those *fer-damn* baggage people again." He smiled. "We'll just give some stinking coolies a better shower." A change of tone. "Valve ballast and prepare to cast off!"

Two hundred men on the ground on either side gripped the landing rails that the airship rested on. They stayed bent in unison, bare brown bodies tense, as cold water from the keel ballast tanks sprayed out over them, rising in unison as the great ship lightened. Then they moved, like one immense caterpillar, backing the ship away from the mooring mast and turning it to face into the light easterly wind.

"Neutral buoyancy, Captain."

"Very well, Number Two. All props feathered."

"All props feathered, aye!"

"Engines to standby."

A low humming filled the fabric of the ship—less than a noise, more than a sensation in the soles of the feet.

"Engines are at full revs, sir."

"Signal *stand by to release*. Release! Valve ballast—establish neutral buoyancy at one thousand feet. All engines ahead one-quarter. Attitude helm neutral. Rudder, left ninety and come to—"

The ground crew let go and stepped back as more water foamed out over them. Freed of the weight of four hundred hands, the huge silvery torpedo surged upward a hundred feet, then began a stately curve to a course slightly south of west. The figures on the ground turned from humans to doll-sized manikins as they rose, then to waving ants. Sound faded away, save for the almost subliminal murmur of cleft air and the working of the hull. Pienaar nodded once to himself and smiled slightly, turning and bowing to Sita and Henri:

"Satisfactory, I trust, *Kunwari*, my lord."

Sita nodded regally. "A very smooth lift, Captain Pienaar. As smooth as I've ever felt; certainly as good as anything Captain Rahungath ever did."

As the Air Service officer straightened, Sita went on: "And Captain Pienaar?"

"Yes, *Kunwari*?"

"As you are new to this vessel, I will overlook the first offense. But you will never, ever, refer to Imperial subjects as 'stinking coolies' again."

Pienaar's face flushed brick red; it ran through shock, rage, and an expressionless mask in the course of a second. He straightened to attention.

"Yes, *Kunwari*," he said woodenly. "I kiss feet, *Kunwari*."

"And by *ever again*, I mean while you wear my father's uniform. If you do, you won't be wearing it any longer. Do I make myself clear?"

Henri wouldn't have wanted to be under the flaying knife of that voice—and a thousand times never in front of men he commanded. The officer's face was like something carved out of lard rather than a living man's. On the other hand . . .

"Yes, *Kunwari*. Perfectly clear."

"Thank you, Captain Pienaar. Thank you all," she concluded, nodding to the rest of the bridge crew.

She turned and extended a hand. Henri put his arm under it, and they walked down the corridor. As the hatchway closed behind them, he heard Sita give a slight hiss; her face was calm as a temple image, but he realized she was furious as he'd never seen her.

"He didn't just mean *sudras*," she said, in a voice that trembled imperceptibly. "Or even untouchables. He meant anyone with a brown skin—and half the crew in that compartment with him are martial-caste Indians, and don't think they didn't know exactly what he meant!"

"Are there many of your, mmmm, *sahib-log* who think like that?" Henri asked.

"Some, although most of those have the sense not to say it. But he's not *sahib-log*—he's barely *Angrezi*. He's a *Kapenaar baas*. They treat all their lower castes over there like dirt, and everyone's lower caste except them, there. It's a . . . Father called it a festering boil on the Empire's arse."

"How does he come to have such a position of prestige, him?" Henri asked.

There were regional differences in France-outre-mer; far more Muslims in Morocco and Tunisia than in the central block around Algiers, for instance, and the special problem of newly conquered Sicily. To know how the Raj handled similar problems was valuable.

"Well, he's a decorated veteran," Sita said. "He was second officer on an airship damaged during the suppression of a native uprising in Kilimanjaro Territory; got her into the air and a lot of refugees out to safety, then went back for more with half his engines out and gas leaking. Lost his own wife and children during the fighting there, as a matter of fact. And he's an extremely good airshipman; he helped with the design for this class. And the Cape holds a quarter of the seats in Parliament—they have to get appointments of honor in proportion . . . Oh, let's talk about something else, Henri."

"As you wish, *chérie*," he said absently, nodding to an Oriental-

looking airshipman who had risen from his cubbyhole of equipment—
one of the also-to-be-envied wireless telegraphs, from the look of it.
Sita noticed his slight check, and paused to give the young man a gracious smile as he salaamed.

The corridor ended with the circular stair of fretted rosewood
that led to down to the deck of the main observation gallery. There
were a dozen or more people there, grouped around the vision wells
set into the deck, or at the long galleries to port or starboard. Sita
took her hand from Henri's arm, and they walked to the vision well
themselves.

Bombay was passing by below; from a thousand feet it looked
like a relief map, save that figures and vehicles moved in the streets;
the storm of gulls over the dock was like flakes of confetti, save
where some came startlingly close beneath the glass. The north–south
hook-shape of the harbor showed clearly, and tiny white wakes from
freighters and ferries and warships. Some of those elevated their guns
as the shadow of the *Garuda* passed above them, and fired salutes
whose thudding bellows rumbled up a perceptible instant after the
flash of red flame and billow of smoke. Henri felt another bubble of
envy at the low-slung gray steel shapes, with their turrets fore and aft
and more heavy guns in barbettes along their flanks; with a squadron
of those, France could smash the Caliph's entire fleet to kindling.

And it is precisely to obtain such help that you are here, he thought. *Not
that this trip has lacked either enlightenment or pleasure otherwise.*

More warships would be out already, strung across the Arabian
Sea toward Aden; the *Garuda* was as safe as a surface vessel, but the
Royal and Imperial Navy was taking no chances whatsoever. Two
more dirigibles curved up from the naval airship base as he watched;
they were slightly smaller than the *Garuda*, their hulls narrower—the
long pencil shape that the Imperials' so-admirable Analytical Engine
had shown was actually less efficient than the portly whale outline of
the newer craft.

"The *Clive* and the *Raffles*," a voice said quietly beside him.

That was the King-Emperor; Henri took his elbows from the railing and straightened, then relaxed at a slight gesture. The ruler of the
Angrezi Raj was in uniform again, a Naval Air Service commander's
light and dark blue this time.

"They each have a company of the Gurkha regiment of the

Guards on board, sir," Lord Pratap Batwa said from beside him. "We have a platoon, here on the *Garuda*. Packed in like lamb kebab rolled up in a piece of naan, I'm afraid."

"Ah," Henri said. Prince Charles and Cassandra King were a step behind the monarch. "Perhaps that was why the ship was slightly heavy, according to Captain Pienaar. About eight hundred pounds— five persons, shall we say?"

None of the faces reacted much; Henri was somewhat impressed. Even Cassandra King, the astronomer and a naïf, only flushed a little at the news that her brother was probably aboard. Sita quickly changed the subject:

"And speaking of Captain Pienaar—"

Her father tugged at the left side of his full cheek-whiskers, scowling.

"Damn the man, and may he be reborn a labor-tenant on his own estate—that would feed him 'some of his own tobacco.' " A sigh. "There's only so much even Parliament can do about the Viceroyalty of the Cape, much less the throne. The way they diddle the franchise laws over there—" He shrugged. "And it's a sensitive time, what with the Egyptian matter, and the clashes with Dai-Nippon. The Empire needs unity."

"I'm afraid it'll always be a sensitive time," Charles said. "Those chickens are going to come home to roost, someday, sir."

"With luck, not in my time or yours," John II said. "And more often than not, if you leave a problem alone long enough, it solves itself—something governments are loath to learn."

A chime ran. "Ah, dinner. My dear?" he said, offering Cassandra his arm. A murmur ran through the watching courtiers.

Cassandra accepted. Henri heard her murmur in turn: "I can see you in your daughter, sometimes, sir."

"Hunf," Athelstane King snarled, straining in the hot stuffy darkness.

The wicker of the baggage trunks around him was both strong and resilient, and that made it a hell of frustration to try to push them apart. They were also closer above than below. With an unconscious Yasmini lying at his feet, he had both knees against one side of his prison and his shoulders against the other. Pushing them apart wasn't the problem—keeping them from springing back as soon as he relaxed again was. At last he managed to brace his sheathed saber crosswise between the sides, hilt and scabbard chape caught by the brass caps at the corners of two of the trunks in the top row.

"Now, carefully, Athelstane," he told himself in a mutter.

He didn't have room to bend; instead he had to squat with his knees apart and reach down to pick the girl up with his torso still bolt upright, lifting with the strength of his arms alone and not dislodging the diagonally braced saber either.

Carefully—how all the *rakashas* in all the underworlds would laugh if he pulled a muscle or put his back out now!—he raised her. The weight wasn't really the problem; she was barely a hundred pounds. The problem now was the utter limpness of her body. Her breath was barely perceptible and her pulse light; it wasn't the only time he'd had a girl faint in the middle of things, but it was most definitely the first time his own heart had nearly stopped in turn because he was afraid she'd dropped *dead*. Inch by inch he pulled her free and slid her onto the top of the upper layer of trunks. There was a gap of a little under a foot between those and the light planks of the decking above it; he could just barely have stood erect if the hold had been empty.

The bulkhead forward was thin metal, probably aluminum alloy— that was too expensive to use for anything but aircraft and luxury goods. From the feel, it held water; ballast, undoubtedly. Something knocked against it from the other side occasionally, with a hollow *bong* sound.

That was the strangest experience I've ever had, he thought. *Not unpleasant*—one of the advantages of being male, he supposed, was that it couldn't be—*but very strange. Very fucking strange in the most literal sense of the term.*

He hooked the knickers and petticoat that went under the sari up from the floor, after a few tries that made him realize the full disadvantages of blindness for the first time; his booted feet had no feeling. Getting the clothes back on her was going to be hard work, even harder than getting them off had been; but first he folded the fresh handkerchief from his uniform pocket into a pad and applied it between her legs. There wasn't much blood, as far as he could tell by touch in near-total darkness, but she'd definitely been *virgo intacta*.

Why losing a hymen should turn off something that happened in the brain he had no faintest idea; but then, since he had no idea of how her ability worked in the first place . . .

Maybe it's like those yogis who can sleep on nails or hold their left arms up for ten years at a stretch, because they believe *they can do it,* he thought. *Mind over matter. Of course, that's just another way of saying I don't know.*

When he'd clothed the girl again and tugged her sari down, he called softly. "Anyone in trouble?"

"Curse these wicker pythons to the pit!" Narayan Singh said, also softly but with total sincerity. "My arse and belly will bear patterns like a reed mat the rest of my life."

Somewhere, Ibrahim Khan chuckled, drawing a volley of whispered curses. King had smiled himself—but only because the darkness hid it. He could get out, and crawl with great difficulty in the space between the top trunks and the roof. Strength would make do where suppleness couldn't, if he didn't mind losing some skin. The Pathan had his own build in seven-eighths scale, and was just as active, so it would be easier for him. Narayan was stronger than either of them—certainly in the arms and shoulders—but also far bulkier. That none of it was fat merely made the problem worse, since muscle didn't compress as well as soft tissue, and bone didn't compress at all.

Warburton would be no problem; the man had the build of a weasel, and the agility of one, too.

As if to confirm his thought, a voice spoke not far away: "How is Miss Yasmini? She sounded . . . distressed . . . for a moment there."

"Ah—" King felt himself flush in the dark. Making love to a woman in a space that required an acrobat's flexibility in both parties to avoid torn tendons, and doing so for *medical* reasons . . . it would be hard to explain.

"She had a convulsion," he said. *True enough.* "I think it had to do with her . . . talent. She's unconscious now."

"And we should act."

"Very well," King said.

Of course, what exactly should we do? Our seeress is out of the Seeing business, if what she said is true. And what on earth did that last thing she said mean? "He is born!"

His hand touched her in the darkness, with a moment's tenderness, then his mind went to work—the one advantage of being in the

354   S. M. Stirling

dark was that you didn't have to close your eyes to visualize. The keel compartments ran from here to the bow of the gondola, but they were useless—this one didn't even have a hatch opening above. Several others could only be accessed from outside the hull, and there was no through passageway; much of the space was taken up with fuel and water tanks. Above that were two decks fore and aft, interrupted by the space of the main observation deck in the middle. There were two vertical ladders at each end of the gondola that ran through the hull to observation bubbles on the upper surface, and internal galleries one-third of the way up on either side that allowed access to the engines.

"Sir Manfred," he said softly. "As I remember the plans, we're directly below the kitchen stores, aren't we?"

A second; Warburton was probably nodding. "Yes," he said. "If you mean the very rear of this baggage compartment, over the ramp."

"All right." He felt upward. "Thank the little gods of vanity this is a luxury vessel. The boards are secured to these metal stringers by screws and the heads are down—improves the appearance of the floors, no doubt."

He felt again. "They'll be the very devil to get lose, though—my hands can't get a tool properly underneath them. And we do *not* want to attract official attention."

"Provided we can get the planks loose?"

"We'll go up through the pantry, through the ceiling of *that*, and then straight up to the rear observation bubble. It's not used except in action or certain maneuvers—and there's room for all of us. That can be our base. You, and Yasmini if she can—"

This time Warburton made an affirmative noise. Narayan Singh cursed again. "And we'll have to get Narayan out—at worst, we can cut him free, but I don't want to do that unless we have to. Noise."

"Like a buffalo mired in a ditch," Ibrahim whispered. "And bellowing . . ."

"Let me get my hands upon you, child of misbelief, and—"

"Silence," King said.

He tested Yasmini's pulse again; a little more rapid, and her breathing was normal. Wriggling, he managed to get the flask out of his back pocket and dribble a little on her lips. For a moment the liquor merely ran down her cheeks; he gently opened her lips with his fingers and rubbed her throat.

Then she coughed, tried to sit up, struck her head on one of the metal stringers.

"*Bozhe moi!*" she said, the last word muffled through his palm.

When he removed it, she spoke again in a shaken whisper, but still in Russian. "My . . . head is empty. As it is between dreams—but more. As if I am *alone* for the first time. A sound gone I did not know was there until it left—"

"Well, you're not alone," King replied. "I'm . . . we're very much here. Can you move?"

"Yes." He could sense her testing herself in the darkness. "Yes, a little sore." There was a smile in her voice. "Not a bad soreness, though."

"Oh, thank Pravati. I was afraid I'd hurt you."

Astonishingly, she chuckled. "That is vanity. After all, even a small baby's head is much bigger than—"

Warburton coughed, and Yasmini was silent for a moment. When she spoke again, her voice was desolate.

"But what use is Yasmini now, without her dreams?"

King reached out in the darkness and found her hand. "You were extremely useful at the fight in the desert," he said. "And I suspect that being able to climb around in small spaces is going to be useful here once more."

"*Da.*" A growing strength. "What can I do?"

"We need some boards removed. About twenty feet in *that* direction."

Vladimir Obromovich Ignatieff was used to cold. Part of his initiation into the cult of the Black God—the one that raised him to the Inner Ring, not the ordinary manhood rites—had involved hours lying naked on a glacier in the mountains on the Roof of the World, using his command of the body's energy to keep him from death. Many initiates did *not* survive that test.

The water in the ballast tank was worse than the glacier; even though this time he was coated in thick grease and wore tight-woven silk that trapped a layer of water between it and his skin as extra insulation. Still, the sluggish movements of the ballast leached away his inner heat, hour upon endless hour. *Patience*, he told himself. *This is the one place that nobody will suspect or inspect.* His hands and feet were numb, and his teeth had begun to chatter despite the iron will that clenched his jaw, when he heard the dogging ring in the hatch above him move.

When the hatch finally opened, only great control kept him from trying to lunge up the two rungs of the ladder that were above the surface and into the dim corridor beyond.

That dimness was bright to his eyes. He saw the square face of the *Kapenaar* captain above him, and an extended hand. Help was hateful, but he took it and lay for a moment on the wooden surface of the corridor while Pienaar hauled on the rope that ran from his waist to the water. A bundle broke surface, fifty pounds wrapped in thick layers of rubber.

"Quickly, into my cabin," Pienaar said, pulling him up and dragging him along with one arm over his rescuer's shoulder before going back for the bundle.

That was a cubicle, enough for a bed and a desk, and a tiny alcove with a shower and toilet. Pienaar pushed him into that and turned on the hot water; it was enough to billow steam and sting, but he scarcely felt it for long moments. It brought strength, though, and after a while he was able to command himself again, turning the handle and stepping out, stripping off the silk and wiping away the tallow. He hid a smile at the thought of what his tool would think if he knew the nature of the beast it was rendered from.

Pienaar was busy slitting open the package, taking out the explosives and blasting caps and detonators. Ignatieff fell on the food set out on a small table—sausage, bread, cheese, chocolate—like a starving wolf, stoking himself.

Pienaar looked up at him. "I wouldn't have believed a man could stay alive in the tank so long," he said. "Particularly a man who wasn't fat to begin with."

Ignatieff grunted—he certainly wasn't going to share any secrets with this ally-of-the-moment.

"The Peacock Angel gave me strength," he said—both truth and a lie, which was delightful, but not missing Pienaar's slight grimace of distaste. "And that belief of yours is why the ballast tank was the best place to hide."

As he spoke he dressed, putting on the plain blue working overalls of an Imperial Navy airshipman. The room was stark, obviously not lived in for long. The only personal touches were a strange demonic mask carved from some dark reddish hard-grained wood, a broad-bladed spear, and a photograph of a smiling fair-haired woman and three small children. The Okhrana agent hid his sneer at that, and watched Pienaar strapping the explosives to his own body beneath the coat. The *Kapenaar* was soft about his woman and spawn; could he not sire more? But that softness had tempered him hard in the fires of hate. He might be an idiot, but he was a useful idiot.

"What news?" he asked, smiling like a shark behind the mask of his face. *Useful idiot. That is a phrase that will bring much laughter, in the Okhrana.* He put on an attentive expression as the *Kapenaar* traitor spoke:

"The *Clive* has already turned back—multiple engine failures," he said. "We'll have to use the fallback with the *Raffles;* probably someone did a just-in-case replacement of the crankshaft lubricant at the very last moment, after our load went through. That was always a risk. Everyone does additional preventive maintenance before an important mission."

"Which is why we have the other. Any problems aboard this ship?"

"Yes," Pienaar said. "Last-minute change in personnel. My man who was to hold down the wireless transmitter was injured in a fall, and they put a damned yellow coolie from British Siam in his place."

Ignatieff scooped up a knife from among the equipment; it was one of his favorites, double-edged and very slightly curved.

"That," he said, visualizing the layout of the airship, "is not a problem."

The wireless telegraph was only ten feet up this very corridor, after all.

The rear observation bubble was a low, domed oval, with seats all around its circumference and a hatch that could be opened to allow riggers and repair crews access to the outer hull. For a moment the huge view of ocean and sky caught Athelstane King. There was a high overcast like milk, and not many stars, leaving the *Garuda* suspended in a world of darkness fringed by pearly light and sea glitter. Then he forced his attention to the task at hand. The forward bubble a hundred feet forward was lit, and he could just see a man there despite the curve of the hull. Off to their right the shape of another airship slid, perhaps half a mile distant and five hundred feet higher. The silvery hull was a hint, a gleam, a thing that the brain sketched from memory more than the eyes.

"Come," he said.

The others came up the ladder behind him, and Warburton let the rubber-padded hatch down again silently. "We don't know how long until it begins," he said. "If they're not just going to blow this up."

"No," Yasmini said. "My dream was definite. Not this—"

"Wait," King said.

A signal lamp was flashing from the other airship . . . and where was the third one, anyway? The lamp was in clear Morse: He read it automatically, as did Yasmini and the other men save Ibrahim:

"Clive . . . will . . . continue . . . to . . . conform . . . to . . . your . . . movements. Suggest . . . you . . . check . . . compass . . . again . . . and . . . attempt . . . star . . . sighting."

The answer from the *Garuda* was hidden. There was a long moment's pause, and then the *Clive* replied: "Acknowledge . . . King-Emperor's . . . direct . . . order . . . will . . . not . . . repeat . . . will . . . not . . . question . . . it . . . again."

"I think it's already started," King said. "*Daffadar*, get to the Gurkhas. You have the letter and the seal? Good. Yasmini, Sir Manfred—best you get started too." He looked at his watch. "Nearly twenty hours . . . sixty miles an hour . . . we could be a *long* way off our course."

Chapter Twenty-two

Henri de Vascogne woke at the light touch on his shoulder, and his hand clamped on the hilt of the blade beneath his pillow. The dark figure skipped backward as the knife came free, and raised its hands soothingly. Henri shook his head once, then reached to turn on the light. It failed with a *pop* and internal spark—reliability as well as expense kept electric light confined mostly to specialty uses such as aircraft and warships, so far.

"It's me, Warburton," a very quiet voice said.

"Name of a dog!" he replied, equally *sotto voce*. "What news?"

"This craft is off course—far off course. And whoever's in charge on the bridge is trying to keep it that way. Are you armed?"

"Knife, and sword. Charles is next door—he has a pistol. So also with Lord Pratap next to him, and his father in the Imperial suite at the head of the corridor."

"Get them. Quickly, man. The airship may already be under enemy control."

He grunted at that, and dressed hurriedly, pulling on the soft-soled boots that were compulsory for wear aboard the *Garuda*. Charles's reaction was considerably slower than his, but then, he had less experience. Enough, though; the pistol was in the bedside stand, not locked away.

"Guard detachment?" he said, sitting up and looking at their faces. *His* light, Henri noted, worked.

"It's being handled," Warburton said. "We'd best get to your father, and quickly."

The King-Emperor's son had no problem getting past the two Gurkhas outside his father's door. It was fortunate that he spoke their language as well, for they could tell him that his father and Lord Pratap had been called to the bridge. The three men looked at each other, appalled, in the light that came through the door and the arched curve of windows around the front of the Imperial Suite. Charles reacted quickly, then: He took the rifles from the two guards, handed them to Henri and Warburton, and sent the two *jawans* running for their comrades at the rear of the aircraft.

"Quickly, but quiet," Warburton said, working the bolt to make sure that he had a round chambered. "I'll lead the way; then you, de Vascogne, then the prince."

Henri did likewise; the thought of a firefight on a flying bomb set his teeth on edge, but the alternative . . . the alternative was likely to be worse. The steep narrow staircase down to the flight deck was shadowed in the early morning hours, only a few lonely bulbs glowing along the corridor below—officers' quarters aft, specialists and equipment forward.

It was the tacky sensation under his feet that made him realize what he was walking in; that, and a whiff of an all-too-familiar smell. He hissed for quiet, and tried the door of the wireless compartment. It gave with a soft heavy resistance, and then blocked half-open. Through the slit into the narrow cubby—the half ton of equipment took up most of the space—he could see the body of the operator, and the thick brown-red pools on the floor.

"Dead," he whispered to the other two men. "At least an hour ago. Equipment destroyed."

They stole forward toward the bridge; no rating stood beside it, another sign of things awry. The Metford was heavy in his hand as he used it to push the hatchway open a crack. That let through voices. The King-Emperor's was unmistakable:

"And for the last time, Captain Pienaar, will you please tell me *precisely* what it was you wished me to observe? Sleep is more necessary at my time of life, and harder to achieve."

"What I want you to observe is—"

The night sky lit, as if the sun had come up to the south. Seconds later, a fist as large as God's struck the *Garuda*.

*   *   *

"What are you taking me to the rear of the ship for, if whatever's happening is happening up front?" Sita complained sleepily.

The *kunwari* was not a quick riser. For that, Cassandra was grimly thankful. She and Yasmini had barely met, but they were moving in perfect unison as they bundled the Imperial princess rearward. It wasn't until they reached the main observation deck that Sita finally mustered the consciousness to dig in her heels and force them to stop.

"What's going *on?*"

"This is Yasmini, didn't you notice?" Cassandra said. "My brother and Sir Manfred are on board. We're supposed to get you to the safest place—"

Boots and bare feet pounded on the polished wooden tiles. A wave of twenty or so Gurkhas went by, many of them half-naked, a few completely so except for cotton loincloths, but all carrying their rifles and *kukris*. Narayan Singh ran at their head, still waving a letter with the King-Emperor's signature at a pink young Australian officer; two of the Gurkhas looked as if they had been told to guard him while official explanations were sought, but at least they were all moving in the right direction.

Sita thought so, too; she made a dash after them. Cassandra and Yasmini grabbed her arms. "You *stupid* bint, what could you do that they can't?" Cassandra yelled into her ear. "Get in the way? Get *killed?*"

The princess sagged into their arms, then broke free as their grip relaxed. "I have to—" she said, darting backward toward the railing to circle around them.

For a moment Cassandra couldn't make out what the flare of yellow light was. She realized it was an exploding airship just as the blast wave hit; a blue wash of hydrogen flame, and then the real punch, as vaporized kerosene from the fuel tanks mixed with air and flashed off all at once. The *Garuda* pitched and rolled like a balloon, rotating on her axis and then swinging down again. Cassandra felt herself weightless, and mountaineer's reflex made her flail for a hold, any hold. The railing that divided the observation deck from the slanting windows struck her across the back of the thighs, and she toppled backward onto the floor as the airship righted itself.

Glass stabbed at her back. *Window blown in*, she thought; but that was not the reason she was slow hauling herself to her feet.

"Oh, Gods, two hundred men," she whispered to herself, clinging to the rail and watching as the flaming debris made meteors through the night. The crew, and the whole company of the Foot Guards, given the nightmare death that had haunted her every time she walked up the boarding ramp of an aircraft. Hatred clenched her fingers on the rail, but only half was for the murderers. The other half was for the malignant fate that had stranded her on this flying bomb.

Dying in an airship crash. How ironic. After years of telling myself how safe it was.

Her mind was functioning. Her body refused, threatening to spew hot bile into the night as she realized that there was nothing between her and the rushing darkened ocean below but air. The sight drew her, despite Yasmini pulling at her and shouting; drew her as the cobra draws the mice, hypnotic.

Not even the sight of Sita's fingers, cutting themselves as they gripped the metal edging of the vanished window below her, could break the spell. The metal bent, and the body of the *kunwari* twisted as well, in the rushing passage of the *Garuda*'s speed. She couldn't hold for more than a few seconds, and then it would be a long fall to the water.

The only reality was the solid teakwood under her fingers as she stood frozen.

"So many men," Athelstane King whispered to himself as he watched the death of the *Clive*, a hand clamping him to the inside of the observation bubble as the *Garuda* wallowed across the sky.

He could see bits of debris go by, flung by the power of the explosion; and in the distance a man jumping from the burning mass of the stricken airship, but *he* was only visible because his parachute was on fire. As the hull fabric curved away in great fluttering patches you could see the gossamer fragility that underlay an airship's bulk; it broke into half a dozen pieces before it struck the sea below.

Then his horror was gone, leaving only a huge and cleansing anger. He turned to Ibrahim Khan.

"I must go forward, there," he said, nodding to the second observation bubble, the one whose ladder led down through the ship to the bridge. "Follow if you dare."

There was no time for anything but the rushing wind, and the feel of the narrow metal track across the arch of the *Garuda*'s spine. Wisps of cloud went by through the air around him, as he crouched and worked his way forward. There were narrow metal loops to either side of the path; probably for crews to clip safety lines to, when they were working on rips to the fabric. Now the gleam of their polished surfaces helped to guide him forward.

"I have the King-Emperor hostage! Nobody move, or he dies!"

Henri de Vascogne recognized the shout; it was the voice of Pienaar, captain of the *Garuda*. Curses followed, and a brief sound of struggle.

He used that to paralyze any loyal men still on the bridge, Henri thought. *His conspirators would be ready to strike.*

The Frenchman looked forward through the swinging hatchway. The King-Emperor and his companion had been thrown to the deck by the force of the explosion. They came slowly to their feet, looking at the pistols in the hands of men in the Empire's uniform. Henri did a quick check of his own; less than a third of the bridge crew present, and a third of those were gagged and bound, one or two dead. All the rest—the mutineers—were armed, though; the captain had a store of pistols under his control. Some of them looked shaky, and he thought he could smell the rank sweat of fear. Pienaar looked exalted, not frightened. His chin was up, and the Frenchman recognized the look in those staring blue eyes.

He'd seen it on *wahabi* fanatics, making a death charge in the face of certain doom, after they slit the throats of their own women in the face of defeat. That was a man with very little left to lose.

Still . . . His eyes met Warburton's, and they nodded together.

"No, you don't," the Political agent said loudly.

The muzzles of their rifles swung the hatchway open as Pienaar started violently. John II and Lord Pratap, with the pragmatism of veterans, went down again to give the men behind them a clear field of fire. There were five potential targets, men with guns—but both muzzles pointed unerringly at the center of mass of Pienaar's body.

The *Kapenaar* looked up at them. "I expected that," he said slowly, pulling his left hand out of his pocket.

With the one that held the service pistol he pulled open his loose officer's jacket. The blasting explosive strapped to his body was unmistakable, and so was the deadman switch that he held in his left hand, the cord running to the first of the cloth-wrapped bundles that were strapped around his waist.

"Yes, I *do* have him hostage," he went on, with a smile. "There's thirty pounds of this guncotton stuff; that's more than two shells from a field-gun carry. You can't save your kaffir-loving Emperor with those toys. Put them down."

Henri thought furiously, not letting the rifle waver from its snug fit against his shoulder. How *did* you threaten someone who didn't care whether he lived or died?

"No," John II said. "You don't have anything of the sort."

"No," Sir Manfred Warburton said. "That's a bomb, you swine, but it isn't a magical spell. If you wanted to kill yourself, you would have already—the way you murdered two hundred men in the same uniform you're wearing."

Pienaar shrugged. "I want to live to see an independent Cape," he said. "One without your coolie Parliament—but I have brothers, a Brotherhood, to see to it. Once the war with Nippon and the Caliph starts—"

"You're mad!"

"No. The evidence has been most carefully planted. We have . . . allies. Then the Brotherhood will seize power in Cape Town, and we'll—" He stopped in mid-rant. "You wouldn't be interested."

"No," the monarch said. He was crouching, but nobody watching his face could mistake it for submission. "Nor surprised."

Henri cocked an ear; the sound of boots came through from the deck above. Shortly thereafter the boards started to creak and splinter under rifle butts and the broad chopping knives—*kukris* had been the Nepalese peasants' all-purpose tool, before they became famous as a weapon. Several of the mutineers in the control cabin looked up in alarm.

"Stop them!" Pienaar said sharply, raising the hand that bore the switch. "Stop your tame mountain monkeys now, or we all die!"

"He means *that*," Henri murmured aside to Warburton, and then looked back over his shoulder.

Charles's face twisted with savage anger, but he called out sharply in Nepali. The sound ceased, and a tense silence fell.

"Stalemate," Warburton said.

"I don't think so," Pienaar said. "I know where we're going. Haven't you looked down?"

Henri did, for a brief second. The clouds had lifted a little, enough for moonlight to show a white line ahead. *Surf,* he thought. *Surf breaking on a shore.*

"The Caliph's part of Baluchistan," Pienaar said, and laughed; it was a sound a drunken man might have made, and he realized it, falling silent for an instant and wiping his hand across his mouth. "Get the prince in here, and I promise the rest of you can live."

"You promise?" Warburton said, lip curling slightly. "On what? On your word of *honor*? As an officer and a gentleman, perhaps?"

Pienaar's florid face went white. Wordlessly, he raised the pistol in his right hand and shot. The sharp *crack* covered the King-Emperor's cut-off cry of pain, as the bullet smashed into his ankle. Henri sensed Charles's forward rush toward his father, and spared just enough attention to push his rifle butt backward six inches, into the young man's stomach right under the short ribs. That stopped the movement, and he returned the weapon to his point of aim with smooth economy.

Pratap whipped the sword belt off from over his sash and looped it over the leg just above the wound, drawing it tight. The motion that would have put his body between the ruler's and the gun was checked with a gesture that set him back on his heels. The wrinkled brown hawk's face of the Rajput lord was no less calm than that of the man he'd served for nearly forty years; they both watched Pienaar with the gaze of birds of prey.

"Get the prince in here, or it'll be his other ankle next. Then his kneecaps. Then his bliddy balls!"

Pienaar's accent had become thicker, but there was no trembling in the hand that held the revolver. The wounded man on the floor spoke then, loudly and clearly; Henri recognized the language but had no more than a few words of it—Nepali. He saw Warburton go pale, and nod once, slowly.

"*Shabash,* Padishah," he whispered, very softly.

Henri thought he heard a soft sound from above, as of many men moving quietly to the rear; and the querulous voices of courtiers awoken. Behind them came a strangled grunt of pain. He turned his head slightly, enough to see the heir to the Lion Throne press trembling hands palm to palm, put them before his face and bow deeply;

the salaam to a ruler, or to the *pitaji* who rules a family. His fingernails stood out white with effort, but the prince's voice was calm and hard:

"No. I will not give you another hostage, traitor, no matter what you do."

"You won't?" Pienaar said, and laughed. "I think you will, kaffir-lover. *I* saw my family burned alive in my own house, and couldn't save them—I know exactly how it feels. Now you'll know, and do as you're told!"

The pistol barked again, and Charles gave a hoarse grunt as if the bullet had struck him instead of his father. Henri looked back at the tableau on the *Garuda's* bridge. The second bullet hadn't been quite as well aimed; it had plowed a furrow through the older man's calf, a little above the first wound. There was pain on the bewhiskered face of the ruler of half mankind, but he forced himself erect, leaning on Pratap's shoulder.

Be as you wish to seem, Henri thought—the ancient philosopher's advice, simple and deadly difficult.

There is a man who has lived his role until he is exactly as he appears, neither more nor less. When the bitter hour of the hemlock comes for me, may I drink it so.

Beside him Warburton's rifle was rock-steady, but Henri could see tears trickling down and dripping onto the polished walnut stock; shocking, on the face of the cynical, self-sufficient Political Service agent he'd come to know over the past half year.

"*Shabash*, Padishah," Warburton whispered again.

"Call him in!" Pienaar said. "And do it in a language I can understand."

It was then that Henri understood what would happen. He saw the beginning of the hobbling leap that John II made, his lieutenant beside him. Pienaar fired four times, and every bullet struck; none was enough to stop the two old men before they grappled with him and toppled off the catwalk onto the great semicircle of glass that surrounded it. There was enough time for Warburton to drop his rifle and drag the hatchway closed; enough for Henri de Vascogne to throw himself flat.

Enough for several of the men on the bridge to scream, as they saw their leader's hand relax and the deadman switch go flying free.

*   *   *

Cassandra King had always doubted tales of out-of-body experiences; the product of minds unbalanced by poor diet and excessive meditation, in her opinion. Some corner of her rationalist soul laughed at that now, as she watched herself acting—her body acting, without the least volition. Against the screaming commands of her own mind, in fact.

Her sari and Yasmini's were both good silk, stronger than rope. She whipped off her own, tossed it into a loose cord, tied off one end around the railing. By then the blond woman had her own off, and the petticoat; the eerie detachment Cassandra felt let her see and feel a flash of embarrassment at a few spots of blood at the crotch of the white underdrawers—she was always finicky about her own periods.

The garments went together with good running knots; she stamped on one end and hauled to draw them tight, took a turn around her body, stepped up onto the rail, and dropped down into the slipstream with a straight rappel. The wind buffeted at her, swinging her like a mountain gust. That thought gave her steadiness; she caromed into Sita and got an arm around her under the rib cage just before her hands released the broken edge of the window framing. It snapped free, tumbling away below, and the princess seized her with arms and legs. The silk stretched, but held; and so did the knots.

Cassandra felt a surge of relief, until Yasmini's shout reached her. She looked up, and felt her face go gray. The silk of the sari was bent over the rim of the window frame not far from where Sita's hands had clung. She could see the first strands fray, even as she watched. Another quick glance down; they were over land, tumbled gray-yellow-brown moonlit desert—and it was a very long two thousand feet.

What to do?

"Sita!" Cassandra called; their faces were virtually pressed together. "Climb up me, and then up the rope—I can't lift us both. I'll follow."

"I can't!"

"Yes you can!"

"No, I really can't!" Sita said, and brought a hand around before Cassandra's face. The rushing wind of the airship's passage blew the drops of blood back into her friend's face, and she moved it immediately.

"Sorry," she half shouted. "But I really can't. Both hands—cut on the broken glass in the frame. I'd fall halfway up."

They both looked up; seven feet, and it might as well have been the surface of the moon. Yasmini was leaning far over the railing, her face a mask of effort as she tried to haul them up. Cassandra suppressed a hysterical giggle at the sight. The Russian girl was strong for her size—but she was tiny, and there was one tall and one medium-sized woman at the end of that fraying silk rope. Call it two and a half times her own weight; utter futility.

Cassandra spoke with more than her usual precision: "Oh, *bugger*."

The man inside the forward observation bubble was Count Vladimir Ignatieff. King sent a brief prayer of thankfulness to Krishna—it seemed appropriate, since the merciful God had appeared to Arjuna and counseled him on a warrior's duty. Of course, he'd also told the noble bowman that he must fight and kill *only* from duty, without personal attachment. That was more sanctity than King was prepared to invest, just now. There were few things in all his life he'd wanted as much as he lusted to kill the Russian at that moment.

King looked carefully before he acted; he had the time, since Ignatieff seemed preoccupied with scanning the northern horizon through a telescope. A savage grin split his face; no gun visible.

Probably only had a limited number, and his wasn't the greatest need, King thought, as he tapped on the rear-facing hatchway with the point of his saber. Behind him, Ibrahim Khan was alternately calling on Allah and blaspheming, as he followed the *Angrezi* with his *chora* in his hand.

Ignatieff started violently as he noticed King out of the corner of an eye, then snapped the telescope shut. He tried to shout through the thick armor glass, and when that obviously didn't work cracked the hatchway open a hair, ready to snatch it back if the other man made a grab for it.

"Greetings, Captain King!" the Russian said jovially. "No doubt you think it fitting for me to come out there, and perish miserably under your good heroic sword! *Spacebo*, but I beg to differ."

"If you're such a mighty warrior for the Black God, why don't you come out and fight?" King called, trying to put as much taunting mockery into the question as he could to no avail.

Oh. Perhaps I was a little hasty in my assumption that he could be goaded, King thought, in the privacy of his mind.

Something of that must have shown on his face; not much, but the Russian was a skilled observer. His laughter was quiet, and in another circumstance might have been charming.

"If you are such a hero, why don't you *make* me come out?" he called blandly, under the rush of the slipstream. Another chuckle, and he went on:

"But forgive me—I was looking for the greeting party I have arranged on yonder coast, to meet you and your Emperor, and to convey me home to Samarkand. When the bodies of your ruler and all the rest of the airship's passengers are discovered, I don't doubt the popular wrath against the Caliphate and Dai-Nippon—not to mention the xenophobic elements in France-outre-mer, also implicated—will be . . . extreme. And meanwhile, there are certain experiments I wish to perform with your sister. As a scientist, I'm sure she will appreciate—"

He roared laughter at King's aborted lunge; hacking through the bubble would be only marginally more practical than chopping through steel.

"Haven't you realized who rules *this* world yet, *Angrezi* hero?" he mocked. "Who else could it be?"

There was nothing of humanity left in the sound his throat made now, a howl of mirth that remained wholly alien even when he modulated it into words.

"I thank thee, Tchernobog, for thy gift of my enemy's pain. I feel their pain, finer than the sweetest of wine on the tongue!"

The thirty-five pounds of guncotton wrapped around Captain Pienaar's belly exploded almost precisely two hundred feet beneath the feet of the men atop the dirigible. Most of that blast went out through the line of least resistance, as the great curving glass windows of the gondola's control bridge shattered. Enough was left to make the whole massive structure flex and buck in midair, driving the nose up until it almost stood on its tail for an instant, then diving forward like a porpoise. The ceiling of the bridge turned into shrapnel, shredding the guest cabins and the courtiers still there. Vents along the keel twisted open, spewing liquid, as the electric controls shorted out and the pneumatic lines lost pressure.

Athelstane King had been moving backward. He heard a despairing yell behind him as the Pathan was flung free of the surface.

His own left hand shot out and slapped on an aluminum ring, clinging with enormous desperate force as he was wrenched, twisted, and slapped back down on the metal walkway hard enough to make his ribs creak and his head ring from the blow his chin had taken.

When he came fully back to himself the *Garuda* was shooting skyward, fast enough that his breath came quick; then vents opened all along the upper keel to release lifting hydrogen—an automatic response from pressure gauges. He couldn't see the gas that roared out, but he could smell it; airship hydrogen was deliberately contaminated with a little sulfur-rich methane, to make detecting leaks easier. He coughed at the stink, chest laboring in the thin air of the heights. But their ascent slowed, for which he was thankful; it had seemed they were going to bounce right up to the moon.

Count Ignatieff had been nearly as lucky as his enemy. The wave of pressure catapulted him forward, but his grip on the handle of the hatchway was already strong and ready. That did not prevent him being flipped out onto the outer hull of the *Garuda*, yet it held him safe until the light metal crumpled and gave way beneath his hand; long enough for the bucking plunge to end, although that was a long moment—nothing eight hundred fifty feet long and many tons in weight could whipcrack swiftly.

Then he slid over the curved surface, hands scrabbling. The ring he seized was not far from King's, and it was the Lancer officer's turn to yell laughter. They swung like pendulum bobs, close enough that Athelstane's wild slash could almost connect. The slack look left Ignatieff's face at that, and since he had both hands free to grip he was able to come to his feet before his enemy—just long enough to draw his saber and face the Lancer.

"So," he snarled, as the motion beneath them died down to a mere tossing. "The Peacock Angel has his joke with us both. It will be you and I, it seems—but His wings will bear me up!"

King's lips peeled back from his teeth. His whole left arm burned from the wrenching it had taken saving his life, and there was a slight blurriness to his vision and a fierce ache in his head. None of that mattered as he closed in for the kill. There would be no fancy footwork here; that was an invitation to go over the side. It would be strength and speed against strength and speed—whether his injuries would be enough to balance his youth and reach. He drew back his blade for the first cut, and Ignatieff's rose to meet it.

Krishna, but he's strong, King thought, as the swords met.

The blades flashed again and again, an unmusical *kring-skrang!* of steel on steel. It was barbarian-style swordplay, not scientific; drunken barbarians at that, because the hull was still pitching and rolling with a slow majesty that sent both men staggering and lurching. One such sent King into the path of Ignatieff's saber, just close enough that the tip of the blade touched the skin over his eyes. Blood poured down from the shallow cut, half-blinding him, stinging.

Ignatieff shouted laughter. "Shall I wait for you to bandage that?" he called. "Shall I be a *sportsman* about it, *Anglichani?*"

He drove King toward the stern with a stamping thrust that made the Lancer shuffle back with a quick foot-to-foot, and almost killed him as his heel skidded off the walkway onto the slick-slippery surface of the hull. King saved himself with a desperate, convulsive leap. Half-blind, he used a trick Ranjit Singh had taught him, something the Sikh had picked up from Eric King and said was an old family legend of the squires of Rexin—whipping his sword in a frantic Maltese cross in front of himself, down and up and over and back diagonally.

It created an impenetrable shield, for the thirty seconds or so you could keep it up before your arm went leaden from fatigue. He used the time to scrub his left sleeve across his eyes, then held it to his forehead to staunch the flow of blood. *Not the best position for sword work,* he thought, and snarled aloud:

"Bugger sportsmanship and sod you!"

For a long moment they stood; the airship was stabilizing, and their sabers just crossed at the point. Ignatieff lunged again, and King beat it aside; again, and again. The Russian's eyes narrowed; his opponent was fighting in a purely defensive style, apart from refusing to give ground, and darting glances to Ignatieff's right and rear.

Mustn't let him suspect, King thought.

"Look behind you," he called, whipping a backhand cut at the Russian. Ignatieff caught it easily, grunting a laugh as the swords locked.

"Look behind you, you stupid sodding cannibal!"

"The oldest trick in the world!" Ignatieff sneered.

"What trick?" King answered, and laughed. The sound was as cold as the Russian's voice.

He was still laughing as Ibrahim Khan rose up the curve of the airship's hull behind Ignatieff, anchored by the dagger he'd driven through the tough multi-ply cotton. His other hand swung the *chora*. Ignatieff sensed it at the last instant and made one last desperate leap. None of his tiger speed had deserted him, and the tip only creased the skin of his left leg, instead of slicing his Achilles tendon as the Afghan intended. That still left him off-balance for the better part of two seconds. For swordsmen at their level, that was an eternity.

King needed no thought for the lunge that extended him forward, knee deep-bent and left leg behind him, the flat of his blade turned parallel to the ground with a twist of the wrist, so that it would not catch on ribs. For one long instant they stood frozen, the Russian looking down incredulously at the blade that drew a silver curve through his body just below the breastbone, and then he toppled backward. King's fingers released the sword hilt, and Ignatieff's body thumped on the drum-taut hull of the *Garuda*, slithered away, gathered speed, twisted for a second as the blade caught in the cloth, then flew free trailing a long scream.

Down toward the waiting horsemen his telescope had sought in vain, flailing the air for two thousand feet of greeting before he landed and spattered before their feet.

No wings after all, King thought, in a single moment of exultation. *Peacock, Angelic, or otherwise. Take that for Hasamurti, you filthy sod, and for my father, and for Ranjit Singh, and for Yasmini—for all of us.*

Then he threw himself flat and hooked his feet into a loop, letting himself slide down and extending a hand to Ibrahim Khan. The Afghan thriftily took a second to clamp his Khyber knife between his teeth and grasped the *Angrezi's* hand in one nearly as strong, using the other man's arm as a lever to swing himself up. When they were both on the flat pathway and hanging on to a metal loop of their own, he turned his face to the officer of the Peshawar Lancers.

"Forget not the two hundred gold *mohurs*," he said. "Or the horse—the food you provide has been scanty of late!"

Yasmini strained until red throbbed before her eyes and her breath rasped in her throat. It was no use; she could see strand after strand of the silk part; perhaps her efforts were merely making things worse, but she *would not stop*—

The universe kicked her, but still she strained, her small booted feet against the railing and her body arched back. She was not aware of the airship's lurch and roll, only of the weight on the end of the improvised rope. It flung upward and back, pivoting her and being pivoted on the fulcrum of her immovable self. When the two saris parted at the weak point chafed by the shards of glass, she tumbled backward utterly spent, every muscle in her tiny compact body slack. All she could do was lie and watch, as the princess and Athelstane's sister tumbled in and lay sprawled together on the floor of the observation deck, identical expressions of stunned bewilderment on their faces.

It is not easy to face death, and then be spared—even for the brave, she thought. *As I know better than any living. For did I not die a thousand times?*

Chapter Twenty=three

assandra King cleared her throat. She sat facing the head of the airship; the end of the observation gallery should have been there. Much of it was missing, and she could look up through the shattered upper deck to the interior of the hull. The gasbag there was notably sagging as the ship drifted nose-down. Every few seconds some bit of dangling wreckage would twist free and fall away downward, toward the rugged hills—or low mountains—below. They were at seven thousand feet above sea level, but much less than that above the ground; the December air was bitterly cold and dry enough to make your sinuses crackle.

They'd seen nomad camps already, black butterfly-shaped tents of goat hair, herds of sheep, men who pointed upward—and sometimes fired *jezails* at the obviously crippled *Angrezi* ship of the air. They passed over fallow fields, leafless trees, flat-roofed stone villages where every house was a fort and thin curls of smoke wound upward. Word would be spreading, as fast as hard-driven horses could go.

"We have seven severely wounded," Cassandra said; all the more senior survivors were grouped in a circle focused on Charles.

"The badly wounded are mostly from the court officials and the Guard officers who were forward when the explosion went off," she continued. "Most of them didn't make it, and those who did . . . I'm afraid a few of them will die, too: The court physician did. There are fifteen surviving members of the Foot Guards platoon, not including their officer—he was last out when your father gave the order to retreat, and the blast got him. Almost all of the airship crew are dead—the mutineers killed them in their bunks, apart from a few servants. Twenty-eight people fit to walk, altogether. And the mutineers are all dead as well."

Charles nodded grimly. "And the *Garuda*?" he said; she was the closest thing they had to a technical expert, and she supposed he wanted confirmation of his own survey, to let the others know their position.

"The bridge controls are gone. You managed to get us on a rough northeastward course when you went aft to crank the rudders before we had to shut the engines down, and the wind's aiding us now. Six of the engines are still functional, but almost all the fuel is gone, and with the ship at this attitude using them would drive us downward."

He nodded again and spoke himself. "As nearly as I and Dr. King can calculate, we're somewhere in south-central Afghanistan. *Over* south-central Afghanistan, that is. From there we can expect to drift northward."

Cassandra winced slightly; that was better than being airshipwrecked over Russia, but only just. There was one ray of hope, though . . .

"I *think* the transmitter part of the wireless was working before we ran the batteries down," Cassandra said. "We were able to keep sending—if we *were* sending, my repairs were by guess and by God—for many hours. The stations in Peshawar and Karachi would have been able to triangulate a location for us. A course, too."

Her heart went out to Charles; his face was seamed with more than the pain of a shoulder broken when the explosion pistoned him down the corridor into Narayan Singh—that had saved his life, that and the Sikh's presence of mind. Grief for his father was there, and more, the weight of responsibility. His kingdom might be only twenty-odd souls at that moment, but it was his, and the *rajadharma* of guiding and protecting. She leaned closer, willing comfort to flow through the fleeting contact of their bodies.

"Could it be intercepted?" he asked, head swiveling to take in all his advisors.

Warburton shook his head. "Probably not. The nearest Caliphate and Dai-Nipponese stations are too far away. Possibly by the Russians—possibly by Russian agents in Afghanistan, though that's a very long shot. What really worries me is Afghans with telescopes."

The others grouped around the young King-Emperor on the observation deck squatted or sat, exhaustion plain on their faces, all of them ragged and drawn, many bandaged. The air carried a scent of dry dust and powdered snow. Mountains floated to the north, white-tipped fangs glinting at heaven.

"*Hendu Kosh*," Ibrahim Khan said, pointing. "Hindu Kush—Killer-of-Hindus. We are not far from my own tribe's lands."

"And not *all* that far from the border," Athelstane King said.

He was lying back on his cushion, while Yasmini changed the bandage around his head. He smiled at her while she worked, although the alcohol—a fine brandy from the pantry—must have stung like fire. Every once in a while he would work the fingers of his right hand, the sword hand, and smile a bit more broadly.

Men! Cassandra thought, with a familiar mix of irritation and affection for her brother.

He killed Ignatieff, and that means everything will come out right, somehow. Males are as silly as rams in rutting season about things like that.

She was heartily glad the Russian was dead, and pleased that Athelstane had done it; but that meant absolutely nothing in their *present* emergency. Servants came in, bearing food—the kitchens were still working, thank the merciful Gods. Cassandra started wolfing down a fiery chicken Marsala, scooping up sauce and rice with pieces of naan; nobody was standing on ceremony now. Henri came in a second later, a rifle over his back and binoculars hanging on his chest. Everyone looked up; he was on sentry-go in the rear observation bubble.

"Aircraft approaching, from the northwest, two." he said. "Two kilometers—a mile and a little. *Merde alors*, I do not like the look of them."

Everyone who could got up and walked over to the portside gallery. Cassandra felt an irrational stab of hope—could it be Imperial airships out searching? That died as the vessels came into view, growing from dots against the blue mountain-fringed sky into tiny model shapes and then silently onrushing sky-sharks. They were four-tenths the length of the *Garuda*, but only a fraction of the breadth, and they were pure blimps, without any internal stiffening save gas pressure. A crisscross net of ropes confined their gaudily painted envelopes, the fabric bulging out between in a diamond pattern like a fat man's flesh between his buttons. The gondolas that hung below—each with a single engine driving a propeller at the rear—were mere copies in wicker and canvas of a Persian Gulf *dhow*, the lateen-rigged craft used for trade—and slaving and piracy.

And I doubt they can do more than forty miles an hour at most, Cassandra thought. *Or travel more than a few hundred miles. Which is forty miles an hour and several hundred miles more than we can do right now.*

Some watchman on a mountaintop had seen them, and flashed signals from height to height with mirrors to the nest of the chief who commanded those blimps. He'd come to see if the wreck was as helpless as reported . . . which, unfortunately, it was. Without fuel or controls or ballast to spare, *Garuda* was a free balloon—and that only as long as it took the remaining leaking gas cells to empty. They had thrown out everything they could, and hacked away bits of the hull, but the inexorable descent continued; or perhaps it was the hills of Afghanistan rising to meet them like a fanged mouth.

Ibrahim Khan spat out into space, studied the heraldry on the blimps, and turned his face to Athelstane King: "Hazaras," he said. "And Durranni Pathans. Jackals—even the Emir has no use for them."

The ship-shaped gondolas of the Afghan craft were packed with men, a hundred or more of them together. As they closed she could hear them hooting and yelling, waving weapons; one near the wheel of the forward blimp was looking at the wreck of the *Garuda* through a long brass telescope.

"See them off," Charles said sharply.

Warburton spoke, reluctantly: "Ransom, Your Majesty. For the good of the realm—"

"No."

The word was not loud, but the Political Service Officer fell silent and bowed his head slightly.

Cassandra felt herself heave a tiny, guilty sigh of relief. Capture by Afghans was a grisly enough fate for a man. For a woman . . .

The Gurkhas snatched up their rifles; so did the other fit men. They lined the rails and knelt; aiming at one moving target from another was no easy task. A slow crackle of shots began; Cassandra could see men yell on the Afghan blimps, and one or two fall. Both drew back, dwindling with a startling speed, and then came alongside each other, obviously making plans via speaking trumpet and hand signals.

"They could try to fire us," Henri said. "We're leaking badly."

"No," Warburton said. "They want to capture the ship intact. The six undamaged engines are booty beyond price—with those, they could get some real range out of those blimps, and go pirating on a grand scale, as long as they lasted."

"*Merde,*" Henri said, looking at Sita.

She had a rifle, too; she glanced up at him and gave a cheerful thumbs-up, looking a little puzzled when he didn't return her gesture.

The Afghans had obviously come to a decision. One kept station with them while the other curved around behind, coming up on their starboard side, just beyond rifle range. Then both turned toward the wrecked Imperial vessel and dropped sandbags full of ballast, bobbing up out of sight.

"That's torn it," Athelstane said grimly, picking up his rifle. "Better get topside."

"No!" Cassandra said sharply.

He looked at her in surprise. "The gasbags are leaking," she said; the tracing-smell was present, faint but unmistakable. "Hydrogen leaks *up*. The upper part of the hull is full of an air-hydrogen mixture, and so is the air right above it. If you start shooting off guns up there, it won't just burn, it'll *explode*."

He gave an exasperated snarl, and nodded. "Sir?" he asked the King-Emperor.

"You're in tactical command," Charles said.

"All right, Your Majesty. You handle things here; they can't get close to the gondola, because of the overhang of the hull, and you can shoot down here. Henri, you take the rear half of the upper hull. I'll take the forward; cold steel only—they may try to board." He raised his voice slightly. "Half with the vicomte, half with me. Unwounded men only. You, you, you—" His finger flicked from man to man.

"Not the Afghan," Charles said quietly. "I have another mission for him, and Sir Manfred. There will be search parties beating the ground all along the Border; someone has to make contact with them."

Athelstane nodded curtly. "Be careful, sir—some boarders may get past us through the hull."

The two parties dashed off, feet pounding on the incongruously festive delicacy of the spiral staircase, shouts tailing off as the two commanders organized them even as they clambered up into the hull.

"Sir Manfred," Charles said quietly. "We must assume that a relief force is on its way." A slight, wry twist of the lips. "Because otherwise we are doomed. Many relief forces, by land and air; but even the Empire's resources are not unlimited. You . . . and Ibrahim Khan here . . . will parachute out now. Make your way eastward; the Border can't be far. Promise whatever is necessary in the way of subsidies and gifts to any natives you encounter; find the nearest relief column, and guide it."

"Yes, Your Majesty," Warburton said, eyeing Ibrahim Khan and obviously calculating if the Pathan would cut his throat the minute they touched ground. "And you, Your Majesty?"

"We will"—a real smile this time—"find the best possible place to crash, and attempt to hold out until relieved."

He shook both men's hands as they left; Ibrahim Khan seemed a little surprised. Then the King-Emperor turned to his ragged followers:

"Everyone who can shoot to the gallery rails. The rest of you, follow me. We're going to put together bundles of what we'll need. Ammunition, food, water, medical supplies—everything in portable bundles. And stretchers for the wounded—"

Cassandra's heart beat a little harder with pride as she rose to obey. Perhaps they would die soon, but at least they wouldn't do it sitting and weeping over their fate. Not with Charles leading them.

Daffadar Narayan Singh grinned as he lay crouched in the stuffy, bad-smelling dimness, clutching at the silken rope netting that confined the gas cell. It arched away from him on either side, like a temple dome for size, with the four men of the section under his command at half-seen intervals. From outside came shouts, muffled by the fabric of the hull; those of his folk, and then the wolfish yelping of the Afghans, a sound he knew of old. For an instant he wondered what Ibrahim Khan was doing, and then there came a massive *thunk-twuuung* sound. Fifty feet away from him light flashed as the barbs of a harpoon sliced through the hull and plunged into one of the spiral girders that stretched from stern to prow of the *Garuda*, or had before the explosion.

He was closest. The Sikh scrambled across the billowy, resilient surface of the cell, his bare feet seeking out the knotted rests on the outside of the netting that were supposed to help riggers crawling about patching holes. Sweat soaked his beard despite the chill of altitude; if he misstepped, his body would probably plunge right through the hull fabric a hundred fifty feet down, and then all the way down below that. He made himself move with careful speed, hands clamping and releasing like mechanical grabs. The harpoon shaft was five feet long, and proved to be deeply embedded in a laminate girder. No time to hack it free, and no use going for the shaft or the line anchored to it; both were wound with iron wire to prevent exactly that.

Instead he waited, out of sight through the hole the harpoon gun had made, drawing the saber he wore slung across his back. The cable running back to the Afghan gondola was taut. Soon . . .

Yes. A yell, and a whirring, rasping sound. Two dirty bare feet landed on the hull on either side of the rent in the fabric.

"*Rung ho!*" the Sikh shouted, and lunged from his crouch.

He felt the point go home in meat, grate on bone—with luck, he thought vindictively, in the Afghan's diseased private parts.

Rotten with a pox caught from his sister, Narayan thought, and wrenched it free while the man twisted and thrashed about, shrieking like a woman in childbirth.

The wounded man's body would give him cover. He slit open more of the hull covering and leaned out. From here he could see the Afghan dangling from some sort of harness arrangement on the line, and more of them at intervals up the long slanting curve of the cable, back to the jagged black and scarlet of the dhow-shaped car of their airship. They screamed curses, thin through the high air, and waved weapons.

Narayan made a broad mocking salute, then edged out with one hand clamped strongly to the cable. As he hacked at the tough hemp, he could see two parachutes gliding in to a landing on the rough ground far below.

"Good luck, Warburton *sahib,*" he grunted, hacking at the tough hemp. "And even to you, child of misbelief—provided you keep faith."

The Afghan yells turned to fear and frustrated fury as the cable parted; the Sikh laughed as he watched it whipcrack away. The reaver airship bobbed upward, and two figures—the man he'd wounded and the one above him—detached from the line to windmill downward to the hard rocky soil. One blossomed out in a parachute of its own, and he cursed as he clambered back into the hull of the *Garuda.*

"And bad luck to you, misbelieving, sister-fucking son of a whore!"

"Here, *Daffadar!*" came a shout; faint from the other side of the gas cell. "They come!"

In Nepali-accented Hindi, followed with a cry of *Ayo Gorkhali!*

Narayan Singh sheathed the saber and began to leopard-crawl rapidly upward, over the curve of the gasbag. He was still grinning.

If he lived through this, he'd have a tale to tell the *pitaji* indeed. And as his father had taught him, while a warrior Sikh was always glad to fulfill his *karman* as a soldier, doing it where your superiors could see your faith and skill was doubly fruitful. Under the eye of a padishah, he supposed, would be the most fruitful of all.

"*Mort de ma vie!*" Henri de Vascogne wheezed.

Another Afghan whirled down the cable just behind the sternward observation post. The Frenchman pushed open the door of the bubble, leapt out, and skidded forward; his own feet were bare, too, but the fabric was slick at the best of times, and there were patches of blood already. The tribesman seemed unconcerned, balanced easily with a curved dagger in one hand and the ugly cleaverlike *chora* in the other, the points moving in unpleasant counterpoint, ready to hold the base of the cable and harpoon while more of his friends slid down it.

"*Allahu Akhbar!*" he shouted—a war cry Henri was only too familiar with.

"*Chingada tu mère!*" Henri replied; not the first time he'd used that reply either.

He lunged, aiming for the face. The Afghan parried with crossed blades, ready to trap the long saber and then free one weapon for close-in work. The Frenchman knew a better trick than that one; his left foot punched out, toes rolled up, and took the tribesman in the stomach—no chance for a groin kick, with the knee-length robe the other man wore.

"*La savate,*" Henri snarled, as the bearded Muslim doubled over in uncontrollable reflex and dropped his *chora*.

Then he yelled again wordlessly as his feet shot out from under him, unbalanced by the kick, and he began to slip downward. A frantic grab took hold of an edge of the pirate's robe, and Henri hung for a moment with his feet scrabbling on a curve above nothing. Then the

Afghan fell, too; Henri used the moment to drop his useless sword, climbing up the prostrate form of the other man. He seemed to be made all out of gutta-percha and gristle and stale-sweat stink, recovering far too fast and slashing at Henri with the curved dagger as he rolled on top.

The Frenchman caught the wrist with a smack and they strained against each other, the Afghan trying to grind a knee into his opponent's stomach, Henri working to get a decent grip. The hooked point came closer to his eyes, inch by inch.

Something flashed over his head and thunked into the Afghan's skull. His eyes rolled up into his head for a moment, and Henri could feel him weaken. He grabbed his own short blade from its sheath and punched it up into the Afghan's body half a dozen times, then rolled him off. The body slid sideways and away, turning and fluttering in the thin cold air.

Henri turned his head. Sita was lying three-quarters of the way out of the open door of the observation bubble, rifle still gripped by the barrel, eyes wide.

There was no time for questions. "Ax!" Henri screamed, then remembered to do it in English. "Ax! By your foot!"

She snapped out of her daze and bent back for it. Henri grabbed it and turned, pivoting on his backside and hacking at the cable just as another Afghan came down it. It parted on the third stroke and whipped away under the strain of the pirate blimp's weight. He could see the Afghan aircraft turning away and climbing; a quick glance showed the other doing the same.

"What are you doing here?" he asked Sita.

The *kunwari* looked older; certainly more smudge-faced and drawn than he'd seen her before.

"Saving your life—again," she said.

A Gurkha's head popped up into the observation bubble behind her, and he called something in his own uncouth tongue.

"Come on—we're getting too low, Charles says."

Henri looked down; the ground *was* a good deal closer. Up, and the Afghan blimps had shrunk to figures no bigger than a man's thumb.

"I don't suppose they're going away?" Sita said, hopefully but with a tone that said she knew better.

Henri shook his head. "Just waiting for us to come down," he said. "Then they can land and come after us on foot."

Athelstane King walked over from the other bubble. "There's a likely-looking valley not too far ahead," he said. "Good as anything we can reach."

Chapter Twenty=four

"*Chalo!*" Athelstane King called.

The remains of the *Garuda* had come to rest in a wide south-facing valley. To the north the ground humped itself up in rocky hillocks, then rose in real cliffs; dark patches hinted at caves. To the south . . .

His mouth tightened. The two Afghan aircraft had circled in on a broad open patch, well upwind of any possible burning debris from the *Garuda* if the fugitives set the wreck on fire.

Which we will; the engines are intact, and a prize beyond price to the wild men.

His mind shuddered at the thought of the havoc they could wreak with craft capable of raiding far into the defenseless provinces beyond the hard shell of the Imperial frontier. They were looking entirely too competent as it was.

Once safely distant, the Afghans had sent down ground parties along ropes, then used the same ropes to haul their blimps down and stake them out. More men swarmed out of them—not all that many, perhaps a hundred all told. Since the remnants of the *Garuda*'s crew totaled twenty fighting men—counting, for the present, the King-Emperor's sister plus Yasmini and Cassandra—the results couldn't really be in doubt for long.

Perhaps Ignatieff was right, and his Peacock Angel is just toying with us, King thought, weariness surging through his body. *Dangling the carrot of hope in front of us to keep us snapping.*

"*Chalo!*" he shouted again.

Gurkhas and women jumped down—he smiled at Yasmini as she clambered past, three rifles in her arms—and pelted by him, heading for the cliffs, the hale helping the wounded. Others carried stretchers, or bundles of supplies. The remains of the airship bounced a little upward as weight dropped free.

Charles III had been on the edge of jumping; with malignant precision, the wobble pitched him forward into empty space. King knew with angry certainty what would happen, and was rewarded with the sound of a stifled cry of pain; when the young ruler tried to stand, his foot wouldn't support him.

"Sprained," he said. "I can hop, I'll use this rifle as a crutch. Go ahead—"

"Maharaj . . . shut up," King said. "*Chup!*"

Charles smiled and did. King began to lay down the ammuniton box that had been his burden; Narayan Singh dropped from the gallery edge, landed with a grunt and a competent flex of the knees, and trotted over to the ruler of half the globe.

"Maharaj," he said, more respectfully, and stooped to throw the smaller man over his shoulder. He rose easily under the weight, a great bundle of food and medical supplies tucked under his left arm, turned and trotted after the others.

King followed him. "*Bhai,*" he gasped, as they panted up the slope—this was the highlands, and the air was as thin as most of the places the airship had taken them. "Why is it, when I am a captain, I find myself never commanding more than ten or twenty men? It is an offense against my dignity."

"*Sahib,*" the Sikh said, "what worries me is that we are become our fathers—trapped in the Afghan country, waiting for Warburton *sahib* to bring us rescue. That ended not well for *them.*"

"At . . . least . . . we . . . aren't . . . badly wounded," King managed.

"Yet. And *sahib*—save thy breath!"

The first Afghan bullet kicked up dust at King's heels as they dived into the cave; it was actually more of a crevasse, narrowing to a slit above them but never actually closing. The Lancer officer flung himself down, behind the rough rock *sangar* the Gurkhas had already started to build. More rocks clacked and rattled; stones were one thing you were rarely short of, in Afghan country.

He put the Metford to his shoulder, peering through the back-sight; the Afghans were deploying with their usual skill.

You couldn't just call them "Pathan bandits," given the means of transportation. Hmmm. Sky raiders? Air pirates?

Their dirty brown sheepskin jackets and dingy robes disappeared against the rock and stunted bushes and pale dirt of the valley floor as well as Imperial khaki would, or better. King licked dry lips, watching the tribesmen skirmish forward from rock to rock; already some with better rifles would be finding hiding spots within sniping range. The depressing truth of the matter was that this country bred the finest guerrilla-bandit-style fighting men in the world. Russia and the Empire had both tried their hand at invading the place off and on for centuries, and neither had had much joy of it.

Behind him, he could hear Charles's voice, tight with pain, thanking someone.

"You're welcome," King's sister said. "And Charles . . . remember that night at the dance, on the terrace? I'm sorry I told you no. Imperial mistress doesn't look so bad, right now."

Even then, King's eyebrows rose. *Well, well, well!*

Down in the open, the remains of the *Garuda* took flame; a small bird of Agni at first, then breaking out in half a dozen places as fuses burned down, then a great soft *whump* of blue flame as the remaining hydrogen caught. An infuriated chorus of howls came from the Afghans, watching precious loot going up before their eyes. Their yelping cries had held a cruel good nature before—all the Imperials had done was kill some of them.

Now they were *angry*.

The new master of the Lion Throne gave a breathless chuckle as Cassandra eased off his boot. "No. I'm not sorry. The position wasn't worthy of you. Only Queen-Empress would be—and to hell with convention. In Delhi *or* Oxford. And that is my—Our—Imperial will."

Cassandra was silent; King looked back to see her kiss the injured man gently on the lips. "I will never forget that," she said softly.

Then she stood and threw a coil of rope over her shoulder bandoleer-style. He looked a question, and she pointed to the back of the cave slit.

"I can go up that like a rock chimney," she said, tracing the route with a finger. "Then work my way forward—there's a ledge on the front face, nearly over our heads here, it'll give me a good vantage point. The rope is to haul up a rifle and ammunition." Softly: "Don't worry, Charles, Athelstane. They won't take me alive."

King nodded, and again when her eyes sought Sita and Yasmini, and a lady-in-waiting with a broken leg, the only female survivor of the court party—the explosion on the bridge had been worst among the sleeping cabins above it.

King tried not to look as his sister climbed; since that last duel with Ignatieff on the dorsal spine of the airship, he found he minded heights a little more. He watched the Afghans instead; they were being very cautious.

A Gurkha licked his thumb, wet the fore-sight of his rifle, aimed, fired. An enemy tribesmen pitched over and began crawling slowly toward cover, leaking, while all his friends and relatives disappeared into the landscape.

"And they're right to be cautious," he muttered, waiting. A few seconds later he saw a flash of movement and snap-shot, swung the rifle and fired again, again.

Narayan Singh came up with a large rock, slung it from behind cover, then crawled forward to push it into the breastwork with his feet.

"They will come in full dark, after moonset," he said, settling in on King's left. "Ah, good—the *sangar* will be chest-high, soon. I shoot better kneeling than prone."

Yasmini leopard-crawled up on his other side, dragging a cloth wrapped around cartridges. King pulled back the bolt of his rifle and thumbed rounds down into the magazine; a Metford held eight .40 in the box and one in the chamber. After that it was nearly as quick to load individually, if you were lying flat like this with loose rounds to hand. Idly, he wondered if there wasn't some faster way. Yasmini smiled at him, and he forgot weapons specifications for a moment.

"That is what the Tuareg would do," Henri said. "Keep us pinned down, then come in the night."

He was a little distance away, leaning back against a cave wall with his rifle between his knees, chewing from one of a selection of pastries someone had thrown into a sack. Whimsically, it occurred to King that they were probably going to be the best-fed isolated garrison in history, with food taken from the pantries of an Imperial yacht. There were even a couple of bottles of brandy; useful medicine, as well as nice to have around for a swallow or two when it got *really* cold, which it would shortly, after sundown. Winter in this country was no joke, even by Kashmiri standards. He frowned at the thin gauzy garments of the women, glad his sister had thought to take a few blankets up with her.

King turned on his back to study the defensive arrangements instead. No way to come over the cliff at them—it had an overhang that curled like a frozen stone wave. More cover than was comfortable in front of them, and that would be a problem in the dark; they'd have to have half the men awake, and watch them like hawks—thank Krishna the moon was nearly full.

But—

"How long . . . can we hold out?" Charles asked.

King nodded at him with sober respect; Warburton had described what he'd gone through in the corridor. He knew it took more courage than *he* had to obey an order like that, and from his own father. All of the Gurkhas would have died, if Charles hadn't ordered them out of the area above the bridge and refused to go in himself.

"Well, Maharaj, it all depends on—"

Two of the guardsmen came back from their examination of the back part of the cleft. Narayan Singh went back with them, and returned himself.

"No, *sahib*," he said.

At the motion of King's eyes, the Sikh turned to Charles, smiling in the dimness and making the salaam.

"Maharaj, as for weapons and ammunition, we could hold them for many days, provided they don't overrun us tonight. This position is strong, and these Gurkhas might almost be Sikhs as fighting men. But we have no water here, only what is in our canteens, and these *banchuts* of Afghans know it, while they have their store of water and all food and supplies from their airships; also there may be wells near here. They will wait for thirst to do their work for them—they wish to paddle their paws in our goods, not shed their blood. They will wait, and test us, and then when we are weakened, and it is very dark—"

The massive shoulders shrugged. "We will not be an easy nut to crack, Maharaj. They will remember the price of their loot."

A silence fell on the chamber then, broken only by an occasional moan from the wounded, and the clatter of rocks as the *jawans* of the Guard built up the *sangar* in front of them. A murmur of voices caught King's attention after a while; Henri and Sita, sitting close. Then he blinked surprise; she swung one of her injured hands in an open-palmed slap across his face. He made no attempt to dodge the blow, merely turning his head and seizing her wrist.

"*Chérie*, you will hurt your hand," he said, gazing up into her wrathful face. "And why are you so angry? Because I did not tell you earlier who I really was?"

"No, because you think I'm an idiot! I figured out who you really were within a *week*!"

With that she collapsed against his chest, sobbing; he cradled her against himself, whistling a jaunty-sounding song. King felt pieces connect in his head, like a rusty clock mechanism.

Oh, he thought, stroking Yasmini's hair where she lay beside him. *Well, the* kunwari *may not be an idiot, but I am. Then again, she had more motivation and more time around the "vicomte." No wonder she wasn't kicking up a fuss the way Cass says she did at first.*

Mind you, the whole question had become rather moot now.

Yasmini put her rifle into position, carefully adjusting the rocks, then handed him a chapati smeared with some sort of meat paste. It was excellent, but salty; he took a small, careful sip of water afterward, holding it in his mouth until it had leached the salt off his tongue before swallowing.

"Well," he said, looking over at those astonishing blue-green eyes. "Since everyone else is making declarations—"

"Oh, that is no matter," Yasmini said. "I knew you would ask me to be your woman . . . wife, you say."

"You did?" He blinked. "You mean you can still, ah . . ."

"No. But I have watched *you* in dreams many times, and I have come to know you a little in the flesh." She gave an impish smile. "Better than I know any other man."

Cassandra King came awake. She felt chilled, though no worse than she often had before on an overnight climbing trip. For a moment, she wondered where she was—why was she sleeping sitting up in a narrow ledge, with blankets around her, rather than in a proper mountaineer's bedroll?

The sound came again. It was hard to pick out among the soughing of the cold wind through the cleft in the rock beside her, and the small noises of the mountain night; also, her face was numb. Only long experience told her; it was the rasp of a rope running through fingers and over cloth. Someone coming down a rope with a half hitch around one leg, at a guess.

Sleep blinked out of her mind in a rush of cold fear at the thought of an Afghan here in this narrow space of stone with her. She jerked up the rifle and rolled onto her back and fired, heedless of the danger of a ricochet.

Crack, and she frantically ripped back the bolt of the Metford and slapped it forward.

The recoil punished her shoulder, trapped against the stone beneath, but the bright stab of light showed her the dark figure just above, coming down a rope that hung from the overhang far above. Steel glinted in his hand as he dropped the remaining distance, landing astride her own feet and lunging forward with a hand reaching for her face. Automatic reflex brought the rifle down toward him, and she jerked the trigger. This time the weapon wasn't at her shoulder at all, but between arm and flank; that didn't matter, since he struck the muzzle with his chest.

The bullet punched through his breastbone and out through his shattered spine, and he fell straight down; blood and fragments spattered across her torso and into her face, horribly salty. Only the leverage of the rifle swung the body sideways instead of straight down on her; it landed beside her on the very lip of the ledge, open eyes staring into hers from six inches away, blood running down into his beard. Then it toppled over, down into the area behind the *sangar*.

Voices were already shouting there. Cassandra reloaded with shaking fingers, trying to look upward to the cliff top and down and out over the stretch toward the besieger's campfires at the same time.

"Oh, bugger," she whispered.

The lumpy rugged ground before the *sangar* wall was coming alive with dimly seen figures. But none of them clear enough for a decent shot—she was an occasional hunter, not a soldier—

From below her, she heard her brother's voice yell out—oddly enough, something like: *"Thank you, David bar-Elias!"*

Then a sputtering spot of light sprang into being, out among the attackers.

Magnesium, she thought, dazed, recognizing the peculiar brilliance from the laboratory. *But what could magnesium be doing here?*

That didn't stop the way her hands swung the Metford around to line up on the backlit figures.

Crack.

"*Thank you, David bar-Elias!*" King shouted, snapping the bundle down on the rock before him and half-rising to give it a cricket bowler's overarm throw. "*And thank you, Cass!*"

Even with Border service he was shocked at how close the Afghans had gotten. They seemed to freeze for a moment as the light revealed them, then charged in a wave. *Jezails* stuttered at the Imperials, lead slugs whickering by or peening off the rocks of the *sangar*, or caroming away in deadly-dangerous ricochets down the cleft cave behind him.

King snap-shot, his second finger on the trigger and the index beneath the Metford's bolt. Shoot, flip the bolt up with your finger, slap it home with your palm, repeat. He had time to thrust one rifle behind him and snatch another and empty it—the surviving servants from the air yacht were loading and passing the extra rifles forward. The Afghans must be taking gruesome losses, caught packed together in the narrow space before the cliff-cleft.

"*Allahu Akbar!*" from a hundred throats, like the yelping of wolves.

Then the Afghans were on them, dark shapes looming through a fogbank of powder smoke turned opalescent by the juddering light of the flare. King clubbed his rifle as the first flung himself up the rough surface of the *sangar*, smashing the man's knees with a sweeping stroke, then breaking the stock as he brought the butt down on his head. The body toppled backward, giving him time to draw sword and revolver; beside him Narayan Singh sank his bayonet through the sheepskin-clad belly of an Afghan and slung him completely over his back with a pitchfork motion, like a countryman throwing hay.

"*Rung ho! Wa Guru-ji ko futteh!*" and "*Ayo Gorkhali!*" rang out over the Afghan shrieks and the cries of the wounded, the clang of blade on blade, the grunts of men in desperate effort.

King caught a *tulwar* on his, shot the man in the chest with the pistol in his left hand, turned and cut down another who was stumbling and yelping—Yasmini was very sensibly staying below the lip of the rough stone wall, slicing at ankles and calves with her dagger as they loomed above. For a moment there was an enormous noise and confusion among the huge leaping shadows, and then like a storm wave recoiling from a beach the Afghans were in retreat, dragging their wounded with them. The flare was dying down, but King saw two more fall as they fled, and heard a steady methodical fire from above.

"*Shabash*, Cass!" he called up. "Are you all right?"

Her voice answered him: "I'm not hurt, but I'm . . . feeling rather ill."

"Don't worry," he said. "That always happens, until you're used to it."

"I have no desire to become used to this!"

King snorted softly to himself and shook his head. *Women*, he thought.

"*Shabash*, Cassandra!" another voice said.

Sounding right royal, King thought with amused admiration, as he turned to look at Charles III. With a broken left shoulder and his right ankle not functioning, the King-Emperor wasn't in much shape to fight. There was nothing wrong with his eyesight, though. *Or his judgment. We'd have been hard-pressed without Cass up there.*

A servant offered the monarch a skin of water. "Take it to the soldiers," he said softly, and then: "That's an order!"

Narayan Singh nudged him softly as they took a careful mouthful and passed it on down the line. "Under the very eyes, eh, *sahib*?"

"Careerist," King chuckled.

Worry ran underneath the humor. Two of the Gurkhas were dead, and another wounded. He had two more of the flares, no more; they wouldn't come again tonight, but . . .

"Any chance of their giving up?" Charles said, sounding unhopeful.

"Not a prayer, Your Majesty," King said.

"Charles or sir will do, Captain King, under the circumstances. And we *are* going to be brothers-in-law."

"Sir," King said, a little flustered. *By Krishna, we are, if we live, and isn't that a strange thought.* Yasmini grinned at him; well, stranger things had happened to him, lately.

He went on: "No, sir, not this breed. Now they've got their blood up and they'll be *really* angry."

Charles shrugged, his eyes going up to where Cassandra waited on her ledge. "Damn, but I wish I could climb," he said. "One of the things we have in common . . . We'll just have to count on Sir Manfred and your man Ibrahim, won't we?"

Narayan Singh winced.

King woke to the sound of gunfire. He winced, as the noise drove needles into his ears, awakening the savage headache of dyhydration. And the shots were coming from the ledge above where Cass had her perch . . .

He blinked crusted eyes. The bodies outside the *sangar* were bloating already. Could the Afghans be trying again in daylight? He felt a stab of savage pain in his leg as he moved; a *chora*-wound on the third night . . . or had it been the fourth?

He looked up, craning his neck dangerously close to exposure. Cass *was* shooting, but up in the air—not trying to hit anything. That jarred him awake, awake enough to hear her croaking between shots.

Of course, he thought, the words crawling through his mind. "Can't talk."

His own voice was nightjar hoarse. He picked up his binoculars and looked down the valley. The Afghans *were* moving! But not forward; they were running back toward their blimps, tugging at ropes tied around boulders and deep-driven stakes. His desiccated brain took in the information, but refused to process it. It was not until the first blimp slumped and then broke into blue flame under a stutter of machine-gun fire that he recognized what had happened; not until he heard the bugle blowing *charge* that he accepted it. Even then, he was too worn to cheer, or do more than shake Yasmini awake.

The Afghans were running, *away* from their burning blimps this time, scattering like quail. Through the smoke of the blimps and the blacker, lower soot of the burning brushwood shelters they'd thrown up came the ordered glitter of lance points, pennants; then the tossing heads of the horses and the khaki turbans. Another bugle call and the trot built up to a gallop; even at this distance he could hear the drumming thunder of the hooves like a humming deep in the earth. The points fell in a rippling wave, and the Peshawar Lancers passed through the loose formation of their foes like a plow coulter through soft earth. Then they were turning, some shaking aside broken lance shafts and drawing their sabers; others let the lances pivot at the balance to drag them free of bodies.

"Slaughter the brutes!" King called in a croak, adding his voice to the other survivors.

Narayan Singh was dancing like a bear, yelling wordlessly, half delight and half aching frustration at missing the all-too-rare chance of a massed charge against Pathans caught in the open with nowhere to hide. His regiment was giving another demonstration of a military lesson three thousand years old: To run away from a lancer is death.

The second pass was more like pigsticking, clumps and pairs of horsemen wheeling and scattering over the rolling plain as the enemy turned at bay or tried to burrow behind rocks and bushes, or in a very few instances called for quarter—but cavalry gives no quarter, and the lances drove down again.

The thought of rescue slid through his mind, like a cold drink of water—very much like a cold drink of water, and he found himself imagining a canteen with a longing like a yogi's for nirvana.

All of them were standing outside the *sangar*-wall when the party of riders trotted up from the valley where twin pyres burned to mark the graves of the Afghan blimps. King saluted as Colonel Claiborne drew rein and growled, taking in his filthy, tattered Guardsman's outfit:

"Not in proper uniform, *and* absent without leave, dammit."

Then his eyes fell on the shorter figure, helped along with an arm over Narayan Singh's shoulder and the other strapped to his chest. All humor left his face: He pressed palms together and salaamed from the saddle.

"Maharaj," he said formally. "I kiss feet. And thank the ten thousand faces of God we were in time."

"Colonel, I'm more inclined to kiss yours," Charles III said.

He looked at the well-dressed Afghan princeling riding beside Claiborne, at Warburton beside him, and the twoscore weapon-bristling *badmashes* behind them both, grinning from their saddles at the *gora-log*, some showing the marks of recent hard fighting.

"And who is this—"

King's surprise pushed aside propriety. "Ibrahim Khan!" he exclaimed.

The ragged Borderer was resplendent now in a knee-length coat of striped silk, billowing white trousers of the same, and soft black knee boots. His horse was not groomed to a shine, but it would have brought approving looks in most of the Empire; and now his *pugaree* was wound about the base of a polished spired steel helm with a neck guard of silvered chain mail.

"I told you my father was a *malik, gora-log,*" Ibrahim said. "Bismillah! It is not my fault if you thought he was chief of one village, rather than twelve . . . and a strong hill fort with a town at its feet. If ever you come in peace to the Tirah country, my house is yours—and if you come in war, be ready for an even warmer reception. But in any case, forget not to send my two hundred *mohurs,* and my horse!"

"I will," King said steadily. "If ever you cross the Border again in peace, a place at my board awaits. And if you come raiding, a rope and a gallows!"

The Afghan chuckled. "If you can catch me!"

Then his eyes sought Narayan Singh. "And now I have saved thy Padishah, idolater. Does that not show how all things are accomplished by the will of Allah?"

Narayan Singh straightened as troopers rushed forward to support the monarch and relieve him of the weight; Charles watched the exchange in silence, but with bright-eyed interest.

"Saving the Padishah is an honor we share, child of misbelief," the Sikh said. "And that is not strange at all—for we both be fighting men, you and I."

Ibrahim eyed the corpses lying shot or hacked before the *sangar* and nodded, slowly; his eyes met King's, and he rode closer, smiling that mocking smile as he offered his hand. Both men shook it.

"Go with God," the Afghan said to the man who had been his lord for a few brief months. "I am not sorry to have fought at thy side." He looked at Yasmini. "May Allah give you many sons . . . and no daughters such as this at all!"

He turned his horse aside to let the doctor of the Peshawar Lancers through, then spurred away with his fighting tail behind him, riding in an effortless torrent down the rocky slopes.

King smiled himself at the brave show, and then again as he recognized the military surgeon; it was the same Reserve "*yoni*-doctor" who had treated his arm four months before. The physician stared in appalled wonder at the work ahead of him, then darted forward, ignoring the King-Emperor for the more seriously wounded behind him and calling for his assistants and their supplies.

Charles glanced after him. "I like that chap's priorities," he said.

His face sobered, as he looked at what awaited the healer. All the drugs and bandages in the world could not repair what lay there, for some.

"And that'll teach me to wish for adventure," he said ruefully.

Cassandra came sliding down the rope from her perch, raising eyebrows among the officers watching. She grabbed at a full canteen a trooper offered, drank, coughed, drank again, forced herself to sip.

"I suspect it's the sort of wish you get granted whether you speak it or not," she said, and walked forward to the King-Emperor's side.

"There's work to be done," the monarch said. "We have an Imperial wedding to organize—two, in fact."

Henri nodded at his glance, and Sita seconded the gesture more emphatically, taking the hand of France-outre-mer's Prince Imperial. The *kunwari* grinned herself, despite dry cracked lips, at the gasps and dropped jaws among the watching soldiers, particularly the officers.

"Sir Manfred," Charles III went on, oblivious of the arm he'd put around Cassandra's waist. "I want you and Detective-Captain Malusre—no, Major Malusre would be appropriate, I think, Major Sir Tanaji Malusre, KCBE—to put together a team to start combing out the secret services—"

King put his own arm around Yasmini's shoulders; she embraced his waist, as high as she could reach in that position, and took some of the weight off his injured leg. Her face gazed up at him silently, gravely happy. King gave her a gentle squeeze and spoke to his *daffadar*:

"Well, *bhai*, now we'll ride back to Peshawar town once more, wounded and victorious. I with a wife this time, though; perhaps you should start looking yourself. My son will need a right-hand man."

Narayan Singh tugged at his dust-streaked black beard and shook his head, his expression mock-grave:

"Ah, *sahib*, the sad duty of beating off the would-be brides I will leave my father and mother to accomplish, while I find solace in mere trifles such as gold and rank. Under the very eye, eh, *bhai*?"

Laughing, they stepped forward into the bright sunshine. A huge cry of *Shabash!* rang out as the ordered ranks of the Peshawar Lancers parted like two great doors to let the King-Emperor and his friends pass eastward to the Border.

Epilogue

"Don't worry," Cassandra Saxe-Coburg-Gotha said. "Mother will love you. She told *me* so, at the wedding. Now you can really get to know each other—and I'll be staying for a week, I promise. Planning the new observatories can wait that long."

Yasmini nodded doubtfully, clutching at her new sister-in-law's hand and looking at her husband.

Athelstane King reined in beside the gig; his face thoughtful as he stroked a hand down the neck of his horse. They had halted for a moment of farewells, as *Rissaldar*-Major Narayan Singh turned up the rutted lane to his father's house. The file of troopers from the Peshawar Lancers who rode escort a discreet distance behind the captain's woman and the Queen-Empress stiffened in the saddle and saluted as he passed—he'd already become something of a regimental legend. He was alone, but the pack saddle on the horse that followed behind him on a leading rein held a number of small, very heavy boxes.

The Sikh had courteously refused transfer to the Guards, but accepted the gold—no fancy modern bank deposits for him!—with equally grave politeness. His charger stepped high, and brothers and sisters were running from the farmhouse to meet the resplendent figure in dress uniform, with the plain bronze medal of the Victoria Cross on his chest; behind them Ranjit Singh stumped, roaring and waving.

The lord of Rexin laughed softly, shook his head, and looked up through the fresh green leaves of the chinar trees and the exploding white and pink flowers of the orchards, up toward the manor and its gardens. A slight wry smile remained on his face, and he took a deep breath of cool air scented with new growth and fresh-turned earth and sweet with peach and apple blossom.

He was in plain civilian garb today, his jacket and turban a forest color that matched the new growth. There would be a crowd to wade through again, but this would be of folk he knew, not the courtiers of Delhi. Then . . .

"Then we'll be home," he said to his wife.

"I've never been home," she said, a hand on the swelling of her stomach. "Never in all my life."

"We're both home now," he said. "Home is where our children are born."

"The hour that dreams are brighter and winds colder,
The hour that young love wakes on a white shoulder . . .
That hour, O Master, shall be bright for thee:
Thy merchants chase the morning down the sea . . ."

Appendix One:

The Fall

On October 3, 1878, the first of a series of high-velocity heavenly bodies struck the earth. The impacts continued for the next twelve hours, moving in a band from east to west and impacting at shallow angles. The scanty and confused records meant that it was never possible to determine the exact nature of the object or objects; the consensus of Imperial scholars a century and a half later was that the Fall was either a spray of comets or a smaller number of large comets (possibly only one) that broke up in the Earth's atmosphere.

The first impact was close to the southern edge of Moscow; later studies by Imperial scholars examining the crater indicated an energy release in the 300 megaton range. A band of further impacts of 100 to 300 megatons swept across Europe, the last striking 50 miles west and slightly south of Paris. Strikes were recorded as far north as the Baltic, and the southernmost fell at the head of the Adriatic; that was, however, the only impact south of the Alps.

The next impact was the largest of all, apparently in the western Atlantic, and the body involved may have been up to a kilometer in diameter. Further large fragments fell all across North America, in a rather wider band than in Europe and as far west as the Rocky Mountains.

Blast damage from strikes on land was the first and most obvious consequence; millions probably died in the immediate aftermath.

Hours to days later, tsunamis struck the coasts of countries all around the North Atlantic Basin. These were most severe along the Atlantic coast of North America, with wave fronts reaching as far inland as the Appalachians in some places. In Europe, Ireland, coastal Scandinavia, and much of the Atlantic coast of France and Spain were wrecked, with loss of life in the tens of millions; the destruction would have been even worse, had not the shallow bed of the North Sea robbed the monster waves of some of their force. The "shadow" of Ireland protected much of western England, and the British Isles as a whole had a similar effect on northern France, Belgium, and the Netherlands.

The impacts—particularly the water strike—released enormous amounts of particulate matter and water into the upper atmosphere. The Gulf Stream was also disrupted for several years, and did not fully resume for a decade.

The climatic effects were drastic and immediate. With insolation reduced by 10 percent or more, winter was exceptionally severe throughout the northern hemisphere, and the southern-hemisphere summer was relatively cool and damp. In Europe, where the warming effect of the Gulf Stream was so important—England is as far north as Labrador, one should remember—the cold season was more than Siberian in its harshness and lasted into April.

Recovery might have been possible, despite the enormous loss of life and destruction of infrastructure, had the next summer been even remotely normal. But it was not. The combination of reduced sunlight and loss of the Gulf Stream made the "warm" season colder and wetter than anything in recorded history throughout Europe, with killing frost in at least a few days of every month as far south as Naples. The following winter was almost as severe as that of 1878, as were those of 1880 and 1881. The summers showed some improvement, but not enough for any appreciable agricultural yield; and there were no sources of imported food available.

By late 1879, with starvation universal, order had broken down throughout northern and central Europe. Mass migrations southward were attempted, but the bulk of the northern Mediterranean shore was only marginally better off in terms of climate, and no better off in terms of food supply when the remnants of the starving hordes arrived. Populations crashed, with only a few small enclaves holding out on the Mediterranean shore. Elsewhere, the only survivors were the most successful cannibal bands.

Even when the climate warmed enough to make agriculture possible again, neither seed grain nor working stock nor tools were usually available; and the remaining population huddled in tiny groups, hiding from and hunting each other in a grisly game of stalking and eating. By 1890, the total population of mainland Europe west of the Urals had fallen to a few million. Here and there tiny hamlets were making attempts to restart farming, but on a level barely Neolithic except for materials salvaged from pre-Fall settlements. Throughout the continent, the forest began its reconquest of the landscape.

North America followed a basically similar trajectory, with patches of settled life surviving along the Gulf Coast. The eastern seaboard remained almost clear of human life for generations; on the interior plains there were small farming enclaves toward the east, with nomad hunters and herders (white, Amerind, and mixed) farther south and west, and a remnant of the Mormons in Utah. Most of the land swiftly reverted to wilderness, and the population was reduced below the levels of 1600.

California suffered less climatically, although the cold and increased rainfall did drastically reduce yields. Attempts to evacuate population from farther east resulted in an impossible overburdening of its resources—a tragic consequence of the survival of the transcontinental railways—and ultimately a number of regressed city-states emerged.

Most of the rest of the northern hemisphere suffered several years of weather wild enough to reduce crop yields by at least 50 percent, with gradual amelioration from 1881 on and more or less normal weather returning by the 1890s. Effects were strongest to the north, tapering off toward the tropics. Mathematically, it might have been possible for a third to a half of the population of, say, northern China to survive; but when it became apparent that massive famine was inevitable, "secondary effects"—chaos, banditry, civil and regional wars—set in, as struggles over the meager yields of food broke out.

These in turn drove farmers off their land, and resulted in the destruction of seed supplies, livestock, and irrigation and distribution systems. The result was catastrophic dieback in the areas south of the worst-hit zone, limited only by comparison to events in Europe; although there was no absolute break in the continuity of agriculture, population declines of up to 80 percent were common in a broad zone that included much of East Asia and the lands between Mexico and northern Brazil. The halting of world trade, and the loss of the only technologically developed part of the world, exaggerated the "crash" to preindustrial, and in some cases prehistoric, levels.

Meanwhile, the southern hemisphere—subequatorial Africa, the southern cone of South America, Australasia, much of Indonesia—were spared the worst effects. Temperatures dropped, but generally not enough seriously to depress crop yields. Floods were a serious problem, but greater rainfall in arid areas actually increased their carrying capacity for most of the post-Fall decade.

Appendix Two:

The Exodus

The British Isles suffered as badly as most parts of Europe from the Fall, but the consequences were not so immediately drastic.

A combination of a dense surviving transport network and prompt emergency measures under strong leadership—Disraeli's government, in which Lord Salisbury quickly became a leading figure—allowed the maintenance of order for some time, and avoided loss of what resources remained by preventing the breakdown of services that swept over most of Europe. Martial law was declared, and the long tradition of centralized authority made it possible to maintain a semblance of civilized life for nearly two years.

Uniquely, the British government quickly became aware (thanks to Professor Thomson, later Lord Kelvin, and others) that the cold weather was likely to last for several years. Once this had been grasped, it was obvious that it would be impossible to feed the vast majority of the British population—still over 20 million, even with the loss of Ireland and much of the west coast. Since the harvest was in and imports had been substantial, there was food on hand for approximately 12 months, which might be stretched to 24 with extremely careful rationing. However, that left a gap of two years in which there would be, essentially, no food at all apart from a small trickle from Australia and the Rio de la Plata countries.

Fortunately, a large proportion of the British merchant fleet had survived the Fall; either in ports on the east coast, on the deep oceans where the tsunamis were merely massive waves (the energy release only comes in shallow water), or in the Mediterranean and southern hemisphere. Together with impounded foreign ships, the navy, and some new emergency construction, roughly 700,000 tons of shipping was available.

In the ensuing three years, this was used to ship out as much of the British population—and of British civilization—as possible. There were three major destinations: India, where Queen Victoria and the government were relocated, southern Africa, and Australia/New Zealand. Roughly 3.5 million were evacuated, a million and a half to India (the closest, through the Suez Canal), a half million to the Cape, and a million to Australia.

By 1881 the rationing system broke down. It had become obvious that it would be impossible to remove many of the remaining people before famine started; there was also considerable resentment over the fact that the Exodus had been socially selective. The aristocracy and gentry—the "upper ten thousand" families—had gone first, and the upper echelons of the middle classes next. Soldiers and their families had followed, together with skilled workers; and the government had allocated shipping space to essential machine tools and other industrial equipment as well.

Rioting broke out and could not be suppressed with the few troops remaining; by the end, the authorities held only London, and Prime Minister Disraeli himself was killed when the mobs overran the last outposts. In the following years, only heavily armed expeditions to retrieve valuable equipment, relics, and works of art set foot on British soil. When the New Empire's soldiers and missionaries returned to recivilize the homeland two generations later, they found a wilderness with oak forest growing over the ruins of gutted cities, and small communities of isolated neobarbarians living amid the ruins.

Most of the actual survivors seem to have been very small groups of country dwellers who managed to avoid hungry notice; the massive town-populations ate each other and died.

THE SECOND MUTINY:

Name given to a series of insurrections and rebellions in India, 1878–1890s; in popular memory, it includes the invasions from Afghanistan and elsewhere.

Minor uprisings began as soon as the extent of damage in England was realized, but they were put down without great difficulty, as more and more of the British army and large numbers of refugees capable of bearing arms arrived.

The first serious outbreaks of unrest occurred when it became clear that the 1879–80 harvest would be catastrophically bad throughout India; crop failures were worst in the mountain valleys of the Himalayas and the northwest, but flooding and unseasonable rain also damaged fields throughout the Indo-Gangetic plain. Only south of the Deccan and in Ceylon were yields sufficient even for subsistence levels, and there was no surplus for nonagricultural populations at all.

Contrary to rumors at the time and legends since, little if any food was shipped to Britain. However, the Imperial government did give first priority to the refugees flooding into India, and to those native peoples of proven loyalty—for example, the Gurkhas, who relocated to the lowlands until it became possible to recolonize Nepal (starting in 1886).

In the abstract, the addition of another million and a half mouths made little concrete difference in the midst of natural disaster on this scale. That was little consolation to those facing starvation, and often seeing what little they did possess confiscated by authorities driven to desperation themselves. Rumors that food was plentiful in "some other province" and that the ships heading back to England were stuffed with grain spread like wildfire.

The result was a series of massive uprisings throughout the northern lowlands, and spreading to some areas of the south, particularly the important Native state of Hyderabad. At the worst period of the mid-1880s, the control of the Raj was limited to the major cities and patches elsewhere—parts of the Punjab, for instance, where the Sikhs largely stood by the Sirkar, the government, and Rajputana, where the local rulers remained loyal.

The military measures necessary to put down the rebellion, and to seize food and supplies where administration had broken down, greatly exacerbated the losses due to bad weather and the epidemics of bubonic plague and influenza that spread among populations weakened by hunger. The overall population of India sank from in excess of 200 million to less than 50 million from 1878 to 1898; and in the middle of the revolt came the invasion from Afghanistan, where conditions in the cold uplands were almost as bad as in Europe. Many of the British refugees also perished, in the fighting and due to exposure to the unfamiliar disease environment.

The crisis was over by the mid-1890s, with regular monsoonal weather restored, and order reestablished throughout the subcontinent. In some respects, the Second Mutiny may actually have helped establish the nascent New Empire. The sheer stark requirements of survival welded the refugees into a nation-army, and solidified their relationships with their local allies; the Sikhs, the upper castes of Rajputana and the Marathas, the refugee population of Nepal, and a number of others. The confiscations which followed revolt provided a solution to one major problem, as hundreds of thousands of square miles were handed out to sahib-log settlers, who formed both a new gentry and, together with their yeoman-tenants, a garrison.

And the absolute necessity of keeping up a flow of weapons, ammunition, locomotives and rolling stock, steamboats and other crucial pieces of Victorian technology was also important in forming the new system. Mines, smelters, and factories had to be maintained, or built if they didn't already exist. The educational system established in the New Empire may well have been more practical, and more science-and-technology oriented, than that of pre-Fall Britain.

Appendix Three:

The Angrezi Raj/British Empire

The state known as the "British Empire" in the early twenty-first century—the term most commonly used by its own population was in fact "Angrezi Raj" with "New Empire" a close second—was a constitutional monarchy centered on Delhi.

Territory and population: As of A.D. 2025, 148 years after the Fall, the Empire (not including territories claimed but not administered) encompassed approximately 17 million square miles and roughly 230 million human beings—40 percent of the Earth's habitable surface, and slightly less than 50 percent of its population.

Roughly in order of importance, its components were:

India: India proper, what would otherwise have become the republics of India and Pakistan, plus Ceylon/Sri Lanka, Burma, Malaysia, and the western half of Thailand.

Area: c. 1.5 million square miles

Population: 130 million, of which sahib-log 10.7 million; Eurasians 6 million; Christians 18 percent, Muslims 7 percent, Sikhs 7 percent, remainder other Hindu and Buddhist.

Viceroyalty of Australia: Australia, New Zealand, with New Guinea and many of the South Pacific islands as colonial dependencies.

Area: c. 3.2 million square miles.

Population: 20 million. Note: This does not include the populations of the interior of New Guinea, most of which were not in contact with the theoretical "government."

In Australia and New Zealand proper the remnants of the indigenous populations had been completely assimilated by the end of the twentieth century, and the Australian Viceroyalty had the most ethnically and socially homogenous population of any large area in the Empire. All were English-speaking, and virtually all were members of the Imperial Church, the Anglicans having absorbed the large Roman Catholic minority after the Fall and the severing of connections with Rome.

Viceroyalty of the Cape: Including South Africa, Namibia, Zimbabwe, Zambia, Angola, and Mozambique, with enclaves farther north to Kenya.

Area: c. 5 million square miles

Population: c. 40 million, of which 6 million were white and 34 million African and mixed. The white population included descendants of the old Dutch-Afrikaner settler population, the pre-Fall British immigrants, and the much larger body of post-Fall refugees; these were gradually homogenized by intermarriage and post-Fall movements. By the twenty-first century Afrikaans had died out except among some remote rural communities in the Cape, and most of the nonwhite population south of the Zambezi had also adopted dialects of English as their first language.

Crown Colonies:

These were areas not represented in the Houses of Parliament, but ruled directly from either Delhi or one of the Viceroyalties.

Britain: Beginning in the early twentieth century, an effort was made to recivilize the British Isles. Small garrisons were established in suitable ports—London, Liverpool, Southampton, Glasgow, Dublin—and missionaries sent out to reclaim and reeducate the savages, seed and stock and tools supplied, etc.; funding was steady but not generous. The total population was less than 200,000 in 1900, when the London base was set up. A scattering of new settlers also arrived, mostly from Australia and the Cape; those from India tended to be in higher-status or administrative positions.

By 2025, this had grown by natural increase and immigration to approximately 6.5 million, and there was talk of eventual promotion to Viceroyalty status. The main concentrations were in the south and east, with outposts in Scotland and a belt of recolonized territory in eastern Ireland. A few bands of wandering savages remained in the fringe zones.

The economy remained largely agricultural, but some railway lines had been repaired, mines reopened, etc. Exports were mainly wool, flax, dairy products, frozen meat, and cloth.

Extensive wilderness areas remained, and there was considerable prejudice in other parts of the Empire against the "Britons," mainly because of their descent from cannibals; the Britons themselves tended to be rather defensive about it. One aspect of that attitude was their insistence on speaking a "pure Imperial" form of English and following Delhi fashions; the post-Fall dialects had nearly disappeared by the 2020s.

After the mid twentieth century, the British operation was used as a base for a similar reentry into Western Europe generally, with outposts at the mouths of the main navigable rivers.

North America: The Empire claimed the whole North American continent.

In practical terms, it controlled a fringe on the eastern and Gulf coasts, outposts at the mouths of the St. Lawrence and the Mississipi, and trading posts inland along the Great Lakes and the interior river systems. The Atlantic coast was virtually empty second-growth forest when Imperial explorers arrived in the mid twentieth century, having no more than a few thousand neosavages. Somewhat larger populations of mixed African and European stock occupied small enclaves on the Gulf Coast, and there were remnant groups of varying background scattered through the interior, some under substantial Imperial influence, others "wild." Colonization of the east coast from Britain began in the 1940s.

On the west coast, city-states of Anglo-Hispano background occupied the coast of California; initially backward, they played off the Empire against Dai-Nippon, and some maintained a substantial degree of independence from both the Raj and the East Asian empire. Explorers and entrepreneurs from Australia had established footholds and colonies along the Oregon and British Columbian coasts, while Dai-Nippon claimed Alaska and had some fishing and fur-trading settlements there.

The Empire's American establishments numbered some 6 million in all; there were probably as many again in the Free Cities of California, and another few million among the wild tribes of the interior.

Batavian Republic: After the Fall, the administration of the Dutch East Indies retained control of central Java, with what aid the Angrezi Raj could supply; there was an influx of refugees from the Netherlands and adjacent territories, although on a much smaller scale than in the Empire.

In 1910, the relationship with the Empire was regularized as a protectorate with a high degree of internal autonomy, and over the next few generations the rest of Java and Sumatra, and the more important islands to the east, were reconquered. Imperial influence grew steadily, with the Angrezi city of Singapore becoming the dominant entrepôt and source of trade and investment for the Indonesian archipelago. There was some speculation that the Republic would apply for formal annexation, probably becoming part of India proper.

The total population was approximately 8 million, with 750,000 of Dutch or mainly Dutch descent; they had been heavily influenced by their subjects, in a manner roughly similar to the sahib-log in India.

Outposts: The Empire had a worldwide scattering of islands, outposts, naval and coaling bases, etc. These ranged from South Pacific islands visited once a year to fairly substantial communities such as Mauritius to fortified ports such as Aden or Bahrain.

Constitution:

Unless otherwise stated, the constitutional status quo given is as of A.D. 2025.

Supreme authority rested with the King-Emperor-in-Parliament; in effect, the King-Emperor was bound by the "advice of his Ministers," who in turn required a majority in the Imperial House of Commons. The King-Emperor had more influence than actual power, although the occupant of the Lion Throne possessed more of both by the early twenty-first century than Victoria I had ever had; the influence of the Indian conception of monarchy probably played a large part in this gradual shift.

The House of Lords occupied a roughly coequal role with the Commons; ordinary nonfinancial legislation required majorities in both Houses. The Lords included both descendants of the original British peerage settled throughout the Empire, and new creations. These included a substantial number of the ancient aristocracies of India, or at least of those who had demonstrated their loyalty to the Raj. However, the House of Commons had a monopoly on financial legislation; it alone could vote taxes or authorize the budget.

Membership in the House of Lords was hereditary, with the exception of Archbishops of the established Imperial Church, of which there were fourteen including the Archbishop of Delhi, the head of the Church under the King-Emperor. Some areas, particularly client states in India under treaty relationships to the Raj (e.g., Nepal) had representation in the House of Lords but not in the Commons. About one-third of India proper in area and population was comprised of such "protected states." The equivalent in the Viceroyalty of the Cape were "native reserves," and did not generally have representation in the Lords.

The House of Commons was elected (with elections at the discretion of Parliament but with intervals not to exceed seven years) on a common Empire-wide qualified franchise. As of 2025, qualifications necessary for the franchise (or for election to the Commons) included:

a) that the voter be male and at least 21 years of age, and a British subject by birth or naturalization;
b) that he be literate and numerate in English;
c) that he possess landed property to the value of 10,000 rupees (equivalent to approximately $125,000 US in 2000 values); or other property to the value of 50,000 rupees;
d) have an income of not less than 2,500 rupees per annum.

Extra votes could be gained in a number of ways; by university degrees, by gaining a commission in the Imperial forces, by securing one
of a number of Imperial service decorations or knighthoods, etc.

In general, the enfranchised portion of the population (including
families) ranged from 20 percent in Australia, 11 percent in India, to
about 9 percent in the Cape. Rather more in each case could have
qualified, but underreported their worth in order to avoid taxation.
This was particularly so among the urban and merchant-industrialist
middle classes; stocks and shares were easier to hide than land.

Local and municipal franchises were generally on the same terms.

Officially, the franchise was open to all Imperial subjects who met
the qualifications. In India and Australia this was so in reality, with the
significant proviso that the one-third of the Indian population who
lived in "protected states" could not vote, since in theory their rulers
were themselves sovereign and represented their peoples to the Imperial government.

The Viceroyalty of the Cape managed, through a number of sub-
terfuges—biased literacy testing, for example—to prevent otherwise
qualified nonwhites from actually getting the franchise, although
there would have been fairly few in any case. In this as in much else, it
was the "bad boy of the Empire," and the source of continual squab-
bles between Cape Town and Delhi.

Appendix Four:

Imperial English and Other Languages

Apart from a few scholars and linguists, the sahib-log of the early twenty-first century were firmly convinced that they spoke English, slightly modified from the time of the Fall and Victoria I.

In fact, the language they used—the spoken form as standardized in the Royal court and Imperial administration, and used by the sahib-log landed gentry, yeoman-tenantry, and urban upper classes of India—was a creolized English-based pidgin, one which would have been barely comprehensible to their Victorian ancestors. It was at least one-third Indian in vocabulary, with major loans from (in rough order of importance) Hindi, Bengali, Punjabi, Bihari, Pashtun, and Tamil; syntax also changed under the influence of Indian languages. In particular most of the vocabulary concerned with food, clothing, and sex had been Indianized, along with many everyday expressions. Tone, stress, and accent had all altered.

For example, the intial "th" sound had dropped out of Imperial English, being replaced by "d" ("dat" and "dese" instead of "that" and "these"); "v" is transposed to "w," ("wery" for "very"), etc.

To a Victorian (or twentieth-century English speaker from our history) Imperial English would sound rapid, with a singsong quality and occasional gutturals. For purposes of comparison, it would be roughly as difficult for a hypothetical observer from our time line to understand as Jamaican Creole is to an American standard English speaker.

The "Imperial" form of English also had a substantial influence in the Cape and Australian Viceroyalties, although their dialects remained more conservative; trade and travel links grew increasingly close during the twentieth century, with many upper-class residents of both the Viceroyalties spending much time in India, as Members of Parliament, students at prestigious boarding schools, Oxford and Cambridge, and the Imperial University in Delhi, etc. The standard speech of Delhi enjoyed a substantial, if frequently resented, prestige throughout the Angrezi Raj.

A notable twentieth-century development was the manner in which the recivilized and immigrant communities in Britain insisted on adopting the Delhi standard wholesale, often taking enormous pains to do so.

It should be noted that Imperial English in turn had a very strong influence on the indigenous tongues of India, as the second official language of education and administration, the language of business beyond the petty-trade level, and through household influence among the numerous servants and dependents of sahib-log households. It also served, together with Hindi, as the lingua franca between Indian linguistic communities. By 2025, about one-fifth of the population of India used Imperial English as its primary language, and another fifth could speak it to a greater or lesser degree.

By the early twenty-first century the educated throughout the Empire spoke Imperial English well enough for easy intercommunication, although strong regional accents often remained to show origins. Lower-class dialects of English in Australia, and especially in the Cape (where the influence of Afrikaans and various Bantu languages was strong) diverged more or less strongly and in some cases they would not find mutal comprehension easy with a native Imperial English speaker.

In the interior of North America, a wild variety of English-based creoles and pidgins were spoken among the neobarbarians; something fairly close to nineteenth-century standard English survived in the Mormon enclaves of the Rockies, which maintained a tradition of literacy; and Spanish-influenced forms were common in the Free Cities of California.

Appendix Five:

Technology and Economy

Post-Fall India was not entirely without a base for industrial development. By the 1870s there were already thousands of miles of railway, and the railway workshops contained a fairly extensive set of heavy machine tools and skilled workers. Mineral surveys had been carried out. There were shipbuilding and repair yards in Bombay, Calcutta, and Madras, and a beginning had been made in mechanized cotton and jute mills as early as the 1850s.

The refugee fleets of the Exodus brought in substantial additional machinery and artisans, as well as examples of nearly every important technical book and drawing in Britain. In many respects, the situation was better in India than Australia, which had been even more dependent on imports. India also had abundant supplies of highly skilled handicraftsmen, who could quickly learn most of the not-overly-complex operations of mid-Victorian machine work.

Still, the early decades were desperate, not least because of the Second Mutiny. All available effort had to be concentrated on building up essentials that were not present in 1878. Exploiting the coal and iron deposits of southern Bihar, for instance, and establishing a small steel mill, required an epic struggle. Once mere survival was assured in the 1890s, emphasis was necessarily on the basics; rebuilding and expanding the railways, dams and irrigation canals, dockyards, housing.

By the 1910s, a surplus over basic needs was available once more, even allowing for the demands of other parts of the Empire. There was also a small but high-quality training system for turning out men of practical learning; engineers civil and mechanical, applied chemistry, and mathematics. What had largely lapsed was any tradition of pure research, of science and scientific research proper. Rebuilding it was a slow process, although it was helped by the increased prestige of scientific-technological careers in comparison to pre-Fall Britain.

In the ensuing decades, Imperial technology tended toward improvements in detail, rather than radical innovation. Steam engines were improved and widely applied, as were telegraphs, steam-driven manufacturing machinery, and basic industrial chemistry. Medical knowledge and biology did rather better, as the sahib-log adjusted to a new environment and ecology; for instance, the etiology of malaria and yellow fever were well understood by the 1890s, and cures for the former (based on Chinese artemisin) were more advanced than in our history. Forestry, plant and animal breeding, and practical agriculture made great strides.

By the 1920s, a recovery to the level of the 1870s had been achieved—in the sense that it was now possible to manufacture without undue strain anything that the European nations of that date had been able to build. Population was growing, particularly that of the sahib-log, and production was consistently greater than consumption, allowing for increased savings and investment.

Yet the economy of the Empire as a whole was quite different from that of Victorian Britain. Even Australia remained largely rural, with the coastal cities smaller than they had been at the time of the Fall; population had dispersed into the countryside and a semi-self-subsistent pattern had emerged in the late nineteenth and early twentieth centuries, and persisted for far longer.

India had a few large cities and a scattering of smaller ones, but it was nine-tenths rural; for the most part a landscape of zamindari-landlords, whether of the sahib-log or native in origin, and ryot-peasants paying rent in shares of their crops and labor-service. A few plantations remained, growing tea and coffee, indigo and jute. Most day-to-day needs, even for luxuries, were satisfied with hand-made goods from small shops. Trade was in exotic materials, and in an official sector supported by rent and taxes rather than consumer demand.

This meant that patterns of demand were also different in the "modern" sector. For long years, the main customer of machine manufacture was the Imperial government, which itself owned much of the basic industry—providing rail and engines for Imperial Railways and the navy, armaments for the military, replacements for its own structure.

However, an urban middle class did survive, even in the deeply rural Cape Viceroyalty; in India it included a substantial native element from the beginning, however shrunken the towns were in the first generations. The financial structure of the Raj was sound, with free trade, free movement of capital, and knowledge of sophisticated banking and the limited-liability company. Trade went on, and as population grew once more in a nearly empty world, standards of living increased and with them opportunities.

By the later twentieth century an exuberant mercantile and industrial capitalism was reemerging, wheeling and dealing, disrupting ancient patterns as men and women began to trickle from the countryside into the growing cities. Knowledge increased, in a civilization where the sciences and their practical application had high respect and much official support.

The roads taken were not always those which would have been, had the Fall not happened.

Differences in detail were many; for instance, metal-hulled ships were uncommon, due to differences in patterns of demand, relative costs, and the availability of abundant and very high quality tropical timbers. Mineral fuels were relatively more expensive than they had been in northwestern Europe, and highly sophisticated sailing ships remained competitive into the early twenty-first century. Weapons technology progressed slowly; until the Asian empire of Dai-Nippon grew into a serious rival in the 1970s, the Angrezi Raj had no "advanced" competitors, and so the venerable Adams revolvers and Martini-Henry black-powder rifles of the 1870s were still being produced a century later at armories in Lahore and Delhi, Cape Town and Melbourne. Almost as important was the absence of a private, competitive arms industry; there the New Empire followed Indian precedent, with state-owned arsenals and strict control.

Chemistry in particular, which had been largely a German specialty before the Fall, was underdeveloped; there was little of the economic drive to develop synthetic compounds which had motivated the research chemists of IG Farben. In fact, the whole German concept of the specialized research laboratory, or of the university as primarily a center of research rather than teaching, was slow to develop. The individualist-tinkerer model of the Anglo-Saxon generalists remained dominant, and was developed to new heights.

In that might-have-been world without the Fall, the internal combustion engine had been a product of France and Germany as well.

The Empire turned to the Stirling cycle instead when the steam engine became inadequate; external-combustion machines, pistons driven by the regenerative heating and cooling of a gas in a closed cycle, most often by air. (Hence their common name of "air engine.") They were easier to manufacture and maintain than the Otto-cycle machines that would have been developed in the 1880s, if slightly less powerful; their thermal efficiency was unrivaled by any other heat engine. And they were silent, using any source of heat from the sun to kerosene; their complete and low-temperature combustion meant that they had few noxious by-products even when burning petroleum. The New Empire's cities would never know smog, although coal smoke was abundant.

By the turn of the twenty-first century, the New Empire was a self-consciously modern society, for all that a man with a wooden plow or woman with a sickle was still its most common figure—the cotton or millet, rice or tea they cultivated was the product of scientific plant-breeding stations, irrigated by mammoth hydraulic works.

The first kinematographic shows were open for business in Delhi and the other big cities, and even the poor could afford a few photographs, could dream of literacy and a clerk's post for their children. Railroads webbed India and the Viceroyalties by the tens of thousands of miles, great articulated steam locomotives pulling expresses at up to seventy miles an hour, and dirigibles driven by air engines floated above; already thousands of motorcars swept with silent speed along its roads. In cities where factories grew apace, daring men of business dreamed of a day when those few thousand motors might be tens or even hundreds of thousands. Steamships and clippers designed with a profound knowledge of hydrodynamics tied colony and Viceroyalty together; telephones were following the telegraphs. Phonographs brought recorded music to remote villages, experiments went on apace with wireless telegraphy, while sanitation and vaccines battled disease even in the slums.

And in the universities, men—and a few women—were growing unsatisfied with even the great Lord Kelvin's picture of the universe. Telescopes probed the sky for the secrets of the Fall; savants tested and doubted the existence of the luminiferous aether, and grew troubled at the implications of the odd behavior of radium . . .

The King-Emperors

Victoria I	1837–1882	Transition from Old to New Empire
Edward	1882–1900	
George IV	1900–1921	
Victoria II	1921–1942	Childless; succeeded by her cousin
Albert I	1942–1989	
Elizabeth II	1989–2005	First son Edward dies in 2000
John II	2005–2025	Children: Charles, Sita, Dalap, Edwina
Charles III	2025–